THE

NIGHT ADVENTURER;

OR, THE

PALACES AND DUNGEONS OF THE HEART.

A Romance.

" Put out the light, and then the life."—BYRON.

' LONDON:

PRINTED AND PUBLISHED BY EDWARD LLOYD, 12, SALISBURY SQUARE,
FLEET STREET.

——

1846.

PREFACE.

IN concluding these brief chronicles of his doings by the light of the moon the "Night Adventurer" has, with a feeling of the most intense gratification, to acknowledge the great public patronage which has been bestowed upon the work.

The extent of that patronage has afforded yet another strong evidence of the fact—the well-known fact we may call it—that these rational episodes of real life, which appeal successfully to the feelings and the hearts of all persons, will ever be the most popular reading.

Even at this time of day, there are those who contend that the masses are best pleased with that wild, romantic literature, which either goes completely into the realms of improbability, or so nearly, that it is a most difficult task to draw the line of demarcation. A more practical refutation of such an assertion could not be found, than in the success of works like the present, which do not deal in the marvellous, but which attract on account of their truthfulness.

Possibly, at some future time, the "Night Adventurer" may, with enervated spirits, renew those scenes of feeling, and, he hopes, of usefulness, through which his readers have so kindly followed. He hopes that once again circumstances will permit him to open the leaves of his chronicles, and to present to his kind patrons —the public—what is there in brief set down.

In the meantime, he can but now, with a most grateful remembrance of the past, say—Adieu! and if any of his youthful readers should feel inclined to make the attempt to follow in his steps, and go out by the

"Glimpses of the pale moon,"

in search of adventure, he advises them to forsake the interesting for the useful, and rather to make themselves knights-errant in the cause of virtue, than be dazzled by any adventure which presents nothing but its glitter to recommend it.

LONDON,
November, 1846.

ADVENTURES BY NIGHT;

OR,

THE PALACES AND DUNGEONS OF THE HEART.

𝔄 Romance.

BY THE AUTHOR OF "NEWGATE."

BOOK THE FIRST—1846.

CHAPTER I.

THE NIGHT ADVENTURER INTRODUCES HIMSELF TO HIS READERS.

THERE are people who have affected to have become acquainted with the habits, the manners, the hopes, the passions, and the modes of life of the inhabitants of this great city, by walking into the broad day-light of existence, and looking around them upon the artificial life that blazes in a noon-tide sun.

Is this the way to dive into that arcana of thought—that depth of feeling, and to explore those hidden recesses of the human heart that contain its choicest treasures, or its most hideous vices? There are birds and beasts that shun the day-light, and there should be men and women who do so likewise : there are, but they are few in number, while the many, the immense majority, wearing a day-light face,

No. 1.

because they know it can be scanned, even as some young beauty puts on her most enchanting simper in the refulgent light of a ball-room, but to whom the expression that they wear belongs not in truthfulness, because it is that which is dictated by the head, and not by the heart. Expediency bids a smile play upon the lips, real feeling will overflow the eyes with tears; but this is in day-light, when all who run may read the human face; when men and women feel that they must seem to be that which is sanctioned by an arbitrary code of fashion or of morals, and not really show themselves as what they are.

He who would seek in the day-light for the romance of existence, may get some of its reflected beams, but he must wait until the sun has really sunk beneath the horizon's verge, ere he can really revel in an appreciation of the heart's joyousness, or of the heart's agony, when it shakes off the weary trammels of deceit that have clung to it for the live-long day, and gives free expression to its pent-up sorrows; or, by the happy fire-side of contentment, expands in beauty, like that fair night-flower we read of, that hides its gentle head beneath the garish light of day, to unfold its sweetest blossoms to the mystic night.

Yes, it is after dark, when toil has ceased its avocations, when there are hours to intervene before active duties summon again to labour those who are weary of the day. It is after dark, when, in a summer's prime, the gentle breezes fan the cheeks of beauty; and when, in the deep winter, in which wild birds of the forest die, the cheerful blaze arises from the genial hearth, and the cold, sterile season is shut out by many a shutter and warmth-giving curtain, that the heart expands and human nature becomes more natural. It is after dark, when maidens listen to their lovers' vows, and not a blush is seen, for though the gentle cheek may be tinged by love's own ensign, the soft shadows from the sighing trees will hide the roseate tinge, while they impart a deeper-whispered tenderness to every gentle word then spoken, to be dreamt of as purest happiness in years to come. It is after dark, when the evil passions that dare not show themselves to the bright eye of the morn, but cower and hide themselves like thieves in a tangled brake, behind fairer and more innocent objects, blaze out again, nor fear detection. It is after dark that those collisions of the passions, which make up some of the most appalling episodes of human life occur. Mankind act a part in the day-time. Put out the glorious sun-light, and Vice stalks abroad, fancying that it makes as brave a show as Virtue, and that in the dim obscurity of earth and heaven it may, for a moment, by some unwary person be mistaken. It is after dark that the assassin lies in wait for his victim; and it is at the soft twilight hour, and in those that follow it, that those moral assassins—those worse than bravos, who arm themselves with the pistol and the knife—whisper to trusting ears of innocence and beauty their seductive counsels, covering themselves with an odium which shall be eternal, and a contempt that shall be withering.

It is at such times that the nearest and dearest connections are uprooted, and when the glossy human serpent, with a frightful practised art, glozes over his subtleties, and does the villain with abundant grace. It is night when the robber leaves the hiding-place in which he has dosed away the day, to pursue his unlawful calling; and it is at night that the timid tremble, for well they know what hosts of evil passions spring into existence when the last bright ray of the departing sun is quenched for many an hour. When night has spread its black and spangled canopy over the green earth—when all is, or should be repose among the good and the beautiful, and when there should be abundance of faith in human nature, because the deeds of men are hidden, but when in reality humanity is armed against humanity, and until the bright sun rises, and again there is doubt, apprehension, and in some cases despair. It is night when the vigilance of those who are appointed to be watchful while others sleep, is considered to be most important, thereby proving that that period is by common consent considered to be likely to be more rife with incidents than the bright and glittering day.

It is at night that one individual, a young, ardent, enthusiastic man—one who has seen much, and profited more, from his intercourse with the great world—rises from his couch, and opens his casement, at that hour when others are closing theirs, and he is our " Night Adventurer." Let him speak for himself.

    *   *   *   *   *   *

The sun has sunk in the glowing west, and the weary are seeking rest. The din of conflict, when conflict has been raging, is over—the night-cloud has lowered, and

> " The cardinal stars set their watch in the sky ;"

but he—the person to whom we have alluded—rises at that hour from the couch on which he has slept all the day, and commences the business of his existence.

It is a strange—a very strange fancy, but it has been his for more than a year —when others rise he retires to rest—when others retire to rest he rises. During the day the shutters of his chamber are closed—the heavy tapestry of his couch drawn close around him, the night-bolt fast at his door, and he reposes, knowing nothing, heeding nothing, of the great world around him, or of all its cares, its hopes, its anxieties, and its follies. The sun may shine, or clouds may obscure its lustre, he cares not—knows not—he sleeps securely.

But what's his object in all this ? Wherefore does he thus turn night to day, and keep himself off, as it were, from the most glorious part of his existence ? Has he no sympathies with the beautiful day-light ? Has he done aught that should make him shun the sweet sunshine ? Is he at war with his kind ; and will he not therefore go forth among them until the sombre shades of night are around and about him ?

No, this is not his reason. No man ever lived who loved his species better. He is no misanthrope, but he is a student of nature, and this his belief—that at no time can he study it better than at night. Therefore is it that he takes that rest in the day-time which is necessary, in order to enable him to be active and alert in mind and body, during those hours when it is his favourite pastime to be out, and observing human nature in such aspects as beneath the light of day it never could show itself.

He has risen, and is rapidly attiring himself, while an old decrepit woman, who attends upon him, prepares what he properly enough, so far as regards the derivation of the word, called his breakfast. But he had a stout battle with this old domestic, to induce her to allow him to give the meal such a name ; she looked not to derivations of words, but would insist that it was his tea, although he took no tea at it, but simply because it happened to be at that hour when she took her meal, which early habit induced her to call it by that name.

" Ah !" she exclaimed, as she laid the equipage for breakfast, " some people are cracked, I think, and completely out of their senses ; the idea, now, of sleeping all day, and getting up just about the time when other people are thinking of going to bed, and then calling his tea his breakfast ! but I won't have that—it is tea, and it shall be his tea, whether he likes it or not ; I will have it so —it is his tea."

And he who will be our hero was talking to himself of his favourite pursuit :—

" Yes," he said, " the time has come again, the delightful time, when I can walk abroad, and feel the delicious cool night air playing upon my brow. The sweet time has come round again, when, with invigorated strength, after many hours' repose, I can go forth to study that most interesting leaf in the great book of human nature which treats of man, his excellences and his frailties, his good and his bad passions, and all the miseries and enjoyments which he is heir to— a delightful time to me—a time full of enjoyment, full of expectation ; I stand as it were aloof from the rest of my kind, a spectator of, but scarcely an actor in, the ordinary affairs of existence ; and what abundant stores of knowledge do I not reap from such a source—stores which shall at one time be opened freely to all who are interested in human existence, and there shall be found pictures drawn from real life, which sometimes, if they shall lack the highest and most gorgeous colouring of art, shall at least be true to nature. And nothing shall be there extenuate, nothing there set down in malice—no false arguments to make the worst appear the better reason—nothing which shall tend to lend an aspect to vice which shall make it seem a libel upon virtue. No, the truth of existence and of incident shall adorn the page, and of truth only. I am the Night Adventurer; and from the records of my existence shall be drawn most rare materials for thinking, strange delineations of character, most remarkable episodes in human life.

"It shall be my task on some day, perchance distant from the present, to place upon record all the strange and wonderful that I have seen and heard. I will write a book, which shall prove that in ordinary life there are incidents more full of existence than the most fertile brain of the novelist ever succeeded in giving birth to. I will prove that fiction presents itself but in weak colours by the side of truth. I will prove, and prove abundantly, that there are heroes and heroines in every day-life far transcending any that can be found in the pages of romance. These shall be my confessions, and they will be such as shall present a picture of the times, that generations yet to come shall study them, and feel that they are acquiring a knowledge most intimate of those who have been before them in the march of mind."

"There's your tea, sir," said the old woman, looking into the apartment.

"You mean breakfast, good Martha—you mean my breakfast."

"Indeed then, sir, I do not; it's tea-time, and therefore tea it is, and you can't make it anything else."

"But it's breakfast, if I break my fast by taking it."

"Rubbish! it's tea, and you know it. Can you mean to say, sir, you are going out again all night long?"

"I am afraid—I do most certainly."

"Oh, yes! you are very much afraid, of course. I do wonder how you can make yourself so ridiculous; you used to have some sense."

"Had I really? Well, Martha, you can enjoy your own opinion, and in the mean time I will enjoy my breakfast."

"Your tea, you mean?"

"No, I don't."

"But I say you do, and I won't be contradicted."

The Night Adventurer laughed, but he well knew the real worth and honest attachment of his ancient servant; he knew that beneath the strange exterior she possessed one of the kindliest of human hearts, and therefore was it that he could well afford most indulgently to put up with her remonstrances, and replied with such abundant good humour to the disapproving remarks she made concerning his habits.

The night was growing on apace. A bank of dark clouds had risen up from out of the eastern sky, the wind was howling by in strange and fitful gusts, and old Martha, as she moved the blind of one of the windows aside, to look out upon the aspect of the night, did so with a sigh at the thought of what she considered her master's mad perseverance, in seeking adventures at such a time. She made an effort to dissuade him from the course he was pursuing.

"Sir," she said; "it's time you gave up dozing all day, when other people are awake, and prowling about all night, like an old tom cat: cannot you do as other folks do, and get up at a proper hour in the morning, taking your breakfast, dinner, tea and supper, like a Christian; and then go to bed like a respectable person?"

"No," said the Night Adventurer with a smile; 'I am afraid I cannot. You know, Martha, that I am alone in the world; you know that I have no relations, and that I make but few intimates—indeed, I may almost say none, but we must all have some pursuit, or we should die of slow *ennui*. Now, my fancy is, to sleep in the day-time, for I don't care about people with their artificial looks, and daylight hypocrisies."

"But I have known you go out in the day-time."

"Exactly, Martha; I seek adventures at night, and, if I encounter one that requires to be carried out in the day, then I do not shrink from the sun-light. I detest oppression, and if, at midnight, I find that it exists, I am happy enough at mid-day, if an opportunity presents itself, to do my best to crush it; so now, farewell, until the morning's light, for I have had my breakfast."

"Your tea, you mean," said the old woman ; for not only was she determined to have the last word, but the question of 'tea *versus* breakfast,' was one she had made up her mind not to be defeated upon.

The Night Adventurer said no more, but went from his house full of pleasing anticipations, that that evening would produce something that would enable him to enter a record upon his projected journal of an interesting character.

CHAPTER II.

THE NIGHT ADVENTURER MAKES FURTHER ACQUAINTANCE WITH HIS READERS.

THOSE who have already perused so much of these pages as have been written, will please to understand that I, the Night Adventurer, myself, penned them as a kind of introduction between me and the reader ; I have no biographer, nor, indeed, do I desire one, for it is not of myself I have much to say, except so far that I become the medium through which the actions and feelings of other persons are apparent. And now that the reader knows something of me, and is aware that I will call my tea my breakfast, in spite of old Martha, my respected housekeeper, and that it is a kind of mania of mine to sleep in the day, and go out in the night in search of adventures, I shall proceed, in the first person, to relate what occurred to me in the course of those expeditions. I shall have no reservation, but in the order that the things happened shall they be recorded : I will insert no falsehoods for the sake of dressing up a story, because I consider myself, and I wish my readers to consider so likewise, that the great charm of these revelations consist in their absolute accuracy. I make no doubt, but most pleasantly together shall we proceed, and, if I make an alteration of a name or of a date in any of my stories, it shall only be upon one ground, and that is one which I am sure my readers will not blame me for considering, because it shall be to spare the feelings of living persons from being hurt by a recital of matters in which they themselves or their most intimate companions have borne a part. And this is the only circumstance under which I shall feel myself justified in not being perfectly candid ; so that I claim great confidence for those who may peruse my pages ; and if any gentleman should become smitten with the idea of becoming a Night Adventurer himself, and go out for a whole month together without meeting with anything more romantic than being told by the policeman to move on, he will not consider that as any reason why I should not have met with the most perilous and moving adventures that can be imagined. And so, without further preface, as I am quite as anxious to get to my revelations as I hope the reader is, I at once commence with a recital of what befel me during the first week that I commenced night adventuring, and as this affair resolves itself into a neat and complete little history, shall call it

"A. B. ; OR, THE BOARDING-SCHOOL AT NEASDON."

I had been out four nights ; unsuccessfully I had traversed many of the London streets ; I had dived into the suburbs, and although once or twice I flattered myself that I fancied an adventure was about to commence of a romantic and poetic character, the circumstances have often resolved themselves into the plainest matter-of-fact prose that can be imagined, and I was all abroad again. I kept these disappointments to myself, for the triumph of my old housekeeper, Martha, would have been prodigious.

The fifth night was one of storm ; it was the autumn of the year, and the fall of the leaf had just commenced ; the weather, like some coy beauty with two admirers, seemed to be doubting and hovering between winter and summer. Sometimes the nights would be calm, mild, and serene, as those of the summer's prime ; and then, again, a marked change would ensue, and, as if the elements had all of a sudden remembered it was the latter end of September, the rain and the wind would make the matter up in earnest and make a thorough uncomfortable night of it.

When I say an uncomfortable night, I do not speak of myself, for I like all sort of weather, and think that, if we choose to look at them with discerning eyes, we shall find that the rain, the wind, sleet, and the snow, have really as much to recommend them to our placid attention as the sunshine.

It has been well said, that the heart, too, creates its own beauty; and, if we will look upon these phenomena, of nature with distasteful eyes, they will appear calamitous, but let us say that we will enjoy them, and they will become forthwith admirable. There was nothing, therefore, in the aspect of this fifth night to keep me from going forth in search of adventure. The wind howled and whistled up and down the streets, and round the squares of London, carrying with it dashing showers of rain, and occasionally sleet and hail, which, at the turning of a corner, sometimes met so suddenly and unexpectedly, that it seemed to have been waiting for me. But I enjoyed all this : it was something like an adventure of itself, to be out on such a night, and then I had none of the consciousness of having to get home for the sake of a night's rest, which I could see painfully written in the serious countenances of the few chance passengers I met, and who seemed surprised at the easy manner at which I strolled along. I took my way towards that district of London which was northward of Oxford-street, comprehending a large locality, with rich and poor for its inhabitants—squalid misery and titled greatness.—The hour was eleven, but the inclement nature of the night had caused the streets to be much deserted, and one might have supposed, to look at them, that a much more lonely hour had been reached. As I walked down a street of new houses, only one side of which had been built upon, I saw standing at the corner a private cab, of fashionable shape and expensive appointments. It was opposite to no one house in particular, but seemed as if drawn up and waiting for some one, who, from the impatience of the horse, for he was fretting and stamping, I conjectured was long in coming. As I paused a moment I heard a voice from within the cab, say :—"Confound her! this is always the way, except when I am not to my time, and then, of course, she would be here to the minute; hang all old women, say I; what on earth can be the use of them? and as for this girl, I don't see anything in her."

I paused, and took shelter in a door-way, and scarcely had I done so, when I saw a portly-looking female figure coming slowly up the street. She was one of those old women, whom you cannot look upon for a moment without knowing they have the highest opinion of their own importance; there was a tremulous movement of her head, and a sort of ancient swagger about her, that spoke volumes as regards her character.

"Hang her! here she comes," said the man in the cab; "there is a deal of assumed dignity; then she is as proud as Lucifer, and thinks herself such a wonderful person, because she is useful to the duke; there is no putting up with her."

The old dame very slightly quickened her pace, when she saw the cab, and paused upon reaching it.

"Now marm," said the servant, for such he was who was in it, "jump up, I have been waiting for you this half-hour."

"How dare you address me in that language?" and her head vibrated like that of some old mandarin in a tea-dealer's window; "how dare you speak to me in that manner?"

"Oh, bother you, get in ; it's more trouble than enough, between the two of you—you and the duke—I have no end of trouble : first of all he is too particular to ride with you, because you cannot hold behind, like any other respectable tiger."

"I hold on behind—you low wretch!" said the old woman, "I stand upon a little square piece of leather, at the back of a cab, and hold by two bell-ropes—how dare you think of such a thing?"

"Oh! I suppose a person may think if they please, Mother Matthews, and not be hung for it; but with you it's nothing else but—how dare one do this and how dare one do the other? till you get as tiresome as the very devil. There, hold on and step as high as you can!"

" I am, you low fellow, stepping as high as I can."

" Then step a little higher, and you will be in the cab in a minute."

After a great deal of scrambling and swinging of the vehicle to and fro, which threatened its destruction, the old woman got in, and down went the spring upon that side with a vengeance that said a great deal for its elasticity.

I heard the groom mutter an oath, and I just saw a bit of his hat, around which was a silver-lace band, when they were ready to start.

On the impulse of the moment I glided behind the vehicle, and seating myself upon the foot-board, that had been so much despised by the old woman, I found myself whirled along at a rapid pace, I knew not where.

Now this was not the most dignified method of proceeding, but then I came out to look for adventures not dignity, and having a strong supposition from what I had overheard that some villany was afloat, I was not disposed to be scrupulous as to the means by which I could become acquainted with it, in order to thwart its progress.

Situated as I was, I soon found that I had great difficulty in overhearing what passed between those two uncongenial spirits, the old woman and the groom, and I feared that if I made any movement to better my curiosity that dissension would be inevitable. Probably, as it was, I owed the impunity with which I travelled solely to the fact that the economy of the cab was so deranged by the old woman, that the groom was no judge as to whether any one was behind it or not. When we got off the stones and into a soft country road, which the rain had made extremely muddy, I found that I could hear much plainer what ensued, and understand in a more connected form the dialogue that took place between the groom and the old woman, whom he called Matthews.

"It is a great bore, Mother Matthews," he said, "for you to put the duke up to an affair so far from town."

" That is no business of yours, Master William," said the old woman, " and when you address me, for the future, I will trouble you to call me Miss Matthews, if you please !"

" Miss Matthews—the devil ! well, that is a good idea. Miss Matthews ! you won't say a better thing than that to night, old one."

" You impertinent wretch ! I shall take an opportunity of telling the duke of your insolence."

" That you may, and welcome ; you are a nice old article—and so we have got to go as far as Neasdon, have we ?"

" Yes, to be sure, and that's not very far ; the girl's name is Amelia Bruton ; she has no friends, so there can be no bother."

" Now, aint you a nice piece of goods? because the poor girl has no friends she is to be picked out by you to be destroyed. I tell you what it is, old Mother Matthews, some of these days my feelings will get the better of me, and then this cab will upset and you will break your damned old neck !"

" Murderer !" said Miss Matthews, " you low wretch ! you nearly had the wheel against a post then."

" And so she's no friends, has she ?"

" No more but an old country curate of the name of Bruton, a tottering old fool, with one foot in the grave ; they do say he supports her at school, but I don't believe that, for he has only eighty pounds a year for himself, I am told ; and is it a likely thing indeed he would keep a girl at boarding-school out of that ?"

" Well he's an old trump if he does."

" An old trump."

" An old trump ! and I wish you were so ; but here we are, I suppose, not far off."

" Not very—you must go down that lane."

" What, that lane ! why it's up to the axles in mud ; the horse will never be able to struggle through it."

" You have got a whip and you can go on lashing him ; what is the use of a whip, I wonder, if it aint to make dumb cattle go ?"

" Bravo !" said the groom ; " humanity all the world over. I suppose you think a horse has no more feeling than you have ; but I can tell you you are wrong then, and as for keeping on lashing him away, it's a thing I won't do ; if he will go through the mud let him, but if he won't—he won't."

They turned now down the lane, which Miss Matthews had indicated, and truly it was in a most deplorable condition, for the few hours rain that had taken place had produced there an amount of mud beyond all calculation.

But yet the horse went through it, although I regretted to add my weight to the cab ; but if I had got down I should have been up to my neck in a few moments, besides running the worst chance of a discovery.

These inducements made me remain where I was and make no attempt to leave my protected position ; so that, at all events, I was conveyed with some degree of safety through the mud, which, although it splashed upon all sides, scarcely reached where I was.

The lane was about three-quarters of a mile in length, as nearly as I could judge, and we were nearly twenty minutes at the very least in traversing it, on account of its dreadfully miry condition, but when we did get clear of it a tolerably firm road presented itself, and besides the night had altered much for the better, and, notwithstanding the wind still blew in blustrous gusts, the rain had ceased, and here and there breaks in the sky indicated a more favourable state of the weather as rapidly approaching—a thing most devoutly to be wished.

Such, I suppose, had been the anxiety of the groom and the apprehensions of Miss Matthews during the progress down the lane, that scarcely a word had been interchanged, but, now that they were clear of it, they spoke again freely although with no better understanding than before.

" Well, now," said the groom, " can you point out the right address ?"

"Of course I can ; it's not likely, Mr. William, that I should not be able to do that—you can drive on, for it's right through the village."

" Further still, is it ?"

" Yes, to be sure; it's a lone house, surrounded by its own grounds—a handsome place—and belongs to some nobleman or other that I did hear the name of, but forget."

" And who keeps it now ?"

" Why the schoolmistress to be sure."

" Well, of course I know that, but I want to know who the schoolmistress is ?"

" Then she is Mrs. Green, if that's any news to you, and the garden-wall we are now passing belongs to the house."

The groom now slackened the pace of the horse, and it occurred to me that the best thing I could do would be to get down, or else, when they stopped, I should run a great chance of being discovered, which was a thing I was far from wishing, because I hoped to be able to circumvent the machinations of that horrible Miss Matthews, who was so evidently bent upon achieving the destruction of the young girl she named Amelia Bruton.

Indeed, if I had got but one more piece of information I should have been contented and have found my way to town, perhaps by some other method than that by which I had reached the village of Neasdon, for my readers may be well aware that I could have no great desire to get back the same way I had come, to say nothing of the risk of discovery, which might completely defeat my scheme I should propose to myself for rescuing the girl from the fate which, it was quite evident, was designed for her by the unprincipled Miss Matthews.

But the point upon which I was still anxious to obtain information was concerning the duke that had been mentioned, and to whose identity I had no clue whatever. I did not attribute this so much to caution, on the part of the groom or Miss Matthews, for they both evidently conversed with the greatest freedom, and like persons who had no suspicion of being overheard ; but, no doubt, the title of the duke was so familiar to them, that they never thought of using it when talking of him, being satisfied that they understood each other by merely saying the duke.

For this reason, then, and with the hope of hearing the title mentioned, I did not leave the place, although I got down from the back of the cab, and walked on under the cover of the wall until I saw it stop, and a whispered conference took place between the groom and Miss Matthews.

They did not wait above five minutes, and it was quite evident to me that the object of the visit at that time was for nothing more than that the groom might be enabled to identify the place again, and conduct his master to it.

With extreme leisure he began trotting the horse slowly towards town, and with some difficulty I followed, and got up again behind.

I suppose now I must have given some unlucky jerk to the cab, for although at the moment of my getting up I had heard their voices, the conversation had suddenly ceased, and all was still.

I held my very breath, with the hope that the suspicion would disappear, and that I should get on as well as I had done before. I began to flatter myself that this was indeed the case, as the horse went on at the same pace, and no remark was made, but I had soon reason to perceive, and to acknowledge the truth of the fact, that it is much more difficult to quell suspicion than to rouse it, for suddenly the groom gave a great lash with his whip behind the cab, and cried aloud—

" I think I had you there ; get down, you boy, will you ?"

" Do you really think," said Miss Matthews, " there is a boy behind ?"

" I am certain of it; I heard him get up."

Another slash with the whip was as unsuccessful as the first, for neither touched me, and this second time the lash got so entangled round one of the large springs at the back of the cab, that William could not recover it ; and I, feeling that my position was now longer tenable, took the opportunity of slipping down, and concealing myself close to a hedge by the roadside.

William was compelled to alight to disentangle his whip, and I heard him say—

" It was a mistake after all, for it was nobody, and yet I would have sworn I heard somebody get up, or rather felt him, for the cab gave a swing back."

" It's really doing nothing," said Miss Matthews, " but swinging backwards and forwards all the time."

I heard no more, for away they went at a smarter pace, and soon drove down again into the narrow lane which led to the London high road.

And here I was at a place I knew very little of, at half-past twelve o'clock at night, without the chance of getting the slightest conveyance towards London, or any accommodation in the way of lodging where I was.

There was no resource. I must walk to London; it had to be done, and therefore the sooner it was commenced the better.

The roads were dreadfully miry, but the sky over head was clear, so, shutting my eyes to the consequences of being bedaubed in mud, I strode on through thick and thin, feeling how utterly futile it was in the dark, and, considering the distance I had to go, to attempt to pick my way.

It was indeed a long and toilsome walk before I got into the Edgeware-road, and even then I was a couple of miles from my house, and, extremely weary, I struck on the nearest way, and passed the end of the same street where I had first seen the cab waiting.

I involuntarily paused and glanced towards the spot, which now was vacant, and no doubt Miss Matthews had been put down a good hour before my arrival on foot along the heavy road I had had to traverse.

" I would give something," I said, " to ascertain who that cab belongs to ; but it was no use lingering there with any such hope, so I walked on, the only persons in the street besides myself being two young women, who were walking slowly in advance of me, and who appeared to be in earnest conversation."

As I approached closer to them I found that one of them was weeping bitterly, and that the other was attempting to overcome her cause of grief by such commonplace and ordinary expressions of sympathy as suggested themselves to her.

" Yes," said the one who was weeping, " but who would have thought it of her—the work-box and the silver thimble ?"

No. 2.

"I won't think," said the other, "I won't think it. Maria, you may depend it is a mistake."

"No, it's no mistake; I wish it was. Joe, you know, had had his holiday, but I was bound to get home by eleven, and Joe is quite willing to swear."

"Well, of course, he is, Maria," said the other; "you know that Joe is rather given to swearing."

"Well, but I don't mean that sort of swearing—I mean in the way of an affidavit. Joe is quite willing to swear that he saw William at the corner of Queen Ann-street with his master's cab."

This sharpened my ears, and I thought to myself—

"Surely they allude to the same circumstance that I myself have observed, and I shall now hear who the duke is."

"Well, but you know, Maria," said the other, "the duke keeps bad hours, and lately he has always taken William with him; so you should think nothing of that."

"Now, Ann," said the girl, who still spoke through her tears, "now, Ann, you are enough to vex anybody; you know as well as I that the duke was at home, and besides, Joe declares it was a woman that got into the cab."

"Confound all these people!" thought I, "there is no getting anything out of them but the duke; they might just as well, some of them, stumble over his title. How on earth now am I to worm myself into the confidence of these girls? If I speak to them they will run off in a great fright. If I follow them home I may find out who the duke is, or I may not; so, what is to be done?"

I reflected for a few moments, but could come to no conclusion, until I heard the girl who was weeping say—

"It's all happened just as the countrywoman in Shropshire said it would. Somebody was to pretend to love me, whose name began with a W., and that means William of course, and then I was to beware of a dark woman, and that's the woman who got into the cab of course, and then I was to have a great surprise."

"Which now comes true," said I, "stalking up to them, and confronting them."

Each uttered a fainting scream, and started back a pace or two.

"Do not be alarmed," I said; "I am your friend. Did you never hear of Rowdoski, the famous conjuror?"

"No, if you please, sir," said one of them; and then she whispered to her companion, "Come along, come along, don't speak to him."

"You are wrong," said I; "and, if you will come to this address to-morrow at two, the famous Rowdoski will tell you who it was got into the cab, and how to save William from being transported."

"Transported," said the girl, who was named Maria, "Heaven preserve us!"

I tore off that part of one of my cards which contained my name, and handed her the remainder, which had only the address upon it.

"Ask for Rowdoski," I said, "and be punctual; you may come without any fear of harm, and indeed you may bring who you please with you to protect you—farewell!"

So saying I turned upon my heel, and walked away; but, after I had turned the corner in the next street, I crept slowly back again, and watched them.

They were in earnest conversation on the spot when I had left them, but in a few moments they walked slowly away, and I was successful, without being myself observed, in seeing them go down the area to the kitchen of a house, the number of which I made a note of, as well as taking a good look at its general aspect. I then felt convinced that for that night I had accomplished all that it was possible to do, and feeling that I should have to rise at two o'clock in the day with the hope of receiving my visitors, I hastened homeward to get my necessary amount of repose, which I never liked, under any circumstances whatever, to cheat myself of. I revolved the circumstances in my mind according as they presented themselves to me, and could come to no other conclusion than that Miss Matthews, as she called herself, was getting a living in the most infamous manner, and that she was in the pay of the duke she mentioned, who I yet hoped to foil in the affair which he had undertaken.

I hope to foil him, too, through the instrumentality of his own servants, who, no doubt, he thought devoted to his wishes ; for it is a common mistake with such men to fancy, that when they hire a domestic all sorts of feeling, honesty, or morality are to be got rid of in the desire to serve them, and that those whom they feed and clothe are from that time forthwith mere abject creatures without the liberty of thought or action. I had, however, great hopes of being able to do something with William, whose hostility to Miss Matthews rather pleased me ; so that, upon the whole, I was well enough satisfied that, if I had not a certainty of being able to foil the duke and Miss Matthews, I had very good ground for hoping such a result. It struck me, before I retired to rest, that it would be a good thing to place the mistress of the boarding-school upon her guard ; but still there was time enough for that, and I did not think it was necessary to do so until after I had had the interview I hoped to have with the duke's servants, so I resolved to put it off until the hour I had fixed for their coming had, at all events, passed away.

There were two or three matters connected with the affair still, which I wanted to know. In the first place, I should like to have written to the poor curate, who, with his eighty pounds a-year, contrived to keep Amelia Bruton at boarding-school, but I knew not where to find him. And then, again, I should like to have been quite sure that the mistress of the boarding-school had nothing to do with the transaction. Perhaps it was very illiberal of me to think she had, and I ought at once, at this juncture, to say that I had no grounds, from what I had heard, for supposing she had. It was to the intense surprise of my housekeeper, Martha, that I rose at one o'clock on the next day. She stared at me when I descended the stairs as if I had been some apparition, and when I said to her, which I did very solemnly,—

" Martha, if one or two more young women should come here and ask for Rowdoski, you will show them into the back parlour ;" she evidently thought my intellects were a little deranged.

" And this is what it's come to at last," she said ; " well, if I did not think as much ! This comes of turning night into day and day into night, and calling his tea his breakfast."

" Don't be foolish, Martha," I said ; " I am not so mad as I was ; I am perfectly serious, so mind you do as I tell you, and let my black cat come up to the parlour."

Martha stared at me as if she were doubting the necessity of calling for assistance ; but, when she saw me sit down very composedly and unlock an old secretaire that I had, which contained, I believe, something of everything, and among other matters some chemical apparatus which I had, at one time, made great use of from attachment to the science, she merely jerked her head a number of times as one who should say, " Well, I give him up ! after this he may do what he likes and say what he likes."

I thought if my visitors came at all they would be punctual, so I got out a spirit lamp, a few chemicals which I knew would make a noise and a smother, an old theatrical wig that I possessed, and a pair of enormous false moustaches. By the time I had completed these arrangements and put on my disguise, Martha came up with the cat ; but, when she saw me, her mouth and eyes opened so wide that it seemed doubtful if they would ever close again, while the cat, who knew me well enough through all disguises, jumped upon the table and sat down at my elbow according to custom.

" Why, Martha," I said, " what are you staring at ? I like to do something useful, as I am going to set up in business as a conjuror."

" The Lord be good to us !" said Martha ; " what next ?"

" A knock at the door," said I ; " don't you hear it ? now recollect, Rowdoski is my name, and whoever asks for me by that name is to be shown in here."

I listened attentively at the door of the back parlour, while Martha opened the street-door, and it was a great disappointment to me when a male voice, instead of that of either of the servants, said, in rather perturbed accents, " Oh ! if you please, mum, does Mr. Rowsey-musky-busky live here ?"

" Something of the sort," said Martha, " lives here, and I dare say you are right ; who are you, boy, and what do you want ?"

" If you please, mum, I am Joe ; they calls me in the kitchen Don Giovanni, 'cause I am quite the reverse, and Maria and Ann was afeard as it was a sell, so they have poked me on at the point of two umbrellas to come and see if Mr. Rowsey-smokem lives here."

" Oh, yes," said Martha, impatiently ; " I suppose it's right enough."

" Thank you, mum—wery much obliged ; you needn't shut the door, mum; they is only round the corner."

Away ran Joe, and presently he came back, accompanied by the two girls, who were whispering together in a terrible fluster. Old Martha was almost too indignant to do the honours of the house ; but, knowing me to be rather a positive personage, she did at last condescend to show them into the back parlour, where I was looking as grave as possible, with my friend the black cat winking and blinking by my side. My appearance evidently made a great impression, and the girls stood very near the door, while Joe, whom they brought with them as a safe-guard, was evidently in a state of great perspiration, for I saw him shake in every limb.

" If you please, sir," said one, and it was she who was named Ann who spoke, " please, sir, are you the great conjuror, Rollan-dusky ?"

" I am," I said, for I thought that quite as good a name as that I had myself invented ; " wait a moment here, if you please, until I have read a letter that has just arrived from the Emperor of China."

" Certainly, sir, we aint in a hurry."

I took a letter from my desk and pretended to read it ; and then, wrapping it up, I threw it upon the floor, and at the same time took care to explode a small quantity of nitrate of silver, which produced such an explosion that both Ann and Maria screamed, and Joe tried to escape. My black cat, too, was so frightened that she jumped upon Joe's back, making him believe that the devil had got hold of him ; for she dug all her claws into him at once.

" Let me go ! oh, let me go !" said Joe ; " I did steal the dripping ; let me go."

It took me some time and some trouble to restore order, and then I said solemnly :—

" Joe, this would not have happened if you had not been guilty of a petty larceny as regards the kitchen stuff."

Joe gave a trembling assent to this proposition, and said he knowed it.

Then I turned to Maria, saying, " Your suspicions of William are not correct, although he is now engaging himself in transactions of a nature not only disgraceful to himself, but such as will separate you from him for ever, and bring down upon him legal consequences. I should like to warn him."

" He wouldn't believe me," said Maria.

" Tell him he shall be made to believe ; you shall give him from me a written paper, which shall explain to him his future fate, and when I tell him of some things which he thinks are now only known to himself, he will be able to put some faith in my predictions of the future."

" Yes, sir," said Maria, curtseying, much struck with what I said ; " please, sir, what have we got to pay ?"

" Nothing whatever," said I ; " you cannot suppose it possible that any one possessed of the amount of knowledge which I profess can require money. Are not all the diamond mines in the centre of the earth at my disposal ? Have I not familiar spirits at my back ?"

" There's every one of them been upon my back," Joe said, " for I feel it now."

I could scarcely refrain from laughing ; but it was so highly necessary that I should keep up my character as a conjuror, that by great effort I did keep my gravity, and wrote upon a piece of paper the following words :—

" To William, the Servant of the Duke,—The most fearful consequences, both here and hereafter, will be the lot of him who leagues with others to betray innocence ; you must no longer associate yourself with any doings with the woman Matthews, except to defeat her, and you must see me, for the purpose of aiding in the preservation of Amelia Bruton.''

I placed a pen before Maria, and said, " You must yourself fill in the surname of your lover, and likewise the title of the duke."

Without making the least question of whether I possessed either of these species of information or not, she wrote the name of Woodward for the groom, and C——as the title of the nobleman, which rather surprised me, for he was a Scotch peer, who pretended, whenever he spoke in the House of Lords, to a great deal of religion.

Maria promised faithfully to place the paper in William's hands, and being quite satisfied that I had done all I could to bring him home, which was what I wanted, I turned to her and said :—

" Now, is there anything that you wish to demand of me ? if so, speak at once, Joe, and speak freely."

" No, no," said Joe, in a great fright ; " I don't want to know nothing, I knows too much already."

" But surely you would like a peep into futurity, Joe."

" No, I wouldn't ; if it's all the same to you, sir, I'd rather go than have any more of that sort of thing. I'm blessed if it don't hurt above a bit."

Joe kept an eye on the cat, who somehow or other seemed to have contracted a great dislike to him, and every now and then she set up her back and looked as if she would like again to put her twenty talons into him.

" Well," I said, " William can be told that I shall be at home to-morrow at two."

I had a taper burning before me, with which I set light to some of the red fire, similar to that which is used upon the stage at the last scene of a melodrama, but the moment Joe began to see it, and the cat began to sneeze in consequence of the unpleasant effluvia, he bolted out of the place like a shot, and the two girls followed him as quickly as they could, which I was glad enough of, for I had really nothing more to say to them just at present.

I hope for the best results from this scheme which I have put in practice, because if I had gone to William the groom at once, and merely told him that I had found out what was going on, it is very unlikely I should have made any impression upon him ; but now that I consider I had enlisted his sweetheart on my side as well as arousing his fears, I did expect a favourable result.

And then I sat myself down seriously to think how I could possibly discover the Rev. Mr. Bruton, who, I had heard, paid for the girl at school. I could think of no way but inserting an advertisement into one of the morning papers, requesting him to communicate his address, for although I might possibly have got it at the school, yet it will be borne in mind that I had not made up my mind, and indeed had no opportunity of doing so in regard to whether the authorities of that establishment had anything to do with the matter or not.

At all events, there could be no harm in the advertisement I considered, as it might at once procure me an interview with the person most interested in the matter. I accordingly drew up an advertisement in the following terms—

" If the Rev. Mr. Bruton, curate of some parish in England, will communicate with A.B., No. 10, Wyndham-street, Marylebone, he will receive some information of deep interest concerning one whom he has befriended."

This I had inserted in a morning paper, and then waited patiently for the result both of that and my interview with William, which I shortly expected.

I did not go out that night in search of adventure, because I had no wish to complicate my affairs, but, on the contrary, liked always to see the end of one thing before I commenced another, so I remained at home and waited for William, being resolved to adopt my course of conduct towards him specially as regarded what he might say or do.

There had fallen from his lips some expressions that gave me hopes of better things from him than what might be merely expected from his fears, but then they were only hopes, and could not be calculated upon.

If, however, I could by any means influence him to act with me, instead of from fear of me, of course it would be much better and much more satisfactory in every possible respect ; but on the whole I congratulated myself that I was doing all I could.

By a little before two o'clock I had got all my arrangements complete for the reception of the groom, if he should come, and precisely at that hour I heard a knock at my door, and listening as before, I heard a man's voice ask for me.

I had, in the meantime, said enough to old Martha to induce her to assist me in what I was about with a good spirit, so that now she played her part better, and bowed William in with all due solemnity.

I received him with perfect coldness and some amount of *hauteur* which had all its effect upon him, and he shook a little as he sat down in a chair which I pointed out to him.

"I have come, sir," he said, "because a young woman of the name of Maria Clements has given me this paper."

" Well ? "

"Well, sir, I—I'm very sorry indeed."

" You ought to be very sorry indeed, for allowing yourself to be made a party to such a transaction, and the only way in which you can help what you have assisted in, will be by doing your utmost to counteract the plans of those who would be the destruction of the innocent young girl you have mentioned."

" Amelia Bruton, sir ? "

" The same."

" Well sir, after what you have said, and after what Maria has said, I quite hate myself for having done anything in it ; just tell me what to do and all shall be right, sir."

"First of all, tell me, does the schoolmistress know aught of it ?"

" She does not. It's all got up by old Mother Matthews, who goes about the out-skirts of London, and sees the girls belonging to the different schools, and if one is very pretty and unprotected, she lets some of her customers know, and an attempt is made to get her away."

"Infamous ! And what may be the age of the young creature, Amelia Bruton ? "

" About sixteen, they say, and as beautiful as an angel."

" And could you for one moment have connived at such villany ? "

" I've got my eyes open now, sir ; just tell me what to do, and it shall be done, sir, you may depend."

"All I want you to do at present is to foil your master, and let me know till I can see the reverend gentleman who has placed the young girl at the school and apprise him of her danger. You can do no more at present ; and you ought to be thankful that you have escaped being led into the ruinous crime contemplated by the woman Matthews and your master. I have advertised for the curate, Mr. Bruton, and have no doubt but he will answer me at once and remove the young girl from the school at the moment, so that then the danger will be over."

" It will, sir; there's no occasion to have any conjuring disguise with me, sir, now."

I was silent for a moment or two, and then I said :—

" William, how I came by my knowledge it concerns myself alone to know. Let it suffice that I do know all ; I shall go to the school to-day, and warn the mistress."

" There couldn't be a better idea than that, sir ; I'm proud to the best of my poor judgment to say the best I can, sir, in a matter like this, where I feel I have done wrong, and if I were you, sir, I'd get a positive promise from the school-mistress that Miss Amelia shouldn't be taken away by anybody but Mr. Bruton the curate."

" I shall," said I ; " and now, William, I shall not detain you any longer ; you may thank your stars, again I tell you, that you have escaped going any further in this nefarious transaction, and mind you do not forget to give me notice of anything that occurs."

"I will not, sir," said William, "you may be assured, and I shall have reason to thank you the longest day I've got to live."

So saying William took his leave, and then I doffed my masquerading guise, telling myself that I should have no further need for it, for that all the proceedings now would be plain and above-board.

I was much gratified, as my readers may well imagine, and having taken an unusually early dinner, I started off to make my visit to the school and place its mistress upon her guard against anything that might occur.

I got into a coach bound for Edgeware, and knowing tolerably well the nearest route to Neasdon, I alighted at the corner of a beautiful lane, and just as the day gave cordial signs of sinking, and a pleasant serene summer-looking twilight very different from that of the preceding evening, was stealing over the landscape. I reached my place of destination, and stood before the massive iron gates of what had no doubt once been the mansion of some noble owner, but which now in course had become devoted to those who reared the tender plant and taught] the young idea how to shoot.

How hold a man feels when he goes upon a great and good errand anywhere! I took a view of Belle Vue House, as it is called, without intending anything in the shape of a pun, which, under the circumstances, would be quite abominable, and then rung with an air of a man who knew of his welcome beforehand, and waited with complacency for the issue.

The people of Belle Vue House seemed in no great haste to answer the gate, for I had to wait a considerable time, until at length a servant girl cautiously came down a gravel path, within two feet of the gate, and suddenly disappeared to my great surprise. Then I heard some whispering, and a voice said, "Push it along!" and then another voice said, "What will he do? and are you sure it's him?" an expression which said much for the mystery, but little for the manners of Bellevue establishment.

"Hilloa!" I cried; "now, are you going to open the gate?"

"I'm sure it's the man," said another voice; "push it along!"

I was completely puzzled, and began to fear I had come across a lunatic asylum, instead of young ladies' boarding school. I seized the bell and gave it a violent tug, and then a female made her appearance, and said in tremulous accents:—

"If—if you please, sir, to give the gate a pull—pull—pull, and then walk in—what a disturbance there'll be!"

"A disturbance," said I, as I pulled the gate, and found that it opened easily, "why should there be a disturbance?" But I soon found out why, for the moment I put my foot in, click went something, and I was caught in a steel trap, the shark-like teeth of which almost went through my foot. Too well then I understood what was meant by "push it along."

"Damnation!" I roared, "what's the meaning of this?"

"Call the constable—call the constable!" shouted two or three voices; and then there came towards me a demure elderly-looking female, carrying a light, who, by the firmness of her aspect, I conjectured to be the mistress of the establishment.

"Individual," she said, "it is to be hoped that your improvement for the next quarter, I mean for the time that you will be consigned to incarceration in a receptacle for offenders, vulgarly denominated a gaol, will be conducive to the two copies of memory may be improved, and do unto others as you would have others do unto you."

"But, bless me, madam, why should I be held by the leg in this way?"

"Young man, young man, control your evil passions, as Mr. Mavor remarks—'honour your superiors,' and in your next vocation, I mean when you are released from that state of bodily thraldom—now, Miss Jennings, what do you want here? Give me leave to say, Miss Jennings, that I really thought and understood you had retired to that repose which is considered essential to the revivification of the juvenescent frame, after what we my call the 'labor omnia vincit' of the day."

"If you please, madam," said Miss Jennings, "that gentleman is not the gentleman who got into Miss Mundell's bed-room, if you please, ma'm."

"What!" exclaimed the schoolmistress; "cerulean powers! that I should live to hear such an expression in this establishment! My brain reels, and despair takes possession of me. Oh! Miss Jennings, you've made me uncomfortable; retire, miss, at once to the dormitorial portion of this establishment," and, assuming a recumbent posture, "do not presume to exhibit your corporeal frame, until after the matitudinal meal of to-morrow morning. And now, sir, what have you to say for yourself?"

"Do you usually, madam," said I, "put every visitor's leg into a man-trap before you ask him any questions?"

"Sir, the profound repose of this establishment, and the high moral influences that pervade it, have been outraged by a fiend in human shape, with, I may say——"

"Two legs, ma'am," put in one of the young ladies, who had stolen down to the gate.

"Legs!" cried the schoolmistress, with a shriek. "Do I inhale the oxygen of the atmospheric air, and do astronomical phenomena continue as heretofore; while the word 'legs' is uttered by any young lady of my establishment You will retire, Miss Bennett, and betake yourself to your repose, without that exhilarating sink of milk and water, of which you are accustomed to become a recipient at this period of the evening. You may imbibe some aqueous fluid, miss, from the canter in your bed-room, but that is all."

"Madam," said I, "I don't know but that I should be so much amused at any other time with your grandiloquent mode of speaking, that I could listen to it for an hour or two, without any trouble; but now, when my foot is in this infernal machine of yours, you can't think how heavily the time lags; and to borrow some expressions from yourself, I will repudiate verbosity, and request the corporeal gratification of having my left pedal supporter extracted from the ingenious mechanical contrivance which has been pushed along."

"He seems quite a gentleman," said the schoolmistress; "this language is highly correct."

I thought it high time to follow up the advantage I had gained already, so I continued:—

"I am quite aware, madam, that this is the first establishment in Europe for morals, philosophy, religion, and the use of the globes; and, therefore, I have come a monstrous distance to make you an interesting communication respecting one of your young ladies."

"Is it I!—Is it I!" cried about four-and-twenty female voices, and a crowd of the scholars showed themselves closely behind the mistress.

"Let me die now!" said the governess. "I often thought, that if three of my young ladies were to speak at once, it would be the death of me."

"What's the communication?" said all the young ladies, as if they'd been practising something for the million. "Is anybody going to be married?"

The schoolmistress reeled again. No doubt she felt like some great autocrat, who, all of a sudden, finds that he is but human.

"This will be the end of me," she said; "I shall turn over the last leaf, and finis, with some flourishes, will be written on my tomb. Ladies, ladies! I'll put you all in the stocks, and you shall wear the back-board for a month a-piece."

"Ha, ha, ha, ha, ha!" laughed all the scholars, very shrilly; exhibiting a memorable example, of how people will do things in multitudes, which alone, they would shrink from with trembling terror.

"Shall I let the gentleman's foot out?" said one of the servants, producing a key.

"Yes, my good girl," said I, "do, it will be a kindly act, and quite consistent with your pretty dimples."

The schoolmistress shrieked, and I saw I was making an unfavourable impression, so I added :—

"Ahem! how the mind is filled with care, when that portion of the person in which the brains are not supposed to reside, treads upon this classic ground."

The servant laughed, and released me from the trap, upon which I advanced, and made a general bow.

"Young ladies," I said, "I hope I have not alarmed any of you. I assure you, however paradoxical it may appear, I am not half so ugly as I look."

The girls all laughed, and the schoolmistress approaching me with stately dignity, said :—

"Sir, two extremely strong constables are now sent for, and if you really have no communication to make, which warrants this desecration of this temple of knowledge and of purity, you will be prosecuted as the law directs."

"Madam," I said, "the communication I have come to make is a serious one; it is one only fitted to your private ear, and if you will grant me five minutes' audience, I shall be able to prove to you that it much concerns the well-doing and stability of your establishment to know it."

I spoke these words so seriously, that she became convinced that I was not trifling with her, and she assumed a more rational aspect, as she conducted me towards the house.

"I do not wish, madam," I said, "at all to take up your time, or to intrude upon your establishment ; but allow me, in the first instance, to ask you if you have a young lady here of the name of Amelia Bruton?"

"We have, certainly."

"Then, madam, I have the pain to inform you that a plan, a most atrocious plan, has been formed for the purpose of taking her from you. Her beauty is the temptation of another which I know nothing of ; but which, I suppose, you will feel probably is a sufficient motive to those whose evil passions prompt them to make war upon that innocence which holds in its keeping so dangerous a gift."

"You alarm me, sir," said the schoolmistress, turning quite rational ; "she is a handsome girl."

"I thought as much ; and now, madam, without reserve, I will tell you all that has occurred."

I then narrated to her the whole facts of the case, only concealing how it was that I had come to a knowledge of them ; for I did not think it necessary to inform her of my predilection for night adventures, which my housekeeper, Martha, once said, in a particularly good humour, were, if I liked them, nothing to nobody.

When I had concluded she looked seriously alarmed, and said,—

"Sir, you would not have been caught in the trap to-night but that the rumour of some one haunting these premises for a bad purpose has been afloat, and it became my duty to catch whom I could."

"Madam," I said, "I think that the parties of whom I speak are not those who would have recourse to violence, it is some stratagem that you will have to apprehend, and therefore it is that I most particularly and urgently beg of you not to give up the custody of this young lady to anyone but the Rev. Mr. Bruton himself, who has consigned her to your care."

"I will not, sir, you may depend," said the schoolmistress ; "and I am very much obliged to you for your caution."

"You know the Rev. Mr. Bruton, of course, by sight, so that you cannot be imposed upon by anyone coming here and assuming the name of that gentleman ?"

"Know him, sir ? Oh, yes! we all know him well here ! The old gentleman comes to town regularly to fetch Amelia away for the vacations. He's as fond of her as if she were his own child, although, between you and I, I do not believe that there's any relationship at all between them."

"Indeed, you surprise me! Why, the similarity of name, one would think, bespeaks that fact."

"Yes, one would think so ; but I believe she is an orphan, solely depending upon him for support, and consequently you'll excuse my feelings."

No. 3.

Here the schoolmistress made up a face that "Punch" in his happiest days could not have rivalled—it was so exquisitely comical an exhibition of grief. If my execution was to have followed upon the spot for doing so I must have laughed. I tried to turn it off into a cough and then into a sneeze. I hope I succeeded, and I think I did, for she made no remark about it, but weut on thanking me, and saying, that she believed old Mr. Bruton was the best of men and a most exemplary clergyman.

"Where does he live?" said I.

"Oh, only in Kent, sir; he's the curate of Margetts-cum-Pumpingale."

"What a night!" said I; "I will write him a note, for although I have already advertised for him he may not chance to see that newspaper, in which case it would be some time, perhaps, before he hears of me; so I will write to him this night, and in the mean time, madam, I can only say that I am much pleased I have come here, and, to say nothing about the infernal machine which was pushed along, I can have no fault to find with my reception."

A glass of marvellously thin wine was given to me, and a biscuit about the size of an acidulated drop, and that was dignified by the name of refreshments. Although like the Scotchman, who had devoured six dozen larks to give him an appetite, I felt much the same.

Of course I did not expect to be asked to remain at Belle Vue Establishment, so I rose and bowed myself out with all the grace I could, hoping that the infernal machine had been pulled along somewhere else, and was not anywhere in my path of regress that I could put my foot in it.

And it was night again when I left the house—my own beautiful night—night that I admired, loved, reverenced! for was it not the parent of all my adventures? the prolific source from whence I drew from time to time mirth-moving incidents, as well as episodes of deep sensibility? Yes, I love thee, Night! and when I love thee not, Chaos shall come again.

CHAPTER III.

THE REV. MR. BRUTON CALLS UPON ME, AND SHOWS ME WHAT A COUNTRY CLERGYMAN OUGHT TO BE.

I REGRETTED now that I had advertised for the Rev. Mr. Bruton, because if he were an aged man—and the schoolmistress had represented him as such—the tenor of the advertisement might give him, what was now, much unnecessary alarm.

But it will be remembered that when I did advertise it was without having any knowledge as to whether or not I could trust the people of the school. The moment I got home now, which I did without accident or adventure of any sort whatever, I wrote and posted a letter for the reverend gentleman, in which I told him that, although I should be glad to see him, he need not give himself any unnecessary alarm, as I considered myself that I had done all that was necessary or that could well be done for the preservation of Amelia. I made some remarks upon the heinous nature of the offence that was sought to be committed by the duke and the infamous Miss Matthews, and concluded by expressing the great gratification it gave me to be able to have so far interfered with the matter, as to save an innocent person from so sad a fate.

And then I felt extremely well-satisfied with myself; my visit to the scholastic establishment had resulted in all that I could wish, and the promise which had been given me by the schoolmistress, that she would not on any account surrender Amelia Bruton to any one but the Rev. Mr. Bruton himself, satisfied me that in that quarter all was safe.

Since I had found that the reverend gentleman resided so short a distance from town, I had every reasonable expectation of an early visit from him, and I gave his name to my housekeeper, with strict injunctions to receive him when he came with the greatest civility, and to show him into my study.

I was seated at breakfast on the following morning—a real breakfast this time for, as I have said, when an adventure did occur in one of my night rambles that I chose to carry out, I by no means scrupled to do so in the day-time like any other Christian, as my housekeeper said.

I was seated at breakfast, then, when a tremulous sort of knock came at the street-door, and in a few moments Martha bustled into my room, and said,—

"He's come, sir, he's come; such a comfortable, old, worthy-looking gentleman!"

"Is it the Rev. Mr. Bruton?" said I.

"Yes, sir, that's what he says he is, and he seems ready to drop."

"Show him in instantly, don't delay a moment; show him into this room, never mind the study; perhaps he will take a bit of breakfast with me."

Martha bustled about in earnest, and soon ushered in one of the most respectable elderly-looking gentlemen I ever beheld.

He was plainly dressed in a clerical suit of black, which contrasted well with the silvery whiteness of his hair. I could perceive that he trembled, and that there was an expression of deep anxiety upon his countenance as he entered the apartment, so that I was most anxious as quickly as possible to reassure him and convince him that no danger could accrue to his young protégé at Belle Vue House after the precautions I had taken.

"Sir," I said, "I perceive that you are extremely anxious, and naturally so, I think; you may dismiss all fears from your mind; but, I presume, from your early appearance here, that you cannot have received my letter?"

"Letter, sir?" he said; "alas, no! it was an advertisement that alarmed me, and has brought me to you; from the first moment that it was pointed out to me, and that was not many hours since, I have endured great anguish, and came directly to you to inquire its meaning."

"Why, sir," I said, "it means that there was great danger to Amelia Bruton, who is at school at Neasdon."

"What!" cried the old man, and tears gushed to his eyes as he spoke; "danger to her?—danger to that innocent and beautiful being, who has been thrown by an unmerciful world upon my care? Surely, surely, there is no human heart could harbour —"

"Calm yourself, my dear sir," said I, "and I will explain to you that this is no false alarm; you will find that there is more wickedness in the world than you have probably ever imagined."

He listened to me with the most painful and close attention, while I detailed to him all the circumstances with which the reader is already acquainted."

When I had concluded, I could see that he had made a violent effort to control his emotion, but he was unsuccessful in doing so, and he fairly wept.

"This is the weakness of age, sir," he said, when he had better recovered; "pray, pardon it as such. I have been in indifferent health lately, and am, I fear, fast failing. You will excuse me, sir."

"Most certainly," said I; "your feelings do you honour, but let me beg of you to be composed."

"I must take the dear child home with me," he said, "it would kill me now to leave her where she is—she must go back with me to the old parsonage-house, where her poor mother breathed her last—that is, for a time; she shall come back when all possibility of danger is passed and over, and I can recover my serenity. Sir, you do not know how dear she is to me; I feel that I have not nerve to do so now, but you shall come and visit us, and as we sit beneath the ivy-mantled porch of my humble dwelling, I will tell you the sad story of Amelia."

"Believe me, sir," said I, "that the pleasure of making your acquaintance will prove to me an ample compensation for any trouble I may have had in this affair. I shall always look upon this visit of yours as one of the pleasantest hours of my existence."

"And is it not something, sir," he said, "for me, an old man, tottering on the grave's brink, to find my confidence in human nature thus restored? Let me hope, sir, that this will be the commencement of a friendship which—although it cannot last long, inasmuch as I must soon leave the world—will gild the remaining hours of my existence."

"Upon my part, sir, you may depend I shall ever esteem you."

"Many thanks, sir, many thanks; and now I must make an effort—weak and incapable as I feel—to go to Neasdon, and fetch the dear child away."

He rose from his chair; but I could perceive that he tottered, as he endeavoured to reach the door. It was grievous to see the state of weakness to which the good old man was reduced; and a sudden idea struck me that I might, at all events, relieve him from the fatigues of a journey to Neasdon, which he seemed so incapable of performing.

"Sir," I said, "are you quite resolved to take with you, to your home, Amelia?"

"Quite, quite," he said, "I should die to return without her."

"Then listen to me: there can be no reason why you should not remain here, and let me fetch her for you."

"Oh, sir! if that could be arranged, I might by rest recover more strength; But I have not come alone to London. The fact is that Mr. Brown, the innkeeper in the village where my curacy is situated, brought me the newspaper containing your advertisement; and, seeing the intense anxiety into which it threw me, he kindly brought me up to town in his chaise; and he is now waiting at an inn-yard not very far from here."

"It is a pity," I said, "that your house don't lie in the same road as the school. By what conveyance do you think of taking Amelia?"

"Why, sir," he said, "there is a stage coach, that starts from the Post-office and goes through the village every morning: but I don't like the dear child to go into a stage coach; they don't go, sir, so slow and safe as they used to in my young days: so I am thinking that Mr. Brown shall take her, gently and quietly, in the chaise, and I will go in the stage-coach myself."

"Very well, Mr. Bruton," I said, "that will do. I will run down to the school, while you make your arrangements. I shall not be above two hours gone altogether."

"And will you," he said, "do so much for the old man who has outlived all his earthly affections but one?"

"With pleasure."

"Bless you, sir; Heaven bless you! But I must write a note to the school-mistress, or she might have some scruples."

"You are right, Mr. Bruton: it would be better to do so."

He took up a pen; but it was pitiful and distressing to see the state of nervousness into which the old man had fallen. He could not write; and I stopped him, saying—

"Do not attempt it, sir. They have seen me once at the school, and know I came upon a friendly errand. Do you go over to your friend the innkeeper at once, and make your arrangements with him. I have no doubt I shall bring Amelia to you shortly."

He grasped both my hands, and I was much affected to see the tears gently rolling down his furrowed cheeks.

"Sir," he said, "the blessing of those who have no other friends save Heaven and yourself belongs to you! May you never know such sorrow as this old heart has suffered! And, when you see the dear girl Amelia, tell her—tell her——. No, no: I will tell her all myself. I can send no message to her but my dear affection."

The old man was pleased to see me make preparations for starting at once; and when I was ready he walked with me to the door, when we parted; he to proceed to where he had left his friend the innkeeper with the chaise, and I to make the best of my way to Neasdon. I could not but look after him as he went—there was something so good, and kind, and patriarchal in his appearance—and I said to myself, "That is the pattern of what an old country clergyman should be, and I fancy it will be long before I look upon his like again." As I went down to Neasdon I quite pleased myself with anticipation of the pleasure I should have some day soon, I hoped, in visiting the old clergyman at his house; and, if I might judge of that by the man, I might well have every reason to suppose it to be a calm, delightful, pleasant place, fitting for so gentle a spirit to dwell in.

* * * * * * *

My object was to lose no time; and, accordingly, I made an agreement with the driver of a hackney carriage to go to Neasdon and back again for a stipulated sum, so that no time would be lost in the proceeding. The distance from Oxford-street to the village of Neasdon is altogther not much above four miles-and-a-half, so that, when I mentioned two hours to the old clergyman, as the time that I should be absent, I gave myself ample latitude, and provided for all exigencies. I need not take up the time of my readers by any detail of what occurred at the boarding-school; suffice it to say that the mistress of that establishment put every faith in me, and opposed no difficulty to Amelia accompanying me to town, in order that the Rev. Mr. Bruton might himself, for a time, take charge of her—a course which, under the circumstances, she, the schoolmistress, considered the very best that could be adopted. As yet I had not had the satisfaction of seeing the young creature who was about to be committed to my charge; but, when I did see her, I at once admitted that those who had described her as beautiful had by no means been guilty of exaggeration. She was of that exquisite order of beings for which nature has done so much that in them are united all the charms of most exquisite delicacy, along with an appearance of healthfulness without which beauty would soon lose its choicest attributes. I might dilate for hours upon her eyes, her cheeks, the flowing tresses of her silken hair, and the musical cadences of her voice, which have left an impression upon my memory I should be sorry indeed to have effaced. The schoolmistress introduced me to her as a friend of Mr. Bruton's; and, without explaining to her any more of the circumstances, merely said that it was the wish of Mr. Bruton that she should spend a few weeks at the parsonage. I saw the young girl's eyes glisten with pleasure at the thought of exchanging the formalities of Belle Vue House for Mr. Bruton's home.

Less than a quarter of an hour sufficed to pack up such things as it was necessary Amelia should take with her, and those were placed on the coach after she and I had entered it. A friendly farewell was taken of the schoolmistress, and then the beautiful object of Miss Matthews's and the Duke's machinations was with tolerable rapidity taken to London, to be placed under the watchful guardianship of the old clergyman. I forebore to ask her any questions as we proceeded, or to say anything to her concerning the cause of this sudden determination of Mr. Bruton to have her at the parsonage for awhile. I considered that what he chose she should know he ought to be allowed himself to communicate to her, so we conversed on rather indifferent subjects; but I was far from being an indifferent listener to the observations of my young and interesting companion. She showed an intellect far exceeding her years, and there was an originality, as well as an amiable and beautiful simplicity about her remarks, that made them irresistibly pleasing. The time seemed to me uncommonly short, and we were in London streets again before I could have supposed we were half way on our journey. She told me she anticipated the delights of meeting her old friend and protector—the only friend, she said, she had ever known, and this was all the remark she made about her personal history. When we reached my home, I saw standing close to the curb-stone, immediately opposite to my door, an old fashioned, roomy-looking chaise, evidently not at all of London manufacture, and in it sat a ruddy-looking man in top-boots, and great white coat on him, and a broad brimmed hat much over-hadowed his rubicund countenance.

"That's Brown, the inn-keeper," I said, "for a thousand pounds! Do you know him, Amelia?"

"No," she said; "I know there is an inn."

He looked very hard at me as I came up, for I was leaning from the coach window, and when Amelia and I got out he touched his hat and said, " Beg pardon, sir, but Mr. Bruton has told me to wait here for a gentleman and Miss Amelia."

" Is your name Brown?"

" Yes, sir ; I keeps the Stag, and if ever you comes down to my place, though I says it perhaps as oughtn't to say it, you won't get better accommodation nowheres than at my house."

" I don't doubt it, my friend," said I ; " but where is Mr. Bruton ?"

" Why sir, you see I put up at the Goat-in-Boots, and when old Mr. Bruton comes to me there I seed as he was overcome a bit, and just as I said to him, ' Lor' sir, you should try and keep up your spirits,' a sort of fainting fit seemed to come over him, and down he went like a shot."

" Good heavens !"

" No harm done, sir; we got him round him again, and I got him an inside place n the stage, so he's gone home quite comfortable, and I promised as I'd bring Miss Amelia arter him as soon as ever I could."

" You are quite right," I said, " here is the young lady, mind you take great care of her, Mr. Brown."

" Care of her," he said ; " trust me for that ; she shall be the apple of my eye, sir, till I gives her to the old man, bless his heart !"

I assisted Amelia into the old-fashioned country chaise.   What she had heard about Mr. Bruton's condition had so much affected her that she could not speak, so I just told her to keep up her spirits, for that there was no real harm, and to give my compliments to Mr. Bruton, and say, that in the course of the next fortnight I would avail myself of his kind invitation and pay him a visit.   She thanked me by a look, then off they went.   I watched them from my door until they turned the corner, and then, giving my hands a rub together of satisfaction, I said, " Well, I think I have done that amazingly clever ; it has been capitally managed from first to last, and if all my night adventures have so pleasant a termination, and do so much real good, I shall set myself up quite as a public benefactor."

My old housekeeper, Martha, was quite delighted to see me look so pleased, and advised me to have a bottle of my old East India madeira, which she knew I never drew a cork of, except upon very festive occasions.

" Well," I said, " I will ; I am quite sufficiently pleased with my morning's work to commit that extravagance, so bring it up, Martha, at once."

The old dame bustled to execute my order, for she knew that she always came in for a glass of the rare wine, so she brought two wine glasses as a thing of course. I tapped the bottle, and filled the glasses, then, pushing one towards her as I raised the other to my lips, " Now, Martha, we will drink to the health of the Reverend Mr. Bruton."

" Very good, sir ; he does seem the nicest old gent. I ever saw——a comfortable old soul, sir, I cal. him ; here's towards the health of Mr. Bruton, and may he live long and die—— Lor' what a knock ! and all of a moment, too."

There was certainly a short rat-tat at the street-door, and we both put down our wine untasted.

" Who can that be now?" said Martha.

" I cannot tell," said I ; " but the shortest way is to go and open the door ; there, don't you hear it's some one who is impatient at being kept so long; we shall have the doors battered down if you don't go at once."

" Drat some people," said Martha, " they expect everybody else to be like a steam-engine."

She went to the door, and I waited with some curiosity to know who it could be, because, as I have before remarked, I had very few visitors ; I heard some conversation going on in the passage, but could not detect its import ; and then I heard somebody shown by Martha into the next apartment.   In a moment after she came to me with a card in her hand, and to my intense astonishment read upon it, " The Rev. Augustus Bruton, Margetts, Kent."   I stared at the card for full a minute, and then rubbed my eyes to know if I was awake.   " Bless me," I cried, " I thought he was half-way home by this time ; what can have brought him back ?" I jumped up, and ran into the next room, exclaiming, "My dear sir, I am delighted to see you, although surprised at your unexpected return!" And then, to use a popular expression, anyone might have knocked me down with a feather, for, instead of the Rev. Mr. Bruton with his silvery locks and venerable appearance, I saw before me a little fat, oily man, with a shining bald head, and a face which looked as if he occasionally sacrificed to the illustrious John Barleycorn.

"What do you mean, sir?" he said, "what do you mean, by not expecting me to come back?"

"Who are you?" said I.

"Who am I? I am the curate of Margetts-cum-Pumpington."

"The devil you are! You are too late, sir; you impudent impostor! you audacious villain!"

"What! impostor, villain; have I been decoyed to London to be murdered? Did you write me this letter, or did you not?"

He threw my letter down before me, and that staggered me for an instant. A most frightful suspicion came across my mind, and I staggered into a seat, as I said, faintly,

"How came you by that letter?"

"Why, by post, to be sure, and I have come to town immediately upon the receipt of it to see you."

"Do you know Brown, the innkeeper, and is there a Stag inn at Margetts-cum-Pumpington? Have you got a porch overgrown with ivy; and did you not see my advertisement?"

"This man is a madman."

"Stop a bit, sir, stop a bit! either you are the most awful impostor that ever stepped, or I have been the cursedest fool that ever breathed."

"It is the latter, then," said my visitor; "and, as I never flatter anybody, I must say that you look it. What do you mean by speaking to me about Staggs—the—innkeeper, with the Brown inn? and as for ivy, I haven't a leaf of it on my premises."

"Sir," I said, frantically, "can you afford me any other proof than your own word, and your possession of this letter, that you are the Rev. Mr. Bruton?"

"What! am I to be dragged all this way to have my identity doubted? But if your scruples be real ones, I will soon set them at rest. There, sir, in that pocket-book you will see a dozen letters addressed to me, some from my bishop, in answer to an application for more money, in which he says that he will see me——blessed first."

I looked at the documents; the evidence was too strong; I had been duped. Like wildfire, through my brain ran the conviction that I had been thoroughly deceived, and, instead of saving Amelia from her enemies, I had actually placed her, at trouble and cost to myself, in their very hands.

I saw how it was in a moment; how I had been duped by the pretended Rev. Mr. Bruton into going myself and fetching Amelia from the school—how cleverly he had avoided giving me a note to take with me, and with what consummate art he had finally kept out of Amelia's way, because she would at once have proclaimed him to be an impostor.

All this came across me in much less time than it takes me to relate; and I really felt, and I supposed looked in such evident distress of mind that my visitor lowered his tone, and said to me—

"Why, bless me, what is the matter? just now you were all violence, but now you are completely prostrated."

"I am," I said, "I am. I will tell you all, sir, and then you may level what reproaches at me you like. I have no other cause but purity of motive; but I have been the greatest enemy Amelia Bruton could have."

Alarm took possession of his countenance; and, as I proceeded to tell him all that had happened, he wrung his hands, exclaiming, "Good God! good God! this is dreadful."

When I had concluded my narration, I remained perfectly silent; for I had lost all energy, and really felt so deeply afflicted at what had occurred that I knew not what to say.

"Sir," he said, "this is a most grievous and melancholy affair; but you did, according to your judgment and your convictions, the best you could. That is all Heaven asks of us, and shall man demand more?"

"Can you forgive me?"

"I can and do most freely. My heart is almost broken by these sad tidings; but let us bestir ourselves, and, putting our trust in Providence, endeavour to undo that which has been done, and recover poor, lost Amelia. Oh! sir, you do not know her as I know her; I knew her mother—poor thing, I closed her eyes, and promised never to desert her infant. That was Amelia; she has grown in beauty and intelligence, and far from being a burden to me has been the delight of my existence."

"I do not wonder at it," I said. "Command me, sir, in any and in every possible way. From this moment I devote myself to the task of recovering for you your lost treasure; I will know no rest—I will cast aside all business, all pleasure—until I have discovered whither she has been taken, and repair in some measure the evil which I have been most unwittingly instrumental in aiding."

"Sir," he said, "you can say no more; you shall never hear a reproach from my lips; but in this very deep affliction I am incapable of advising what to do; I have however, some friends in London to whom I will instantly go, and, among others, I hope the bishop of the diocese in which my living is situated will not refuse me his aid in such a matter; I will come to you again in a few hours, when I have set every inquiry at work that I can for the discovery of poor lost Amelia."

His voice was cracked and broken as he spoke, but he struggled with his grief, at least in my presence, and hastily left me. When he had gone, I felt if anything more than I had done when he was present; I could have struck myself for my folly; I was nearly raving, but by a great effort I controlled myself, and hastily putting on my hat I rushed into the street, making my way towards the house to which I had dogged the two servant girls. I was in no humour for temporising, but in my half-maddened state of bitterness I was capable of anything. I rushed up the steps, and seizing the ponderous knocker in both hands, I executed such a series of bangs upon the door, that the whole street echoed again, and windows were thrown open in all directions. Then observing a little brass plate beneath the knocker, with the words, 'ring also,' upon it, I seized a bell-handle that was close at hand, and gave it such a terrific pull that I broke it, and rolled down the steps with it in my grasp like a dagger. The door was opened at this moment by a terrified looking footman, and without asking myself whether I was hurt or not, I sprung to my feet and rushed into the hall.

"Where is the Duke of Choldcarle," I cried; "I will see him; the desperate old villain, where is he?"

"Lor' sir!" said the footman, "he e'ent here, why you have broken the blessed bell, sir, and in all my life I never heard such a knocking."

"He is here," I shouted; "where's the Duke—where's William—where's Ann and Maria—where's Amelia Bruton—and where's the desperate villain that played the parson and the thief, that did Brown, the innkeeper?"

"You have been done brown yourself sir," said the footman, "if you expect to find the duke here. He has been staying for about three weeks; this is a private hotel."

"An hotel! then where's the master of it?"

"We have no master, sir; but a mistress, and here she is."

"And pray, sir," said a woman of portly aspect, advancing, "what is the cause of all this uproar in my house?"

"I want the Duke of Choldcarle."

"Then you can't see him, for he is gone; you can leave your little bill, and when he comes to town again, no doubt it will be discharged."

"I have no little bill, madam."

"Aint you the newspaper-man; John, did you ever see such a likeness?"

"Never, marm; but we shall have a little bill for the gentleman, if he is a gentleman—he has broken the bell."

"It is impossible," I said, "that I can tell whether it be truth or falsehood that is coming from your lips; but be assured, this matter shall not rest here; there has been foul wrong done, and those who are injured shall have justice. If you don't know where the Duke of Choldcarle is, you had better find out, for it will be the worse for all of you."

Away I walked, quite unconscious at the moment that I carried the bell-pull in my hand; nor could I flatter myself that I had really done anything towards the emancipation of Amelia Bruton, beyond making a disturbance, if that was calculated to have any beneficial result upon her fortunes—a proposition which admitted of much doubt. But the fact is, I had not acted at all from reflection in the

business, since I had seen the real Rev. Mr. Bruton; but from a violent impulse that had hurried me onward, perhaps, into an indiscretion. And here I was, completely abroad to the subject, and without the real clue to the place where Amelia Bruton had been hidden by those who had taken great pains, and employed so much confederacy to obtain possession of her.

I felt desperate, and, but for my promise to be at home in about a couple of hours to meet Mr. Bruton, I should not have thought of bending my steps in that direction, but as it was, I felt bound to attend to the kind appointment he had made with me. The day was yet young, and I could not at all anticipate that the chapter of

No. 4.

accidents would throw anything in my way, so I hurried homewards as fast as I could. I had not been there very long when Mr. Bruton arrived. He told me that he had met with every sympathy and encouragement from those to whom he had applied, and that the bishop in particular, whom he had seen, had promised to interest some of the higher authorities in the matter, and that the most vigorous steps should be taken to bring it to a favourable result."

"Did you think," said I, "of mentioning to the bishop the name of the Duk of Choldcarle?"

"I did; and he could not believe it possible that that nobleman was the guilty party, for although he had heard, he said, that in his youth the duke had led a dissolute life, he now felt conscious of his error, and was now rather religiously inclined."

I quite forgot for the moment the character of him who was with me, as I said—

"Ah! you may depend that is a bad sign; I generally suspect a man who has been leading a bad life and affect to turn religious."

"But surely," said the clergyman, "that is not always the case; and, as regards this duke, I think, when we consider his rank, there ought to be very little difficulty in discovering whereabouts he is."

"We can make the inquiry," said I; "and as I am, perhaps, more active than you, and more capable, consequently, of moving about with quickness from place to place, let it be my duty to discover that fact."

"Be it so," he said; "I am half distracted, and feel myself quite unequal to the task of prosecuting such an inquiry. Here is where you will find me"—he laid a card before me as he spoke—"and may Heaven prosper your endeavours!"

When he had left the house, and as I was reflecting in my own mind where I should go first in order to prosecute my engagements, old Martha made her appearance.

"I put back the two glasses of madeira in the bottle," she said, "and co ed it up and put it away. I thought you would not want it till next time, since you owned to having made such a fool of yourself."

"How do you know," said I, "that I owned any such thing?"

"Why, I listened, to be sure, at the folding-doors, and it saves you the trouble, you know, of telling me all about it."

"You may drink the madeira," said I, "so do what you like with it; only don't trouble me about it, that's all. I am sick of everything and everybody. I am going out now, and don't know when I shall get back, if I ever get back at all."

"Very good," said Martha.

CHAPTER IV.

THE DUKE OF CHOLDCARLE ASSERTS HIS INNOCENCE, AND REPUDIATES WILLIAM.

THE first thing I did, when I left my own house, was to proceed to some place where I could see a court guide, and there I found that the Duke of Choldcarle was one of the representative peers of Scotland, and that his town-house was in Burlington-street. Under the circumstances I had not the remotest hesitation in calling upon him, because, if he were innocent, he ought certainly to be made acquainted with the unjustifiable use that had been made of his name, and if he were guilty, I need have no scruple at all with regard to him. With these sentiments I walked off to Burlington-street and knocked at the door of one of the handsome mansions which occupy that locality. The door was opened into a spacious and elegant hall, and the porter, whose station it was to sit in it, at once admitted that the duke was within. "I am a stranger to him," I said, "but the business I come upon is not only one of importance, but one which I think he will be well pleased to have communicated to him." I gave my card, and the porter, calling to a footman, desired him to take it to his lordship. The footman demurred a little, saying that he thought some one was with the duke, but when upon that, I said I would wait, for that I must see him, he went, and in about five minutes returned to say that the duke was just disengaged, and that he would see me. This was all very well, and I followed him up a handsome staircase into a drawing-room, which was replenished with luxuries. I was not left above three minutes when an elderly pale-faced man made his appearance.

It is wrong to be prejudiced against any one merely for their look, but there was something about the countenance of the duke, for it was he, that I certainly did not like. I think it must have been the curious manner in which his teeth projected, that gave him an odd cannibal-like look, but certainly it is wrong, and illiberal as it was I did not feel prepossessed in his favour.

"I presume, sir," I said, "I have the honour of speaking to the Duke of Choldcarle?"

"I am the Duke," he said, "of Choldcarle—pray be seated."

"It would have been very wrong of me, your grace," I said, "to intrude upon you, being, as I am, a complete stranger to you, without a sufficient motive; but the fact is that your name has been made use of in a manner which you ought to know and which more than justifies me in coming to you on the present occasion."

"Sir," he said, "I shall listen to what you have to say, and I can have no doubt, from your appearance, that this business is quite justifiable."

"Will your grace permit me, before I proceed any further, to ask you a few questions?"

"Sir," he said haughtily; "it seems rather a strange mode of proceeding to come to me, professing to give me certain information, and to wish to cross-examine me."

"Then I will tell your grace my errand at once, and leave it to you to answer my questions afterwards, as you please."

I then related to him the story of the abduction, which he listened to with the greatest attention, and when I had concluded he said—

"And did you imagine, sir, for one moment, that I could be the hero of this disgraceful abduction?"

"I imagined neither one way nor the other," I replied; "you were named, and that is all I know about it. I am bound to believe your denial, but, at the same time, I feel that I am authorised to expect that, as your name has been so unwarrantably used, you will assist me in rescuing the young girl and in discovering the perpetrators of the outrage."

"Most certainly; to the utmost of my ability will I do so—that is what you might have calculated upon, apart from every other special circumstance. I was staying a short time at the house you mentioned, while some of the principal apartments of this were under repair, but I have no person by the name of William in my employment, nor have I the slightest acquaintance with any one by the name of Matthews."

"It is quite needless for me," I said, "to apologise to your grace for giving you this trouble; because I consider that I should have been not at all justified in keeping from you the fact that so scandalous a use was made of your name. I cannot help thinking that you are bound to resent, to the utmost of your ability, such an attack upon your reputation."

"You may rest assured, sir, that I shall resent it: I shall consult my professional adviser upon the subject, and, of course, any thing that I succeed in doing must be favourable to your own object."

"Precisely. Your grace has my address upon the card, and, should anything occur worth communicating, I hope I shall have the gratification of hearing from you."

"Most unquestionably you will."

I rose as I spoke and bowed myself out, and if any one had met me at once, probably, and asked me if I was quite pleased with the interview, I think I should have said no; for there was a coldness of manner about him which was certainly not pleasant, and which no one would like in conversation. I partly, however, attributed this to his nation, for I well knew that in their interviews with strangers Scotchmen are mightily reserved; therefore, I ought not, perhaps, to blame the Duke of Choldcarle entirely upon such a score.

My next idea was to call upon one of the servants, Maria or Anne, to try and settle the point as to whether the man called William was actually in the service of the duke, or not. I was pondering over this and had turned into Oxford-street, when a public-house door suddenly opened and out came two servants in livery; they were washing their mouths as if they had just been solacing themselves with something very pleasant and delightful at the bar. I shrunk back in an instant, for in one of them I recognised Master William. They walked up Oxford-street together, talking loudly, as if one or both of them were a little the worse for their potations.

Like young Norval, ' I marked the road they took,' and was disappointed to find that it did not lead to Burlington-street; but, on the contrary, to some other public-house, into which they turned, after expressing to each other a hope that they should find Bill Somebody there.

I waited for some time at the door, but neither of them emerged, and I began to think I might have a long job of it, before I could get speech of Mr. William alone. I was quite satisfied that I should not be known by William, because I had been so completely disguised when he saw me at my own house, and not liking to wait in the street, I walked into the public-house, and stood at the bar, purchasing the permission so to do by ordering something of a very mild and quiet nature to drink, and there I waited, sipping cold sherry and water, and anxious to see Mr. William make his appearance. Nearly half an hour elapsed, and I was begining to think it would become necessary for me to order a fresh supply of the tolerably harmless beverage, when a door, which had already attracted my eyes, by having the word "Parlour" written upon it, was opened, and the same two persons made their appearance, only, to all outward showing, much more inebriated than on the preceding occasion. They paid for something which they had had at the bar, and although William must have seen me, he evidently knew me not, but walked past me with perfect unconsciousness. I followed, without betraying any appearance of haste, and had the satisfaction of seeing him part with his companion at the door, and that they both proceeded in totally different directions.

William walked down Wardour-street rapidly, and continued right on, till he came to Pall-mall. He then made his way by Charing-cross to the Strand, and finally, down a narrow street, at the bottom of which was a stairs, and a landing-place of the river. He did not pause, but, walking a few steps down the stairs, he called aloud, " boat, boat!" He was soon answered by some of the men waiting about the spot, and in a few moments he had procured a wherry, in which was a man with a pair of oars, who simply rowed out into the stream.

I had fully made up my mind to follow William, let him go where he would, and I called another boat, but could get no one but a lad to attend to me.

" You can pull an oar, I suppose," I said.

" Yes, sir," was his reply, " or a pair of sculls either."

" No," I said, " oars; I will take one myself, and 'pull away after that boat you see."

" What, Jem Atkins's boat, sir?"

" It may be Jem Atkins's, or Jem anybody-else's, for all I know; what I want you to do is, to pull after it."

" Very good, sir," and away we went into the stream.

The preceding boat had got some distance, for the tide was with it, and the evening was rapidly advancing, so that it would be difficult in a short time to keep anything in sight, at a distance. I pulled rather vigorously, which put the boy upon his mettle, and, to tell the truth, he did wonderfully well, considering that he was but a lad, and rowing is a thing which depends, after all, so much upon downright stamina.

When I found that we had decreased the distance between the first boat and our own, I relaxed a little in speed, which the boy observing, induced him to do so likewise.

"You will understand," said I, " I don't want to overtake the boat, I only want to know where they are going."

"I could have told you that at the stairs, sir," said the boy, "for that man has been twice before, and Jem Atkins told me he took him to Hood's house."

"And where may that be?"

"Just by Chelsea."

"And what sort of house is it?"

"I can't say, sir; it's a nice place, and has a private water-gate down to the river."

"Well, at all events, I will go on, so that I may know the place myself, and if you will promise me to say nothing to any one about my having asked a question upon the subject, you may depend it shall turn out to be the best evening's work you have done for many a day."

"Depend upon me, sir."

"Then pull away, and let us just keep as far off only as not to seem to be watching them, but yet, if possible, near enough to enable us to see precisely where they land."

"We will take the other side of the river, sir," said the boy, "and pass them, and after that we can drop down again without being at all suspected. Jem Atkins is none such a beauty, nor yet so civil, that I mind getting the better of him a little."

This was the best plan, unquestionably, so we pulled out of the wake of the advancing boat, and, getting right across the river, we soon came abreast of it, and then, as we were two rowers to one, we got past, and I was enabled, without looking behind me, to notice exactly where the other boat went in.

I could perceive in the very dim and uncertain light a low brick wall, and immediately beyond it some stately trees, and it was immediately under this wall that the boat turned its head to shore, and I distinctly saw William jump out. I looked carefully about me, so as to mark all the bearings of the spot, in order that I might know it again, and then, very well pleased with the result of the adventure, I desired to be rowed back again to the stairs at which we had started. I gave the boy double what he asked me, and although it was quite night when I landed, I determined upon taking some immediate steps for the recovery of Amelia, if, as I strongly suspected, she had been secreted in that house to which I had traced William.

CHAPTER V.

THE WARRANT AND THE SEARCH.—A NIGHT OF DANGER.

It struck ten as I emerged from the narrow street leading down to the river's brink into the Strand. I knew that one of the most active and gentlemanly of the Middlesex magistrates lived in Craven street, because it had so happened that I had applied to him once before for his assistance. I did hesitate a little about the lateness of the hour, but then when I reflected what agony and suspense and apprehension poor Amelia might be suffering, I no longer paused, but, proceeding at once to Craven-street, I knocked at the magistrate's door, and sent in my card I was instantly admitted, and found him in his study surrounded by papers. He received me with kindness and cordiality, and then, as shortly as I could, I made him master of the whole of the circumstances attendant upon the case of Amelia Bruton, and how I had traced William, the groom, to the house by the river's brink, where I strongly suspected Amelia might be concealed.

"That is quite sufficient," he said, " to induce me to grant a search warrant. I have heard something of that house you mention, and the Thames Police have been ordered to give an eye to it. It purports to be inhabited by a Mistress

Frith, but nobody sees anything of her, and the neighbours say that sounds of contention and strife have been heard at all hours of the night issuing from it."

" Can you accommodate me with force to execute the warrant ?"

" Most certainly. I will send a couple of officers with you that you may thoroughly depend upon."

" 1 should like much to go at once."

" There can be no objection. I can send for the officers, and a boat will take you all up."

He rung the bell as he spoke, and ordered that the officers who both lived in the immediate vicinity should be sent for.

" You may make," he said, " your own arrangements ; and if you can find at this time of night the Rev. Mr. Bruton, I should advise you to take him with you in the execution of such a warrant, for he having legal castody of the girl can put an end of cavil as to who is to take charge of her, and besides, from what you tell me, it would require some experience on your part to convince her that you had nothing to do with her abduction, because you will perceive that to all appearances it looks as if you had every thing to do with it."

" True, true," I said, " that did not occur to me ; of course it looks so to her. I know where to find the Rev. Mr. Bruton, and have no doubt but he will obey the call instantly. I will come back, with your permission, and meet the officers."

This was settled accordingly, and I hastened to where Mr. Bruton told me he would be staying, and, to his great joy, gave him hopes of the speedy liberation of Amelia.

" You seem certain," he said, " about the connexion of this man William with the affair."

" I do; indeed, he has never been near me again, according to promise, and I thoroughly believe that, when he did call upon me, he was playing a double game, and that it was merely for the purpose of discovering what I knew."

" It looks like it, indeed. Heaven send that this expedient may be successful in rescuing to me my poor Amelia, who must have suffered now within this last few hours more acutely than she ever in her life did before."

An unusual energy seemed to actuate the old man, and came with an alacrity one could hardly have expected from his years.

When we reached the magistrate we found that both the officers were waiting, and that they were armed with the search-warrant as well as other means of defence and offence, should such chance to be required.

We were a party of four, and we went down to another stairs than the one at which I had embarked, for we wanted a couple of watermen, and I had no inclination to get Jem Atkins as one, because I could not tell how far he might be in the enemy's confidence, and so, perchance, be to us of worse than no assistance. We looked out a good-sized boat, and with two stout watermen, who were to pull a pair of sculls each, we started, at a quarter past eleven o'clock, for our place of destination.

Since I had been upon the river before, the aspect of the night had greatly improved, and the moon, which was gently rising above the horizon, had begun to cast its calm, sweet light over all objects, and presently it fell upon the ripples of the water, and, as it rose higher and higher in the clear blue heavens, a thousand objects that had before been dark and obscure, and mingled together in inextricable confusion, became clear and distinct, standing out in bold relief of light and shadow against the night sky. The tide was at its full, and there was scarcely the slightest impulse either way, so that the boat had to be propelled by its oars alone, meeting neither obstruction nor assistance from the stream. The old clergyman for some time was silent, and then he whispered to me, " She whom we are going to attempt to rescue is sixteen years of age to-day."

" Indeed," I said, " is this Amelia's birth-day ?"

" It is ; and on this day, at the request of her mother, I was to have enclosed her a sealed packet, which with her dying hands she gave to me, and which she enjoined me to keep sacred until that time should arrive."

" I have forborne, sir, asking you any questions regarding Amelia; may I now ask what degree of relationship she bears towards you?"

" None whatever," was his reply, " excepting that relationship of distress which the unhappy should always bear towards those who are capable of rendering them assistance."

" You surprise me much; she bears your name."

" Yes, poor thing; for want of a better."

" And do you mean to tell me you do not know her name?"

" That is the fact; her mother came to the village of which I have been the curate for about seventeen years, and took a humble, cheap cottage, living alone and in great seclusion: she gave the name of Wilson, and a settled and deep grief seemed constantly to be preying upon her, from which nothing could move her. Time passed on until this child was born; the mother survived that event only one month, and on her death-bed she implored me to succour and protect the infant, and not to leave it to the unkind mercies of a workhouse. I promised her that I would be its protector; and then she placed in my hands a sealed packet, saying, ' If this child should reach the age of sixteen years give her this packet; in it she will find papers and documents that will tell her who and what she is; but if, upon her attaining that age, you shall think proper to withhold that information from her, do so. Come to me yourself in another hour, and you shall hear from my own lips the contents of those papers.' "

" Then, she did tell you?"

" No, in the hour she was speechless; and, after a vain effort to communicate something to me, she breathed her last."

" And you fulfilled your trust?"

" I did, with the means that Heaven had given me to do so; those means were scanty, but I willingly shared what I possessed with Amelia. Now you know why it is I have given her my name for want of another."

" And how old should you have supposed her mother to have been?"

" Scarcely twenty; grief had evidently bowed her down, but she was still very beautiful, and as amiable a creature as ever stepped."

" It is a sad tale, and if we knew it all you may depend it would contain some particulars of heartlessness and criminality on one side, and unsuspecting innocence upon the other, of a most painful character."

" Of that there can be no doubt; but Amelia may keep her own secret if she please, or communicate to me the particulars of her history."

By the time he had communicated thus much to me, in every word I felt deeply interested; we had arrived near our place of destination; and by the moonlight, which was now bright and clear, I could perceive the water-gate, the brick wall, and the tall trees which I had before noticed as the landmarks of the place at which William had been put ashore.

" That is the house," I said, to Mr. Bruton; and then, turning to the officers, I pointed it out to them, saying, " Is that the same house which is considered by the police suspicious?"

" It is," said one, " and this is no bad opportunity for going over it. It is a large place and surrounded by at least three or four acres of ground."

" I cannot see the house from here."

" No, sir; we are low in the water, and the trees hide it. It's a mean-looking mansion though, and such a one as anybody would be glad to have. Pull in as quickly as you can, waterman."

It being high water, we were landed quite close to the wall, and there we found a gate which had a padlock upon it, but which presented no great difficulty in the way of scaling, so we all got over it, after telling the waterman to keep charge of the boat until we returned, and made our way along a gravel path of considerable width. We were rather surprised to find the place so unprotected, and just as I had made such a remark as that to one of the officers, a gun was fired off so near at hand that we all involuntarily started. One of the officers ran forward in the direction from whence the sound proceeded, but he found no one, and came back, saying, truly enough, that it would do no good for him to lose himself among the thickets and trees, and so divide the party, for a person who knew the place well might dodge him in the ground for hours.

"Do you think that gun was a signal?" I said.

"It is very difficult to say; there's some waste land close at hand, and bad characters of one kind and another are often about it; it might be a shot at some poultry, or a dog, for what we know; but come on, and we will soon see what sort of people they are who inhabit this house, and I think we ought to be close upon it now."

In another moment we were clear of the tall bushes through which the pathway meandered, and then came full upon a view of the house, which burst upon us suddenly in the moonlight, clearly and distinctly, and, I may add, with much romantic beauty. We all involuntarily paused to look at the place, and well worthy was it of the passing tribute of approbation which we paid to it. It was a large buil ding composed of red bricks, which are now so seldom used, but which, when they are used, are always used with so much effect and beauty. Different generations might have added to the original building, but all who had done so had had the taste to consult the essentials of the original style of the house's architecture, as well as the materials of which it originally was composed, so that there were no incongruities in the whole structure. The deep shadows which it cast upon an ample green lawn in front of it, brought out in bold and clear relief that portion of the house on which the cold but beautiful moonbeams fell, and many of the windows looked like sheets of burnished silver glistening in that placid light, which is ever associated with calm delicious feelings. But this was no time for reflection; on the contrary, it was one for action, and diligent action too; and I felt it to be my duty to break off the spell which the calm and quiet beauty of the spot had cast over all our faculties.

"Come on, Mr. Bruton," I said, "this may be a sweet place to look upon, but, unless I am much mistaken, it is the prison of Amelia."

"Yes, yes," he said, "lead on and rescue her. Let me place in her hands the packet that contains the intelligence connected with her mysterious birth. Heaven knows I would barter the remainder of my existence to look upon her once again, and hear her speak, if that felicity was to be obtained upon no other terms."

"I think," said one of the officers, breaking in upon the romance of the thing, "saving your presence, gentlemen, that the least said the soonest mended; them people here are wide awake, no doubt. It's a devil a bother that the moon's shining so, because they'll just see how many there is of us."

I looked no longer with rapture on the moonlight. All the romance of the affair seemed cut short in a moment by this matter-of-fact proceeding of the officer, and we walked towards the house in perfect silence. It was not so easy as in daylight to estimate distances at that moonlight hour, and I found we were not so close to the mansion as I thought we had been by a considerable distance; and as I neared it I found it lost much of its beauty of appearance, in consequence of the eye not being able to take in the whole of its details at once. Moreover, the officer's caution had not been thrown away upon me, and I said no more, but turned my whole attention to what was about to ensue. I could perceive that old Mr. Bruton trembled very much as he leant upon my arm, and I almost regretted to have brought the old gentleman with me, even although the magistrate had suggested it, and although I knew the sight of him would afford as much gratification to Amelia as she would to him.

"We may have some difficulty in getting into the house," said one of the officers, "so I advise that you all step aside and let me knock, and if the door is opened I'll give you a signal, when you can come in at once."

We admitted the justice of this proposition, and all stepped aside accordingly, while the officer alone ascended three or four stone steps, and applied for admission. There was no knocker, but he rung a bell, the sound of which was sufficiently loud to come upon our ears, and then a pause ensued of several minutes' duration, and the light I had observed in one of the upper windows was suddenly extinguished. The officer rung again, and scarcely this time had he taken his hand from off the bell-handle, when the door opened, and a man stood on the threshold. We could all see him quite plainly, because there was a lamp hanging in the hall, which threw his figure into bold relief, although, of course, it left his face in shadow.

"What do you wan" h e said.

"Oh! it's only I and a friend or two," said the officer, " who want to speak to the lady of the house."

" Well, it's an odd time to come at," said the man ; "have you any objection to state your business ?"

" None in the least ; you'll be so good as to consider yourself my prisoner ; we have a search-warrant, and if we find nothing suspicious on the premises, why, we'll let you go again."

The man put on an appearance of great astonishment, and on finding that the officer had thus thrown down the gauntlet, all advanced at once, and assembled in the hall.

"Why, what's the meaning of it?" said the man, who had been captured ; "if you are thieves you'll be disappointed, for I assure you, we keep nothing valuable upon the premises, except a few spoons and forks for ordinary use."

No. 5.

" No," said the officer, '' we are police, and I insist upon seeing the person who represents herself as mistress of the house."

'' Certainly, sir, you shall if you please ; but I beg you'll talk gently, for my mistress is an elderly woman and in bad health ; any sudden surprise, the doctors say, or shock, might have a very serious effect upon her."

" Oh ! you need fear nothing of that kind.   Show the way."

The man preceded us, and flung open the door of a handsome dining-room, into which we entered, and there, sure enough, sat an elderly looking lady with a pair of gold spectacles on—black silk mittens—and a work-box open before her.

" Gracious goodness ! Jackson," she exclaimed, " what's this, oh ! my side."

" this is some dreadful mistake,'' whispered the clergyman to me.

'' Never mind, we can't help it, you know, if it is. If people will live in suspicious houses, and have suspicious visitors, why, of course, they'll be suspected, and it's no use saying anything about it."

" If you please, ma'am," said Jackson, who looked like a respectable butler; " these gentlemen say that they are officers and talk of a search-warrant."

" Officers ! " said the old lady; " a search-warrant here ? oh, my side ! "

" We are very sorry, madam," I said, " to intrude upon you, and if this be an error, no one will more sincerely apologise to you than myself ; if it be otherwise I give you great credit for being an accomplished actress."

" I an actress ! Oh, my side ! this will be the death of me."

" Proceed with your search," I said to the officers ; " I've been so taken already by appearances, that I'll trust nobody ; and in the first place, here goes for an experiment ; Mr. Bruton, do you think you could aggravate your voice to such an extent as to make it sound all over this house ? "

" I'll try," said the old man.

" Then call upon Amelia as loud as you can; she'll know your tones ; and if she be hidden anywhere you may get an answer."

" Call upon whom ?" said the old lady ; " you'll be the ruin of me, all of you, and my sides never been worse.   Are these thieves, Jackson ? because, if they are, give them everything, and tell them to spare our lives ; oh, dear ! my spasms are coming, I know."

Old Mr. Bruton went into the hall, and raising his voice as loud as he could, he cried—

" Amelia ! Amelia ! ''

" Hush ! " said I, and we all listened attentively. From afar off, as if the sound had been conveyed miles by the wind, there came a faint cry, which we could scarcely shape into a word, and yet it sounded like " Help ! "

" Call again," said I, " call again."

He did so and when he had concluded, I raised my own voice and shouted, "Amelia;" I am sure in a tone that the people at Putney must have heard.

Then we all listened and the faint sound came again.

" It's from above," said one of the officers; I'll swear it's from above."

" Hold, hold !" cried the old man; " I hear it nearer.   There is a light foot-step too upon the stairs.   She comes—my own—my beautiful—my child !"

An immense tom-cat, with a brass collar, came down stairs, and stared at us all ; and most particularly did he seem to look at old Mr. Bruton, who had addressed such endearing expressions to it.

" Thomas," said the old lady, appearing at the door of the dining-room, " come here, my Prussian."

Thomas held up his tail as perpendicular as a flag-staff, and came down, rubbing his back against the balustrades all the way, every now and then looking at us, and opening his mouth a short distance to emit a noise something like the expiring sound of a catherine-wheel ; until, at last, Thomas, the Prussian, reached the hall, where some of the officers received him with a great many oaths, and then he walked into the drawing-room.

" Who'd have thought of that?" said old Mr. Bruton.

" Never mind," said I, " call again."

He did so, and I listened with more interest, if possible, than before.

There is no sound—yes, there again that faint, annoying cry, where can it come from? We looked at each other bewildered ; it might be above, below, on one side or the other ; so faint was it, and indistinct, that we could come to no satisfactory conclusion.

" Mr. Burton," said I, " what is your opinion of that ?"

" I know not what to think," he said. " I'm like one in a dream ; restore to me my child, she who is as dear to me as if she were my own flesh and blood. Where is my Amelia—why do you mock me, all of you—why do you mock me ?"

He sat down in one of the hall chairs, and wrung his hands, when out came the desperate character Thomas, the Prussian ; and walking up to him, he deliberately attacked the calf of one his legs.

" Get out," said I, " you feline monster—you've no more feeling than a brickbat."

Thomas the Prussian swore, and lifted up his back like a viaduct ; after which he walked into the dining-room again.

" What's to be done ?" said I, to one of the officers ; " I can assure you that the people among whom we've got are the most accomplished dissemblers you can imagine. I have been myself deceived by such acting as I scarcely ever saw on any stage."

" We have no resource but to search the house, sir ; my companion here will remain as a guard to the lower portion of it, and I'll accompany you, gentlemen, if you please, through the different rooms."

" Damn that cat !" said I ; " here he comes again."

This time Thomas, the Prussian, only came as far as the mat that was outside the dining-room door, and gave a sort of spit at us all ; after which he turned and walked in again with great placidity and dignity.

" You're better hands at a search," said I to the officers, both of you, than we ; suppose I undertake to keep guard below here, which I think I can undertake to do efficiently, while you search the house ?"

" I had no sooner uttered these words than the report of another gun somewhere in the grounds came upon our ears ; and the old lady cried, " Jackson, Jackson, you know that my nerves and my side won't stand that sort of thing. Why don't you go outside, Jackson, and see what it is that's going off with a pop? Oh! my side, Jackson."

" Please, marm, I'll go directly," said Jackson.

" I beg your pardon, Mr. Jackson," said one of the officers, pulling an extraordinary face as he spoke ; " but, when we were coming to the house, Mr. Jackson, something went off with a pop."

" Did it, sir ?" said Jackson.

" Yes it did ; and it struck me at the time, that whenever anybody came who wasn't invited, something went off with a pop. Do you know, Jackson ?"

" Lor!" said Jackson ; " you confuse my mind, gentlemen, you do—but, however, I'll come back and tell you what it is."

" No, excuse me," said the officer ; " we'll wait and see, and you'll wait with us, Jackson. If nothing comes of it, you know, it's no matter."

" Oh, my side !" said the lady ; there's no such thing as feeling in this world Come here, Thomas, my Prussian, come to your mistress."

Thomas, the Prussian, was on one of the window seats, which were very deep and capacious, covered with cushions of faded crimson velvet ; and, with malice aforethought, he was working his front claws into one of the cushions, to its great detriment. But he came away at the sound of his mistress's voice, and stayed by her for a little while ; and then we heard the sound of feet upon the gravel path outside the house, and I, who was keenly watching the countenance of Jackson, saw an uneasy expression steal across it.

He even tried to get towards the hall-door, no doubt to make a bolt out ; but the officer had his eye upon him, and suddenly stepping between him and the means of exit, he said,—

" Mr. Jackson, I have already told you I consider you my prisoner ; and as sure as you are a living man, if you attempt to escape, I'll shoot you dead upon the spot ; for I've neither time nor inclination to come after you."

As he spoke, he took from his pocket one of those powerful, short, thick holster pistols, such as would have been thought neat and elegant in the days of Dick Turpin, and presented it at Jackson's head.

" I aint going," said Jackson, retreating, " I aint going."

In another moment a man walked up the steps, and the officer springing upon him just as he was about to retreat again, brought him into the full glare of light.

" What is the meaning of this ?" he cried.   " Ruffians, unhand me."

" Close the door," said I ; " this is the man we want."

" Who is he ?" said one of the officers.

" His grace the Duke of Choldcarle."

" The duke !" said the officer.

" Well," said his grace ; " and if I am, my rank protects me.   Who dare lay hands on a peer of the realm ?"

" I dare, villain !" said Mr. Bruton, springing forward, and confronting him ; " I dare, who am a poor, weak old man.   This withered arm shall hold you as with a grasp of iron : were you twenty peers of the realm—were you a king, I denounce you to your face—were you an emperor, I brand you as the suborner of innocence, an enemy of all that is good, and all that is beautiful.   In the name of the Most High, whose poor servant I am, I accuse you."

" Accuse me !"

" Yes, if there be justice in Heaven !"

" Old man, you rave—you know not what you say.   What on earth is the meaning of all this ?"

" It is your grace," said I, " who perhaps may find it difficult to explain your visit here."

" And why so ?   Surely, although I am a peer, I have the ordinary right of visiting whom I please.   Woe be to him who so much as places a little finger upon me."

" It's an awkward thing to touch him," said one of the officers, " if he be a duke, without a warrant."

" Pshaw !" said I, " you know better than that—he's only a Scotch duke."

" What !" said the officer, " not a downright English nobleman, but one of them there brimstony lot ?   Why, you humbug !"

I laughed in spite of myself, but the duke turned pale with anger, as he exclaimed—

" I command you all to leave this house, it is mine."

" Oh ! it's yours, is it ? why, that's what we've been wanting to know for a long while whose it was.   What's he the duke of, sir ?" to me.

" Choldcarle," said I.

" What the duce is that, I wonder ?"

" Lor'," said the other, " don't you know that ? it's yesterday's greens not warmed up."

The duke dashed into the dining-room, and we all followed him.   He flung himself upon a window-seat, without observing that Thomas, the Prussian, was there ; but that artful individual saw the danger and escaped, all but his tail, and then not fancying at all to be detained by that flexible portion of his body corporate, he turned and attacked the Duke of Choldcarle in a manner highly insulting to the peerage, and made him roar again.

" My lord duke," said I, " the mask is off—let us understand each other— restore Amelia Bruton to her friends, as the only reparation you can attempt to make for the evil that you have done, and the only chance that you can possibly hope for, as likely to awaken their merciful consideration."

" Was there ever such insolence heard of ?   You're the man who called upon me, and I believe wanted to rob my town house."

"You know that is untrue," said I; "it is nothing but a mere bold-faced lie, at the moment, and I declare that you shall go to town with us, in custody, and I will make such a substantive charge against you on oath, as shall warrant your detention; and to-morrow a reward of five hundred pounds shall be offered for the man William, or for either of the parties who acted the parts of the Rev. Mr. Bruton, or of Mr. Brown, the innkeeper.

He looked a little staggered at this, but the assurance of the man was wonderful, and he quickly recovered.

"I cannot understand," he said, "what is meant by all this; but, I am willing to give you the benefit of believing that you must be labouring under some great mistake. Call all of you, if you please, at my town house to-morrow, and we will talk it over."

"On one condition," said I.

"Name it."

"The instant surrender of Amelia Bruton."

"My good sir, I cannot surrender to you what I don't possess. You keep talking to me of an Amelia Bruton, of whom I know nothing. You will pardon me for supposing, that is to say, provided I do you an injustice by so doing, that you are of the upon that point. If any of those who are with you will confirm that view insane case, I can, of course, excuse anything."

"That infernal cat," said one of the officers, "has been giving me a claw on the sly, so I've made up my mind, to do what I always do in those cases, that is, shoot it."

He winked at me as he spoke, so as to hint to me there was a hidden meaning in his words.

"Shoot Thomas, my Prussian!" said the lady with the gold spectacles. "I dare you to do any such thing. What can such a poor creature do to you? besides, he's left the room."

"Not quite, madam, he's gone into yonder closet, and I'll have a shot at him through the panelling—here goes."

"What, and smash my old china, that would be the death of me in one moment."

"Oh! never mind the china, ma'am, I'll make that all right. I dare say Thomas, the Prussian, breaks more in a few weeks than I should in a year."

He shut one eye, and levelled one of the awkward looking pistols, when just as he was upon the point of firing, the closet door opened, and out came two persons,—one a stout-looking, large, elderly lady, the other, a small, sleek-looking man, of a very common-place looking aspect.

The lady sunk into a chair with a groan, and the man gave a sort of circular bow to every body in the apartment; and with the most consummate assurance he said—

"Ladies and Gentlemen, I trust that this sudden and unexpected appearance on these boards will not be productive of any unpleasant consequences to those friends whose patronage, I am proud to say, I have experienced on more occasions than one; but, ladies and gentlemen, the idea of being shot, instead of Thomas the Prussian, was too romantic—upon my soul it was."

"Damnation!" said the duke, and putting his hands in his pockets he walked up the apartment.

"Your grace seems discomposed?" said I.

"Not a whit, sir, not a whit; your penetration is at fault. Pray what is to be the next scene in this extraordinary drama of your getting up?"

"I hope that the next scene will be your grace's humiliation and defeat. In a word, it will be far better for you, and for all concerned with you, that you at once give up the secret of the hiding-place, for such, I'm sure there must be, of Amelia Bruton."

"Then once for all," said he, "this to me is the most arrant nonsense that ever passed the lips of man. I know nothing of it—I want to know nothing of it—and I will know nothing of it."

In marched the cat again, and to the great surprise of all of us, she went direct up to the window-seat, which she had before attacked, and standing opposite to it she put up her back as if it had been a living opponent, and then he swore a great number of cats' oaths, so that we were quite astonished to know what she would be at, and looked on in silent wonder.

"Thomas," said the lady, "come here, my Blucher, come to your own Buonaparte, come here, my Prussian."

Thomas only growled more energetically, and then springing upon the window-seat, he began clawing it as he had done before.

"There's something extraordinary in all this," said I : "what on earth can be the meaning of it ?"

"Why it looks," said one of the officers, "as if there was something in the window-seat that Thomas wants to get at."

"Yes ; and there is too, gentlemen," said Jackson. "Tommy knows his meat's kept there. May I give it him out, marm, and then he'll be quiet ?"

"Certainly," said the lady, "yet stay—not yet—when did he have it last ?"

"Only one hour ago."

"Then how can you think, Jackson, of giving him any more? you know, as well as I do, that too much meat makes these creatures vicious, you know that, or you ought to know that, Jackson, quite as well as I know it, only you've no sympathy for my side, not you. This night'll be the death of me, I'm certain."

"That's quite correct, marm," said Jackson, "quite correct it is ; so you may say indeed, he has had plenty of meat, and as you say, marm, very correctly, too much meat does make those creatures furious."

"Well, then, don't give him any more, Jackson."

Jackson and the lady preserved such imperturbable countenances while this little dialogue was going on that I really was much amused at it and gave them infinite credit for the manner in which they played their part, that was none of the most easy ; for acting in real life, when some uncomfortable consequences may arise from a failure, is a very different thing from a stage performance.

I could see that the Duke of Choldcarle looked confused as if he knew not what to make of the transaction ; but the two parties who had just come out of the small room preserved an equanimity that under the circumstances was really surprising.

I whispered to one of the officers—"don't you think there is some mystery connected with that window-seat ?"

"I do, and will soon find it out."

At this moment the stout, big woman, who had made her appearance from the china closet, walked up to the window-seat and placed herself down upon it.

"What is all this disturbance about ?" she said, "I never knew anything like it in this quiet house before."

The moment she spoke I knew her voice ; I had heard it before, and it sounded quite familiar to my ears.

"Madam," I said, "I quite congratulate you upon our meeting again. I hope I see you well ?"

"Sir," she said, "I don't know you ; you have the advantage of me."

"I hope to have," said I, "you may depend ; and perhaps, as you say it, I have now."

"I don't know you, and never saw you in my life."

"Not know me, Miss Matthews ? now that is really too bad of you to say so."

She started at my thus suddenly pronouncing her name, and the Duke muttered a terrific oath.

"I am surprised at you," I said, "my lord duke, swearing in that manner, because you know in the House of Lords you have quite a character for religion."

"It is time to put an end to this farce," said he, "and I desire that you leave the house instantly."

"It will soon be left," said I ; "but first it is necessary to come to some explanation, which I shall now proceed to do at once. In the first place, this is Mrs. Matthews, who likes to be called Miss Matthews, and who prowls about as procuress to your lordship. In the second place, Mr. Jackson here, who has played his part extremely well, I begin to recognise as William the groom, who has done quite enough, connected with these transactions, to make him amenable for all their consequences. Then, in the sanctified-looking gentleman, who has come out of the china closet, I think I can have no difficulty in recognising the individual, who played the part of the Rev. Mr. Bruton to me, and who, for all I know, likewise played the part of Mr. Brown, the jolly landlord of the Stag Inn. And now, ladies and gentlemen, I think I have got through the matter pretty well, with one exception, I must confess I do not know who the lady is in the spectacles."

"Stop a bit then," said Jackson, "and I will tell you."

"The wretch is going to turn upon us," said the lady with the gold spectacles.

"Not in this world," said the earl, and drawing a pocket-pistol he levelled it at Jackson's head.

"Hold, my lord," said I, as I dashed it from his grasp, "this is already quite a bad enough affair for you, without your taking the trouble of making it worse. Speak, Jackson, and speak freely, you shall be protected, you may depend."

"I am tired of this kind of thing," said Jackson, "it's troublesome, dangerous, and not well paid, and as a proof of my sincerity, allow me in the first place to present you all with the fair object of your search uninjured, however much she may have been alarmed. The Duke has this night paid his first visit here, since she has been in this place, so that he has had no opportunity of attempting a persecution."

As he spoke, he advanced towards the window-seat, and throwing off the velvet covering, he raised the lid of it, for it was wide, and as large as a considerably sized chest, and capable of containing at least two persons.

"Don't be alarmed, miss," he said, "your friends are here."

There was no reply. I and Mr. Bruton, sprang forward in a moment, and then we saw, to our inexpressible grief, what appeared to us to be the dead body of Amelia.

"They have killed her, they have killed her, cried the old man; they have murdered the dear child. Oh, that I should live to see this day : she is no more ; Amelia, Amelia, when will the world look upon your like again."

Almost convulsed with agony, he knelt down by the side of the window seat, and then I said to one of the officers,

"Help me to lift her out : after all she may but have fainted ; do not let us presume that she is dead because she looks so calm and still."

The officer assisted me, and we gently lifted the insensible form from where it had been concealed. I supported her on a chair, and then I had the inexpressible gratification of hearing a deep sigh come from her lips.

"She lives, Mr. Bruton," I cried, "she lives, your child, upon whom you have showered so much affection, will yet live to repay you with gratitude for all you have done for her : do you not see she lives ?"

With a cry of joy the old clergyman sprang forward.

"Amelia, Amelia," he cried, "speak to me, if it be but one word to assure me of your existence."

"She cannot speak, but she is recovering. Is that wine upon the table ?"

"It is," said Jackson, " and some of the best."

He poured out a glassful and brought it to me ; with some trouble I induced Amelia to swallow a small portion, which revived her greatly, and she opened her beautiful eyes, and looked around her with confusion and dismay.

"There is nothing to fear," I said, "all danger is passed, you are with your friends, friends who can and will protect you."

"Yes, dear Amelia," exclaimed Mr. Bruton, "I am here, and you need now fear nothing. Oh, what a happy moment is this ?"

She was sufficiently recovered now to know him, and she clung to him with frantic eagerness, weeping bitterly upon his breast. During the time I had been thus actively engaged, it appeared that the duke had made an attempt to leave the place, which one of the officers observing, had induced him to lock the door and place the key in his pocket, so that none of the persons connected with the singular scene that was taking place, could leave the apartment; but all were compelled to wait the end of a scene, which by no means had as yet reached its climax.

"Does not this shame you, sir,' said I to the duke, as I pointed to the weeping girl. "Have you no sensations of remorse for what you have done—or of thankfulness for what you have escaped doing?"

"This is a conspiracy," he said, "to bring my name and title into discredit. It is a conspiracy among you all—but you shall suffer for it, I swear."

"Swear as you please, my lord; 'tis you, and you alone who will suffer; and, notwithstanding your present haughty boast, in vain, the time will come when you shall sue for mercy from this young creature, whom you have attempted to injure; and who, but that Providence would not see its fairest works defaced, would by you have been destroyed."

Old Mr. Bruton now gently disengaged himself from the clinging embrace of Amelia; and, looking in the face of the Duke, he said—

"I will not launch curses upon you; but I will pray that Heaven may forgive you your great wickedness. I have now a sacred duty to perform to the dead. This is Amelia's birth-day—she is now sixteen years of age—and the communication which her mother desired should be made to her on this day shall be made at once. Amelia, this sealed packet contains the secret connected with your birth, which your mother would have revealed to me; but that she expired ere she could do so. I promised that on this day it should be delivered to you; and, wishing to perform my promise to the very letter, as well as to the spirit, as it is now midnight, I hand to you the packet, and call upon all here to witness that I have kept my faith with the dead."

Amelia looked much affected, as she took the packet from the hands of the old man.

"And is this," she said, "in the hand-writing of my mother, concerning whom I have heard so little, but yet ever felt so intense a desire to know more."

"It is, Amelia: it is."

"Oh! then, let me at once gratify an impatience I cannot attempt to control. Let me at once see who and what I am, and end this frightful state of suspense and anxiety. Shall I—may I—break the seal, Mr. Bruton, at once."

"Most certainly, my child—most certainly: do so, if it please you. There is no place and no time unfitting for the truth."

"What is all this to me?" said the duke. "A likely thing, indeed, that my house is to be made the scene of such tricks. I suppose all this will end in a demand for money." -

"No," said I, "it will end, as it began, in a demand for justice—a demand which shall be answered to the full by you. Heed not this man's interruptions, Amelia; but read, if it please you so to do, the document which has been handed to you."

She broke the seal; but tears evidently blinded her, and she was incapable of perusing the written paper.

"Read it for me, dear Mr. Bruton," she said: "my hand trembles, and I cannot see through the blinding tears. Read it for me, I pray you."

The old man took the paper, and in a tremulous voice read as follows:

"'I HEREBY declare, with my dying breath, and truthfully, as I hope for happiness hereafter, that, although I have passed in the village of Margetts as a Mrs. Wilson, my real name is Matthews——'"

"Matthews!" exclaimed the duke.

"Proceed, Mr. Bruton, proceed," cried I.

There was a breathless stillness, and the old man proceeded.

"' My real name is Matthews. I am the daughter of a Mrs. Matthews, who kept a hosiery shop in the Haymarket, at London. Heaven forgive her! but I have indubitable evidence—such evidence as I dare not doubt—that she bartered the honour and virtue of her child, for a large sum of money, to the seducer. I fled—and have hidden myself and my sorrows in the village where I write these lines.'"

The portly woman, who had played so vile a part in the whole transaction, uttered a shriek, as she exclaimed—

"I am that Mrs. Matthews!—Heaven have mercy upon me!—This girl is my grandchild,"

"Woman!" I said, "do you not see that this is retribution. You betrayed your own child, knowingly ; and now, in pursuit of the same frightful trade, you would have destroyed this fair young creature, who is so nearly allied to you. You may well tremble."

She shook so, that I became seriously alarmed about her, and thought it best to say no more ; but, turning to Mr. Bruton, I added—

"Read on, sir ; you have not perused all the paper."

"I—I—I have not," he said, falteringly : "it is terrific.'

Speak ! This suspense is more terrific still."

Listen. There is but one paragraph more. It is this—"

"'The father of the child whom I leave behind me to the care of strangers is the Duke of Choldcarle, and may Heaven have mercy upon him."

A wild cry of despair burst from the lips of the duke, and he made a rush forward.

"My daughter—my own child! oh, no, no, no! do not say so ; that cannot be it is too terrible !"

No. 6.

"It is too true," said the old clergyman.

"My father!" exclaimed Amelia; "and have I found a father?"

The duke seemed as if he would have flown to her, but he paused, and a death-like paleness came across his face.

"Let me go," he said, "let me go; to-morrow, to-morrow, I will talk of this—to-morrow. Let me go now, I pray you let me go now. A boat, a boat! I must reach town at once—at once."

There came a howling gust of wind past the windows, and a dashing shower f hail against them proclaimed that a storm had arisen suddenly—one of those storm incidental to the period of the year, and which come and go in so short a period of time.

"Let him go, let him go," I said; "things have taken now too strange and dreadful a turn for us to think of prosecuting. Let him go at once."

The officer, in obedience to this desire of mine, unlocked the door, and the duke rushed from the house.

"Have mercy upon me," cried Mrs. Matthews; "stay, my lord, stay. It is of you I want justice—justice for my child's child; I must, I will speak with you."

She rushed after him just as Amelia recovered sufficiently from the shock she had experienced to rise and call loudly to her father to speak to her."

"Do not let him go," she said; "be he what he may he is still my father. Let me speak to him—let me hear his voice. I can forgive and forget all but that I have found a father."

"It would have been better," said one of the officers, "to have detained him; he seems rash and desperate."

"Then I will pursue him," said I, "and bring him back. Come with me, some of you."

One of the officers accompanied me from the house, but when we reached the outside we found that such a remarkable change had taken place in the aspect of the night that it was with the greatest difficulty we proceeded. The beautiful moon-light which, but a short time since, had invested everything with so many charms, was completely obscured. Heavy drifting clouds were careering along the sky, and such dashes of hail, rain, and sleet came in our faces, that for some moments we scarely knew in which direction we were proceeding.

The officer seemed to know the path better than I, which was probably in consequence of his being more in the habit, from his profession, of taking accurate notice of anything that came in his way.

"Come on," he said, "come on, follow me, we are going direct towards the water gate."

He was right, and four or five minutes' running brought us to the gate, over which we had clambered upon our arrival. To our surprise it was open, and when we reached the water-side the boat we had left was gone, as well as the men, whom we had ordered to await our coming.

"Why the watermen must have taken the duke and Mrs. Matthews away; it is very odd, for we had not paid them for bringing us here."

I had scarely uttered these words when I heard voices, and in a few moments the two men made their appearance, looking not a little surprised to see us.

"Hope we haven't kept you waiting, gentlemen," said one of the men, "but it turned out such a queer night that we moored the boat, and just went up to the public-house yonder to get a pint of beer."

"And during your absence," said I, "the boat is gone."

"Gone, sir! it arn't possible!"

"Look, do you not see a black speck upon the water? Is that your boat? Look, you have sharper eyes perhaps than I have."

"It is," he said; "and there is a man and woman in her; why I would not have gone on the Thames such a night myself till the storm had blown over. My boat is as good as lost, and I am a beggar. They will never get through the bridge."

I watched the dark object on the water as well as I could, for every now and then I was nearly blinded by the hail and sleet, and at last it disappeared from my eyes, I knew not where.

"You neglected your charge," said I to the watermen, "and you must do the best you can."

I walked towards the house again, accompanied by the officer, and then, leaving the confederates of the Duke of Choldcarle, to make the best or the worst of the matter they could, we, that is, Mr. Bruton, the officer and myself, took charge of Amelia, and made our way through the grounds inland, until we came to a high road, and presently to an inn, where, by great good fortune, we succeeded in hiring a glass-coach, which conveyed us all to London.

Mr. Bruton had succeeded in restoring Amelia to something like equanimity; so that, although the traces of tears were in her eyes, she was able to talk to us.

She informed us that by the man who had personated Brown, the innkeeper, she had been conveyed direct to that house, where she had been kept and threatened with death if she attempted to escape.

* * * * * * *

The boat in which the duke and Mrs. Matthews had left the house was found floating, bottom upwards, off the Temple. The bodies were not found for a considerable time; and even then we contrived to keep the sad catastrophe a secret from Amelia.

The most gratifying thing I have to relate, as a finale to the affair, was, that Mr. Bruton's bishop, being made acquainted with the particulars of how he had maintained Amelia at boarding-school out of his eighty pounds a-year, promised him the first living in his gift, and that turned out, as accident would have it, to be one worth fifteen hundred pounds a-year, which the bishop, in a very handsome letter, at once preferred him to, and Amelia, still retaining the name of Bruton, resided with him, not in a little country cottage, but in a handsome parsonage-house, surrounded by its own fertile fields and majestic trees, and replete with luxuries and comforts, while she became its chiefest ornament.

CHAPTER VI.

THE NEXT ADVENTURE :—THE MAD STUDENT.

It is night again; the stars are looking out sweetly from heaven's vault; a gentle and refreshing air is blowing, and the midnight hour is near at hand. I arose and dressed myself in silence. It was the first time I had gone out seeking adventures since that which I have recorded to my reader, in which the beautiful and amiable Amelia Bruton played so important a part.

The gratifying termination of that adventure, for, although I did not exult in the death of either the Duke of Choldcarle or Mrs. Matthews, I could not say that they were either of them a very great loss to society, and that Amelia was much happier without relatives of such equivocal character than she could have possibly been with them

"Now, Martha," I cried, as I opened the door of my bed-room, "now, Martha, are you stirring? I want my breakfast."

"Oh, yes; I am stirring," said my housekeeper; "but it aint your breakfast you want; it's your supper? Aint it getting on to twelve o'clock at night, when Christians are going to bed, and how can you call it your breakfast?"

"Easy enough, Mrs. Martha. That meal at which I break my fast is, of course, my breakfast."

"It's no such thing, it's your supper—it's supper time, and I don't see how you can make it anything else."

"Very good, then; I will be down to my supper in a few moments."

I had had a long, sound, refreshing sleep all the day, and was ripe and ready for any adventure that might befall me, so I proceeded down stairs to my breakfast-room, fully equipped for the street; but this time I took care to carry arms with me, for the experience I had had of some of my adventures had shown me that they were not always unattended with danger, and that it was better to be provided against any such contingency.

I was in possession of a small pair of pocket pistols, upon which I knew I could perfectly rely; and these I loaded and placed in my pocket, feeling, as I did so, that I had with me two friends, each of whom was capable of taking a life in defence of mine.

It is astonishing what an increase of confidence a man feels in his own resources when he is well armed, and I sat down to my breakfast, hoping that the night would not be unproductive of some adventure of a most deeply interesting character.

Martha stood for some time looking at me, and giving her head an occasional jirk, which was indicative of her strong disapproval of my night adventures. I made no remark, however, and I knew that that would annoy her, because she was waiting anxiously for me to do so I felt certain, so after a time she was forced to speak herself.

"Well," she said, "you are going again, are you?"

"Yes," said I, "I am going again, Martha."

"To make yourself ridiculous in interfering with other people's affairs? For my part I wonder what pleasure you can feel in it. I think that you ought to be called The Buzzeybody."

"Yes, Martha, I think so, too; I am quite of your opinion, we are unanimous for once in a way."

"Are we? I tell you what it is—some of these days you will get into a nice scrape, and then you will wish you had not made tea and suppers into breakfast, but had gone to bed and got up like other Christians, at reasonable hours; that's my opinion."

"Well, I think so, too," said I, "it's just my opinion; we never agreed so well before, Martha."

"Then, why do you go?"

"Ah! that's the question, and it couldn't have been put better."

"I know it's the question."

"Well, I say it is the question; I am quite of your opinion, it is the question."

"Hum! why don't you say something to it?"

"Say something to it? that would be the answer and not the question. How can the answer be the question, Martha, when the question is not the answer? You talk about me getting into some scrape, but I really think you have got into one yourself."

"You are enough to aggravate a saint," said Martha, "and make him tear his hair out by the roots! You will be brought home on a shutter some day or in a shell."

So saying, she bounced out of the apartment in more of a passion than I had ever seen her, but I was really getting tired of her remonstrances, and wished, if I could, to put an end to them; so I took no further notice of her, and sallied forth into the streets.

It was indeed a lovely night, for although the month of September was nearly gone, a more beautiful and serene atmosphere I had not seen, even in the height of summer. It seemed as if the richest summer-time had come back again for a moment or two, to see how the world looked without it.

There was sufficient coolness in the air to make exercise invigorating and delightful; and I walked along without the least symptoms of fatigue, and feeling as if I could go hundreds of miles without requiring rest.

It is only in certain states of the atmosphere that this invigorating and delightful feeling comes over the system, and it seldom lasts long; while it does, however, it's quite a treat, and should be made much of and enjoyed in the open air.

This time I took my course in another direction, walking eastward from where I resided, and making my way imperceptibly towards the city.

"The city," I said, "by common consent is considered an unromantic region, but there are beings in the city as well as elsewhere, and human passions will develop themselves as well in one locality as in another, so to the city will I bend my steps in search of adventure."

There is something to me very delicious in strolling along looking for an incident to attract the attention, instead of having the mind fixed upon one place of destination

There is all the pleasure of conjecture, and the imagination is actually set to work to consider what is likely to occur.

Reflections arise as to the class of adventure, whether it shall have a comic or a serious tendency, or whether, as is most commonly the case, it shall combine those tears and smiles which make up the sum of human existence.

And I have always found that I have had a sort of presentiment or inward certainty that something was about to occur when an adventure was near at hand, while on other occasions, I have felt a certainty that my night peregrinations were in vain, and that nothing, on that particular occasion, would occur worthy of a place in my journal.

This night, however, I told myself there would be an adventure, although I saw not the slightest symptom of one, as yet.

I walked onward and reached the Strand, intending to take my way by that great line of thoroughfare into the city; there were but few persons at present in the streets, for the theatres had not given up their audiences nor had the public-houses closed their doors against the crew of wild revellers who at such a time are always to be found quaffing liquid poison in those establishments, consequently those who were in the streets consisted of the very few who were returning home from late employment, and some others who had been visiting their friends and were now making their way to their own homes to prepare themselves, by sleep, for the duties of the next day.

It was too early for the robber to be abroad, and almost too late for the honest man.

I was involved in such a train of reflections, as these and similar thoughts suggested, when I reached Fleet-street, and I was just passing the gates of the ancient Temple when somebody darted across the road, and addressing me in a hurried manner, said—

"You are the fourth man I have asked if he is bold enough to come with me to Fig-tree-court, number 12. Answer me quickly, yes or no?"

I was very much startled at the suddenness of his address, and started back a step or two. We were close to a lamp, so that I had an opportunity of observing the appearance of him who spoke to me. He was a young man, well attired, and of a pleasing aspect. There was about him all the appearance of careful culture, both mentally and physically, and, in fact, a glance would have been quite sufficient to have convinced any one that he belonged to an extremely respectable class of society. His face was intelligent, but his manner somewhat excited, as if something had much disturbed him, and caused great mental uneasiness. He paused after thus addressing me, as if awaiting my answer with the greatest anxiety, and, I must confess, I was much puzzled to know what to say.

"Sir," he said again, "may I hope that you will accompany me to number 12, Fig-tree-court, in the Temple? I occupy chambers there; I should not proffer to you this extraordinary request, were it not that I feel convinced a dreadful deed has been committed in the chambers immediately adjoining mine, and I wish to consult with you as to what can be done."

"A dreadful deed?"

"Yes; I am confident that murder has been done."

"Murder!"

"You may well start, sir, at the mention of that terrific crime, but I am so convinced of it that I have run out of my chambers with the resolution of importuning the first intelligent and gentlemanly-looking stranger I saw to come back with me."

"But the police, sir," said I, "are the proper persons in such a case."

"Not so, sir," he replied; "the circumstances are peculiar. I am almost certain, in my own mind, that such a deed has been done, but yet I have no evidence to satisfy the police of the fact, there yet requires some observer and a careful analysis of the circumstances. I do not like to trust my own judgment entirely, but if you should be of the same opinion as I, we will no longer hesitate, but call in the police at once."

There was something so rational in this that I, seeking for adventure as I was, could not resist the application, so I at once replied—

"Sir, you are an utter stranger to me, but your appearance so much bespeaks the gentleman, that I cannot but believe the story you tell me; I will accompany you with pleasure, more because you request it than from any idea that I shall be able to throw a light upon the subject you mention and expect you must certainly be a far better judge than I."

"This courtesy, sir," he replied, "I assure you is highly appreciated. I am a humble student of the law, and likewise of natural philosophy, which I am more fond of than I am of legal subtilties. I have no friends in London, my family and connexions are all residing near Exeter, so that I trust you will excuse my addressing you."

We were but a few paces from the Temple entrance, and as I knew that emporium of law was closed against strangers after a particular hour, I thought that if my new friend was admitted, without question, by the porter, it would be tolerable evidence that he was known, and had described himself to me correctly.

The gate was opened in answer to his knock; the porter glanced at him for a moment, and then stepped aside to allow him to go in. As I was about to cross the threshold, the man seemed about to make some little demur; but, upon the young student saying, "This is a friend of mine," there was no more notice taken, and we both walked into the Temple.

Fig-tree-court is not very far from the Fleet-street entrance, and we soon reached it. My companion spoke but little as we went, until we reached the door or rather the door-way, for door there is none, of No. 12.

"This is the place," he said, "and I think we had better ascend with caution. My chambers are on the second floor; and if you follow me, although the staircase is dark, you cannot go wrong."

He walked slowly and cautiously up the stairs until he reached the second floor, and I followed him in the same manner. Then I heard the rattle of a key in a lock, a heavy door swung upon its hinges, and the student said in a whisper, "Come in and tread lightly."

I did so, and he closed the door behind me, locking and double locking it—a precaution which gave me some uneasiness at the moment; but I reconciled myself to it by thinking that no doubt he would give me some satisfying reason for so doing in a few moments.

"I'll get a light," he said, "in an instant; don't move, or you may fall over something."

"Thank you," I said, "I won't."

He procured a light; and then, as it slowly burnt up, I saw that we were in a apartment, decently furnished, and well provided with books.

"These are handsome chambers," he said, "but rather dull, and it was a great change of life for me to come and live in them; it was not intended that I should be any profession, but some family circumstances altering my prospects a little, made it necessary that I should take to something, so here I am, a student of the Temple."

"He is wonderfully communicative," thought I, "to an entire stranger."

"Well, sir," I said, "I hope you will prosper in the profession you have chosen; it may be made a highly honourable one, and in this country it is the high road to great preferment."

"It is indeed, sir; but how few reach to anything like distinction?"

"Well, sir," said I, "you have brought me here under the impression that I might be instrumental in preventing some murder, or in punishing those who had perpetrated one. You will excuse me, therefore, for calling your attention to that subject."

"You are right," he said; "now I will show you in a moment what I mean; you perceive that the matches for a fire are laid in the grate?"

"Yes, I perceive that."

"Well, then, now for a phenomenon."

He took up the light and set fire to the paper and wood that was in the grate, after which he put the light upon the table again, and sat down opposite to me with a very triumphant look.

In a moment out came a puff of smoke which filled the room and set me coughing and sneezing violently.

"I am glad of that," he exclaimed; "now are you convinced?"

"Yes," said I, "I am convinced that your chimney smokes most awfully."

"But the murder, sir, the murder."

"Well, it's enough to murder anybody to live in these chambers."

"Yes, but do you know the reason?"

"Yes, because the chimney smokes."

"But do you know why it smokes? Hush! speak low, our lives may pay the forfeit of an indiscreet word. Let us discourse in whispers; we are surrounded by an atmosphere of murder. The very air we breathe is heavy with the scent of blood and the groans of the dead, lingering in every cranny and crevice of this ancient building. Blood spilt cries out for justice; but let us be very cautious. Hush! did you hear nothing?"

"Nothing alarming."

"It must have been the wind rattling the window-frame; it sounded like a voice from the grave. Did it not strike you so?"

"I really don't know; for I never heard one. I wish you would put that piece of fire out, for the smoke evidently mistakes the room for the chimney."

"That is my evidence," he said. "I am able to have no fire here on that very account. The chimney smokes, and for days and days, and nights and nights, I thought over it till I found out why."

I began to get a little uneasy, for there was a strange, wild glare, in the eyes of my new friend, that made me shudder to look at them.

"I will tell you why," he continued, "and let the impression sink deep into your heart. I will tell you why this chimney smokes, and it will show you how curious and mysterious are the ways of Providence—it will show you how murder will out, let it be hidden how it may—it will show you what great events spring from the most trifling causes, and how, most strangely and mysteriously, the crimes of those who consider they have committed them, with impunity, will come forward to the light of day."

"Very likely, sir; but what on earth can that have to do with your chimney smoking?"

"Everything. Don't be impatient, and I will tell you."

"I am all attention."

"My neighbour in these chambers is a Mr. Lee, a sinister-looking man, with one eye. Now, the reason my chimney smokes, is simply this:—he has murdered somebody in his chamber, dragged him up his own chimney, and put him up mine, and I am convinced that there the dead body sticks, just out of reach of my arm and the poker."

"What, do you mean to tell me that Mr. Lee crept up his own chimney, and dragged a dead body after him? the thing is impossible."

"Not at all impossible. He has nothing to do but to get two iron hooks, with a screw at the end of each of them. Those he screws into the heels of his boots, you understand, and then he fastens the hook part in the sockets of each of the dead man's eyes, and so he dragged him up the chimney after him, and puts him down mine. A most ingenious way, you will perceive, of disposing of a dead body."

This fellow is a thorough madman, I thought. The conviction that I had fallen into the hands of a dangerous lunatic, had been each moment growing stronger upon me since I had entered the chambers. I felt the perspiration break out upon brow, as a full conviction of my own danger came across me. I thought of my house keeper's prediction, that I should come home on a shutter, or in a shell; one of which results seemed likely enough to ensue, unless I could free myself from the company of the lunatic into which I had fallen.

"Do you doubt it, sir?" he said; "and he dashed his fist upon the table so furiously, that the candle jumped again, and I felt that my only chance of escape was in temporizing with him.

"Do you doubt it, sir?" he again repeated.

"My dear sir," I said, "pray be calm. How can I doubt it? no rational man could doubt it for a moment."

"Ah! that is well."

"And I think it very ingenious, sir indeed—extremely ingenious, I may say so much so that I highly applaud the great talent you have shown in discovering it."

"That is well," he said; "and now I will tell you, sir, what I want you to do."

"Thank you, I am very much obliged; but don't you think, now you have told me thus much, that we may as well take a little quiet walk and talk it over?"

"No, we are better here. Now look you, sir, if I was to go up the chimney and pull down the dead body by the legs, people might say that, out of dislike to Mr. Lee, I had been over all the house-tops, and into some attic window, to get a dead body; but, if you go up and pull him down, as a disinterested party, you know your evidence will be good upon the occasion, and we shall get Lee comfortably hung."

"A capital idea," said I; "but I tell you what, I don't live far from here, I have got a curious apparatus at home, for getting dead bodies out of chimneys. I'll just run and get it."

"No," he said, "that would be a waste of time."

"Oh! not at all, I will get it in a moment; just unlock the door, and I'll soon return."

"If I let you go," he said, "it shall be in two pieces."

He dived his hand into his coat pocket as he spoke, and produced a razor.

"Now," he added, "which shall it be? I will cut you in two, but you shall have your choice: shall it be done perpendicularly, or laterally? You can't get out, you know you can't. I have got you safe, and, now I come to look at you, I can see that your eyes are bits of coal, and that you are one of the fiends that mock me."

I can give no expression upon paper, it would be hopeless to attempt it, of the manner in which these words were uttered. They partook of something between a yell and a shriek, and really had a most startling effect. The frightful conviction came across my mind, that I should have to kill this maniac in self-defence; but yet, that was better than being frightfully murdered by him, and at the moment I deeply congratulated myself upon having my pistols with me, upon which I could so well rely. And yet I determined, of course, only to use them in the last extremity, when every scheme I could possibly try had failed to free me from the danger I was in. He kept making cautious approaches towards me, with the razor in his hand, but I kept my eye steadily fixed upon him. I slowly moved round the table, which I considered my principal safe-guard.

"And so you won't," he said, "you won't get up the chimney and pull down the dead body?"

"I did not say I would not," said I; "although I do think we could do it so much better; but I only ask to go home first."

"And that then convinces me of what you are. Once before I had somebody here, and was foolish enough to let him go, he never came back again. I will not be served so again. Ah! now I know you are a fiend!—gleams of light come from your eye-ball. You shall die, if it be possible for human means to take so terrible a life."

"Hold," I said; "I do not know if you are accessible to fear. That you are a madman, I am convinced; and since temporizing with you, and talking kindly to you, is of no use, I must endeavour to see what fear will do."

I took one of my pistols from my pockets, and presented it at him.

"I will shoot you," I added, "if you do not give up the key, and let me go."

"And do you think I care for such a threat? I have a charmed life. No one can kill me. Your pistols are harmless; and now I sacrifice you to the remembrance of many wrongs."

At this juncture there came a knock at the door of the chambers, and I thought it a blessed chance that any one should be there.

"Force the door," I cried. "Help! Murder!"

The madman closed the razor carefully, and put it on a shelf.

"Somebody is coming," he said. "I shall let them in."

"Do so," I said.

"Oh, I intend." He then walked towards the door, and, to my great surprise called aloud,—

No. 7.

"Hands off, madman, hands off! Help is coming. Give me the key. Ah! now I have it. Come in ; whoever you are, you are welcome."

I had heard much of the cunning of the insane, and how frequently, when they find themselves in danger of being detected in an act of violence, they will, with the most consummate art, turn aside suspicion from themselves, and make it light upon others ; but never had it been my fortune to see such an instance of it as this.

He unlocked the door, flung it wide open, and then affected to sink, exhausted, into a chair, as two stout, common-looking men entered the chambers.

Seize him !" said the madman, pointing at me—" seize him ! He is quite out of his senses, and will do some one a mischief."

I was disarmed of my pistol in a moment by one of the men, for I made no resistance, being too much astonished at the effrontery of the madman, to think of doing so.

" Come, come," said one of the men to me, " this sort of thing won't do with us. Did you ever hear of a straight waistcoat ?"

" Why," said I, " you must be made likewise to speak to me in such a way. That is the madman sitting yonder on a chair by the door."

" Oh, that's a likely joke. I say, Bob, he's one of the cunning ones, aint he ?"

" It is astonishing," said the mad student, with all the calmness in the world, " it is astonishing how cunning these mad fellows are. I merely dropped in upon a visit to him, and I believe, if you had not arrived so opportunely, he would have taken my life."

" I am glad we have come, sir," said one of the men. " The fact is, that some of the gentlemen connected with the inn wrote to his sister, Mrs. Manning, at Exeter, explaining what a strange state of mind he had fallen into, and she has come to town. We belong to Dr. Watkins's asylum, and will soon have him there, all right."

" But, good God !" said I, " it's a mistake—that's the madman who is speaking to you ; now call in who you please to identify him."

" How cunning of him," said the mad student ; " and don't he speak rationally ?"

" He does, sir," said one of the men ; " but we are used to that. Bless you, sir, we knows 'em as well, that the more rational they speaks, the more madder we knows they is."

"That's a convenient doctrine," said I, " for keeping people in a lunatic asylum ; but I warn you—you shall have to take the consequences of an action at law, if you lay hands on me."

"Yes, yes," said one, " we'll take all that—just you be quiet. Bob, he is getting obstropulous ; just give him one of your looks, will you ?"

Bob came up to me, and fixed his eyes upon me with such a dead stare, that I laughed in his face as I said—

" Do you fancy that such a stupid stare as that has any effect upon me ? You have now tried your notable experiment, and I suppose you are now convinced you are wrong."

" Not at all, my man ; only you are more wicious than we thought you. Come along, it's high time you was put under what we calls straint."

I felt my patience getting rather exhausted, and I said—

" Now, once for all, I tell you you have made a mistake ; that is the real madman, who tells you he is only a visitor here, thus affording a proof of what you say you know so well, viz., the cunning of lunatics ; and if you still continue obstinate, I tell you I will not come further than my own fancy suits. Of course I am rejoiced to leave these chambers, when I consider I have incurred great risk ; but that man who has so successfully imposed upon you is, I assure you, as mad as he can be."

" Artful !" said one of the officers, winking at the other ; " but it won't go down with us and Dr. Watkins—oh, dear, no, we're used to those sort of customers."

" My good fellows," said the maniac student, as he handed them some silver, ' get yourselves something to drink ! I really believe you have saved my life— take him away—take him away !"

I resisted a little, and the effect of this was, that one of the men took from his pocket a stout elastic belt, and fastened my arms with it in a moment.

"Now," he said, "we'll see what's what! We goes upon the soothing system; damn you, come along!"

"How do you like it?" whispered the mad student to me. "You are a mad fellow, aint you? and if it wasn't for an insane spider that has built a nest in one corner of my brain, I should be mad, too; but that saves me, and makes all the difference!"

"Do you hear him?" said I.

"Oh, you be bothered!" said one of the men. "Come on! Shut the door, Bob, we'll soon get a coach in the Strand, and pop him off to Peckham."

What could I do? and what could I say? Then, I was as helpless as any human being could be, and if I got into a furious passion, which I naturally enough felt very much inclined to do, that of course would be considered at once proof positive of my insanity; and from the experience I had of my own sensations at that time, I am quite convinced that a charge of insanity against any man is nearly sufficient to induce such a state of mind.

It required all the resolution I was master of to prevent myself from seeming furious, and from an exhibition of the rage that filled my mind.

In procession—I going first with the two keepers and the real madman following afterwards—we reached the gate of the Temple, and then I thought a chance presented itself to me of extrication from the difficulty into which I had fallen.

"Tell me," I said to one of the men, "for whom do you take me?"

"Why, for mad Mr. Manning, to be sure!"

"That will do—that will do! Here, gatekeeper, just come and tell these men which of us two happen to be Mr. Manning."

The madman knew his danger now at once, and in an instant he turned and fled.

"Why, that's Mr. Manning," said the gate-keeper, "running away. We all think he is a little out of his mind here, at times."

"The devil!" said the man who had hold of me, "here's a-do, but never you mind, sir, it's only a mistake; don't you say another word about it, sir."

"I will, though," said I, "say a great many words about it; these kind of mistakes must not be made, for they might be more serious than the present one."

He did not wait to hear what remarks I made, but set off at once after the real lunatic. He, however, had the start of them, and perhaps a better knowledge of the Temple than they, for the pursuit seemed a long one, and the worst of it was, that they had left the elastic-belt upon me, so that I was perfectly helpless, until the gate-porter cut it off, after trying in vain to find the proper way of releasing me from it.

I then waited in his little lodge the result of the chase after mad Mr. Manning, and in about ten minutes the officers returned with their prisoner. They had him firmly secured, and now he had all the wild appearances of a furious maniac. I shrunk back, appalled at the sight of him, and of course I said nothing to him of the trick he had played me.

"Pull him down!" he shouted, "pull him down! pull down the dead body from the chimney! you will find the hooks sticking in his eyes! drag him down! and then the chimney won't smoke. Kill—slaughter—blood for blood!"

"He's a nice article, sir, arn't he?" said one of the officers to me.

"That's perfectly true," said I; "but you must recollect, a little while ago, you told him that I was a nice article."

"Oh, but, sir, that was a mistake."

"It is a mistake that Dr. Watkins must hear of: you had no business to have jumped at a conclusion that I was a madman, merely because you were told so. You must be very indifferent judges of the calamity, which in all its various aspects you ought to be acquainted with."

"Well, but, sir, it wasn't our fault, you know. How came you there?"

This question put me upon thinking that I certainly had, rather imprudently, accompanied a perfect stranger to his chambers; so that I thought, after all, the old proverb, of 'the least said being the soonest mended,' came in tolerably well. I said no more to the men, but putting on my gloves, I walked out of the Temple, feeling that in one short hour—for the whole affair did not occupy much longer time in enacting—I had been threatened with death and the mad-house; and really had very narrowly escaped both, or, at all events, the third alternative of shooting Manning, the mad student. If I had done so, being as I should have been, without witnesses of any kind, I might have found it very difficult to clear myself of the consequences of the deed.

"Truly," I said, as I wended my way homeward, for I had had adventure enough for that night, "truly, Martha is, to a certain extent, right, for these adventures are not unattended with danger, and some of these days I may certainly fall into some serious predicament on that account."

But still, nothing could quench my ardent desire to carry out the adventures which might from time to time occur to me. Let there be what danger there might, I felt that I ought not, and would not shrink from it, and that I would place the exciting affair as that which had just occurred to me against the much more gratifying episode connected with Amelia Bruton; for, after all, although my judgment at one time had been at fault with regard to that transaction, I believe that I ultimately was the means of her preservation, and likewise, indirectly, the cause of the comparatively brilliant fortune that had fallen upon old Mr. Bruton.

I wish that my next adventure had terminated as easily as this one with the mad student; but it was of a more serious aspect, and involved many more serious considerations, making, if anything, a greater impression upon my mind than the tale connected with the beautiful Amelia.

CHAPTER VII.

MY THIRD ADVENTURE, WHICH I CALL " THE BROKEN CHAIN."

MARTHA was curious. It was evident to me that she wished to know something of the particulars of what had occurred to me on the last occasion of my going out in search of adventure; but, as I had really achieved nothing, and only after all encountered an incident, I told her that I would not occupy her valuable time with a detail of what had occurred, and she, as might be expected, took such a reply as a grievous sarcasm, and one which she ought to resent accordingly.

I always knew when I had done or said anything to give Martha serious offence, for when, on ordinary occasions, she by no means paid a great deal of attention to anything I said to her—when she was offended, everything was done in the most punctilious manner, and with a degree of frigid formality, that, if I had not steeled myself against it, would have been peculiarly annoying.

But when these little ebullitions of temper took place with Martha, I found the best plan was to leave her alone, and let her come round again slowly and comfortably as she pleased.

To oppose her was only adding fuel to fire, and after a while I knew that her better feelings would rise up in my favour, and that she would do something of a conciliatory character.

I retired to rest at early morning's dawn, closing my shutters as usual, and lighting a chamber-candle, so that my room had all the appearance of night, and I retired to rest without caring one straw about all the din and bustle of active existence out of doors.

And my readers are now aware that I do not dislike daylight, but simply that I sleep in it, in order to be awake at another time, when I thought I should be more likely to fall into adventurous episodes, which, if they required carrying out in the day-time, those who have indulged these pages with a perusal know perfectly well I did not shrink from doing.

In ten minutes I was sound asleep; and although towards evening I did have a confused tumult of dreams, in which the mad student, a dead body and a chimney, the Duke of Choldcarle, and Mrs. Matthews bore a part, I awoke tolerably refreshed, and rung, as usual, for my breakfast.

My housekeeper Martha was never tired of insisting that it was my tea, on account of the hour at which I took it. But as my readers now know Martha sufficiently well to be almost of themselves able to tell what she would say upon such and such particular occasions, I need never trouble them with her garrulity, unless it should happen to have something fresh in it.

On this evening it had nothing of that character, and I left home, accompanied by the usual running fire of remonstrances, which I always received upon going forth on one of my night adventures.

I debated with myself, for a short time, as to which direction I should go in, and at last I resolved to take a course which I had not done before, and which consisted in prowling about all the streets at the back of the Strand, quiet and sedate as many of them are, with the hope of picking up, in some one or other of them, material for action, and food for reflection.

There is something, to my mind, always solemn and thoughtful about streets such as those which lie in the neighbourhood of the Adelphi, and which, of themselves, are so calm and still, although in the immediate vicinity of such a torrent of animal existence.

Their solitude is made so much more complete by the roar of human life, softened down into a composed and gentle murmur, that reaches their inmost recesses; and in such places one can fully feel that sensation which has been described as the solitude of a crowd.

It was to this neighbourhood, then, that I betook me; and as I strolled up Adam-street, it certainly at that moment did not seem likely to be prolific of adventures, considering that I was the only person throughout its entire extent.

Not for long, however, did I possess that street alone, for two figures came hurrying out of the Strand, and proceeded directly towards the Adelphi-terrace.

They were both women; but one evidently considerably the elder of the other, for she had to run to keep up with the hasty walk of her companion; but the latter suddenly seemed to become aware of this circumstance, for she relaxed her speed, and, placing her more elderly companion's arm within her own, she seemed, by her gestures, to be talking to her in a kindly manner, and apologizing for neglecting her, or forgetting her.

Here, at all events, was some food for reflection for me. I quickened my pace and approached as near as I could to them without seeming to follow.

They turned on to the Adelphi-terrace, and I went after them for some distance until I feared, from the slowness of their walk, that they intended to turn again and pace that quiet place, awaiting the arrival of some one.

Fearing this, then, I shrunk into a door-way, and the moment I did so I found that my conjectures were correct, for they both turned and walked slowly back again.

The door-way was large and ancient, and very deep. The people who occupied the house were evidently economists, for no lamp was in the passage, and for once in my life I applauded an act both stupid and stingy, inasmuch as it enabled me to be securely hidden from observation.

There never was such a lucky chance, that is to say, for my love of knowing what other people were about, as now occurred, for a slight shower came on, and the women took refuge in the very door-way where I was ensconced.

They had scarcely done so when I found that one was weeping. It was the young one, and in the intervals of her sobs she spoke.

"No, aunt," she said, "no, I admit the truth of all you can say—I fully and freely admit it, but what can I do? my heart and faith are pledged to Lionel; he may, as you say, never return to claim my plighted troth. The wild waste of waters may have entombed him, and I may never look upon his face again. He may have fallen in deadly conflict. You have told me all this, aunt, and I agree with you that there is abundant food for such suppositions ; but I do not know anything, and therefore I am bound to keep my faith."

"But, Florence, I am getting old, and soon must leave you. Mr. Grantley is young, handsome, wealthy. I'm sure he loves you—loves you in spite of your harshness towards him, for you know he has been compelled to leave our house in consequence of your behaviour to him."

"I know it, I know it, aunt ; I did give way for a time and forget Lionel—no, no, not forget him, but did not think of him as I ought. I ought to have thought of him continually, by night and by day; he should never have been absent from my mind ; I ought never to have forgotten him for a moment, nor ever to have dreamt of the possibility of his forgetting me : it was treason, aunt, it was treason to the affection which Lionel always had for me, that I should for an instant dream of another."

"But Mr. Grantley was led to think you loved him—no, I will not say so much as that, but that you might love him—and that you did not look with altogether an unfavourable eye upon his evident admiration of you. Oh! think again, think again, Florence—it is now two long years since you have heard of Lionel."

"And is that the date of earthly affections?" said the young girl; "is it wonderful that love should maintain itself pure and inviolable for such a space of time as two years. Aunt, aunt, you cannot mean what you say—you cannot wish me to forget Lionel, because I have neither seen him nor heard of him for two years?"

"My dear Florence," said the old woman, and her voice trembled with emotion as she spoke, "my dear Florence, you know that I think of nothing—I wish for nothing in this world, but your happiness ; consult, my dear girl, the dictates of your own heart, they will guide you right, although all the world should attempt to lead you astray."

"I know, dear aunt, that I have had a mother's love from you, and I know that the advice which it hath pained me much to hear from your lips in relation to this affair, has been dictated with the purest and best affection for me ; and so it was, aunt, that the advice did pain me, for if any one but yourself had asked me to forget Lionel, more anger than sorrow would have stirred me."

"Let it rest, my dear, let it rest," said the old woman, "I pity Mr. Grantley, for I know he loves you."

"It is because I think he loves me, aunt, that I have consented to this meeting. It is because I think him noble-minded and sincere, that I have come here to tell him I can esteem, nay, almost reverence him, but that I cannot love him."

"Well, my dear, you shall tell him so, and I am sure you will never regret meeting him. Remember, too, that I am with you, and as I hope and trust I have stood in the place of a mother to you, you may consider this meeting with Mr. Grantley as sanctioned, and as in every respect one which you will have little occasion to look back to with regret."

"I know not, aunt," said the girl, speaking in a low tone, as if rather communing with herself than talking to any one—"I know not how it was, but, from the first moment that Mr. Grantley came to us, his company gave me pleasure, and some hidden train of old recollections seemed to rise up in his favour. The very tones of his voice sounded familiar and pleasing to me ; and every now and then there was an expression upon his countenance, which so overcame my reserve, that I spoke to him not as though he were a stranger, but as if I had known and esteemed him for many years."

"It was so, my dear, I saw that it was so."

"And then he told me that he loved me."

"He did, but he told it to you respectfully, and at the same time painted to you the happy home he could give you."

"He did, he did ; and for a moment I listened like one fascinated by the recurrence of some well-remembered strain of music. More than once, I was inclined to think that Lionel himself spoke to me, and to ask him how he could for a moment doubt my faith."

"But now, you are resolved?"

"Quite, quite resolved; and bear in mind, aunt, that I never wavered really, though I seemed to waver. I never did for one moment, from reflection, yield to a new passion, and that is what I wish to tell to Mr. Grantley. Is he not late in coming?"

"No, my dear, 'tis we are early; but see, does not some one come; surely that was his tread."

"Yes," said the girl, and there was agitation in her tone, "'tis he; I may not love him, but I do not blush to say I know him well, and can recognise this footstep."

I glanced out as cautiously as I could from the doorway, and saw advancing rapidly from the other end of the terrace a man enveloped in a cloak.

He paused when he got half way, and looked around him anxiously.

Then the girl said to her aunt, "He does not see us, let us meet him, aunt!"

"Nay, my dear, see how the rain comes down; there, I will wave my hand to him—now he sees us."

With a sudden exhilarating movement the man with the cloak made his way up to the door; his voice had a pleasant musical cadence with it as he spoke, saying—

"A rough evening, Miss Deerbrooke, a rough evening, and I regret to have brought you abroad upon it. I hope you are well, madam," to the aunt; "will you walk?"

"Nay, the rain still falls," said the old woman, "and there is a good shelter here."

"But we may be enlightening the inhabitants of this house with our private affairs."

"Not so," said the girl, "it is empty and to let, do you not perceive? Let our interview, Mr. Grantley, be a brief one, and let it be here."

"You know, Florence," he said, "you have but to dictate your wishes to me, and they become my holiest purposes."

The circumstance of the house being to let had certainly escaped my observation, when I had been abusing the people who I supposed inhabited it for not having a light in their hall, but I was pleased to hear the fact mentioned, because it encouraged these parties, whose conversation, Heaven knows, for no evil purpose, I was anxious to hear.

There was a pause of some moments' duration, and then it was broken by the girl, who said, rather hesitatingly—

"Mr. Grantley, I have, at your and my aunt's request, consented to this interview. I think that, for both our sakes, it had better be the last."

"Heaven forbid, Florence," he said, "that I should gainsay you; I have no hope now, and if I tell you again that I love you, I do so rather that it is a melancholy fact as regards my own feelings, than with any hope or expectation of making you my own."

"Do not use that language, Mr. Grantley; I came principally to tell you that I think myself to blame—much to blame—for, upon reviewing my own conduct, I fear that I led you somewhat astray, inducing you to fancy that my heart was not so entirely fixed in its affections but that it was capable of being assailed by another. That was what I fear I led you to think."

"I had a hope of happiness," he said.

"Can you forgive me?"

"Nay, Florence, nay; it is I who ought to ask forgiveness if I have cast for a moment a cloud over the sunshine of your heart; but from the first moment that I saw you I found that you possessed that grace of person and beauty of feature that all might admire, and when I found that the fair face was but an index to the mind within, I loved you."

The girl made no reply, and after the pause of a moment he continued :—

"Yes, I then loved you; and bright and beautiful visions of future happiness came across my soul! I loved you—and the whole world altered its aspect to me! I loved you—and I became an altered being; for until then I had led a sad and solitary life. But I offend you?"

"No; go on—go on!"

"I had lived surrounded by my books—those treasures of past ages—those shrines in which are deposited the purest and the holiest of relics; but when I came to know you, and love you well (and I will not say I loved you at once with a fever-gush of passion), all was forgotten! I lived only for you; I dreamt only of the joy of making you my own! But I know I ought not to say this to you now."

The girl sobbed.

"I distress you; but remember that this occasion will be the last on which I shall permit myself to utter such sentiments and thoughts; and being so, I pray you to let me tell you all."

"Go on—go on! I will listen."

"It was not until after I loved you thus—not until after I had drunk in the inspiration of your beauty—that I heard you were another's—that you had plighted your faith to one distant — pure and holy faith, which you mean to keep."

"You could not know, nor could I tell you; these are things not spoken of idly. Alas, alas! that in this case the knowledge should have come so late!"

"It was late. But you are right. I could not expect—I ought not to have expected—that you should carry, as it were, your heart in your hand, to be inspected by every passing stranger; that is what I could not expect nor wish, Florence. I only say, and complain not of you as I say it, that most unhappy has it been for me that I plunged too deeply into the sea of affection for extrication. Florence, I loved you; and then, but not till then, did I know that your heart was not at your disposal, and that another claimed its fealty. Do not, oh, do not, fancy that I say this to give you the slightest pang! It is not so; I simply say it because it is true, Florence."

"And I believe you with my whole heart—with my whole soul."

"You exculpate me at once from the supposition that I came to enthral your affections and divert your sympathies from the proper channel; thus laying up in your heart cause for much future misery."

"I acquit you of all—all that."

"I tell you freely, Florence, that it is the honour and the purity of your mind, which to me is your more beautiful and better self, and that is why I love you. And I love you more that you cling to your religion and early faith, than as though for me you had cast it aside, and made me what I must have been, happy in the society of such a one as I shall never meet again."

Florence sobbed as if her heart would break.

"No more—no more," she said. "Do not—oh! do not speak to me in such a strain as this—do not, Mr. Grantley, make me think that if I could divide my heart one portion would be yours—another devoted to my early, unextinguishable love."

"Oh, those words of rapture! Speak again, my Florence, speak again!"

"Heaven help me! I have already said too much."

"No, no; do not retract a word—not a tone, upon which memory may yet linger in years to come, when it were criminal to look upon you with eyes of such affection as those which now beam the light of holy love upon you. Guileless, pure, and beautiful being, you may speak to me most freely; retract nothing that is the emanation of that divinity of soul which is all truthfulness. Florence, I can love so well that the happiness of her I love shall be as transcendant over my own feelings as is the glorious light of heaven over the puniest contrivance of man to chase the darkness from his mind."

"Mr. Grantley, Mr. Grantley—cease, oh, cease."

"I've done: and I will bid you, Florence, if it be your sentence, an 'adieu'—so complete and so eternal, that the faintest echo of my name or of my existence shall never again intrude upon you."

"Heaven, Heaven," she cried, "now grant me strength to go through this sore trial. The chain—aye the chain—there shall be magic in the touch. And the broken chain—I have it here: each link of it binds my heart yet dearer to him who is away."

She kissed something that she took from her bosom, fervently.

"And is that the gauge of your affection?" said Grantley.

"This, Mr. Grantley," she said, and she spoke through her tears—"this is one-half of a chain that he presented to me ere he left me. We rent its links asunder—each retaining a portion—and vowing that, as we looked upon it, we should, from time to time, renew our faith and constancy—that we should never, never forget."

"A chain!"

No. 8,

"Yes: and there is not a link of it but has a hold on my very heart. It is entwined so closely around it, that the attempt to withdraw it would be to break both. I thank Heaven that I have this memento of my affection and my duty near to me now; and that the happy remembrance of the past may enable me to resist successfully all the present, that would withdraw me from my heart's devotion."

"Will you let me see the chain, Florence?"

"Yes, yes! Look upon it as long as you will, Mr. Grantley. Heaven knows that I feel I owe you all the courtesy it is in my power to bestow upon you."

The portion of chain she had around her neck; and now she withdrew it, and handed it to Mr. Grantley, who held it up to the dim light, and looked earnestly upon it.

"And this," he said, "is your *gage d'amour*—this reminds you of the absent form of him to whom you have pledged your best affections?"

"It does."

"It is very strange."

"Strange!—what is strange?"

"Florence, I am the last one who would wish to inflict a pang upon you; but if you will examine a portion of chain that I have, you will be surprised that the abundant faith you have had in one whom you would have trusted with your heart's best happiness, is a false light, and one which you ought to discard from your heart."

"A false light?"

"Yes, a false light, Florence, and such a one as it is well to awaken to a due appreciation of. You are deceived, and that feeling of trustfulness which induces you to stake so much upon the honour and reputation of the absent, is surely misapplied."

"No, no, that cannot be; do not, I implore you, Mr. Grantley, do not attempt to deprive me of any portion of the deep respect I bear towards you, by making me believe that it is possible for you to stoop to jealousy."

"I have no jealousy, because I have no hope. I cannot, after what you have said to me, indulge in the most distant expectation that you can ever be mine; for me, therefore, to make any attempt to turn you from him who is the real object of your attachment, without full and adequate reasons, would be futile. When I tell you, however, that your lover has parted with the chain, a portion of which you now show me, you will not be surprised that, feeling as I do so intent an interest in your fate, I should call upon you to hesitate before you put continued faith in him."

"Parted with that chain which he swore would be his while life continued to him? Oh no, no! that is impossible."

"The presumed impossibility, Florence, is best tested by the fact. Look upon this which I now produce to you: tell me that it is not the other half of the chain which you have shown to me, and I will not say it is."

As he spoke, he took from his pocket something wrapped in paper, which carefully unfolding, he handed to the girl, who eagerly looked upon it with such an expression of horror, mingled with incredulity, that it was painful and dreadful to look upon her face.

I saw it by a gleam of light that shot across it, and I waited with breathless anxiety for the verdict she was called upon to pronounce concerning her lover's faithfulness or deceit.

"Look upon it well," cried Mr. Grantley; "mind that you have no doubts; assure yourself that it is or it is not the corresponding half of the chain which you have shown me."

She was still silent. It seemed too dreadful a thing for her to decide, or, if she had made her decision, it seemed too dreadful for her to utter it. I knew not, for a time, which was the case, but I saw her tremble, and for many minutes there was a perceptible silence.

"Have you decided?" he said.   "Can you not come to a conclusion?"

Florence did not speak, but her aunt suddenly flung her arms around her, crying—

"Help, Mr. Grantley, help! I fear she faints, and I am unequal to the task of supporting her."

Mr. Grantley stepped forward, and apparently only just in time, for I saw Florence hanging over his arm, apparently lifeless.

"My poor child, my poor child," cried the aunt. "Oh! Mr. Grantley. why did you tell her of this? the knowledge will destroy her."

"No, no, you are wrong, it will not destroy her; this is a subject upon which she ought to know the truth, and it is better by far for her to know it from friendly, than from unfriendly lips."

" But it is very dreadful."

"She will recover. See, even now, the rain as it falls upon her cheek revives her, she will soon be herself again."

"What is it?" said Florence, in a low tone—"what has happened?—did I dream that Lionel was false?   Oh! no, no, no—it cannot, must not be."

"Listen, now," said Mr. Grantley, "and believe me, Florence, that it is with abundance of grief I say to you what I now say.   This chain came into my hands some months since ; but, before I proceed, tell me if you have any certain means, beyond its mere general appearance, of identifying it.   Speak to me, Florence, and command your feelings, for this is a subject which, indeed, demands your most serious attention."

" I have such a means," she said, " on one link, namely, the first one of the broken chain, my own initials are scratched.   Look, look for me, aunt, and tell me if they be there."

"My dear child," said the aunt, "my eyes are old, I cannot see."

"You will not trust me," said Mr. Grantley ; "already I find I am received by you as an enemy, because I bring to you an unwelcome truth."

She made no reply, but eagerly examined the chain, holding it up so that the link she looked at might catch a few rays from the nearest lamp.   Then her hands trembled, and she said faintly—

"It is too true, it is too true.   Oh! why has this knowledge come upon me, to embitter a future existence?"

"Nay, do not say embitter," remarked Mr. Grantley.   "Why should your future existence be embittered, because you have discovered that one whom you thought worthy is not so?   If there be any bitterness, let it fall into the cup of him who has deceived you; it is not you who should suffer it, for Heaven knows you have kept your faith—it is him who should suffer it, who has broken his.   That you should suffer, Florence, from finding yourself deceived, is natural, but that you should soon shake off such a suffering is likewise natural, or I am much mistaken in your disposition."

"Mr. Grantley, listen to me," said Florence, "and you, too, my aunt.   The weakness of human nature made me yield to a momentary impulse—an impulse that made me think it possible Lionel had deceived me ; reflection, however, has now come to my aid, and all is calm again within my heart.   I do not, I will not doubt his faith."

"Not doubt him, Florence?   What say you to the chain?"

"I say that it is the same chain, the other half of which is so dear to me ; but I say likewise that there are a thousand accidents beyond all human cont.ol that might have deprived him of it ; and it is not for such evidence I will pluck him from my heart."

"Rare and unexampled being!" exclaimed Grantley, " why, oh, why, do yo thus force me to love you by an exhibition of such traits of nobleness and gen - rosity as I could not believe the world had to show me?   Why are you not s others are?—swayed by circumstances that would seem to bring conviction ; but which you, with such a nobility of soul that, had I read of it, I should have deemed it fabulous to reject.   Can you forgive me for presenting to you the apparent evidence of the worthlessness of one whom you love?"

"I can forgive you truly, Mr. Grantley; indeed, I ought not to use that phrase at all, for there is nothing to forgive; it would have been strange indeed, very strange, if, possessing the other half of the chain which I have shown you, you had not not proclaimed the fact."

"And are you not curious to know how it came in my possession?"

She was silent for some moments, ere she replied.

"It did not come direct from Lionel."

"It did not."

"Then I ask no more. I wish to know no more, but I am satisfied in the abundant faith I have in him."

"Be it so. And now, Florence, and you, Mrs. Russell, I have one great favour to ask of you. I was lodging, as you know, in your house, and some of the happiest days I have ever known have been passed beneath your roof before this explanation took place. My quitting was a voluntary act of my own, arising from deep disappointment at finding your affections, Florence, were no longer at your own disposal. I have repented of that hasty act, and wo uld feign now return. Do you think that you could bear with me?"

"Our means of subsistence," said Mrs. Russell, "depend, as you know, Mr. Grantley, upon letting some portion of our house; but, as this is a matter entirely of feeling, and connected with Florence, I consider that she alone ought to have the power of decision; I therefore leave it entirely in her hands."

"Then from you, Florence, I await the decision of my fate. Believe me, you have nothing to fear from persecution. I admire too much that noble clinging to a faith in him to whom you have pledged your affections, to seek to shake it. Nothing, I presume, but death would have the effect of making you abandon the hope of being one day the wife of Lionel Feversham."

"Nothing but death," said Florence, "nothing in the world but death. I will not, Mr. Grantley, say that you shall not reside in our house, if you think proper so to do. I will leave the decision of that subject to yourself."

"But you do not object to it or oppose it?"

"I know not why I should."

"Then to-morrow allow me to hope that I may occupy my old apartments, from which I have been absent now sufficiently long to make me feel how unhappy I am elsewhere."

"All shall be ready for you, Mr. Grantley," said the aunt, "and most glad shall I be to have you again under our roof. The house will seem more like itself again, and I shall feel the satisfaction of knowing that we are not quite lonely, but have a friend beneath our roof."

"Believe me," he said, "a most sincere one; and now, that the rain has passed away, I will leave you, for I have kept you a most unreasonable time here. To-morrow we shall meet again. Good night!"

He shook hands with them both, and then hurried off towards Hungerford-street.

Florence and her aunt paused for a moment, while the old lady adjusted her shawl, and then they walked slowly into the Strand, which they traversed until they came to Surrey-street, down which they turned, and entered a tolerably-sized house, near the termination of it. I saw that there was a bill in the window, announcing apartments to let; and, as I stood with my back against the railings of the opposite house, I pondered in my own mind over what I had overheard.

Of course I cannot hope to have transferred to paper anything of the manner in which the conversation I have reported was conducted, although I have made a faithful transcript of the matter of it; but if it has awakened in the mind of my reader but half the interest it did in mine, it would be sufficient to make him wish to hear more of Florence.

But, as I said, I stood there deeply pondering over the possibility of acquiring further information with regard to her, and rather puzzled in my own mind upon the question of whether Mr. Grantley was really the sincere and kind-hearted individual his conversation would lead any one to suppose, or r ot.

There was something in my mind of a contradictory tendency. At one moment I thought it almost impossible that any individual could behave with such an amount of apparent greatness of soul, and be really otherwise; but when I came to reflect that, during even my brief experience in the world, I had found the most remarkable instances of the most refined hypocrisy, my doubt would revive, and I knew not what to think.

It seemed to me so wonderful, too, that Mr. Grantley, of all men in the world, should have possession of the chain that had belonged to him whom they called Lionel: it puzzled me amazingly to think how he could have got it, and I knew not whether to believe his admiration of the manner in which Florence had received the information was real or feigned.

But at last, without coming to any conclusion upon these questions, I came to a determination myself as to what I should do to solve them.

"This is an adventure," I said, "which I will carry out; it is one which I should like much to see the end of. I am an idle man, and have nothing to do but to carry out such affairs at my own pleasure. What is to hinder me from taking a lodging here in the house of Mrs. Russell, and then trusting to good luck to get me on such terms with the family that I shall acquire a knowledge of all that is proceeding?"

And now, having arrived at this point, I will adopt a different course in the relation of the remarkable incidents connected with this tale. Without troubling my reader with all the little steps by which I, in course of time, acquired the full information which I did really obtain, I will proceed to relate the circumstances as I placed them together in my journal, in all their details, which, from time to time, I was enabled to procure, and put together in the form of a complete story.

My readers will, therefore, please to forget me for a time, and to suppose that they are listening to a regular narrative told by a third party. I did take a lodging with Mrs. Russell, and I did come at a knowledge of the whole circumstances, some portion of which I had heard detailed during the agitated interview on the Adelphi-terrace.

*　　　*　　　*　　　*　　　*　　　*

When Florence reached home she at once, on the plea of fatigue, retired to her own chamber, and there, burying her face in her hands, she gave free vent to those pent-up feelings which she would not exhibit in the presence of Mr. Grantley.

"Lionel, Lionel!" she exclaimed, "why do you not write to me? why not send to me, if it be but a word, to put an end, not to doubts of mine, for I have none, but to the possibility of others insinuating a doubt of the truth and purity of your affection? For two long years, Lionel, have I waited, and waited in vain, for news of you! Shall I ever look upon your face again, or are you indeed numbered with the dead?"

A copious flood of tears came most seasonably to her relief, and as she wept she found the fever of her heart and brain gently subside, and a calmer feeling creep over her.

"I will not be impatient!" she said; "I will still wait, and wait patiently. When he left his native land to seek his fortune among strangers, he told me that it was possible, although he hoped not likely, that circumstances would occur to make him seem neglectful, but that, should the whole world conspire to tell me he was false, I should not believe it, but with a holy, clinging faith in his constancy, still believe that he was all my own. And I promised. Shall I—dare I doubt him?"

*　　　*　　　*　　　*　　　*　　　*

On the following morning, true to his word, Mr. Grantley took again possession of the apartments he had occupied in Mrs. Russell's house, and for the remainder of that day his usual quiet and familiar intercourse with the aunt and niece was established.

Towards evening a stranger called to visit him, with whom he remained closeted for a considerable time, and, apparently fearful that he should be recognised on some future occasion, he, Mr. Grantley himself, preceded him to the door, and showed him out.

Neither Florence nor her aunt paid any attention to this circumstance, for they were not, in the ordinary sense of the word, curious people, but still they could not but be aware that mysterious communication had taken place between the stranger and Mr. Grantley.

At supper-time he was more than usually reserved, and it was evident that something painful was upon his mind, for now and then he answered abstractedly, as if his thoughts were far away.

When it was time to retire to rest he paused and seemed upon the point of making some revelation, but he checked himself, and after bidding them good night, walked from the apartment.

"To-morrow, to-morrow," he said, " will do as well ; let her, at least, have one night more of peace."

They did not hear him utter these words, but still they could not but feel some disquietude from his manner. They well knew he was not the man, if he had any gratifying or pleasant communication to make, to keep it from one day to another, and, therefore, the presumption was, that what he had to say was of a painful tendency.

In the morning he looked pale and agitated, and after partaking of but a scanty breakfast, he took occasion, when Mrs. Russell had left the room for a few moments, to say to Florence—

"Will you, at your own time, and when you please, grant me this morning half an hour's attention ?"

"Not to renew, Mr. Grantley, let me hope, that subject, which is interdicted between us."

"Florence, I have not deceived you yet, and I dare not now commence to do so : what I have to say relates to that subject ; I have a piece of information which you ought to know."

"Your manner, Mr. Grantley, indicates it to be disastrous ; suspense is dreadful. I will come to you in the dining-room in half an hour."

He bowed his acquiescence, and then left the room, followed by an afflicted and an alarmed glance from the beautiful eyes of Florence.

She shook like an aspen leaf after he left her, and, clasping her hands, she exclaimed—

"What is this—what can this be—that he has to tell me ? It sits heavily upon his own mind ; it must be something dreadful, or it would not move such a man as he is in the manner that it does."

She said nothing to her aunt ; but, when the half-hour was nearly over, she walked with trembling steps to the dining-room, where she found Mr. Grantley pacing to and fro, evidently in great agitation.

He started upon the entrance of Florence, and, placing for her a seat, he said, in as composed a tone as he could assume,

"Florence, let me pray you to call your firmness to your aid, and to be calm."

"Are you calm, Mr. Grantley ?" she said, as she looked at him.

"I am not," he said, " but I have seen enough of you to know that you have a spirit superior to my own, and that what would have crushed me only inspires you with a nobler confidence. Florence, I have great faith in your mental power, or I would not make to you the communication I have now to utter."

"Is it disastrous, and can it be concealed ?"

"It is disastrous, most bitterly disastrous ; and likewise, for a time, it could be concealed ; but it must come at last, with accumulated power ; and, until it did come, you would suffer abundance of those pangs which, I have heard you yourself say, are the worst of all to bear, namely, the pangs of suspense."

"They are the worst. Let me know all at once, Mr. Grantley. I will not shrink from the information."

"You shall. And first, I have a confession to make, and forgiveness to seek."

" Confession and forgiveness !   Do I hear aright, or have my ears deceived me?"

" Your ears have not deceived you. The words I used were, confession and forgiveness ; and, when I make the former, and ask of you the latter, I can but urge my motive as a good one, for concealing from you that which I have known some time, and which I now purpose to relate. You will listen to me?"

" Most assuredly."

" When first I saw you I loved you, as you are well aware. I did not know you were another's. But, when I found that you had really fixed your affection upon some one who was far away from you, I reflected deeply upon what I ought to do, loving you as I did, and esteeming your happiness far more than I did my own."

" Say on."

" With me to love, is to sacrifice all feelings of self; it is to concentrate all thought and feelings in a loving object ; it is to live for her alone and to esteem her happiness with another even as of the first importance. It was with such a love as that, that I loved you."

" No more, no more of this, Mr. Grantley ; do not permit me to suspect that you have merely sought this interview to renew a theme you told me you had abandoned. If you have news for me let me hear it."

" Your reproof is just ; but when you hear my news you will wonder not that my tongue lingers over its utterance, and that I am loth to say the words. My confession is, that I knew, before I sought the interview with you on the Adelphiterrace, what I am now about to tell you : the forgiveness I ask is, that I have kept it so long from your ears."

" You have that forgiveness most freely. I cannot, will not doubt but the motive was a kind one."

" It was ; and as I tell you, when I heard from your own lips that he who had won your heart was named Lionel Feversham, and that he had gone on a marching expedition with a view of bettering his fortunes, I conceived the romantic idea of communicating with him, and at once, for your sake, place him in a position of making you his own."

" Mr. Grantley, this noble generosity goes to my very heart."

" I loved you, what other could I do?"

" But such is not ordinary love."

" Be it so : but to continue. My extended resources gave me a means of acquiring information, which otherwise I could not have availed myself of, and at last I was introduced to a man who had sailed in the same vessel with Lionel Feversham."

" You did ! " exclaimed Florence, with enthusiasm, " you did? you found one who had known him—one who had heard his voice, and associated with him amid dangers? Oh, tell me, tell me at once, what said he of Lionel Feversham?"

" You shall hear," he said, " that the vessel sailed towards the Greek Isles, and that all went well with Feversham, until they reached those classic shores of ancient Greece, which will ever have such a charm to the imagination ; but there a deadly sickness spread its ravages among the crew."

" God of Heaven ! " cried Florence, " what would you say?"

" Hear me out ; I have commenced, and I must finish."

She gazed at him with distracted eyes, and every pulse seemed to stand still, as she waited, in horrible suspense, for what should next come from his lips ; and it seemed to take him some moments to recover himself before he could proceed with what he had to say. When he did speak, it was in a tone of deep emotion.

" Some died : and the first corpse that was committed to the deep was Lionel Feversham."

Poor Florence sat as motionless as a statue. It seemed as if those few words had completely stunned her faculties, and as if she had no ears to hear what he continued to utter—

" The half chain which I exhibited to you upon the occasion of our interview at the Adelphi-terrace, was taken from around his neck by the man who told me the tale."

" Oh, Heaven, can this be true," she gasped.   " Mr. Grantley—Mr. Grantley—on your soul's dearest hopes, tell me if this be true."

"On my soul's dearest hopes, it is true."

" Then I am desolate."

" Not so, Florence—not so : he whom you loved best is gone from you; but you cannot be desolate while there is one heart still living that clings to you in pure and holy affection."

" And you kept this from me ?"

" I did : but listen to my reasons.   Perhaps I was wrong ; for I have been bred up among books and in seclusion—I know not much of human nature—but I kept it secret from you because I did think that the pang of thinking Lionel Feversham was false would be less to you than the pang of knowing he was dead.   I pray you pardon me that I made such a mistake ; and when I found that, in spite of all, you still clung to a belief in his affection, I felt that the communication I now make to you must be made ; and therefore it was that I asked leave to return again to this house, in order that I might take the opportunity of making it."

" Lionel, Lionel ! and have you indeed gone from me ? Alas, alas ! that it should be so.   Heaven grant that the grave may soon close over me ; for I can now know no joy.   But, Mr. Grantley, is there no room for doubt ?"

" I can produce to you the man who saw him draw his latest breath. I thought you might require such a confirmation, and I can produce it.   He has been here, and I have appointed him to call again at the hour which is fast approaching.   It may pain you to see him, and to hear that which he has to relate ; but if you please to do so, and if it will remove any doubt existing in your mind, 'tis better that you should hear his statement."

" No, no, his possession of the chain is sufficient ; that mystery is now frightfully cleared up ; it was a piece of evidence of his faithlessness that I could look upon with scorn, but it is an evidence of his death which I cannot resist.   I know enough, I have heard enough, Mr. Grantley ; leave me, I pray you, leave me !"

" And can you pardon me for the part that I have played ?"

" I do, I do ; it was a mistaken one, but I can see its motive."

He saw that she was overwhelmed with grief ; he heard, by the strange tone in which she spoke, that it was with the greatest effort she did so, and he left the apartment at once.   He sought Mrs. Russell, and merely telling her that Florence was in the dining-room and he thought required her presence, he then left the house, and strove, by violent exercise and the physical exertion of a long walk, to get rid of the state of mental excitement into which he had been thrown.

*   *   *   *   *   *   *

Five days have elapsed, and Florence has just risen from a sick couch, to which she has been confined during that period.   She is very pale, and there is an air of settled sorrow upon her face ; her aunt is with her, and tears are standing in the eyes of the old lady.

" Florence," she said, " did you hear what I was saying to you ?"

" Yes, aunt, I did," she replied, faintly ; " what was it ?"

" Alas, alas ! my dear Florence, you were not attending ; I must tell you again."

" Do so, dear aunt, do so ; my thoughts were far away."

" Then, Florence, it is with grief I say it, we shall be compelled to leave here. Circumstances with us have been getting worse for a long time past, and the small means with which we commenced in this house are absorbed completely.   Its expenses overpower me, and we are on the brink of ruin. Do you understand me ?"

" I do, aunt, I do ; Heaven help us !"

" Alas ! my dear, there are no miracles now-a-days, and nothing short of one can save us from absolute want."

" It is dreadful !"

" It is, and more dreadful to you than to me, for I am old, and it matters little now what I am called upon to endure."

" No, no, aunt, you shall endure nothing ; I shall soon be well, and the dreadful shock which the tidings of poor Lionel's death has given me will pass away. I

can then toil for you; and surely, with youth and willingness to back me, I shall
be able to earn sufficient to support us both."

"Florence, Florence, you know not what you say; you are totally unacquainted
with the world and its ways; you know nothing of the frightful difficulties
which you would have to encounter."

"But those difficulties are all conquered by resolution?"

"I don't know that, Florence; it by no means follows that they are so, although
resolution may do something towards accomplishing such a result; but there is one
mode—a mode terrible and just, of relieving yourself and relieving me from all
care."

"Indeed, aunt? and what mode can that be?"

"It is one, however, by which you make the happiness of another. Can you
not guess it now, Florence?"

"Perchance I may, but I will hear you speak. Go on, aunt, I will listen to you,
No. 9.

I will not be impatient; I am too much bowed down with grief for that; I will listen to you calmly, say to me what you may."

"Then, my dear, I will speak to you freely. It is useless for me to say that Mr. Grantley loves you; that is a fact of which you are sufficiently well aware, and I think, if I were to tell you that no man ever lived that is more worthy of your affection, you would not disguise the truth of the assertion. He is acquainted with all the circumstances of your life; he knows that you have loved another, and therefore there is nothing to explain to him—there is nothing to conceal from him. He loves you with an affection, I am confident, of the most enduring character. You may trust him most implicitly; and if you would be his, it would be his greatest pride and his greatest pleasure to place you very far above all the exigencies of life."

"I understand you, aunt; but ought I, in common justice to one whom I respect as I do Mr. Grantley, to give him such a withered heart as mine?"

"He knows the circumstances, Florence; and there is one thing which you, as well as he, will always recollect."

"What is that?"

"When you met him on the Adelphi-terrace, and he spoke to you such words of affection, you told him that if you could divide your heart in twain, one-half of it should be his, while the other remained still devoted to Lionel Feversham."

"I did so—I did so."

"Then he will be content to receive from you the amount of affection which you will be able to bestow upon him; an amount not regulated by any love for another, since the only other who could have come into competition with it, is no more."

"Would it be just of me?"

"It would be generous as well as just. Will you promise me to think of it, Florence?"

"I will. Heaven knows, it matters little now what becomes of me. You have played the part of a mother to me for that period, when I was deprived of the care of one. Mr. Grantley's character is entitled to my approval and admiration; and it is impossible, widowed as my heart is, that I could feel otherwise than most grateful towards him for any affection which he could bestow upon me. I will think of what you have said, aunt, but I feel now that I ought not to bestow upon such a man as Mr. Grantley an affection second to any other feeling."

With this Mrs. Russell was satisfied; for, although she certainly had not been prompted by Mr. Grantley to make this appeal to Florence, she could read well the state of his feelings, and she well knew how gladly he would make her his wife, notwithstanding she could only give her the second affection she mentioned.

Mrs. Russell wished that Mr. Grantley had been in the house, that he might have backed what she said, by pleading his own cause with Florence, but he was from home; and she waited with considerable impatience for his return, in order to communicate with him, and let him know precisely what had transpired.

Mrs. Russell fondly flattered herself that this short conversation we have recorded was quite a confidential and private one between herself and Florence; but in this she was mistaken.

The one servant of all work whom they kept, fancying that affairs were not going on so swimmingly as they might do with old Mrs. Russell, had lately taken to acquire useful information by means of listening at key-holes, and otherwise ascertaining what other people were talking about.

In the pursuit of this inquiry she ascertained that somebody of the name of Lionel Feversham was dead—that that news had come from Mr. Grantley, and that a marriage between the said Mr. Grantley and Florence was most unquestionably upon the *tapis*.

All this was very well, so far as this girl was merely concerned, and she might, without doing any very great damage to anybody, have gossiped about it among her own class.

We shall, however, soon perceive what "great effects from trifling causes spring," and how a most dreadful conjunction of circumstances arose from this simple fact.

But it would be premature just at present to detail them, until we ascertain precisely what conclusion Florence came to, with regard to the proposition made her by her aunt.

We cannot take upon ourselves to say but even that, amid that dreary latitude of mind which had followed the certainty of Lionel's death, she had conjectured the possibility of a distinct offer from Mr. Grantley, and had asked herself what she should say to him, so that her aunt's proposition came not upon her quite unawares, and she did give it all the consideration she could be supposed to do, under the circumstances.

She thought, then, that she came to a conclusion firmly to reject the offer, and that principally upon the ground that it would be doing Mr. Grantley a great injustice to accept it.

She yielded, however, to an interview, at which she explained to him her reasons, and implored him not to press his suit.

But he did press it, and pressed it so affectionately, that she yielded her reluctant consent to become his wife.

"But, Mr. Grantley," she said, "although you declare that you will be satisfied with my respect and my esteem, you must permit me to give the usual period of mourning to him who is no more."

" I can prove to you," said Mr. Grantley, " that poor Lionel's death happened more than a year ago, and consequently that that period has passed away. Give a right at once to remove you and your aunt from this place, which I am sure is distasteful to you both, you know I can only acquire that right by calling you my wife. Let me pray you, therefore, to allow me to do so with the smallest possible delay."

The argument concerning her aunt's necessities was a powerful one to Florence. She yielded, and the day of the nuptials was fixed to be one week from that time.

"And now," said Mr Grantley, "I am going to ask you, Florence, if you have sufficient faith in me, personally, to say that you will forgive the withholding a secret from you concerning myself, which I do not wish to tell you until after we are married "

" I have sufficient faith," she said. " Tell the secret when you please. I am certain it is not an unworthy one."

" That it certainly is not. But as there is such a secret, and as it is a mere personal one to myself, I thought it just that you should know it as something which had to be communicated afterwards, and which it would please me to think you had sufficient faith in me not to insist upon knowing before."

This, then, was all settled, and nothing could appear to be more straightforward than the circumstances attendant now upon the projected union. All seemed arranged in the most perfect and satisfactory manner, and probably never had Mr. Grantley felt so happy in his life as upon that evening when it was thoroughly arranged that he was to become the husband of the only person for whom he had ever entertained a deep and sincere feeling of affection.

And now two circumstances occurred which materially altered the whole aspect of affairs.

It was the first evening since Florence had heard of the disastrous death of Lionel that she could be persuaded to leave the house, but at the earnest request of her aunt and of Mr. Grantley she accompanied them to take a quiet stroll in the Temple Gardens, which were close at hand, and to which they had access. The evening was uncommonly serene and beautiful, so that, in more cheerful conversation than she would have thought it possible for her to engage so soon, Florence remained later than she had at all intended, and during that time we will turn our attention to the house in Surrey-street.

First of all there came a large packet bearing a country post-mark, and addressed to Mr. Grantley; this the servant took in and placed upon his table, and then, just as the twilight was stealing on and she was thinking of lighting candles, there came a hurried double knock at the street door, and such a sudden pull at the bell that the alarmed servant hesitated for some few moments before she would answer the summons.

"Now, who can that be," she said, "coming just between lights, and giving such a pull at the bell; I wonder who it can possibly be !"

Whoever it was seemed not blessed with any extraordinary amount of patience, for another knock, louder than the first, and another pull at the bell, satisfied her of the fact, that, be he who he might, he thought he had waited quite long enough.

Under these circumstances the girl was forced to go to the door, and she comforted herself as she did so with the thought that thieves and murderers did not usually knock and ring when they came to make victims of anybody, which was a very sensible idea, considering the person from whom it emanated.

CHAPTER VIII.

THE UNEXPECTED ARRIVAL.

WHEN Maria, the servant, opened the door, she saw standing upon the step a young man well attired, but in something of a naval uniform. His manner was hurried and impetuous.

"Is this Mrs. Russell's ?" he said, and then glancing round him as he stepped into the passage, he added, "oh, of course it is ; of course it is. I know it now, and every object within it. Is Miss Florence within ?"

"Miss Florence did you say, sir ?"

"Yes, confound your stupidity ! didn't you know what I said ?"

"Yes, sir, and as for being stupid, I aint so stupid as some people is uncivil. Miss Florence aint at home, if you must know ; she is gone out with her aunt to take a walk, and with Mr. Grantley, her husband as is to be."

"Husband! Grantley!"

"Well, sir, husband and Grantley. I suppose a person may speak what she knows without having her eyes tore out of her head."

"Woman! what do you mean ? Tell me at once all that you do know. I have already heard enough to drive me distracted."

"Have you really, sir ? I should think then that ought to do ; and if you'll be so good as to get off the mat, I'll shut the door."

He clasped his head with his hands, and looked in such a frightful state of excitement that Maria got alarmed, and would have rushed into the street and called for assistance, but he seized her by the wrist, crying—

"Hold—I mean no harm to you, but I must know more of this. Here is gold for you—tell me all."

He placed in her hand several sovereigns as he spoke, and the sight of them had such a magical effect upon Maria, that her voice sunk lower to quite a respectful whisper, and she said—

"Oh yes, sir, certainly; please sir to walk into missus's best parlour; you wouldn't like to take anything, would you, sir? there's a cask of small beer tapped, that was remarkably good till the thunder-storm came and turned it to cider."

"No, no, I want nothing; tell me about this Grantley and the marriage that you spoke of—be brief about it, or I shall do something desperate."

"Well, sir, if so really be that you want to do something desperate, then the kitchen chimney hasn't been swept for six months."

"Peace, peace, with this folly. Tell me, is it really true that a marriage is contemplated between Florence and this person you speak of ?"

"Well, sir, that I can't tell you. It's a going to be, that's all I know ; but whether it's 'templorated or not, I can't tell you."

"Who is he?"

"He is our first floor, sir."

"The devil! and how came you to know it?"

"How should I, but through the key-hole of the back dining-room? I heard Miss Florence say, 'that me,' says she, and then Mr. Grantley, he says, 'I mean,' says he, 'and no mistake;' and then the old lady, she says, 'what a blessed thing it is to have managed it all so nice while Mr. What's-his-name was dead.'"

"What name did they mention?"

"It was Mr. Lion—Lion somebody."

"Lionel Feversham, was that the name?"

"Ah, to be sure it was, that was it; and they quite 'gratulated themselves about it."

"They thought him dead?"

"Very dead indeed, sir."

"And this from Florence, upon whose faith I could have staked my life!"

"You, sir, you stake your life! why, you don't mean to say you are Mr. Thing-umbob, and that you haven't been dead at all—what a miscovery!"

My name is Lionel Feversham; but keep the secret of my presence here, and you shall be amply rewarded. The tale you tell bears an impression of truth about it, dreadful though it is to my ears. Tell me, if, in course of the conversation, you overheard anything was mentioned of a chain?"

"A chain; do you mean the street-door chain?"

"No, no, no, a gold chain. Did you hear the word mentioned?"

"Well, now I think on it, I did; there was a something said by somebody, but who said it, and what it was, I really don't know."

"Listen to me," said the stranger; "I will leave you an address, where you can communicate with me; you must ascertain the precise day on which this marriage is to take place."

"Oh! it's to be this day week, they settled all that first of all. They thought of waiting a good while, but at last it was brought down to a week. I'm to have a new gown, and old missus is coming out strong in a wiolet satin."

"Then will you, for any sum of money you like to name, admit me secretly into this house on the evening before the marriage is to take place?"

"To be sure; you can come down the area steps."

"I will; and I will do something that shall make me remembered."

"Well, I would, sir; and if you don't find nothing else you likes better, there's always the kitchen flue to rewert to, and I shall remember you as long as I live, for what with the smoke—and what with the blacks—and what with the fat frizzling up when you don't want it—and the biling of one thing, and the biling over of the other, it's not a very quiet life a servant gets here; and then, the second floor back expects its boots before anybody else; and when the first floor gets hold of the bell, he don't know when to leave off. Lor', he's gone; what a violent sort of gentleman he is, it's quite a romance in seven volumes. I shouldn't at all wonder now, but Mr. What-you-call-'em will say something unpleasant to Mr. Thing-a-me."

It was a sad trial to Maria to be forced to keep the secret which had occurred, and yet she feared that if she told any one, it might very possibly get round to the ears of Mr. Lional Feversham, and prevent her from receiving any more of the gold, of which he appeared so lavish.

When the party came home from the Temple Gardens, the mysterious manner of Maria could not but attract their attention.

She walked about like a bandit in a melodrama, and assumed such mysterious attitudes, that Mrs. Russell thought she was going mad, and determined upon giving her a month's notice at once, rightly considering that a lunatic was not at all desirable as a servant of all work.

Mr. Grantley went up to his apartment, and perhaps he had seldom felt so happy as he did on that particular evening. He felt confident, and he looked forward with pleasure, for he was yet a young man, to many years of unalloyed happiness, with the object of his choice.

He had declined a light, because, in the first place, he had the means of igniting the candles that were in his own room, and, in the second place, he was particularly fond of the twilight hour, considering it always as favourable to reflection.

He threw himself upon a chair, without seeing the packet that had come by post to him, and he gave himself up for nearly half-an-hour to the happiest thoughts.

"She is mine," he said, "she is mine, and I, who have hitherto courted solitude, thinking that the world would never show me one I could love sufficiently to make me wish to call her my own, have at length won, certainly, one of the best and fairest of human beings."

"How different an aspect will my ancient home in the country now wear, when I place a mistress at its head. How happy am I that I mingled in the world more than was my custom; inasmuch as it has enabled me to discover so much beauty and so much excellence. Poor Lionel, I have a tear for thy memory; but, of all sorrows, that for the dead is the least tangible, and I rejoice to see that Florence is beginning to assume her old aspect of cheerfulness."

He rose and approached the window, which commanded a partial view of the busy river, upon which he gazed for some moments, still wrapped in contemplation.

He then turned his attention to procuring lights, and, when the rays from a candle spread themselves over the table, his eyes, for the first time, fell upon the packet that had come to him by post.

"Ah," he said, "from my agent in the country. An accumulation of letters, I presume, since his last dispatch to me."

He sat down and broke the seal, and then, with an appearance of perfect indifference, he perused several epistles, all of which, however, he was careful to return back into the large envelope which had contained them.

Then he came to one, upon the first glance at the exterior of which he gave a slight start, and exclaimed—

"How like the hand!"

He then hurriedly opened it, and the moment his eyes fell upon its contents, haalf-suppressed shriek burst from his lips, and he sat looking the very embodiment of despair.

This strange apathy lasted but for a few minutes; he then rose, and lifting his hands above his head, he cried, "Oh, Heaven! have you no friendly lightning flash with which to strike me dead? it would, indeed, be merciful to kill me."

He then, with a deep groan, dropped into the chair again, and resting his head upon his hands remained in that attitude for more than an hour. For the most part he was quiet; but at times a convulsive agony seemed to shake his frame, as if he were going through some terrific struggle of the mind, which required more power than he was master of. Then he rose and placed the letters carefully away, with the exception of the one which had caused him so much bitterness of feeling. He crept carefully down the stairs, making the least possible noise, so that no one heard him, and he left the house. He did not return until Florence and her aunt had retired to rest, and then he proceeded direct to his own room and locked himself in. On the following morning he made his appearance at the usual breakfast-hour, for he boarded with Mrs. Russell, and the only change which was perceptible in his appearance consisted in the fact that he was somewhat paler than usual, and that now and then his voice had a mournful pathos in it which was most sad indeed to hear.

But still he spoke with his usual kind gentleness to Florence, and when the breakfast was over he said to her, "Various concerns of great importance, dear Florence, will take me much from you between this and that day on which you have consented to make me so happy; but do not fancy that because I am not with you I am unmindful of you. On the contrary, believe that you will always be present to my thoughts."

"And you to mine," she said; "perhaps I am too critical, but to my eyes you look ill."

" Nay," he said, with a forced smile, " how can I look ill when I have such felicity in store for me ? I will wear a gayer aspect when you see me next, and you shall then own that I look better than, perchance, I have looked for years; because I shall be enjoying that truest of all felicity, which consists in the fact that my heart cannot sum up against me one item of reproach." And so he kissed her cheek and left her.

CHAPTER IX.

THE NIGHT BEFORE THE WEDDING.

So far as regarded his absence from the house for a considerable period during the few days which were to intervene before his marriage took place, Mr. Grantley was as good as his word, and up to mid-day on that preceding the day of which the ceremony was to be performed, Florence could hardly have said that she had had ten hours of his society. And when he did come to the house he certainly did not seem to be near carrying out what he had said about his own improved looks, for he was paler than before, and evidently deeply agitated.

The unequivocal symptoms of a mind ill at ease were a great distress to Florence, as well as to her aunt, but they hoped to see them pass away, and attributed them to some circumstance, the annoying effects of which would soon disappear.

" Florence," he said, as they sat together after their mid-day meal was over, " Florence, you may be assured I shall not sleep here to night, because I have some business to transact a short distance from town, and there I shall remain until the morning, when, at ten o'clock, be assured your bridegroom will meet you at the church."

" How strange you have seemed of late," said Florence, kindly ; " if anything disturbs you, can you think it right to keep it from my knowledge?"

" Nay, there is a secret; I told you there was one, but you must not know it yet."

" And it is that secret which disturbs you."

" It is, in part, dear Florence ; but don't vex yourself with any anticipation of uneasiness, but believe, as indeed you well may, that all will be quite well and as happy, aye, more happy than your anticipations bid you hope for."

With such an answer, unsatisfactory as it was, she was compelled to be satisfied, but she certainly endured much uneasiness from the conviction that there was some mystery which was painfully pressing upon the mind of Grantley.

The day wore on, and towards evening Maria became seriously alarmed and fidgetty about the promise she had made to admit Lionel Feversham into the house.

Visions of blood and murder had floated across her bewildered imagination ever since she had made such a promise, and as the time approached, not even the prospect of the gold she was to get from Lionel was sufficient to reconcile her to the circumstance.

She had, for a wonder, kept her word, making a confidant of no one ; and now it was too late to do so, as regarded any one out of the house, and, if she told any one in it, the question became an anxious one as to whom that should be.

She did not like to speak to old Mrs. Russell, nor to Florence ; but at last, perhaps with a dim prospect of getting well paid for her intelligence, she thought that she would communicate what she knew to Mr. Grantley.

She felt that, if she carried this resolution into effect, she had little time to lose for the evening was coming on.

Then, as if the Fates would have it that she was to have every opportunity of making him a confidant, as regarded what had occurred between her and Lionel Feversham, Mr. Grantley rang his bell.

" That's his bell," said Maria ; " and, as sure as eggs is eggs, I'll tell him."

Mr. Grantley only wanted the fire seen to ; but, after she had accomplished that object, Maria lingered, and commenced by saying—

" Mr. Grantley, perhaps, sir, you isn't aware as you stands upon a lot of gun-powder, which is, in a manner of speaking, ready to go off, and blow you, sir, into never-so-many small bits."

Mr. Grantley looked at her amazed, as well he might.

" Ah, sir, you may look ; but, as I always say, there's wheels within wheels, and crankums, and all sorts of things, continually agoing on."

" And pray, what do those mechanical remarks apply to ? "

" Why, sir, I've found out as we lives in a world as doesn't always stand still."

" I think, Maria, that discovery was made some time ago."

" Was it, sir ? Perhaps you're right, and perhaps you're wrong. But I have got something to tell you, sir, as ought to be enough to make you open your eyes and your hair stand on end."

" Indeed, Maria !"

" Yes, sir—Mr. Lionel Feversham has been here."

" Lionel Feversham been here ! You cannot mean it. Here !—actually here !"

" No—not on that corner of the table, Mr. Grantley, as you was a pointing to—but he's been down stairs."

" When was that ? "

" One day when you was all out—so that he seed nobody but me."

" Oh, indeed ! Close the door, then, and tell me what he said."

" Why, first of all, he gave me three sovereigns."

" Tell me all that passed, and I will give you six."

" Won't I ? and more— "

" No, no—I want to know nothing but what actually took place."

" Well, sir, he comed with a sort of knock, and another sort of ring, and he asked for Miss Florence."

" Yes, yes."

" But it warn't my business to say nothing to him about other people's affairs ; so all I told him was—bearing in mind there is nothing so bad as gossiping—that she was going to be married that day week ; that your name was Grantley ; and that the old lover was supposed to be dead ; and that——

" In fact, you told him all."

" I tell him all ! I didn't tell him anything, I think I know better. I tell him, indeed ! I only said as misses was coming out in a wiolet satin, and about the kitchen flue, and then he flewd away, but he said as how he'd come here to-night, and do something desperate."

" And did he not tell you what it was to be ?"

" No, and I can't think unless he whitewashes the area ; that will be a desperate job when it is done, for it is black enough, and I wonders as he declined the flue. Howsomdever, he's to come here to-night, if so be as how I'll let him in."

" And you must keep your word ; and now tell me truly, and you will get more by doing so than by prevaricating. Have you told this to any one else ?"

" Not to a blessed living soul. I couldn't bemean myself to do so. I hadn't nobody to tell, unless it was the servants up and down the street."

" Well then, listen to me, and I will give you your instructions."

" Well, sir, I don't mind taking my destructions from a real gentleman ; and you may depend, sir, as whatever you tells me to do, I will do. It's been on my mind nearly a week, and I'm uncommon glad as somebody else knows of it at last, so that the 'sponsibility is off me—that's how I looks at it, sir—'sponsibility's the thing ; and if so be as you has that, you has everything—and if you hasn't it, you hasn't nothing."

" I will take all the responsibility," said Mr. Grantley ; " you shall have none of that, believe me, and moreover, you shall be amply rewarded, and in addition to all that——"

" That'll do, so I don't want anything else, so long as I get's rid of the 'sponsibility and gets the handsome reward, that's all I cares about; so now, sir, what's to be done—and as regards them six guineas as you spoke of?"

"They shall be made into a ten pound note at the end of the transaction, if everything goes properly."

"Well, sir, there's something in that; but do you think a ten pound note, at the end of the transaction, is quite so good as six guineas at the beginning of it?"

"If you are dissatisfied, there's the money."

"Much obliged to you, sir; and now, what is I to do to Mr. Lionel Feversham when he comes?"

"There will be nobody at home when he does come, but you will admit him into the house as quietly as possible; at least, when I say that there will be nobody at home, you are not to make him believe so, but to direct him up to my room, where you are to tell him he will find me. You will take no notice of whatever passes—indeed, if you hear any noise, it is not to alarm you, but you will let him, leave the house as noiselessly as he came, and remember that he is a man of wild,

No. 10.

headstrong passions, and he may do something extremely desperate if you impede him; remember that—you can tell him that I'm rather indisposed and am in bed, and, should he ask any previous questions whatever, assure him that it was I who promulgated the story of his death."

" Yes, sir, I'll do all that; you may depend, sir, upon me."

" Very good ; and if all turns out as I expect, you'll be further rewarded, and make, eventually, a good thing of it."

Instead of leaving the house, as he had announced it to be his intention to do, Mr. Grantley went down stairs and said to Mrs. Russell and to Florence—

" I have quite set my heart upon your seeing the first piece at Drury-lane theatre to-night. I will come to you as soon as I can, which, I think, will be in about an hour after you have been there."

" But cannot we go alone?" said Mrs. Russell.

" Certainly ; I can give you a note which will procure you every attention and a private box. Pray expect me there very shortly, and I shall leave town as I intended to do, at about half-past nine o'clock, when the first piece is over."

This was acceded to, for it was not likely that, under these circumstances, a proposition of such a nature would be objected to, on the part of Mrs. Russell and of Florence.

At about a quarter before seven o'clock Mr. Grantley saw them safely into a coach, and when they were clear of the house he again gave some instructions to Maria to be particularly careful what she should say and do as regards Lionel Feversham when he came, if he should persevere in his intention so to do.

He then retired to his own room, on the mantle-shelf of which he lit an extremely feeble night-light.

About a quarter of an hour passed off very uninterruptedly, and then, as Maria was waiting in a state of great fever and impatience, there came again that hurried startling knock, and the sudden ring at the bell, which had before announced the arrival of Lionel Feversham.

" That's him for a guinea," said Maria; " Lor' what a twitteration I am in, to be sure; there'll be wheels within wheels to-night, as sure as I am a sinner."

She opened the street-door, and there, sure enough, was the object of her ruminations.

" Lor' sir," she exclaimed, " how could you be so impudent? what if missus was at home—as she isn't. Didn't I tell you, when you came again, I'd let you in at the front area."

" I know as well as you who is in the house and who is not," said Lionel, and his voice was indicative of suppressed passion. " I know, I say, as well as you, who is here. Florence and her aunt were handed into a coach by some one a short time since ; I could not see him distinctly, but it was a man, and, I doubt not, my rival."

" Well, sir, I shouldn't wonder; that is strange. Do you know, sir, they've gone to the play. I should like to go myself, for I haven't been I don't know how long, but when I does go, no Drury-lane for me, sir, but give me the Wictoria."

" And where is this Mr. Grantley ?"

" He's in his room, sir, and it's a most remarkable thing—"

" What's a remarkable thing ?"

" Why, sir, you'd hardly believe it, but, about half-an-hour ago, he comes down stairs to me, and ' Maria,' says he. ' Yes, sir,' says I. ' Maria,' says he, ' put this here letter in the postesses, and I did, and who do you think, sir, that there letter was drestified to ?"

" Was what ?"

" Who do you think, sir, the prescription on the back was ?"

" I cannot tell."

" Why then, sir, it was to you. ' Lionel Feversham, Esquire,' was written upon it, and after that it said, ' care of Mr. Plumpy Brown, the Beatle of Saint Clement Danes, at the Westry.' Now, there's a go, sir, for you !"

" It's very strange, a letter addressed from him to me. But it only shows to m that the base tale he fabricated of my decease is known to be a falsehood, and he thinks by my receiving that note, in case I should make my appearance at the church, that I will accept some promise of future satisfaction instead of interfering with the ceremony, and telling Florence what I think. But he little guesses the purpose of my soul. I will have revenge!"

"Well, I would, sir, if I was you."

"It shall be a desperate act—an act at which men may well marvel."

"There's ever such a load of marvels down our area, sir, as the little boys drops; and if so be as you is still bent upon that desperate act you speaks on, there's the kitchen chimney, sir, hasn't been swept yet, and agin you get to the top of there, you would be desperate."

"Where is Mr. Grantley?"

"He's in his room, sir. He don't seem to me to be very well, and he spoke of going to bed."

"And which is his room?"

"The first floor front, sir, is his sitting-room, and the back his bed-room."

"Enough; say nothing, and mind, let you hear what you will, and think what you will, I will have no interference with what I purpose."

He immediately walked up the staircase; and Maria, looking after him, remarked to herself—

"Well, it's a very odd thing, but they've both of them been uncommon anxious to tell me to hear nothing, and do nothing. Let me see: three guineas first of all from Mr. Lionel, then six guineas from Mr. Grantley, and what more I've got to get from him, and leastways another three from Mr. Lionel, perhaps a six. Oh, Thomas, you dear barman of the Pig's Tail and Cowcumber, that'll be a fortun to you and me; we'll go into the blessed greengrocery line as sure as pancakes isn't Flanders bricks, and I thinks I sees us with a cask of small beer always on tap, and that permission of Providence a-waiting on us as sends a thunder-storm in the very heat of the weather to turn it into cyder. Oh, what a wision—what a wision!"

While Maria is indulging herself with these felicitations of the glorious future, Lionel Feversham has made his way to the apartments occupied by Mr. Grantley.

The light that is burning is so dim that he can only just discern objects generally, and when he got into the apartment a creeping, shuddering sort of horror came over him, for his soul was oppressed with guilty ruminations. All was still, and he walked to the doorway which divided the two rooms, and glanced into the bedchamber. There lay his rival, sleeping quietly in his bed, while he, Lionel Feversham, felt his heart tugged, and his brain racked by a thousand demons.

"Speak, speak," he cried, "or your blood be upon your own head!"

All was still, save the regular breathing of the sleeping man, who lay wrapped up in the bed-clothes, with his back towards him.

"Grantley, villain!" he cried; "liar! speak to me, and tell me that, even now, within the small limits of these apartments, I may have that satisfaction I require, for, by the God above us, one or both shall die to-night."

There was no answer, but the regular, quiet breathing continued.

"He mocks me, he mocks me," exclaimed Lionel, and he staggered back into the front room. "I cannot bear it—my brain's on fire. What have we here, glittering on this table before me?—A sword, and drink, my ancient enemy? Welcome both. Brandy, by Heavens! sparkling nectar—life-giving, soul-inspiring draught! For two long years I abjured thee for the sake of my dear Florence, and not one drop of poisonous alcohol passed my lips; but now—welcome again, thrice welcome, thou only true friend to the unfortunate. Thou art no deceiver; thy smiles are as bland, as with a gentle ripple they dance upon the surface, to the veriest wretch as to an emperor; thy aroma as full of fiery beauty to Lazarus as to Dives. Come, let me clutch thee. I will quaff resolution from the cup—resolution to do a deed that, while it damns my soul for ever, shall teach a lesson to the treacherous, traced by the grim hand of Death in steaming blood!"

He drank deeply from a tumbler of the contents of a decanter of brandy.

"Ha! ha!" he laughed, "I feel it flowing through my veins. It warms me into life and energy, it stirs my blunted purpose, quickens my revenge—one blow for life, for love for Florence, and for the punishment of hellish deceit and treachery."

He seized the costly glittering sword and flung the scabbard from it.

"Help, Florence, help," cried a voice from the bed.

Stung to madness, furious with passion, wild with the excitement of the ardent liquor he had swallowed, the name of Florence ringing in his ears, and that, too, in the accents of a man who had made her valueless to him, inasmuch as her faith was broken—he made but one rush into the apartment, and passed the sword up to the hilt through the back of the sleeping figure, pinning it by the bright blade to the bed on which it lay.

"God! oh, God!" groaned a voice.

"'Tis done," cried Lionel, "'tis done!" and he flung up his arms; "the deed is done, and the curse of Cain is upon me; I am a murderer. I will live long enough to meet Florence at the church to-morrow. I will tell her of her infamy, I will tell her of the vows she has broken, and then death! death! death!"

He sprang down the staircase—he passed the screaming Maria, he gained the door, opened it, and rushed like a madman into the street. She heard his wild shrieking laughter as he went, she heard him shouting death! death! and half fainting with terror she leant against the passage wall, bewildered beyond all possibility of explanation.

CHAPTER X.

THE CHURCH.

The morning came, bright and beautiful. A sweet sunshine rested upon all objects, and the gay, inspiriting appearance of the town presented under that aspect a pleasing contrast to the more natural delights of the country.

And it seemed as if upon this occasion Nature chose to assume her happiest aspect, as though nothing should be wanting to the felicity of Florence, who surely could not but feel happy at the idea of wedding one in every way entitled to her respect.

The various circumstances which appear incongruous in our narrative will now be soon explained, and we shall find how evil passion, fostered by maddened impulses, might have produced the most exquisite misery. We shall find how such a lesson was read to the intemperate and the violent as was not likely ever again to be effaced from their memory.

The chamber-door of Mr. Grantley was securely locked on the morning of the marriage, so that if Maria, whose curiosity to know what had therein taken place must have been most powerfully excited, had not the opportunity of being gratified; and as regards Florence and Mr. Russell, they were evidently in ignorance of the dreadful meeting that had taken place between Lionel Feversham and Mr. Grantley, for at the appointed hour they left their home, and proceeded to the church.

This was at ten o'clock; but a full hour before that, as some persons were sweeping out the sacred edifice, there entered it a man, whose appearance was sufficient to strike terror into the heart of any one.

He looked half famished; his eyes had a wild and staring aspect; the matted hair hung in disordered masses about his head, and altogether he presented such a picture of wretchedness and desolation as was most painful to look upon.

This man advanced, staggering, into the church, and leaning against one of the upright columns for support, he said in a feeble tone—

"There is a letter in the hands of a man named Brown—give it to me, give it to me."

It was a woman to whom he spoke, and she was so terrified at his appearance that she could scarcely reply to him—she thought that he must be some madman newly escaped from some place of confinement, and that perhaps half a word he did not like might drive him to absolute desperation. She trembled as she replied to him, saying—

"There is a Mr. Brown, sir; he is the beadle. Perhaps it's him you want?"

"That is the man," said the stranger.

"Then, sir, if you will be so good as to wait for a few minutes he will be here, for there is to be a wedding this morning, and he is sure to come some time before."

"Peace, woman, peace," cried the man in loud and startling accents, "peace, I say; talk not to me of weddings, unless you would make me a worse madman than I am."

The woman shrunk back, and looked upon him from a distance as he paced the church with disordered steps, now and then muttering exclamations of despair, and by every action betraying the greatest possible amount of mental disquietude.

It was a fearful thing to look upon him—fearful in every respect, because he seemed like a man who could not possibly long continue in his present state without committing some desperate act, at which humanity might well shudder.

He spoke aloud, evidently heedless of who heard him, caring nothing for the consequences of what he said, and utterly heedless if he criminated himself or not by the expressions that fell from his lips.

"What could he write to me!" he exclaimed. " I have killed him; but what could he write to me previous to that act? How could he know that his letter, addressed to an official of this church, would find me; and yet the information of that servant-girl was too circumstantial to doubt; it must be true, and this man, who stole from me the affections of her who was the brightest spirit of my happiest dreams, must, with a devilish art, have discovered all my movements. Oh! Florence, Florence, why did you make so little of the faith you pledged that you could not keep it for a brief space longer, but must throw aside, upon the mere pretended rumour of my death, all your boasted faith and constancy?"

Our readers have no doubt, previous to the utterance of these words, recognised in this stranger Lionel Feversham. Where or how he had passed the night, Heaven only knows; but his predominant idea now was evidently to get possession of the letter which Maria had said she had posted to him by order of Mr. Grantley.

Perhaps the thought of the deed he had committed was already beginning to bring with it a terrible retribution. Perhaps, even now, he felt that he would gladly give his own life, provided by that sacrifice he should be enabled to obliterate that one act which had stained his name with murder. But whether that was so or not, he certainly waited with a restless impatience, that would scarcely brook control, the appearance of the man who, he had been told, had the letter for him.

It was half-past nine before the beadle, who was a portly, and, in his own eyes, most important personage, made his appearance; but when he did so, Lionel Feversham, who at once recognised him by his official costume, rushed up to him, crying out,—

"The letter, the letter—give me the letter! Do not tamper with me or hesitate, for I am a desperate man. I must, I tell you, and will have the letter."

The beadle staggered back until he came to a wall, which supported him, and then, as he was rather a slow thinker, he only stared without being able to arrive at any rapid understanding of what was demanded of him.

The principal feeling of his mind consisted of a vague sensation of danger and an impression that there was somebody who did not entertain that marked and powerful respect for a beadle which he considered all the world ought to do.

" The letter, the letter," again cried Lionel; " idiot, give me the letter."

"Did you speak to me, young man?" said the beadle.

Lionel glared at him for a moment in silence, and then he said, slowly and distinctly—

" Fool, you do not know your own danger. My name is Lionel Feversham Speak at once—have you, or have you not, a letter for me?"

" Oh ! well, certainly; I didn't know, but there did come a letter to my house. I'm sure you needn't be in such a passion about it; there's twopence to pay, that's one thing."

" Produce it quickly."

" What! the twopence? I begs to say, sir, that you are to produce that; and as for the letter, why here it is."

The beadle as he spoke slowly produced from a capacious pocket a letter, but before another word could be spoken Lionel rushed upon him, and wrenched it from his hands, and then, with trembling eagerness, he tore it open.

Fives minutes' attention sufficed to read it through, and when he had completed that operation, he uttered one loud cry of despair, which so terrified the beadle, that he rushed out into the Strand, and then Lionel Feversham fell upon the stone pavement of the church in a state of perfect insensibility.

The two women who had been cleaning the sacred edifice, and who had been silent spectators of the short conversation between Lionel and the beadle, now advanced full of curiosity to know what that letter could contain that had produced so remarkable an effect upon him who had received it.

One of them suggested to the other that a doctor ought to be sent for, as the young man might die in the church; but curiosity overcame humanity, and the desire to read the letter, while there was an opportunity of doing so, banished every scruple.

One of them took it from the nerveless grasp of poor Lionel, and read as follows :—

          " Surrey-street, Strand.

" MY DEAR LIONEL,—It becomes necessary now that I should explain to you some circumstances which have induced me to act a strange part towards you, but I hope a part which will eventually tend greatly to your happiness; and if I say anything in this epistle which shall seem in the slightest degree harsh towards you, I pray you to believe it is said by one who has been always willing to act a brother's part towards you.

" When our father died about two years ago, you are well aware that on account of your great irregularities, and the frightful life of dissipation you had led, he left no provision for you whatever in his will, but was satisfied that I would exercise a kind and a sound discretion as regarded you.

" You cannot but recollect that we had a stormy interview, at which you accused me of injustice, and then left me, as you said, to seek your fortune elsewhere.

" But do not suppose that I was unmindful of your movements; on the contrary, I made every inquiry, and learnt that you had gone abroad.

" Then came a long interval, during which nothing was heard of you, and I came to London myself about two months since to institute inquiries as to your fate, for if you, Lionel, could forget the ties of kindred that bound us together, I could not.

" I thought it advisable, in the prosecution of those inquiries, to change my name, and instead of calling myself Feversham, I assumed the name of Grantley.

" Chance directed me to lodge with a Mrs. Russell, whose niece, Florence, in a short time imperceptibly gained so strong a hold upon my affections that, for the first time in my life, I thought of altering my condition, and giving Feversham Hall a mistress.

" It was not until I proclaimed my secret wishes that I was informed of a prior engagement which Florence had entered into, and to my intense surprise your name was mentioned, coupled with information from Mrs. Russell, that you had omitted your faults of temper, and that you had led a life of intemperance, but that you had made a solemn promise of reformation, and had gone abroad to better your fortunes.

" I immediately left the lodging, determining to forward your happiness in every possible way. I renewed my researches, in order to discover whither you had gone, that I might send to you, and tell you that you need not prosecute more adventures abroad for the acquisition of those means, which, if you were really the reformed character you're represented, I would gladly place at your disposal at home.

"During those researches a man was introduced to me named Matthew Horn, who stated that he had sailed in the same ship with you, and that you had fallen a victim to some contagious disease at sea, and your body had been committed to the deep. He described you accurately—he told his story circumstantially and well, and in proof of what he said, he produced one-half of a gold chain, which, he said, you had given to him out of gratitude for his kind attention to you previous to your death.

"I bought the chain of him, and then, feeling that the only obstruction in the way of my prosecuting my suit to Florence was removed, I sought another interview with her, in which I committed the only great error of judgment I can charge myself with, and which consisted in concealing your death.

"At length, however, it came out; and from respect and esteem, rather than from affection, she consented to become mine.

"Preparations were made for our union, and then among a package of letters that was sent to me by my steward in the country came one from you, announcing the fact of your arrival, and that you had repented of your past errors, that you had made a small competence, and came to be happy, and with the object of your warmest affections.

"Lionel, the struggle I went through was a most severe one, but I triumphed; and I made a resolve that means should be taken of fully testing whether you had indeed conquered the irritable disposition you once had, and then I fully intended to place the hand of Florence within your own.

"You wrote to me again, saying that you had discovered the falsehood of Florence, and that a Mr. Grantley was about to make her his wife; and you added that you would do something of a desperate nature to be avenged upon the man who stood between you and your happiness.

"I wrote you an answer, Lionel, in which I asked you to do four things : firstly, to have faith in Florence ; secondly, to show that you had conquered your worst propensity by abstaining from wine and other stimulants ; thirdly, to commit no violence whatever against your supposed rival ; and fourthly, that if you controlled yourself to all this extent, and then met me at the church where Florence was to be married, I would undertake that everything should be arranged to your satisfaction.

"Lionel, you sent me no reply; consequently, I presume, you reject the offer ; and I enclose this letter to Brown, the beadle, in case you should keep the appointment, and not finding me there, feel disappointed of an explanation.

"Thus you see that there is no Mr. Grantley—that you have no rival—that Florence is and has been true to you ; so that, when she comes to the church, you can meet her and wed her yourself, if you think that you deserve her.

"I feel unwell to-night ; and, as the evening is creeping on, when I have sent the servant to post this letter I shall retire to bed.

"Farewell, Lionel, and believe me to be yours over,

"GEORGE FEVERSHAM."

The two women who read this epistle made nothing of it, but to the reader it will be intelligible and explanatory of some important circumstances connected with this singular and eventful story.

By the time the women had finished the perusal of the epistle, Lionel Feversham showed some appearance of recovering from the death-like stupor that had come over him.

Having more the appearance of a ghost than of a living man he rose to his feet, and tottering along until he came to the altar-steps, he sunk down upon the lowest of them, and wringing his hands, while hot scalding tears flowed from his eyes, he gave fevered utterance to the agony of his soul.

"Lost—lost—lost !" he said, " lost here and hereafter ; wretched—wretched

Lionel!—murderer! fratricide! there is no hope—nothing but despair, and I have done all this from my two old faults, drink and precipitancy. I have raised to my lips the stimulating cup of delirium to dash that of pure and holy happiness aside. I would have no patience; I would trust no one; accept no guide but my wild, unruly passions; and what is the result? I am a murderer! I have slaughtered George as he slept. I have taken the life of the only being who was plotting and contriving to give to me the greatest possible amount of happiness—why do I not die here at once, and not be preserved to add one other to the crimes I have already committed, as I most surely shall by self-slaughter?"

He paused a moment, and just then the bells of the church struck up a merry tune; they filled the air with joyous sounds, making the old steeple ring again, and awaking every echo within the sacred pile. It was a bridal peal—but, oh! what a frightful mockery to the wretched—wretched Lionel!

"Strike me dead, just Heaven!" he cried, "strike me dead! Have you no red lightnings to launch at the head of a murderer? I shall go mad—mad—mad!"

He crouched down upon the altar-steps with his head resting upon his hands and bowed down so that nothing of his face was visible.

He looked like some wretched outcast—some one repudiated by Heaven—forgotten by man.

And now the church-doors are opened wide and a crowd of idlers line the aisle. Mrs. Russell advances in that very violet-coloured satin that Maria had spohen of, and on her arm leans Florence, dressed in purest white and looking so beautiful that the spectators blessed her as she passed, and youth and age alike join in wishing that the union of one so fair, and with a look of such heavenly gentleness upon her brow, should be propitious and full of happiness.

They advanced slowly, and Florence whispered to her aunt—

"He is not here!"

"He will be sure to come, my child. Look, Florence, what a strange and miserable-looking man is sitting upon the steps; he shakes as if he were in some strange convulsion!"

"He does indeed. Heaven have mercy upon him!"

At this moment a hurried footstep sounded in the church-porch and a man, so closely enveloped in a travelling cloak that none could see his features, walked up to where Lionel Feversham sat trembling in his despair.

The horror-stricken man saw him not, but when the stranger allowed the cloak to fall at his feet, and then said, in a voice, clear but low, and full of the most exquisite pathos—

"Lionel Feversham, will you not rise and look upon the face of your bride?" Lionel sprung to his feet, and with glaring eyes and such horror upon his countenance as was sufficient to strike terror into the hearts of all who saw him, he confronted the speaker, who was no other than his brother, George Feversham, whom we have known as Mr. Grantley.

"Brother Lionel," cried George, "you have suffered enough; your lesson is over; if it has been a severe one, recollect that it had to correct severe faults."

"Do I hear aright?" cried Lionel. "George—George—do you live? and do you really lift from off my heart this load of guilt? I am a murderer, but not your murderer, George; who was it that I slew?"

"Lionel, you slew no one; those things which were left upon the table in my apartment, namely, a decanter of ardent spirits and a sword, were typical of your character—intemperance and violence—you drunk of the one and you drew the other."

"I did! I did!"

"I saw it all, for I was crouched down by the bedside. I saw you pass your sword through—"

"Through some one who then slept?"

"No, Lionel, no; a bolster certainly reposed in the centre of the bed, and that you pierced with the sword."

"Oh, joy! joy! my hands, then, are stainless of blood?"

"What do I hear?" cried Florence; "what voice is that which brings the memory of the past back to me? Can it be possible that the voice of Lionel, at such a moment as this, rings in my ears."

"It is true," said George Feversham; and, stepping aside, he disclosed to the view of Florence him whom she had supposed numbered with the dead.

"Lionel?—and living!" she exclaimed.

With joy beaming upon his countenance he rushed forward three or four steps but then he paused, and, shrinking back, he said—

"No, no: I am unworthy, brother—she is yours! I—who have given way to such unruly passion! I—who have shown how little I can control my wildest impulses—am unworthy of snch a treasure. Florence, farewell for ever: take to your heart a nobler, better spirit than I can offer you."

"No," said George, "no; I can accept of no divided empire. While you were

L No. 11.

supposed to be no more, Lionel, I would have made myself happy with Florence's esteem : but you live—her love is yours. Your renunciation of her, at such a moment as this, proves to me that the severe lesson has not been thrown away upon you. You are now beneath the roof of God's temple, Lionel—will you again, think you, be intemperate !"

"I dare not promise."

"That is better than if you did. Florence, you have come here to wed with me —with Mr. Grantley ! I grieve to tell you that there is no such person : he is a being of the imagination, and has resolved himself in to thin air."

"And you," said Florence, "you are ——"

"The brother of Lionel, who is now here—I hope redeemed from all his errors, and likely to make you a happy husband. Much that is now obscure to you in these affairs will be explained as we proceed ; but if, Florence, you still retain the same attachment to poor Lionel Feversham, which made you, while you thought him living, refuse the hand of the rich Mr. Grantley, give him your hand at once, and let the ceremony of this morning unite you, never more to part."

Bewildered by surprise, and completely overcome by a rush of joyous feelings, Florence gave her hand to Lionel ; and George turned aside for a moment to hide a sudden gush of emotion, which else would have been but too visible.

Florence then turned to him, and seemed about to speak, but he said—

"Not now, not now, dear Florence ; we shall have ample time for explanations when you and Lionel come to Feversham Hall, and then they shall be complete."

"And you have parted with the broken chain, Lionel," said Florence.

"It was stolen by a man named Matthew Horn, who deserted from our ship after committing numerous robberies. But how was the deed I supposed I had committed at Mrs. Russell's kept secret ?"

"Simply because when you had left I locked the door and came down stairs and quieted the fears of Maria," replied George Feversham, " and then I proceeded to Drury-lane Theatre—met Florence and her aunt there as if nothing had happened, and slept last night at an hotel in the neighbourhood."

"Gentlemen," said the beadle advancing, "gentlemen and ladies, I mean ladies and gentlemen. The Reverend Mr. Snuffles says as he can't wait no longer, so if any body is going to be married let them come at once."

"There Lionel there," said George Feversham, "I expected it would come to this, and provided you with a special license."

At this moment a female rushed into the church and laid violent hands on Mrs. Russell, exclaiming—

"Oh ! marm, marm, the kitchen flue is gone at last ; the street is full of engines, marm, you see marm, the fat would boil over, and up it went with a phiz, so we sent for the plug and he pulled up the turncock."

"Young woman, young woman," said the beadle, " do you remember where you is ; don't you see there is a awful ceremony going on. Just hold your blessed tongue will you, we knows nothing about flues here ; I say, where does you live."

"No 7, in Surry-street."

"Good, there will be a jollification, I suppose. I'll just pop down the area in the evening, and you can tell the old lady now, that if so be she stands two bob and a tanner, there won't be no marrow-bones and cleavers out of Clare market, but if she don't, my eye wont there."

"You are a wretch, I never allow beetles or policemen to speak to me."

This short conversation lasted seven minutes and a half, and that was likewise the exact duration of the ceremony which made Florence Mrs. Lionel Feversham, a change which she never had occasion to regret, for the lesson which had been taught to Lionel by his brother George, was indeed too severe a one to be forgotten. And in that moment forthwith he became, not only the most temperate, but the most considerate and carefully patient of men.

CHAPTER XI.

MARTHA'S REMONSTRANCE AND THE GREAT CHANGE OF OPINION.

THIS adventure, which I have just related to my readers at such careful length, occupied my time for about three weeks, and although there were periods during its continuance in which I experienced acute mental suffering, because I knew not how the various circumstances would end, the gratification which I eventually experienced in a conviction of the happiness of Florence, amply repaid me for all that I endured.

And although I have not troubled my readers with a detail of all the troublesome means which I was forced to employ, in order to arrive at the knowledge I did obtain of the affair, those means were such as to keep me almost constantly from home to the intense dissatisfaction of Martha, my housekeeper.

Indeed, I think she was never so displeased with me before, and had I not been a little explanatory upon the subject, and awakened her sympathy, I verily believe she would have left me.

But when she came to hear what Florence had suffered, and how noble and high-minded George Feversham had achieved every body's happiness but his own, she no longer blamed me for being deeply interested in such a circumstance, but on the contrary, expressed an ardent desire to see some of the parties connected with this strange eventful episode of human existence, that I recorded to her.

"Ah!" she said, "now if all your night adventures were like that, and you came home at once and told me all about them, I should not say so much upon the subject."

"We cannot expect," said I, "that every collection of strange events should end as happily as this one, which I have related to you. It but too often happens that abundant misery arises from the collision of human passions, for how rare is it that we find such a being as George Feversham—a man, who had it in his power, as he unquestionably had, to unite himself to Florence, despite his knowledge of the certain existence of his headstrong brother."

"Well, that's true enough," said Martha, "but mind if you find out anything miserable in your night adventures, you can keep that to yourself, for I don't want to hear it, as it sets me dreaming at night of all sorts of disagreeables when I ought to be enjoying my repose, and making myself as comfortable as I can."

"Well, Martha, you may depend that you would sleep none the worse for knowing a great number of these affairs. If anything more than another be injurious to the mind, the morals, and the repose, it certainly is to concentrate to much of our attention upon ourselves individually."

"Well, I don't understand that; it seems to me that if we don't attend to ourselves, most certainly no one will attend to us."

"You misunderstand me, Martha, what I mean to express is, that an acquaintance with the habits, the feelings, and the adventures of other persons, prevents us from giving an undue importance to our own, for we shall find that in many cases, what we thought affairs of great magnitude, sink into insignificance, when compared with other matters in which other people are deeply concerned."

"Well, now I do think I understand you, sir, and after all I may become reconciled to your night adventures; but for all that I can't consent to your calling your tea your breakfast, when it is no such thing. I say it is no such thing, it's your tea, and if you were to go on calling it your breakfast till you were quite black in the face, it would still be your tea."

"Well, Martha, don't get in a passion about it, you can call it my tea, and I will call it my breakfast. Pray be a little tolerant."

"I won't be any such thing. I attend the parish church regular, and I won't be tolerant; I don't see why I should, except when people are right, then I don't mind being tolerant."

" That is to say, Martha, like all the rest of the world, you are tolerant when an opinion jumps with your own."

"Well, of course I am, I never said I was not."

"That's candid at all events."

"And that I always was too, you know that. I think what I say and say what I think; and if your were to go on argufying for hours, you would never convince me that your tea was your breakfast and your breakfast your tea."

" Very good; but at all events it is something to have your free consent to my night adventures."

" Well, I dont't mean to say they are all quite so bad as they might be, and you may go on with them a little while longer, but always provided, you tell me about them when you come home."

"It's a bargain, Martha. You shall know all; and this night I hope to meet with some adventure which, in it's result, would be as gratifying to you as [that which I have related as terminating so happily in the marriage of Florence."

" Take of yourself then, and go at once; it's a shocking thing to be so given to curiosity as you are; if that was a woman now that meddled in other people's affairs as you do, all the world would be in an outcry, and they would say, ' Oh, of course, that's woman like, fond of gossiping and meddling,' but now, I suppose, because you are one of the he sex, it's quite another thing."

Feeling probably that there was some truth in what Martha said, as well as being anxious to get out into the streets to see what adventure might befall me, I made no reply but left at once, and Martha became misstress of the field.

The night was one of those dubious ones on which the weather is in that changeful mood, like a spoiled child, when it knows not when to laugh or cry.

Now and then a twinkling star would peep out from a cloudy sky, but scarcely for a few moments would it have time to show its radiant face, when careering clouds would come across it, and all again would be in darkness.

It mattered however, little to me what was the aspect of the weather; that was a matter which I always held in tolerable indifference, and as I have had once before occasion to remark, I could extract some instruction and some pleasure from hail, rain, wind, or sunshine.

Without, then, much more than a passing glance upwards to the changing sky, I pursued my way towards the outskirts of the metropolis.

By walking rapidly, I soon got clear of the regular lines of houses and found myself in the pleasant enough district of Holloway, among a number of detached residences, with their trimmed gardens in front of them, and presenting, many of them, aspects of great beauty and cheerfulness.

I passed on for about half a mile, until I was pursuing my solitary way along a garden wall, I was suddenly attracted by hearing a loud crash as of broken glass, then a scream sounded in my ears, and a garden gate was opened, from which rushed, with frantic haste, a young, and as far as I could trace by the hasty glance I got of her, beautiful female.

She did not seem to have observed me, but rushed past me several yards distant and then she glanced eagerly around her, as if looking for some one, and cried with frantic eagerness—

"Help! help! oh, help! Will no one part them? they are incensed, and there will be bloodshed."

" What is it?" I cried; and, at the sound of my voice, she turned and rushed towards me, seizing my arm with eagerness, as she cried—

"Help! oh, help! if you have any of the seeds of holy compassion in your heart, let them now burst forth. Follow me at once. I pray you to follow me."

Without a moment's reflection, I said to her, "lead on and I will follow you."

Then she rushed through the garden gate again, and I, keeping her in view as well as I could for she went with amazing swiftness, ran after her towards a large and handsome looking house.

As I neared the structure I heard voices in contention, and now and then a clashing sound as if parties were fighting with swords—a thing so very unusual in this country that it filled me with curiosity and astonishment.

The young lady who had summoned me paused only a few moments on the steps, as if she made sure that I was following her, and then crying—

"This way, this way—quick, quick;" she darted into the house, the hall of which was brilliantly lighted by a lamp which hung from its centre.

She dashed open a door upon the ground-floor, and then a most singular scene presented itself to me.

An elderly man, most elegantly attired in evening costume, was half supported by a chair, and holding a drawn sword in his hand.

Opposite to him, at some few paces distant, was a much younger person, and his appearance too was of the same character. He was gesticulating furiously as I entered the room, and I could perceive that upon his white waistcoat there were several drops of blood.

"Will nothing satisfy you but my death," he cried; "was it not only necessary that you should deprive me of the affections of her whose heart I had won, but you must likewise endeavour to make a beggar of me by depriving me of my just inheritance, and you already so bloated with wealth that you know not what to do with your accumulated hoards. You are a villain, but I will yet have a revenge that you will feel keenly."

"Part them, part them," cried the girl. Oh! father, father, you promised me that this should not be."

"I did, my darling," said the old man, "but I stand extenuated in consequence of the circumstances."

"You think so," said the young man. "I admit that you are a better swordsman than myself." He picked up the sword that lay at his feet as he spoke, and of which I conjectured he had been disarmed by his aged antagonist. "I own that you are a better swordsman than myself, and consequently I think I am entitled to take what advantage I can."

"There was something in his eye which made me suspect he meditated an act of treachery, and the result proved that I was correct. He suddenly darted forward with the sword pointed full at the heart of the old man, and he would eventually have run him through had I not stepped forward, and, turning the blade slightly aside, received it under my own arm, which was only slightly scratched, although, such was the vehemence with which the thrust was given, that the hilt of the weapon struck forcibly against my breast. I was at the moment greatly incensed at such a piece of heartless treachery; and as I had no weapon at hand, except pistols, which I did not like to use on the angry impulse of the moment as the assailant was just within striking distance of me, I gave him a blow in the face with my clenched fist which made him reel again.

"Assassin," I cried, "what may be your cause of quarrel I know not, but the act you attempted was assassination, and stamped you as a villain."

He tried to draw the sword back again, with fury flashing from his eyes; and no doubt, if he could have done so, he would have taken my life, but I turned sharply, and the sword blade, being closely confined between my arm and my chest, broke short off, leaving nothing but the hilt in his hand.

He shrunk back, and then, addressing the girl, he said—

"You see, Linda, you see, it is my life that is aimed at."

"Gilbert," she said, "we now part for ever. In a cowardly and a dastardly manner you have raised your hand against my father's life, and, but for this stranger, you would have made me an orphan. I have myself witnessed the deed, therefore it cannot be extenuated or explained away. I cast you from me for ever."

The young man's countenance assumed a livid expression, and he said—

"I will be revenged of you all. You do not know what is in my power. Look your last upon the magnificence with which you are surrounded, you will see but little more of it; and woe be to all of you for crossing me thus."

"Do you mean to let him depart in this way," said I, "after such an attempt upon your life?"

"Yes, yes," said the old man, "let him go. He bears a name which is his safe-guard."

"Gilbert Lincoln, let me never look upon your face again, and speaking now as patiently as I can with the full recollection that you have attempted to take my life, I advise you to retire to some distant country, and when I hear that you have done so, you shall receive from me sufficient to support existence, but not to support extravagance or dissipation. Go at once, go at once, and thank heaven that you have fallen into merciful hands to-night."

"I scorn your offer and laugh at your advice," said the young man; "I go, but it is to take measures that will soon open your eyes to the extent of my power. Beware, I say, and look your last, and make your most of what you now have."

So saying he turned abruptly, and dashed out of the room.

The young girl, whom he had called Linda, sunk upon a sofa and burst into tears, while the aged man, who still held the sword, looked at me for some moments in silence.

"Sir," he said, "I know not who you are or how you came here so providentially, but you have saved my life, and I am bound in gratitude to express to you my deepest acknowledgements."

"I am happy, sir," said I, "to have been useful. How I came here is easily explained. I was passing your garden-gate, when this lady implored my aid to prevent bloodshed within. Immediately I followed her, and I rejoice that I was in time to interpose with some effect."

The girl rose from the sofa, and, approaching me, she clasped my hands in hers,—

"Sir," she said, "I owe you more than life itself; for, I owe you the life of my dear father, which would this night have been sacrificed to the insane rage of Gilbert Lincoln, but for your presence."

"Say no more," I said. "As it turned out it was a very simple thing to do, and quite undeserving the thanks you bestow upon it; besides you must know I have a fondness for adventure, and if you really wish to confer upon me any favour in return for that service, which I am so glad it has been my good fortune to be able to render to you, I can point you out a way at once."

"You have but to name it," said Linda.

"Certainly," said the father. "All we have is at your disposal."

"I want nothing," I said, "but your confidence; if you will bestow that upon me, I shall be satisfied; but, at the same time, believe me, I shall consider you abundantly justified in witholding it, because no service whatever can bestow upon me the like of making such a demand."

"It is but a poor thing to ask," said the old man, "when you have saved my life; what were the circumstances which led to its being threatened you shall know all, sir; and it is as well that you should, in other respects, because you have heard some violent threats used; and if any act of criminality does arise from them, your assistance may be required."

"Oh, father," said Linda, "do not let us live in dread of anything. Let the past be as soon as possible forgotten; and when calmer judgment comes to Gilbert, as it must come, the folly of attempting anything against you will be sufficient to deter him, if the criminality of it has not that effect."

"I will hope so, Linda—I will hope so; and now, sit sir, down with us, and take some refreshment. We have had a few friends here, who have just left us, and we were about to retire to rest."

"Do not let me then," said I, "break in upon that intention. I will pay you some other visit, at which you can give me the confidence you promised me."

"No, let it be at once," he said, "let it beat once. I am too much disturbed now by what has happened, to seek immediate repose. I must sit up until my mind is calmer, but we will not detain you my Linda."

"Nay, father, let me stay," said Linda; "believe me that this dreadful circumstance has had to the full as great an effect in banishing sleep from my eyes as from your own. I shall be full of apprehensions, if I retire to my own apartment."

"Remain with us then, darling, and see about some refreshment for this gentleman."

"I want nothing," said I. "I only had my breakfast an hour ago."

"Your breakfast!" said the old man, "why 'tis a little after midnight."

"Yes, I call it my breakfast, more from the proper derivation of the word, than from the time of day or night at which I take the meal. I break my fast, and the meal at which I do so, I call breakfast."

"Oh, you are quite right, sir. Ring the bell, Linda, I believe we have some servants at home, although some of our guests being ladies, residing in this immediate neighbourhood, and alone, we have sent two of our domestics to see them to their doors." After ringing twice a female servant made her appearance.

"Why, how is this?" said the old gentleman. "You used not to be so inattentive.

"Oh dear no, sir, I would not be inattentive for all the world, but as I heard a disturbance was going on, I thought there was some danger, and hearing young misses cry help, I shut myself up in the butler's pantry."

"By way of rendering us assistance, I suppose," said Mr. Lincoln, for that was his name. "Why, we might have had all our throats cut while you were in the pantry."

"Yes, sir, that you might."

"Well, you take it cool, certainly ; but go into the next apartment, and bring in some of the wine you'll find there."

"Certainly, sir."

The girl left, and presently returned with some wine, biscuits, and some dried fruits, which she placed upon the table before us, and of which, certainly, I partook with some degree of relish, notwithstanding I had had my breakfast, or my tea, which ever people may please to call it.

Old Mr. Lincoln drank some wine likewise, and Linda was prevailed upon to take a glass. Then as I was acquainted with their name, I tendered my own card, and in a little while, we all seemed to know each other as well as though we had been acquainted for twenty years, which, by-the-by would have been rather difficult, considering that Linda could not be above seventeen, at the outside.

She was a most beautiful and interesting looking girl, and now that her alarm had somewhat subsided, and her natural colour was in a measure restored to her, I was much charmed with her appearance.

The old man too, was one in every way calculated to command respect. There was a kind of rough, honest bluntness about him, which, combined with the fact, that he knew how to use a sword, induced me to think that he had been in the army, nor was I wrong in that conjecture, as will be presently seen.

Both father and daughter won upon me much, and the more I saw of them the more I liked them ; but this, under the circumstances, was rather natural, when we come to consider that my last interview with both had been under circumstances of danger and excitement, during which people certainly cannot be expected to show themselves to advantage.

And so it was, that as the young girl improved in beauty, the old gentleman assumed an appearance of frankness and hilarity such as was quite pleasant to look upo.

He insisted upon me taking a second glass, and then he said—

"Sir, you must know that that young scapegrace, who, in his vindictive passion, would certainly have taken my life had you not interfered, is my nephew. He is my younger brother's son, and, of course, is the same name as myself. Why it is that you found him thus arrayed in hostility against me I will shortly detail to you :—

"I have been with my regiment abroad, of which I had the honour to be colonel for a number of years ; in fact, almost from the birth of my little girl here, Linda, who is at once to me such a plague and such a consolation.

" I arrived home home with rather shattered health and not very improved fortunes, for, to tell the truth, I never was of the most saving disposition, and some how or another had a wonderful facility in getting through with great ease, whatever might be the amount of my incomings.

" I found, however, upon my arrival in England, and that you will bear in mind was not very long ago, that my brother, who had pursued a mercantile career, had made a far better thing of it than I in the army ; for he was, in fact, a man of fortune, and with all the luxuries of life about him.

" Like myself he had an only child, and was a widower, but his was a son, and the same young man whom you saw aim at my life to-night with such a desperate purpose of carrying his intentions into effect.

" He received me—that is to say. my brother—with open arms, and the first act of his munificent kindness was to present to me this house, which was his own property, with all its contents.

" We became great companions, and Gilbert, whom you have seen to-night, visited us continually, and, of course, was always welcome.

" I was not long, however, in discovering that his visits were far more destined for Linda than to myself, and when I found this out, it became to me, as a matter of fatherly prudence, to inquire into the life, character, and general habits of Master Gilbert.

" Alas ! I soon found that he enjoyed, if I may use the term, a most unenviable reputation. I found that he was a man full of vice, and, what was worse, that they were somehow or another not the vices of a gentleman—trickery, crafty, profligate, deceitful, bah ! I didn't like the fellow a bit, so, the next time he came, I said—

" ' Gilbert, my boy, the air of this place don't agree with you ; it's too clear and transparent, and I would advise you the next time you pass this house to take as attentive a study as you please of the outside of the door.' You see I was very mild and temperate with him. ' For damn your blood,' said I, ' if ever you see the inside again.' "

" Mild and temperate, papa ?" said Linda.

" Yes, my dear, some men would have got into a passion—some men would have fumed and pelted, and got the roof of the place off, but there was no occasion for that. My gentleman saw I had found him out ; he tried to bluster a little, and asked me for my meaning, but he did go.

" The next day his father came to me. It appears that he had heard of Master Gilbert's disgrace ; he wanted to know the reason, and I told him.

" ' Brother,' he said, ' are these youthful follies, are they mere extravagancies of hot blood, generated by idleness, or are they pieces of treachery and villany ?'

" ' That was a sad question for the old man to ask ; it was not one for me to answer.

" ' Brother Gilbert,' said I, ' do not put me, I pray you, upon this painful inquiry. Do it yourself, and draw your own conclusions. I have done all that it was requisite for me to do. My little girl here, Linda, is dearer to me than all the world. I live but for her ; she is my life, my every thing, aint you, Linda ?' "

Linda's eyes were full of tears, and she nodded her head, which did quite as well, perhaps better, than as if she had uttered the most eloquent affirmative that ever come from human lips.

" Well, that was all that passed at that time, and my brother went away. I did not see him for a week, and except that Master Gilbert waylaid Linda once out of doors, we saw nothing of him.

Well, one evening my brother came to me ; I saw that dejection was upon his visage. He sat down, and after a few casual remarks, he said,—

" You're right, my son Gilbert is a villain. Oh ! what I have heard within the last week is enough to break my heart. Never—oh, never mention his name to me again."

" Yes, but I will, though," said I, " we must do something with him—we must

try and reform him; nobody's so bad but they may be made a little better or a
little worse by the circumstances in which they are placed."

"If anything is to be done with him," said he, "you must do it, and not I;
it is out of my power; I cannot, I dare not, and I do not think that I shall ever
set eyes upon him again.

"Well, he died that night."

"Your brother?"

"Yes; he went to bed, complained of a slight indisposition, and was ound
dead and cold in the morning. But scarcely had his lifeless remains been placed
in order for interment and the news became general, than I received an insulting
letter from my nephew Gilbert forbidding me his house and claiming back from
me this place which we inhabit, unless I could produce a regular deed of gift, and
likewise rent from the time we had lived in it, charging it as a furnished mansion
at a most extravagant rate."

No. 12.

" That, indeed, was infamous."

" It was rather ; and then on the day of the funeral of my brother we met.

" ' Gilbert, my boy,' said I, ' now for to-day you know you're a damned scoundrel ; but we'll sink our quarrels.'   You see I was quite calm but resolute. ' You blasted villain,' said I, ' don't you say anything to me and I won't say anything to you ;' and so it was proved how fair words turned away wrath, for he said nothing till the funeral was over and we all got back to the house."

" Ah, I recollect the undertaker, as if I saw him at this moment—a little roly-poly man, with black silk stockings and silk breeches.   Well, what must he do but pour out about twenty glasses of wine and put them all on to one tray for the purpose of handing them round to the funeral guests ; when, just as he'd got it all in his hands and was very ticklishly tottering along, Gilbert Lincoln gives the table such a bang with his fist that the old undertaker dropped the tray, and then, in the most comical way in the world, he turned round and sat down among the glasses, and then, when everybody was looking at him, what do you think that damn'd rascal Gilbert said !

" ' Uncle, old boy,' he said, ' the air of this place don't agree with you ; it's too clear and transparent,' said he, ' and the next time you pass this house you may make as long a study as you like of the outside, but dam'me if you ever see the inside of it again.'

" Then just as I was about to say something, old Kinder, my brother's lawyer, stepped forward, and he said,—

" ' Master Gilbert, master Gilbert, is this the sort of language you use to your poor old uncle?'

" ' Damn you,' said he, ' Mr. Kinder.'

" ' Hush, sir, hush,' said Kinder, ' will you be quiet; let me beg of you, Mr. Gilbert, to retract what you have said, and likewise I assure you, that although no deed of gift was prepared about the house at Holloway, that your father, who is now in his grave, did give it to your uncle.   It is true that he did not convey it to him in a regular manner ; it is true that the title deed to that property has been found among your father's papers ; all that cannot be denied ; but he did give it him.'

" ' I tell you what, Mr. Kinder,' said Gilbert, ' and all of you, I'll not only have it back, but I hope to have the satisfaction of seeing this old boy here, who thinks himself so clever, in prison.'

" ' Now, really,' said Mr. Kinder, ' really, this is a sort of thing that's wrong.'

" ' You get out of the house,' said Gilbert, ' will you; I want no lawyers here.'

" ' Well, after that—after that,' said the old man; ' but first of all it's my duty to read your father's will.'

" ' What ! my father's what ?'

" ' No, Mr. Gilbert, it's not his what, but his will.'

" ' He left no will.   It's the first I've heard of it.'

" Ah !" said the old lawer, " but it aint the last.   Do you think now, that I could be your father's professional adviser, and his intimate friend beside, for this forty years, and he die without a will.   Its very seldom I use strong language, but Mr. Gilbert Lincoln, you're a humbug—that's not actionable, and therefore I repeat it—you're a humbug, sir."

You may guess how pleased I was, so I said " he was a damned humbug," but no one else said a word, and then old Mr. Kinder began to read the will, which contained the following words.

" I, Gilbert Lincoln, of Godsdon House, Surrey, hereby give and bequeath of my own free will, and without condition, the whole of my property, real and personal, whereever and whatsoever, to my brother, George Lincoln, of Mordon House, Holloway, and should he in his judgment, think proper to bestow upon my son, Gilbert Lincoln, either in a whole sum by way of annuity or gratuity from time to time, I hereby state that such a plan meets with my cordial concurrence, and that

I trust he will do so to the extent that my son Gilbert may be deserving, and repent him of his evil ways, but no further."

"Repent and be d——d!" shouted Gilbert, furiously. " I don't believe it is my father's will—its a forgery."

Well then at that moment, you wouldn't credit it, but everybody turned round and looking at Gilbert they said—

" Well, you are a damned humbug."

" What do you mean to give him, sir," said one to me.

" Nothing, said I."

" Then he's an infernal humbug," said that man, " such a humbug as I never saw in my life. I wish you joy, sir, and I consider that you act with all the liberrality you ought.*

" Well now Gilbert," I said, " my boy, the air of this place does not agree with you, it's too clear and transparent; and the next time you pass this house—"

" A thousand curses on you all." said he. " D—n you every one of you—you may all die and go to h—ll," and then away he went.

" Well then everybody began congratulating me, but I got rid of them all as soon as I could, and when old Mr. Kinder and I were alone, I said, Mr. Lawyer, I said, what's to be done ; I know well enough, my brother wants me to take this young fellow in hand—of course he means this as a lesson to him, and how am I to set about convincing him that he ought to have his property back again, and making him the sort of man to deserve it."

" My dear sir," said the lawer, " 1 shall begin to think you're a humbug, too, if you talk in that way. I do not meant to say but that it would be a great thing, and a noble thing of you, to give Gilbert back his property, provided always such a miracle occurred as his being deserving of it, but all you're called upon to do is to support him, sir, like a gentleman ; but he must be humiliated, he must be let see for once in his life, that his conduct cannot be pursued with impunity. You have no idea, sir, of the life that young man has led—he's a heartless young man, sir."

" Well," I said, " l've not the highest opinion of him, I will write him a letter though, and tell him what I think, letting him know that all his future prospects depend upon himself, and as regards money matters, Mr. Kinder, he shall be compelled to call at your office every day for a guinea."

" A guinea, it's too much, sir; it's too much."

" Oh, no, oh, no. Let him have no cause of complaint, he has been brought up with the habits of a gentleman, and a guinea each day will enable him to continue in those habits. Now, Mr. Kinder, I shall not touch my brother's property, although of course, I shall keep what he gave me."

This did not please the lawyer at all, he wanted me, at least, to take half completely, for said he—and that was true enough. " If your brother had not left the sort of will he has, he would have left you a handsome legacy, which, of course, you would have accepted without scruple."

" Very likely," I said, " but as things have turned out, its different. I'll leave every thing in your hands, Mr. Kinder, I shall not live here at Godsdon House, but I shall go back to my own place at Holloway, and there I will remain."

" Well, sir, of course you can do so at your please ; but be sure when you write to Gilbert, that you write a strong letter, so as to let him know thoroughly your intention. And pray, sir, if he should not reform at all, but on the contrary, his bad and wicked nature should triumph over his love of money, what will you do then with your brother's property."

" I really don't know," I said ; " I must be guided by circumstances, and in the meantime, if there are any private papers of consequence, pack them in a tin box and send them to my house at Holloway, and as for the will, I suppose, no steps need be taken in it immediately."

" Not certainly to-day nor to-morrow ; but you must administer within a certain time."

" Very well then, let the matter rest for the present; when I must take any step in it I will."

Agreeably to my directions, the private papers and the will were packed in a box the removal of which I superintended myself, and got packed in my bed-room

" Well, sir, after that I made the most disagreeable discovery of all, and that was that my little girl here had really thought more of the scoundrel than he deserved."

" But why, papa," said Linda, " and why was that? Was it not when I thought he was my worthy and exemplary cousin? but why I knew him as he really was, believe me he held no place in my affections; do not think so meanly of your Linda as to suppose that she could love such a man."

" I don't suppose it now, my dear, I merely say it was a pain to me to make the discovery at the time I did make it. But that soon passed away after I had had a little conversation with you about it; and then we understood each other perfectly, although it seems the young scamp reckoned strongly upon the supposed predilection which Linda had for him."

" And did he take any measures presuming upon that predilection ?"

" He did, and was a source of annoyance; but Linda could well be trused to take her own part in such persecutions, so I resolved not to interfere until the very last extremity."

" And did he go for his guinea a day, sir ?"

" Yes, but made a most infernal disturbance at poor Mr. Kinder's chambers."

" And what did you do, sir ?"

" Mortified him by reducing it to seventeen and sixpence; it was the only way to do with such a blackguard, and I gave him an intimation likewise that for the future, unless he behaved himself, a shilling a day would be taken off regularly."

" Why the next week he flung the seventeen and sixpence at poor Mr. Kinder's head, whereupon he very prudently picked up a shilling of it, and said to Master Gilbert,—

" Now, sir, your sixteen and sixpence lies on the floor; if you cannot stoop to pick it up you may go without it."

" And did he ?"

" Did he? yes, to be sure; and then I lost sight of him for a time, until this very night, when my little girl here had a few friends, young ladies, who go to practise music and dancing at a seminary in the vicinity, to see her, and I, being quite delighted with the society of young girls, as I always am, did my best to please them, and invited an old friend or two to assist in that purpose."

" Now we have so little ceremony here, and we conduct everything in such a quiet, free, and easy sort of way that we have no master of the ceremonies and nobody to announce that anybody or their carriage either stops the way; and that unrestrained manner in which we receive our guests accounts, I think, for the accident that occurred to-night."

" Indeed, sir, how could it do that ?"

" Why, simply this; Gilbert Lincoln got into the house, dressed as for an evening party, and my servants admitted him without a word of question or explanation."

" That was a rare piece of impertinence, indeed."

" It was, but I can account for his appearence here in no other way; for, in order to amuse the young people, I popped up into my bed-room for a microscope I have, and I went in the dark, because, being well accustomed to the place, I knew that I could lay my hands upon anything in the place in a moment. But I had not been in my apartment many moments before, from something I heard, I felt convinced that I was not alone in it, and that conviction by no means pleased me.

"I made up my mind what to do in a moment; I had the young people then you see, and did not want to make any disturbance, so I took no notice, but walking quietly out of the room I locked it up and went down stairs, saying nothing about it to anybody.

" In about an hour after that my guests retired; and then, without saying anything to Linda, I popped up stairs, taking with me a sword which I kept in my study in one hand, and a light in another.

"I forgot, however, that there were arms in my bed-room, but I found them at the moment I opened the door, for a thrust was made at me that had very nigh proved fatal, for I had enough to do to defend myself from it.

"A sort of running fight then continued down the staircase. I retreating, and my opponent, whom I soon saw was Gilbert Lincoln, pursuing and poking at me all the way, having the advantage, which was no trifling one, of standing so much higher than I did.

"But he had an old soldier to deal with, and I was not going to fight at disadvantage when I could get on to better ground, so I said nothing, but let him thrust away, and contented myself by parrying his assaults until we reached the part - ment into which he pursued me, presuming, I fancy that he was getting all the best of it, and that the old boy was nearly done up.

"Then I had him, for I disarmed him in a trice, letting him see a trick of fence such as probably he had never witnessed.

"Then I gave him a slight flesh wound, as a sort of reminder that he might by possibility get a worse one.

"And how terrified was I father," said Linda.

"Yes, you were poor Linda; she set about screaming and kicking up no end of disturbance, and where she went I could'nt tell, for she ran out of the room."

"Oh, papa, that was when I laid hold of this gentleman and dragged him in, and you know he was of service to you."

"He was, most certainly he was, for if he had not been here, that treacherous scoundrel Gilbert, contrary to all rules made and provided in such a case, would certainly have taken my life after I had fairly beaten him, and when I was authorised under such circumstances to be off my guard."

"Yes, he certainly had the move of treacherous intentions. But what, now, sir, candidly speaking, do you suppose was his intention in coming to your house to-night."

"Well, I really can't take upon myself to say, unless he thought he'd catch my little girl here, Linda, and frighten her.'"

"Do you think it likely, sir, that could have been his intention.''

"Why; what else could it have been?"

"I don't like to state disagreeable surmises, but you know it just possible he might be fully aware, by some means unknown to you, that his father's papers were in your room, and that among them was the will: a will not yet done anything with, but merely an instrument, as it were, *in terrorem*, which, if destroyed, is powerless."

There was, indeed, silence for a few moments, and then the Colonel exclaimed,—

"By heaven! you've hit it, and he's done me at last. Give me a light. You stay, Linda, and keep this gentleman company, while I go and have an examination."

He jumped up, and seizing a candle from the table, rushed from the apartment, leaving me *tête-a-tête* with the beautiful girl, whose ingenuous disposition, sweet looks, and gentle innocent remarks, were enough to make her beloved by any one capable of appreciating real beauty.

But the supposition that I had myself started concerning the possible abstract of the will, and other important papers by Gilbert Lincoln, gave me so much uneasiness, that I could only wait with a feeling of intense impatience for the return of the Colonel.

He was about ten minutes, and when he returned, he put down the candle with a bang upon the table, and clapped his hands together with a noise as loud as a pistol shot.

"Well, sir," I said. "Well, sir."

"All's right," he said, "he's got it. I thought he had. Now he's all right. Upon my word it's too bad. The fact is, I'm a damned old fool; and that's quite evident, and I shall think myself offended if anybody disputes the proposition. I'm an old ass, that's settled. Nothing can be a clearer fact. It would be absolute folly to dispute it. I say it, and, therefore, I believe it."

" Well, but Colonel, I cannot say that to me it follows, as a thing of course, that because you have not shown all the caution you might have shown, you are to be so cruelly stigmatized.   This is a most lamentable affair."

" Oh ! not all.   Never mind, let the fellow go to the devil his own way. I really do not care one straw about it.   He will now, of course, be able to claim the property, and all I have to say about the affair is, that he may do so just as soon as he likes for me ; and, perhaps, after all, he has spared me a great amount of trouble."

" Well, sir," I said, " you take it extremely easy, much more so, I can assure, than I could, under the circumstances ; but, in what position do you suppose you stand, with regard to this house ?"

" Why, I suppose he will take it from me as soon as he can, that's the position, I presume, I stand in.   If I know anything of Gilbert Lincoln, he will not be a long time in accomplishing that object, unless Mr. Kinder has settled that part of the business by some legal movement of his own."

" But, father," said Linda, " we were very happy and comfortable, although by no means very rich before all these circumstances took place, and, therefore, I shall rejoice for one, if the possession by Gilbert, of his father's will, and his father's property, frees you from the possibility of the recurrence of such a scene as that which has taken place to-night."

" It certainly, my dear, is not worth the risk, and, it would, I admit, be rather a hard case for me to come by my death about some money matters here, after escaping with my life through so many engagements as I have been connected with. I am not so foolish as to say that I set no value upon my existence, for I do. You know, Linda, that you have made it valuable to me, so let Mr. Gilbert, in the name of heaven, have his money, and leave us in peace."

" Well," I remarked, " I do hope, most sincerely, that Mr. Kinder, the attorney, has, at all events, taken pains to secure to you the undisputed possession of this house ; for, although to deprive you of it would be certainly a heartless piece of villainy on the part of Gilbert, it seems to be unfortunately just the sort of thing he is capable of doing."

" That he is, most truly ; but—come, sir, take another glass, and as I could not think of turning you out of the house at this hour of the night, or rather of the morning, we must try to find a bed for you, and you will breakfast with us, when we can talk over this affair again."

" But, sir," said I, " you spoke of the papers which had been brought away from your bed-room, as having been contained in a box."

" Yes, truly ; but when I say a box, I mean a small one."

" But did he take that with him as well ?"

" Oh, no ! he had wrenched it open, and removed from it every scrap of paper it contained, so that he had the will, as a matter of course."

This was desperately provoking, but what could be done ?   The circumstances spoke for themselves, and were too clear to be disputed ; my only great dread was, that in addition to losing his hold over his brother's fortune, and his power of punishing Gilbert, Colonel Lincoln would likewise be deprived of the house which had been presented to him as a free gift by his brother, for, probably, the contents of the box comprised the title-deed of that property, as well as other matters of importance.

I accepted the colonel's hospitality, as regarded procuring me a bed, for now the morning was actually getting advanced, and the adventure I had already met with was quite sufficient for one night.

The last words he said to me, as I retired to rest, were,—

" You may depend upon it that by this time my brother's will has been consumed, and is nothing but ashes."

" It is more than likely.   We cannot suppose that Gilbert would keep so dangerous a document in his possession long.   Good night, colonel."

" Good night—good night ; and a pleasant repose to you."

Before retiring to rest I could not help thinking what an amiable frame of mind

Colonel Lincoln had to enable him thus readily and easily to throw off the pressure of circumstances, which would have produced so great an effect upon most persons.

"This man," I said, "whatever may be his income, may be called rich, for he is contented, and evidently cares nothing for the frowns or smiles of fortune.

It was certainly some alleviation of my annoyance to be possessed of this idea, although to think that such a thorough scamp as Gilbert Lincoln should thus get the better of anybody was a mortifying circumstance.

Reflecting upon these matters I soon fell sound asleep, but how long that sleep continued I knew not, for I was suddenly aroused from it by a tap at my chamber-door, and I heard the colonel say,—

"I am sorry to disturb you if you have not been disturbed before, but has any attempt been made at your window?"

"At my window?" I said, springing from the bed and opening the door, "certainly not that I am aware of, colonel."

"There has been at mine."

"What, Gilbert Lincoln again?"

"Scarcely possible. I can't see what object he can have; it's most likely some common ordinary thief, who fancies the house perhaps more unprotected than it is. But the fact is somebody attempted to open my window, and to do so he must have climbed upon the balcony for I distinctly heard him drop into the garden again when I spoke. and then fearing that the attempt might be carried out at your room, while perhaps you were sleeping, I have come to warn you."

"I thank you; I have heard nothing, though, and seen nothing."

It was not yet quite daylight, but fast approaching thereto, so that objects were dimly discernible, and from the window the garden in front of the house was plainly visible—it was a French casement, and I opened it to look out, when I thought I saw something like the figure of a man crouching down behind a thick lilac-bush, about twenty feet from the window.

"There is some one there," I said, "but in the dim uncertain light, I do not recognize him exactly as Gilbert. Stand aside, now I see him plainer, and be it who it may, he has a pistol in his hand."

"The vagabond, I suppose, wants to take my life still," said the colonel, "let's try him, he knows that I always wear a green silk nightcap, and probably he may have a shot at it if he sees it."

The colonel took up his nightcap, and putting it on the end of a stick, which he took from a corner of the room, and slowly and cautiously projected it forward until from the garden it must have had the effect of a head peeping with extreme circumspection from the window.

Scarcely had he been in that position a moment, when the sharp report of a pistol came upon our ears, and the night-cap was dashed off the stick to the further end of the apartment.

This diabolically murderous attack incensed me to that degree, that I snatched up one of my own pistols from the dressing-table, on which I had laid them, and at once fired in the direction from whence the shot had proceeded.

I always kept one of my pistols loaded with ball, and the other with shot, it so happened, that in this instance, I took up the latter, which no doubt gave me a far better chance of hitting my man. I heard the shot rattle among the leaves of the lilac bush, and likewise I heard a sudden sharp cry of pain, and the figure I had before observed crouching down among the vegetation, made a sudden rush from his place of concealment, and gaining the garden-gate, almost immediately escaped.

"I have not hurt him much," said I, "but I have marked him, it is too dark to however, to identify him, unless you can do so."

"No, it is like Gilbert Lincoln, and that is all I can say; so as there is a doubt, he must have the benefit of it."

"But this is most monstrous," I said, "that you are to be continually made the subjects of these attacks; it is, colonel, a state of things which must not be endured, and if your individual feelings and your military habits prompt you to disregard the ferocious attempts upon your life, you nevertheless owe it to society at large to take some steps in the matter."

"I will think of it," he said, "and see what can be done; it puzzles me, however, to imagine that this can be Gilbert Lincoln, when we consider he has already been successful to the greatest possible extent, in what must be his primary object?"

"It only shows you how revenge, when once it takes possession of the mind of such a man, becomes a predominant feeling, and overpowers all other considerations, and besides, I think you owe something of this second attempt to yourself."

"Indeed! how so?"

"Why you allowed the first to be made with such perfect impunity, never even hinting at what you ought to have done; namely, an appeal to the laws, that you gave Gilbert Lincoln every reason to think he might with impunity, pursue any desperate course that his evil passions could point out to him."

"I admit all that, and as regards the reasoning of the matter, you are quite right, it is very irksome, however, for a man of my habits to appeal to the law, but I will talk to you of it, after you have had some more rest, and then we will decide upon what is to be done, which I fear will be nothing because you must not forget that I cannot recognise in the man who fired the shot at me to-night, my nephew, Gilbert, with anything like sufficient precision to enable me to swear to him."

This was true enough, and when the colonel had left me, although I laid down, I did not attempt to sleep. but could not get rid of the strong impressin which had taken possession of my mind, to the effect that sooner or later Gilbert Lincoln would murder his uncle.

And it seemed such a gratuitously rascally deed, when we come to consider that he had actually got possession of the will, and consequently had placed himself, by its destruction, exactly in the position, which his complaint was that he had been driven from, but all that I set down to the score of his desperate wickedness.

In the morning, at about half-past eight o'clock, I was summoned to breakfast, and upon repairing ro the room where we had passed some hours the precedeing night, I found the colonel trying to make light of the attack upon his life, while Linda was bitterly weeping at the very thought of it.

"Father," she said, "we must not stay here, consideration for me should induce you to remove from here."

What reply the colonel was about to make was stopped by the entrance of a servant with a letter, which he stated had come by the earliest post delivery that morning.

The moment the colonel opened it, he exclaimed—

"It's from Gilbert, and only think what must be his amount of impertinence in sending me such an epistle, and how he must have calculated upon his chances of success in getting possession of the will."

He read as follows:—

"Sir,—The air of Morden House will not agree with you any longer, and unless you produce the will and administer to the estate of my father, as you allege you have it in your power to do, I shall, as heir-at-law, claim and take possession.

"I am, sir, your's, &c.

"Gilbert Lincoln."

"P.S.—I desire that any communication respecting this affair, be addressed to my solicitor, Mr. Peter Macconnich, Thavies Inn."

"He thinks he has us now," said the colonel, "and I suppose he is right; the will is no doubt destroyed, and as heir-at-law, of course he can claim the property."

"If you please, sir," said the servant, coming into the room, "Andrew, the Gardener, says, he found this paper lying near the gate this morning."

"Oh, did he; give it to me—something of not much consequence, I dare say."

The colonel took the paper in his hand, and the moment he glanced at it he gave such a shout that I was positively alarmed that he had gone mad suddenly.

"Hurrah!" he cried, "hurrah, hurrah! here's a discovery! Why this is the will the fellow has dropped it in his hurry, and taken off instead a lot of old papers, of no value to him at all. This is glorious—a famous idea! Who would have thought of such an accident occurring to undo all that the vagabond thought he had accomplished! Look, it's the very document itself, a little soiled from being trampled upon, which most likely he has done himself in his haste. This is glorious!"

"It is indeed," I said, " and now I think you can perceive into what a stupid dilemma Gilbert has placed himself; this letter you have received, he had posted

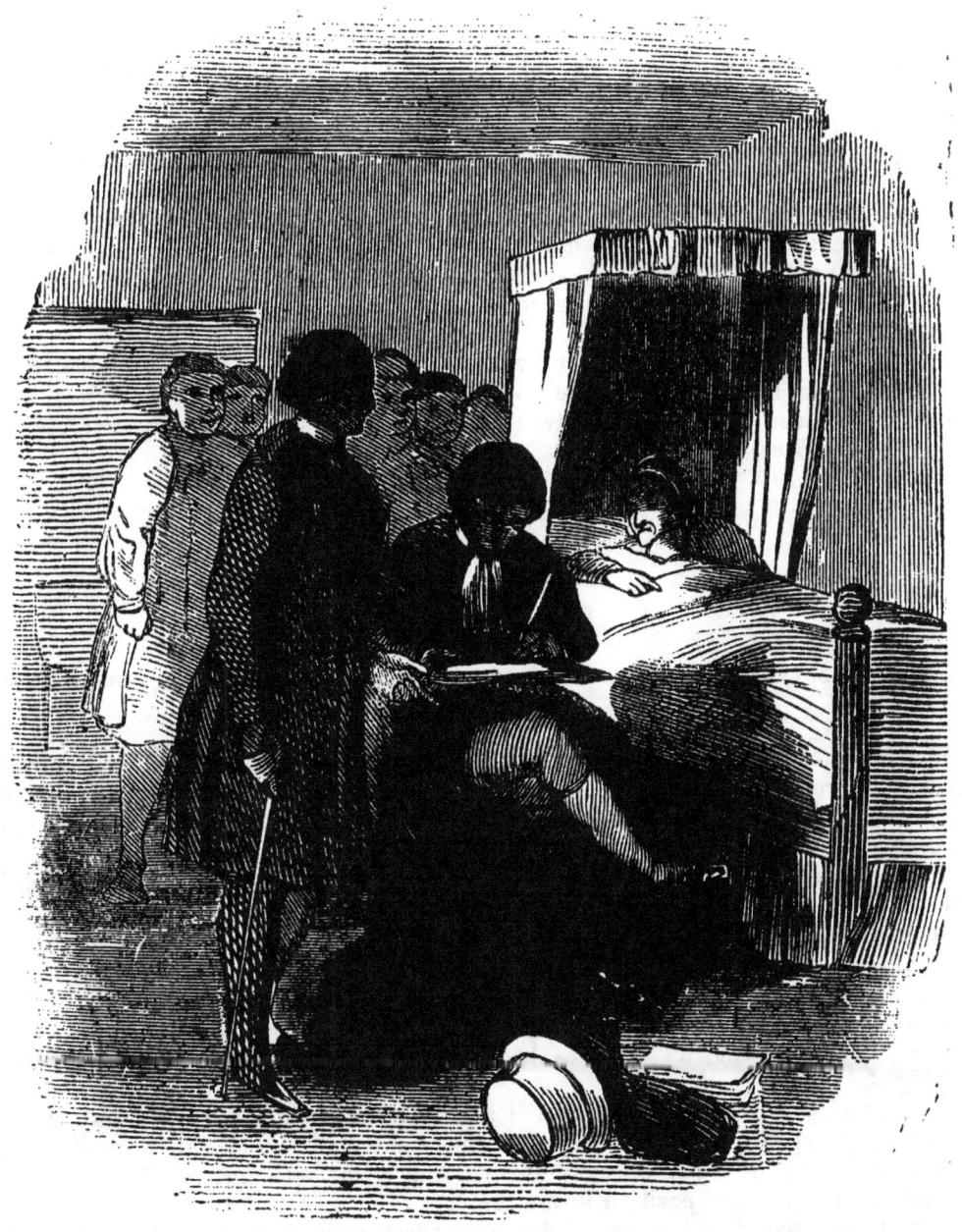

last night, believing that you were completely at his mercy, while by this time probably, he has made, to him, the most uncomfortable discovery, that he has got every document but the right one. I should recommend that you send at once for Mr. Kinder, and take steps for placing the validity of the will beyond all question and preventing the possibility of the recurrence of such a circumstance as this."

"I will, you may rest assured ; but first let me answer this note."
No. 13.

The old colonel then wrote as follows :—

"**To Mr. M'Cormick, Solicitor, Thavies' Inn.**

"Sir,—I have received a letter from one Gilbert Lincoln, who desires that the answer should be sent to you ; I therefore request you to inform him that the air of Morden House agrees with me perfectly well, and that I have instructed my solicitor, Mr. Kinder, to take immediate steps for proving the will of my late brother.   "I am, sir, yours, &c.,

"George Lincoln."

This letter was despatched, and the lawyer was sent for, who was so indignant when he heard what had occurred, and the atrocious attempt that had been made upon the colonel's life, that I could see he had great difficulty in keeping the expression of his indignation at all within ordinary bounds.

"Well, gentlemen," I said, "I shall now leave you with the pleasant conviction that Gilbert Lincoln has been most signally defeated. Of course, colonel, nobody can make you, if you are not yourself inclined, prosecute him ; but, for Heaven's sake, be careful, for there is no knowing what extent of violence his disappointed malice may now urge him to. You know, gentlemen, the man you have to deal with, and, therefore, being forewarned, you ought to consider yourself as forearmed.

Mr. Kinder very much approved of what I said ; and I took it kindly because of the inhabitants of Morden House ; hoping, and, indeed, fully expecting that the circumstances which had involved them in danger and difficulty were, at all events, nearly over.

CHAPTER XI.

DETAILS SOME FURTHER PROCEEDINGS WHICH GILBERT LINCOLN TOOK TO RECOVER HIS PROPERTY.

When I reached home I was not unmindful of the promise I had made to Martha to relate to her any adventure which had a pleasant termination, so I told her at once how Gilbert Lincoln had tried to get possession of his father's will, and by what a strange accident he had failed in attempting that purpose.

"But," I added, "I have a strange feeling that this adventure is not over, and I cannot help censuring what I consider the really criminal apathy of Colonel Lincoln as regards these attempts upon his life : he has certainly no right to allow them to pass unnoticed."

Martha fully agreed with me, at the same time that she added a prophecy of her own, to the effect that she was quite sure Gilbert Lincoln would come to some bad end, and that end, let it be as bad as it might, would unquestionably serve him right.

The latter part of the proposition I fully concurred in ; but, as regarded the former, my experience of society gave me some doubt, and the doctrine that, in the long run, guilt was always punished and virtue was always triumphant, by no means held a strong position in my mind.

I had seen too many cases of the direct contrary, and, if Gilbert Lincoln chose to be quiet, I should not have been surprised at his getting a large sum yet out of his uncle, and entirely escaping the consequences of the nefarious acts in which he had been engaged.

The only chance that I considered there was of his reaping the reward of the crimes he had already committed, consisted in the probability that he would perpetrate, or endeavour to perpetrate, some new ones.

About a week elapsed, during which an adventure occurred to me, which I will not now relate, because it would break the regular thread of this narrative, and always, in case of an episode of human life having such an hiatus in it that there was time for me to commence another, I shall postpone the relation of that other in order to keep up the completeness and integrity of the first.

A week has elapsed, then, and I was sitting with a newspaper in my hand, listlessly glancing over its pages, before sallying out on one of my adventurous expeditions, when the following paragraph caught my eye, and soon absorbed all my attention :—

"SINGULAR CASE.—Our courts of law will in a short time be occupied with a very remarkable case. It appears that the eminent merchant and banker, Mr. Gilbert Lincoln, executed a will, leaving the whole of his property to his brother, Colonel George Lincoln, (the gallant officer whose name is so favourably connected with our military operations of the last quarter of a century,) to the exclusion of his only son, whose conduct, it is asserted, had given his father great displeasure.

"But it now appears that an action has been instituted of ejectment by Mr. Gilbert Lincoln, the son, against Colonel Lincoln, who is now asserted to be illegitimate, and, consequently, so wrongly described in the will as not to be able to maintain his claim to the property."

I read this paragraph twice over with absolute wonder. I was quite petrified at the amount of assurance which must have been necessary to induce Gilbert to take so extraordinary a step for the purpose of harassing his uncle.

I debated with myself whether I ought not to call upon the Lincolns. And, after a time, although it certainly was rather a delicate matter to interfere in, I made up my mind that I would, because I was not really aware but what this newspaper paragraph might indeed be but a hint upon the subject, and possibly the first intimation that anything of the sort was contemplated.

It was sufficiently early in the evening to make a call with no impropriety—so I started off at once to Morden House, Holloway.

I found the Lincolns at home. And when speaking to the colonel upon the subject, and showing him the paragraph, I saw pride and passion struggling upon his countenance.

"I certainly was not aware," he said, "of the thing assuming this shape, I look so little at newspapers, that this paragraph has escaped my observation : there can be no doubt from whence it comes."

"But is it the first you have heard of the affair ?"

"I suppose not," for yesterday a legal paper was served upon me which I did not understand. At the top of it were the words, 'Doe on the demise of Lincoln,' which was all Greek to me."

"Let me recommend you," I said, "to take immediate advice. Put the affair into the hands of Mr. Kinder at once, for the meaning of the words, 'Doe on the demise of Lincoln,' simply is, that the whole of the property is claimed of you by John Doe, who is a legal fiction ; and when you are dispossessed, the heir-at-law can institute his claim without opposition."

"Confound the property," said the colonel, "it's no end of trouble ; and now this scoundrel, when he cannot succeed in any other way, begins by attacking the reputation of his grandmother."

"Mr. Kinder, sir," announced a servant.

"Ah! in good time," said the colonel. "How do you do, Mr. Kinder? Pray look at that. What do you think of 'Doe on the demise of Lincoln?"

The old attorney put on his spectacles, and carefully read the paper.

"Somebody is claiming the property," he said, "and it's Gilbert, of course."

We then showed him the newspaper paragraph, which, he at once said, proceeded from the same source, and explained fully the legal document that had been served upon the colonel.

"This is a most extraordinary thing," he said ; "to dispute the legitimacy of a second son is so unprecedented. If any trouble of that sort occurs, it is generally about the first. Are you aware, colonel, of any family circumstances that will tend to throw a light upon the matter."

"Damn it, no," said the colonel, "I know nothing about it. I know I was born somehow, somewhere, and that's all I can tell you. What the scoundrel means about illegitimacy I cannot imagine. It is a piece of the greatest impudence I ever heard of. But you must do whatever is necessary; and for my part, I am not a little curious to know what the fellow can have the confounded impertinence to say."

"We shall soon see, he will put in an affidavit, and we must answer him; after which witnesses will be examined; and then they will proceed in due form, the whole family history being raked up from every imaginable source."

"Devilish pleasant upon my word," said the colonel; "here, first of all, I am pushed into possession of property, which I neither wanted nor expected, and then I am shot at as if I were a Tipperary land-owner, and, when I object to that, this Mr. John Doe that you talk of, steps forward to dispute my being the son of my father; and pray, what recompense am I to have for all the trouble?"

"Why, if he can't make out the case, Gilbert will have to pay costs; and, if this be a protracted suit, they are just as likely to swallow up half the estate as not."

"What a pleasant idea; but, however, if we must, let's go at it tooth and nail, if necessary, and we will see what the rascal has got to say."

"He may not proceed, perhaps it's only to frighten you."

"No, I think he knows better than that; that fellow of a lawyer has put him up to something."

"Most certainly," said Mr. Kinder; "if anybody is highly qualified to carry out a piece of great roguery, it is that Scotch lawyer, M'Cormick, who is as great a vagabond as ever stepped; but, be patient, we shall soon see what they mean."

I will pass over the intermediate stages of this matter, and briefly state upon what evidence it was that Gilbert Lincoln relied.

His statement was this :—

"In the June of the year before George Lincoln was born, old Mr. Lincoln, the father of the banker and the Colonel, had occasion to proceed to Dresden, on business, where he was detained eight months and then returned to England. George Lincoln, being born four months after that, and a great number of witnesses' names were put down, who it was stated, could and would, all of them, depose to that fact."

Now the colonel was fifty-eight years of age, so that the witnesses who could prove anything in such a case must necessarily be extremely aged; but still, there was a goodly collection of them, varying from the age of seventy-two, the youngest, to that of ninety, the eldest.

This was a most stunning allegation, and if it could be proved, there was no doubt of course, as he knew the case must necessarily go.

"I never heard," said the colonel, "of my father having been to Dresden. He was certainly engaged in mercantile transactions connected with shipping matters, but all this is news to me, nor is it likely that the most good natured man alive would put up with a child presented to him four months after he had returned from an absence of eight months."

"He would indeed," said I, "be one of the most confiding of individuals."

"Oh, it's rubbish—rubbish, and nothing but a rank lie from beginning to end."

Notwithstanding this opinion of the colonel, proceedings went on, and, in the course of numerous examinations, three witnesses deposed as follows :—

An old woman, of the name of Mary Saunderson, said—

"I am seventy-three years of age, and when I was about sixteen, I went as nurse-maid into the family of Mr. Anthony Lincoln, who lived in a house in the fields, where Russell Square is now, and who, likewise, had counting-houses in the City. I always heard that he had ships of his own, and that he was very well to do. There were only four persons in family, and they were, Mr. Anthony himself, his wife, Miss Smith, his wife's sister, and a young child named Gilbert."

"Do you recollect any occasion on which Mr. Anthony Lincoln was abroad?"

"I do; I recollect one night, there was a good deal of contention in the drawing room, and, after that, a coach was sent for, and my master got into it, and was driven away along with two boxes. On that same evening my mistress said to me—

"'Your master has gone to Dresden, Mary, and may not be back for soe tme should any one ask for him at the door, you will say so.'"

"When was that?"

"In the June of the year I was sixteen, that's fifty-nine years ago."

"And when did you next see your master?"

"Not till the February of the next year, when he came home, and brought the same boxes with him that he had taken away."

"Are you aware after that of any disturbance or contention having taken place between your master and mistress?"

"None in the least."

"And when was the next child born?"

"On the last day of June in that year. Master seemed very much pleased, and rode thirty miles to get misses a cucumber, as they were very scarce that year, and she had a great fancy for one."

This was all this witness had to depose, and it certainly said a great deal for Gilbert's case, and made the colonel look very queer.

But, if this witness answered well the purpose of the nephew, the next answered it better still.

She was a very old woman indeed, verging upon ninety, a little, thin, ancient, withered creature, with sharp, cunning features, and eyes that still had about them a fierce lustre.

She seemed in full possession of all her faculties, and likely, as the leading counsel remarked, to live twenty years yet.

"My name," she said, "is Fanny Cook, I was a confidential servant sixty years ago, when I was twenty-eight years of age, to the Lincoln family. I was with them at the birth of Gilbert Lincoln, and I was likewise with them at the birth of George. There was another child afterwards, but it died in its infancy."

"Were you aware of anything remarkable occurring in the family, between the births of these two children, Gilbert and George?"

"Yes, I am aware of the absence from England of Mr. Anthony Lincoln, during a period of eight months."

"Are there any particular circumstances which make you peculiarly aware of that fact?"

"There are. On the evening previous to my master's departure, my mistress called me into her own private apartment, and, closing the door carefully, she thus spoke to me,—

"'Your master has occasion to proceed to the continent, to a city called Dresden, he will remain for a considerable time, and, what I want you to do is, to pack up for him in a box, that you will find in his dressing-room, all his linen that is in good condition, in order that he may take it with him, for he will be absent, perhaps, a number of months."

"I did as I was desired, and packed up a number of shirts, stockings, and other articles; indeed so many as to fill a chest, and then my master took them away with him in a coach, which was sent for for that purpose."

"And when did you see your master again?"

"In the February of the next year; and on the last day of June a child was born, who was named George."

"Did you not consider it extraordinary that the child should be born at that period?"

"I did; but it was no business of mine, and I was well provided for."

"How do you mean well provided for?"

"Captain Blue gave me fifty pounds."

"And, pray, who was Captain Blue?"

" A gentleman who lodged in the house while Mr. Anthony Lincoln was away."

" And when did he leave ?"

" The evening before my master's return."

" And did Mr. Anthony Lincoln make no remark about this remarkable twelve months or four months' child, which ever the case was ?"

" None to me, it was not likely he would. I never heard anything further about it. They are all dead now, and, therefore, it cannot matter."

" But, you are aware, that this enquiry is very important to Colonel Lincoln."

" Well, I cannot help that ; what I say is the truth, and there is an end of it. There was no use in cross-examining such a witness because her deposition was uncommonly clear."

The statement of the third was to a similar effect, with the addition that she produced a letter dated Dresden, and signed Anthony Lincoln, so that it seemed, without question, to have come from the party who was sought to be proved, to have been in that city at a particular period. She accounted for the possession of this letter, by saying that, when she left the service of Mrs. Lincoln, she gave her a number of articles of clothing, and that, in the pocket of a dress, she found this epistle, and considering it of really no importance, she did not take the trouble of restoring it. The contents of the letter itself went far towards proving this assertion ; a less important epistle could not very well have been conceived, it was as the witness had stated, dated Dresden, and expressed a hope that the writer would be able to return to his family. About the genuineness of the letter no one so much as hinted about, and if they had they would have been wrong, for it was a *bonâ fide* epistle, and one that was in no way open to any objection of any kind whatever.

And this was the whole of Gilbert Lincoln's case, and a very strong case it certainly was, such an one, indeed, as I could not help feeling the Colonel would have a great difficulty to get over. The affair was so precise and clear in all its bearings. There was nothing left to conjecture—but all seemed as plain and aboveboard, as such a case could by any possibility be, when I heard the evidence I trembled for the result, and, indeed, considered that the last statement, which was made by a woman of the name of Haddington, was so conclusive, that the less was now said about the matter the better it would be for all parties interested.

The illegitimacy of the Colonel, however annoying it might be to him was, of course, no real consequence, because he was the last man to care about the property, and, as far as regards those kind of prejudices which some people might entertain to his disadvantage on account of the peculiarly uncomfortable circumstances attendant upon his birth, I will venture to say, that he did not care a straw about them.

" It's rather annoying," he whispered to me, " though to have all this thing dragged forward, when really it would have been just as well left alone, but there's an end of it."

" I beg your pardon, sir," said Mrs. Kinder, who heard him make the remark, " there is not an end of it yet, nor shall there be, and I will trouble the enemy certainly to prove their case a little more strongly before I give in, I shall give notice of an appeal to a higher court than at present, and then we see what is likely to become of the affair."

" As you please, as you please," said the Colonel ; " I suppose I shall be ruined with costs."

" Certainly not, this is a case in which in any court in Christendom the costs would be ordered out of the estate."

" Oh ! well, if that's the case bleed the estate as long as you like."

The attorney was as good as his word, he did move the cause to a higher tribunal, although against the advice of several counsel learned in the law, who considered it useless so to do, and about a month after that, I was somewhat surprised one day to receive a visit from Mr. Kinder. I was in bed and asleep, but he was so urgent to see me, that Martha came and rattled   my bedroom door and mentioned his name, upon which I arose instantly; for I conjectured he had something important to say as regarded the Lincoln family.

When I appeared before him I saw that his countenance wore an anxious expression. I begged him to be seated, and when he had done so he entered at once into the subject of his visit.

"Sir," he said, "the kindly interest which you have shown for Colonel Lincoln and his daughter, has induced me to call upon you; but, I fear very much by finding you in bed, you are too indisposed to assist me."

"Oh no," said I, "not at all—finding me in bed is nothing. I always sleep all day and get up all night."

"You astonish me, sir."

"I dare say I do, but it is a fact for all that. I have been in the habit of it for some years. I like to ramble about at night, seeking for such adventures as may befall me, and from time to time getting such glimpses of human nature in its strangest modes, has given me abundant food for reflection. It was on one of these occasions that I made the acquaintance of the Lincoln family. How is the colonel?"

"He is very well, but, contrary to my advice, he has determined to give up the contest in which he is engaged with Gilbert. I would fight it out to the last, but he is tired of it; and to-morrow morning he is to surrender, at the chambers of Mr. M'Cormick in Thavies' Inn, the will, and renounce all right to the property."

"I am very sorry for it."

"And so am I; but if he will do it, who is to help him? I shall be present, and I want you as a disinterested witness to go with me."

"With great pleasure," I said. "If my presence will not be considered an intrusion by the remainder of the party, I will be there. At what hour do you meet?"

"At twelve, precisely; and I trust that the matter will go off, at all events, smoothly and easily, if it presents no pleasant features to one of the parties."

"I thought the old lawyer's manner was very dejected, but I promised to be punctual, and so we parted."

    •   •   *   *   •   •   •

Martha was quite astonished that I did not go to bed again, but remained up and took my proper meals like a Christian, and went to bed like a Christian after taking my supper, which I admitted to be that meal and not a breakfast, and, moreover, got up again in the morning like another Christian and took a real breakfast.

The fact is, I was extraordinarily anxious to be present at the scene which was about to take place at the Scotch lawyer's, and, as is usual with me, I made up my mind rather to be too soon than too late, so I started in good time and reached Thavies' Inn a quarter of an hour before twelve o'clock.

I easily found Mr. M'Cormick's chambers, and, as I was debating with myself whether I should wait until the hour actually struck or go in at once, I saw Mr. Kinder approaching along with the colonel.

"Ah! well met," said the colonel. "You are determined to be in at the death. The fact is, my little girl and I are thoroughly tired of all these lawyers, and we have made up our minds to put an end to it, so Mr. Gilbert may have his property and, as I said before, go to the devil with it precisely in his own way."

"Well, colonel, you have made your own determination," I said, "and no one has a right to dispute it with you. I regret much that such a man as Gilbert should obtain any triumph, but I suppose it is one of these things which must be put up with and borne with as good a grace as possible."

"It is so; but there is twelve o'clock striking, so let's go in at once."

We knocked at the chambers of Mr. M'Cormick and were shown into a private room, where we found that worthy affecting to be immensely busy with a great number of papers before him.

He had the insolence at the moment to pretend that he really did not recollect who the colonel and Mr. Kinder were, or what cause it was they came about, and when it was explained to him, he said—

"Oh, certainly—yes—I recollect—a will case. I believe the affair was to be arranged this morning."

"This is great nonsense Mr. M'Cormick," said Mr. Kinder. "You know perfectly well all about it; and, before we proceed, allow me to ask if your client is here or if you expect him?"

"I dare say he will be here," said Mr. M'Cormick. "He is a remarkably clever and punctual young man."

"Now, sir, there is some more of your nonsense," said the colonel, "for you know very well the only thing remarkable about him is his roguery."

"Really, sir, really this language is very—I may say wrong. I presume you intend to pay costs, as between attorney and client, for it would not be allowed you know out of the estate."

"I will not pay one penny piece," said the colonel; and, unless a conveyance in due form is made to me of the house at Holloway and all its contents, I will make no compromise. That house was the free gift of my brother, as such I accepted it, and as such I intend to retain it."

"But you must be aware, sir, that that house is worth a large sum."

"It may or may not," said Mr. Kinder. "We don't come here to argue that point."

At this moment Mr. Gilbert Lincoln was announced, and with unabashed effrontery, attired in the very height of fashion, he made his appearance.

"Now, sir," said his uncle, "I hope that we meet here for the last time as well as the first, and, as I have no desire to remain one moment longer in what I consider the contaminated atmosphere you breathe, give me an answer at once. Yes or no, will you execute a conveyance to me of the house at Holloway or not, if I abandon opposition to your suit and give you up the will."

"Then in a word I will do no such thing. I wonder what you should see in me to fancy that I am such an idiot as to make you a present of a house at Holloway, which I am told is at the very least worth £2,000."

"Very well, sir. If that be your answer our presence here can be no longer required, and the suit must now take its course."

"Well," said Mr. M'Cormick, "you will do as you please, gentlemen; but, as you are relatives, I advise a compromise of the nature mentioned, and I hope that Mr. Gilbert Lincoln will see the propriety of executing the conveyance required."

"I know you advise it," said Gilbert; "you told me so before, but I have thought over it and I won't do it—he shan't have a sixpence. I have the law on my side, and I don't see why I should make any compromise whatever."

"Very well," said Mr. Kinder, "then we need not stay. There can be no use in protracting an affair of this kind, and all I hope and trust is that the day will come when you, Gilbert Lincoln, will bitterly regret the words you have just now uttered."

"Do you," he said; "but you will find yourself mistaken; and, although for the present, in consequence of your protracting the suit, you hold possession among you of my property, I will exact an account of every farthing you receive upon it when the day of reckoning comes, which assuredly it shall."

We could perceive that the Scotch lawyer was decidedly in favour of the compromise, and that it was nothing in the world but the brutal obstinacy of Gilbert that prevented it.

I abstained from saying anything, but I thought the colonel had acted quite right, and I applauded him for the spirit he had shown when we reached the street.

"It's time enough, colonel," I said, "to give in when there is nothing to fight for, but certainly I could see no utility in sparing Gilbert Lincoln trouble literally for no object whatever, because, as Mr. Kinder says, you will have no expenses to pay."

"The scoundrel," said the colonel, "I am only sorry that I condescended to meet him at all, and I should not have done so but that confounded Scotch lawer made a proposition to the effect I have mentioned, and new his principal departs from it.''

" Yes, said Mr. Kinder, "and on the part of the Scotch lawyer you may depend it was a *bond fide* thing, and what makes me think that there must be some hitch

in the business somewhere, is that that individual has an evident desire to compromise the matter if he can. Now, I have a proposal to make to you."

" Go on," said the colonel, "what is it?"

" During the examination of the witness Cooke, she twice or thrice congratulated herself upon what she considered the certainty of her at least living for twenty years to come, and she always brightened up and looked uncommonly pleased when any one intimated how well she bore her years; so that I arrive at the con-

No. 14.

clusion that such is her weak point, and she is well paid and expects to live long to enjoy the produce of her villany.''

"Well, but what is your scheme."

This was a necessary preface to it, that woman resides some short distance from town, and she prides herself very much upon her capability of walking once a week a mile and a half down a lane to borrow a Sunday paper, which lasts her the whole remainder of the week for news, as she reads it very slowly and at her leisure.''

'' But the scheme, the scheme," cried the colonel.

" Don't be impatient, it is this."

Mr. Kinder then propounded to us a plan of operation which the reader will better understand as it was carried out, and as they were attended with signal success, I shall proceed to detail them in due order.

It was a singular experiment we tried, and one which at the first, I had my doubts of, but which as it proceeded, presented itself to me in more feasible colours, and seemed full of the elements of success.

I gave the attorney great credit for the ingenuity of the plan, and I still do so whenever I think of it, although he has more than once assured me that it was not original with him, for he heard of it having been done on another occasion with complete success, which encouraged him in this instance, likewise, to hope for a similar result.

CHAPTER XIII.

THE THREE MEETINGS IN THE COUNTRY LANE.

THAT same afternoon about an hour before sun-set, found us about four miles from town, at a country village, which was a mile and a half from a place of greater importance, and which mile and a half had to be traversed through a beautiful and winding lane, margined on each side by tall trees and the most luxuriant growth of underwood I had ever beheld.

It was in this village that the woman, Cooke, resided, and it was down this lane she went to borrow her Sunday paper, this being Monday, was her proper day to do so.

Mr. Kinder had evidently been careful in his inquiries, for he not only knew the day on which she went, but he evidently knew the hour, and when he got down to the village he pointed to a pretty little cottage, the window of which was shut up, saying—

"That is her place, and that is how she leaves it always if she is away for more than a few minutes at a time, she has now gone for her newspaper, and will be back in the course of an hour or so.''

We were a little astonished at the extent of this information, but we said nothing, and then we proceeded to carry our scheme into effect; we stationed ourselves at different points in the lane, down which the little old woman must come on her return home, and I shall relate what occurred just as I was able afterwards to put it together from information I received from the different parties concerned.

I was first, and after I had waited about a quarter of an hour, I saw the little curious aged creature toddling along with the newspaper tucked under her arm. We all knew her by sight, although she knew not one of us, and as soon as I observed her coming, I walked out into the middle of the lane and advanced leisurely to meet her with my walking stick in my hand, as if I was taking a country stroll merely.

In a very short time we met, and she cast a mere casual glance at me, and was about passing on, when I gave her such a start that I made her jump again, and then fixed my eyes intently upon her face, and shook my head from side to side with great gravity. When I saw that I had fully attracted her attention, and that she made a dead halt to look at me, I spoke to her saying—

"My good woman, I don't know who you are ; but being a physician, I feel myself justified and authorised in giving you an opinion. It is impossible for me to look upon your face one moment without knowing, from experience in these matters, that you are a dying woman."

"Me, sir !" she cried, " I shall live these twenty years."

"Not twenty hours," replied I ; "not twenty hours—good day ; you look awfully ill ; don't tell me that you don't feel ill, for I know better. I ought to know, as a physician, whether you feel ill or not."

She stared at me as I passed on, but when I got a short distance, she called after me.

"It's not true: I am quite well, at least I am pretty well—but yet I do feel a sort of something ; I'll get home as fast as I can—but I shall live for twenty years yet—quite twenty."

So saying, she hobbled down the lane, but I could observe, by a sly glance which I cast after her, that she did not go with half her usual confidence, but on the contrary, seemed depressed and unsteady.

"It will do," I said to myself; "it will do, we shall frighten her. What a strange looking old creature it is, hovering between this world and the next, and to talk of living twenty years; it is most singular that she should cling to life with so much pertinacity, when it surely can have but few charms for her, if any : but it is always the case—youth despises existence, but age clings to it as its last and only possession."

"Of course it would not do for me to follow ; so I must relate what happened as I heard it."

Old mother Cooke, as I found she was called in the village, although she stuck out stoutly for being Miss Cooke, walked on until she was met by the colonel, who pursued much the same plan as I did, as far as regards accosting her—that is to say, he took care to walk out from his place of concealment before she got up to him, and strutted up the lane."

He saw that the countenance of Miss Cooke was very much disturbed, and as he approached her she was muttering to herself—

"Die indeed ! die indeed ! I'll let them see that I'll live all the days of my life in spite of them. Die ! oh no—I shall live for twenty years yet, and then I shall be a hundred and—never mind what I shall be—but as for being ill, I aint ill at all, and there's an end of that. I wonder who this is coming? I don't know him— He don't belong to the village—he's a gentlemanly looking man though; but what is the matter with him—how he jumps ? "

By this time the colonel had arrived sufficiently close to Miss Cooke to enact his part in the drama ; he gave a great start and exclaimed—

"Good God !"

"Aye! aye !" said Miss Cooke, " what's the matter ?"

"I hope you're going home. Gracious Heavens ! madam, you can have no conception of how ill you look ; death is stamped upon every feature."

"Death !"

"Yes ; and your eyes are glassy, and your nose is pinched, I don't pretend to a great deal of experience in these affairs, but my wife's uncle, whom I never saw, was a medical man, so I ought to know something."

"Yes, yes," said Miss Cooke, trembling ; " what was his name?"

"H. Walther, Esq.; and I'd advise you, if you wish to die in your bed, and not drop down a blue looking corpse upon the queen's highway, to hurry home as quick as possible—to go to bed and make your peace with Heaven."

Miss Cooke wrung her hands.

"It must be true ; you're the second gentleman I've met in the lane that has told me so—I'm a miserable woman."

"You are : a leaden hue is coming over your countenance, Do you feel nothing about your chest, your head, and your internal arrangements generally. I say do you feel nothing ?"

"No—o—I don't feel anything; and yet when I come to think—Gracious

Providence! when I come to think, I do feel a kind of creeping of the blood, and a sort of sensation of—"

"That's the worst symptom," said the colonel. "Good evening; I don't think it at all likely that you and I will ever meet again in this world."

So saying, he walked on, leaving Miss Cooke all of a tremble.

"It must be true, and I shan't live twenty years. I did not feel quite well when I got up this morning, but I didn't think I was going so quick. The Lord have mercy upon me, miserable woman that I am!—what will become of me— where am I to look for assistance now—what's the use of my money—my hundred pounds buried underneath the hearthstone? but after all, is it true? It may be a mistake; I don't feel any worse, and I think if I could get home and have a glass of the old shrub that the housekeeper at the great house borrowed for me, and I borrowed of her, I should get a little round again."

She went on more unsteadily than before; and now Mr. Kinder, who had seen the interview between her and the colonel, went bustling up the lane with an umbrella under his arm.

When he got sufficiently near to her, that he was just himself upon the point of addressing her, she spoke to him, saying,—

"If you please, sir, if it aint taking too great a liberty——"

"Gracious Providence," said the attorney, "how ill you look."

"I'm a lost woman," said Miss Cooke, and she sat down in the middle of the lane. "The Lord have mercy upon all miserable sinners! Amen! I was going to ask you how I looked, sir; for I met two gentlemen in the lane who said that I am dying."

"I don't know who those gentlemen may be, but if they are not medical men, they have made a good guess; for dying you are. I'm chief doctor to the Megatherian Museum, and ought to know a thing or two. You're a dying woman; and if you've not wound up your earthly affairs, it's time for you to begin to wind them up."

Miss Cooke fell back with a deep groan, and then she lay upon the green sward of the lane, really looking so unwell, that the attorney was particularly glad, when a couple of countrymen passed along a meadow on the other side of the hedge, to hail them, and request that they would come to his assistance.

"Who is it?" said one.

"Why, it's Miss Cooke," said the other.

"I don't know her name," said the attorney; "but whoever she is, she is dreadfully bad."

"Yes," said Miss Cooke, "I'm a dying woman. Everybody says so, and what everybody says must be true. You know that, I believe, Thomas Jones, for I think that's Thomas Jones that spoke."

"Ah, Miss Cooke," said Thomas Jones, "it's plain to see—all be over with you."

"There's another," she moaned—"they're all alike. Take me home—oh, take me home."

"Can't thee walk," said one of the men; "can't thee move thy little bits of legs, Mother Cooke?"

"I'll haunt you, Jacob Singleton," she said, "when I'm a ghost."

"Haunt and be damned," said Jacob Singleton.

"It would be better," said the attorney, "to carry her home, poor thing, and not let her die here in the lane."

"Come along, then," said one of the men, and stooping, he lifted up Miss Cooke, and flung her over his shoulder with the greatest ease in the world, and trotted towards the village.

The other man ran on before, and spread the alarm that Miss Cooke had been found dead in the lane, so that the whole village turned out to welcome her arrival, which, added to the shock her nervous temperament had already received, went a long way towards destroying her.

She could scarcely speak by the time they reached her cottage-door, and for the want of the key of it, they burst it open, and laid her upon her humble bed within.

There was a raw sort of a boy, who had set up as a medical practitioner in the village, and he was immediately sent for; but when he saw Miss Cooke, he shook his head as if there were anything really in it.

"How old is she?" he said.

"Ninety," said one.

"Oh, it's a decay of nature. Nature, my friends, is like anything else, decays occasionally; and when nature decays, the animal functions become, in a manner of speaking, slowly done brown. It's impossible to do anything for this good woman. If I were to bleed her it would kill her, and if I don't bleed her she'll die, so if anybody will say they'll see me paid, I'll send her an effervescing draught.

"Get thee out for a fool," said one man; "thee sent me a fizzing draught, and much good it did me, filling one up with smoke."

"Hush, hush!" said Mr. Kinder, "the dying woman wishes to speak."

"I know I'm going," said Miss Cooke—"I know I'm going now fast. I don't think I've got any inside now left—it's quite gone.'

"I should say it was," said Mr. Kinder.

"I see about me," said Miss Cooke, "a great many faces that I know, and I begin to fancy that there are some in the room that have been dead years ago!"

"Poor thing," said a woman, "she's deleterious! Ah, dear, it's a shocking thing when one's latter end flies in one's face."

"Hush, hush! listen to her."

"I've done some things in my life," continued Miss Cooke, "that I'd better have scratched my own eyes out than have thought of."

"We'd better send for the parson," said one.

"No," cried the old woman, with energy, "I've done without parsons ninety years, and I'm not going to be troubled with one now."

"That's, now, what I call dreadful," said a man—"dreadful, sir. Does this, sir, remind you of the dying Christian to his soul? No, sir, it does not; it's more like St. George and the Dragon—a great deal more like St. George and the Dragon; for old Miss Cooke's St. George, and the dragon's the devil!"

"Pray be quiet," said Mr. Kinder, "and hear what she's got to say, will you. People haven't got time to look after their souls when death's treading on their heels."

The man looked puzzled, but he made no reply; and Miss Cooke continued,—

"Beneath that hearthstone will be found——"

"Gracious! a dead body!" screamed a woman.

"No," said Miss Cooke—"a hundred pounds—a hundred devils; for they've been my ruin. I sold myself to the devil for a hundred pounds, and they're under that hearthstone."

Mr. Kinder was poking curiously about the cottage in search of pen and ink, which he at last found, and then sitting down by the bedside of the terrified woman, he said,—

"Miss Cooke, if you have done anything in your life which, at such an awful moment as this, presses heavily upon your soul, and if you feel that you can make any atonement for it, there is in Heaven such abundant mercy, that you may hope for the happiest results, by doing justice to the innocent."

She looked at him for a few moments in silence, and by that time some of the officious people had pulled up the hearthstone, and there, sure enough, in a little red bag, was found the one hundred pounds in gold.

"Throw that into the roadway," she said, "cast it out of the cottage; it is accursed."

"No, no," said Mr. Kinder; "let it be, let it be."

"Thank Heaven," said the woman, "that is gone," for she seemed to think that her orders had been obeyed; and "now, whoever you are, write here—I shall dictate to you."

"I will," said Mr. Kinder; "but tell me, do you really consider yourself a dying woman."

"I do; and let what I say be taken as the declaration of one who believes herself not long for this world."

"You all hear that," said Mr. Kinder, "you're all witnesses to that."

"Yes, yes," said everybody.

"What has happened—what has happened?" said a gentleman, coming in at the moment.

"Oh!" said one, "here's Sir John Leveson."

"Are you a magistrate, sir," said Mr. Kinder.

"Yes."

"Then, sir, this woman's extremely ill, believes herself to be dying, and wishes to make a declaration concerning something which presses heavily upon her mind."

"Indeed. Why it's Miss Cooke, surely; she is very aged. I shall listen to what she has to say, and strive to give effect to anything that is requisite."

Miss Cooke took no notice of his presence, but after a short pause went on to speak,—

"Now that the accursed gold is cast away, I will tell all :—Three months since there came at night when I was asleep in this cottage, a heavy knocking at my door, and when I arose thinking that fire, perhaps, or some disaster in the village, was the cause, a man spoke to me saying,"—

"Get up—get up, and admit me to the cottage; I have something to say to you that shall enable you for the remainder of your existence never to know what it is to be without gold." I rose, for the words were pleasant to my ears, and dressing myself hastily, I opened the door to the stranger, for what had I to fear? I had neither money nor beauty to tempt him with. Ha! ha! a poor, miserable, lone, wretched, old woman like myself could have nothing to fear.

"He was a tall thin man, dressed in black. Curses on him—curses! he laid on the table a handful of bright glittering gold, and then he said,—

"You must come to London, and say as I bid you say, and then you will have as much again as the fifty pounds I now lay before you."

"I was sorely tempted: the sight of the gold dazzled me: I'd never seen so much before even in a dream; and I asked him what I had to do to get more of the same glittering metal which I loved so much; and he told me that all that would be required of me, was to swear to much that I knew to be true; but to suppress something else which would give it a different complexion, and I consented."

"After a time then, when I had given him my solemn promise, he told me what was he required of me , it was as follows :—

"You were once," he said, "many years ago, in the service of a Mr. and Mrs. Lincoln."

"I was," I said.

"And a circumstance occurred which brought letters from Mr. Lincoln, from Dresden, where he was supposed to be for eight months; and you know well what the circumstances were under which he was away from home; will you tell me what they were?"

"I did tell him, and they were these :—

"Some time after the birth of his eldest son, Mr. Anthony Lincoln got into some difficulties in consequence of engaging in some speculation which had a promising aspect, but which turned out to be extremely unfortunate, so much so indeed, that it became necessary, in order that he should avoid legal proceedings to absent himself from his home for a considerable time, until various sums of money which, in course of time would become due, fell into his hands, and enabled him to liquidate certain claims."

"He remained away for eight months."

"At Dresden," said Mr. Kinder.

"At Dresden! Pshaw! at Camberwell, where he had a lodging, and where Mrs. Anthony Lincoln repeatedly visited him."

"Go on—go on."

"During the whole of that period, whenever it was necessary to make any communication to him, I used to do it—that is to say, I used to carry notes from Mrs. Lincoln to him, and bring back the answers; and those answers were always dated from Dresden, in case by any accident the letters should be mislaid or seen by another person."

Mr. Kinder wrote all this down carefully, and Miss Cooke continued,—

"This man who called upon me at night, told me that there was a law-suit going on in London about the property of the Lincoln family, and that I should have a hundred pounds, fifty of which he had laid before me, if I gave my evidence to the fact that Mr. Anthony Lincoln had actually gone to Dresden at the time when he really only was at Camberwell. He told me that people were attempting to deprive young Mr. Gilbert Lincoln of his property, and that, combined with the one hundred pounds, induced me to swear to the circumstances."

"And can you tell me," said Mr. Kinder, "if there was ever such a person as Captain Blue?"

"There was never any such person. I invented that name myself."

"Will you sign this document when it is read to you?"

"She signified her assent, and Mr. Kinder read it carefully to her, after which she affixed her signature and the magistrate witnessed it.

"That'll do," said the attorney, and wrapping it up, he bolted out of the cottage and went to the inn, where he had left a horse and chaise, and when it was agreed that I and the colonel should wait for him, he related to us all that had happened and showed us in triumph the confusion of Miss Cooke.

"Here now," he said, "is one of the most important documents that for many a day past has been in my hands. It legitimatises you all and places at your disposal the whole of your brother's property, and in this case it saddles your worthy nephew, Mr. Gilbert, most unquestionably, with the costs, which, as he will not be able to pay, will expose him to the same fate he so urgently wished should be yours, namely, a residence in a prison."

"I never was more gratified," I said, "in my life. What will you do with him now, colonel?"

"I'll try the vagabond again," he said, "and begin upon him with the guinea a day, decreasing it a shilling each day for any kind of misbehaviour whatever."

"Really, colonel, you really are one of the most extraordinary of men! Here's this fellow has behaved to you in an outrageous manner; attempted your life—insulted you—behaved with the greatest illiberality and selfishness, and taking every possible advantage when he thought he had it in his power to do so."

"But there is one thing that I do not forget, let him be what he may and who he may, the property is his father's and I really have no right to it."

"You have the right of bequest?"

"Yes, yes, but that was done in a passion; and my brother always considered that it was possible Gilbert might reform and, at all events, he never intimated that he should be left by me destitute."

"You're right—you're right," said Mr. Kinder, "and while I confess that the course you've pursued is not one which I could have had the moral courage or temper to pursue myself, I admire it for all that."

"Well, well, enough of that," said the colonel, "it will be necessary to ascertain how far fright has really acted upon this old woman, Cooke, and whether she is likely to die or to live."

"You may depend that shall be ascertained. I will send somebody down in the morning to the village with full instructions what to do, before we take any actual steps contingent upon this confession; he must be a sharp fellow who will let nothing go past him."

"Then," said the colonel, "we will wait for his report at head-quarters before we do anything more, and when we receive it, I certainly must say, I should like to have a bit of amusement at Master Gilbert's expense, and above all things I do want to identify the thin gentleman in black, as Mr. M'Cormick, of Thavies' Inn, for that to my mind, is a consummation devoutly to be wished."

"Nothing can be easier," said Mr. Kinder, "in my opinion, than the management of such an affair. We have but to intimate our readiness to accept of some compromise, in order, I apprehend, to make certain of another meeting at Mr. M'Cormick's chambers. The anxiety of that practitioner to make terms, must be evident to us all, and I dare say, at the least hint of a likelihood of the affair being settled without further warfare on our parts, he will arrange a meeting."

"I should like that meeting to be one," said the colonel, "at which a further proposition from us could be made to Gilbert, in order really to see if he is so obdurate as he represents himself."

"What proposition would you make?" said I.

"Why, suppose I was to bring down my demands from an absolute concession of Morden House as a perpetuity, to an indemnity against proceedings for any rent during the time I have occupied it."

"That is being immoderate, indeed."

"Yes ; but I want to give Gilbert an opportunity if possible to make some concession."

"Have your own way," said the lawyer. "It's not of the slightest consequence what opportunity you give him, or what concession you make to him; he will remain obstinate as long as he thinks he has power to be so, and he is one of those kind of men who become only the more obstinate and tyrannical the more concessions you make to them. They construe everything of that sort into weakness, and then they triumph."

"Well, if your opinion be a correct one, and I am not the man to dispute it exactly," remarked the colonel, "it only affords me a stronger motive to test it. Let a meeting, such as I have proposed, take place again at Mr. M'Cormick's, as soon as you have received the report of the party you send down to the village, and we will consider that this last experiment will be final, as regards the character and habits of Gilbert Lincoln."

We all agreed upon this, and proceeded to town greatly pleased with the success of the plan which had been put in practice, having the truth from the reluctant mind of Miss Cook ; and Mr. Kinder and I agreed to dine the next day with the colonel at Morden House, in the hope that possibly Mr. Kinder might be prepared with his report.

I think I passed one of the pleasantest afternoons and evenings I remember ever passing in my life, on that occasion of dining with the colonel and the pretty, amiable, and beautiful Linda, who just lent that charm to the little company which such female society as hers was so highly calculated to give it.

Mr. Kinder would say nothing to us until after dinner upon those subjects, which of course were uppermost in all our minds ; but then, when Linda had left us with our wine, and we were sitting as comfortable as emperors, and a great deal more comfortable too, for we had not state to keep up, and nobody watched us or cared what we did or what we said. Mr. Kinder spoke, saying—

"I think I have all the news for you that, as reasonable men, you ought to require. In the first place, after a good night's rest, Miss Cook has recovered, and still talks of living her twenty years, although she declares she is so much happier since making the confession of the part she played in the nefarious transaction of the will, that, far from detracting from it or placing any difficulty in the way of proving it, she expresses her satisfaction and her willingness to come forward and re-state personally what was taken down in writing from her dictation, so that we most certainly now have Mr. Gilbert completely on the hip, for his own witness has turned against him."

"That's famous," said the colonel. "I presume we may consider him now as thoroughly defeated."

"Thoroughly and completely, colonel," said the lawyer ; "and now it becomes your duty, whatever may be your own feelings in the matter, and however you may act, as regards money matters, and indict Master Gilbert for a conspiracy."

"Oh, no, let him be, his failure is enough."

"Well, if you let him be, you must likewise let Mr. M'Cormick be, for Miss Cook is ready to swear that he was the individual who called upon her, and gave

her the fifty pounds, making to her the distinct proposal, and the promise of another fifty pounds, if she carried it out, which resulted in the hard swearing that made you illegitimate."

"No, hang it," said the colonel, "we can't let the lawyer escape."

"Then you are called upon in a private way to prosecute his client."

"Well, well, give it another thought, and, for the present, please to consider that nothing is decided whatever upon the subject."

It was now agreed that Mr. Kinder should make for us an appointment, at No. 15

Mr. M'Cormick's, for twelve o'clock the next day, at which the presence of Gilbert was to be particularly requested.

All the minor arrangements we left to the attorney, and the reader will suppose that he made them with an amount of discretion that was highly calculated to produce a satisfactory *denouement*.

From a hasty note I received in the morning from the attorney, I learnt that he had made the arrangement with M'Cormick, who had with great eagerness jumped at the idea of another meeting, and expressed his satisfaction at the prospect of an amicable settlement to the affair.

The fact is, this lawyer was much wiser than his client: he knew well upon what a tissue of falsehoods Gilbert's case rested, and how it consequently must be at the mercy of any accident that might occur, of the most trivial nature, as all fine-drawn plots always are, even if conducted with the greatest skill and judgment.

        *   *   *   *   *   *   *

It is twelve o'clock midday, and once more the chambers of Mr. M'Cormick, attorney-at-law, are honoured by the presence of far honester men than their actual occupier.

The colonel, myself, and Mr. Kinder, arrived together, and were at once shown into the same private room, where the former conference that had ended so unsatisfactorily had taken place in.

Mr. M'Cormick was there alone, and I thought, from the first moment that I looked at him, there was an air of suspicion and mistrust about him, as if he suspected that all was not right for the interests of himself and of Gilbert.

He was manifestly fidgetty, and the courtesy with which he requested us to be seated, was of a strikingly overstrained description.

"I sincerely hope, sir," he said to the colonel, "that these unhappy little family difficulties will now cease entirely. I can assure you, sir, that, although I am a professional man, and of course, to a certain extent, interested in the progress of litigation, I have, from first to last in this case, advised Mr. Gilbert Lincoln to compromise it."

"Have no doubt of that at all," said the colonel, "and, from my knowledge of him, I can easily imagine how his obstinacy overcame your prudence."

"It did indeed, sir; and I can only say, that whatever may be your proposition to-day, it shall have my most cordial support. Mr. G. Lincoln is in the next room, sir; shall I call him in?"

"Oh! most certainly, do so by all means."

The attorney opened the door of communication between two apartments, and called to Gilbert, who, as before, showily dressed, and with an extremely insolent deportment, made his appearance.

"Well, nephew," said the colonel, "we have met again."

"Sir," said Gilbert, with a great assumption of insolence, "this is the second time I have given myself the trouble of meeting you here. My attorney tells me you have some proposition to make, to stop litigation. I have an appointment, at one, westward, and therefore desire that you will be as brief as possible."

"Yes," said the colonel, "and as humble as possible, of course; you have rejected my former proposition, which was, to confirm legally the gift of Morden House, which my brother conferred upon me. Do you still persevere in that refusal?"

"Unquestionably I do; and it is a most strange and inexplicable thing to me, how you can take upon yourself to ask the question."

"Very good. I dare say it's like my impudence."

"Come, sir, your proposition—quick, quick."

"Will you then come to an arrangement, by which you indemnify me from any claims for rent of Morden House, during the time I have occupied it?"

"Indemnify you! most certainly not. It's a large and handsomely furnished house; the rental I expect for it is three hundred pounds per annum, and as I consider you must have taken it for a year, I shall charge you three hundred pounds."

"But I can't afford it," said the colonel. "Three hundred pounds is a very large sum for me, and I tell you I can't afford it. You surely would not distrain me for it?"

"Such power as the law will give me, no man can blame me for exercising, and if I make the slightest concession to any one, it would not be to you."

"Then that's quite settled. I am to expect no consideration whatever from you?"

"None in the least."

"And this will," added the colonel, as he drew the document from his pocket, "this will, which you made such an audacious attempt to steal from me, becomes valueless, if my illegitimacy be proved?"

"Which is proved, as you know perfectly well."

"Well, I believe Mr. Kinder has a few remarks to make. I have said all I can, Nephew Gilbert, and you will take your own course. Nevertheless, I advise you now, I advise you for your own good—I am an older man than you, and I think I may say a wiser one—I advise you, therefore, most sincerely, to take another thought of this affair, and to do something which shall look as if all feeling was not dead within you."

"I hold you and your advice," replied Gilbert, "in equal contempt; you have been an annoyance to me, and, let it cost me what it will, I am resolved upon having my revenge."

"Now, really," said Mr. M'Cormick, "really, Mr. Gilbert Lincoln, I cannot approve of this. I go with you as far as I can, of course, but you are too violent, and I tell you my candid opinion is that it would be better to accede to your uncle's proposition, and put an end to this uncomfortable business."

"You are afraid," said Gilbert, fiercely, "but I am not; you have been doing nothing but harp upon the subject of compromising for some time past, but my mind is fixed—I will have all or nothing."

"We will take you at your word," said Mr. Kinder, "you shall have all or nothing. It appears that a woman, named Cook, along with others, proved your case, and swore to certain statements. Now, some people, when they begin swearing, take a fancy for oaths and declarations, and that has been the case with regard to Miss Cook."

Mr. M'Cormick groaned, and Gilbert looked terrified.

"Miss Cook states in this paper," continued Mr. Kinder, "a paper which is witnessed by a magistrate of the county, that, having the fear of death before her eyes, she wishes to do an act of justice."

"Stop a bit," said Mr. M'Cormick, "stop a bit, my client, Mr. Gilbert Lincoln, consents to give the indemnity against any charges for Morden House."

"She further states," continued Mr. Kinder, without taking the slightest notice of the interruption, "she further states, that she was induced, by the bribe of £100, to swear that Mr. Anthony Lincoln really went to Dresden, when, all the while, in consequence of his commercial difficulties, he only had a lodging at ———"

"Stop a bit—stop a bit," cried Mr. M'Cormick, "my dear sir, stop a bit, my client consents to execute an assignment of Morden House, and all its appurtenances, fixtures, decorations, and furniture."

"Camberwell," said Mr. Kinder, paying no attention to the interruption of M'Cormick.

"Damnation!" said Gilbert, as he sunk into a large chair, and turned of an ashy paleness.

"Gentlemen," said M'Cormick, "my client consents to divide the property. You see, as it is a family affair, he thinks there ought to be no more contention about it."

"It's too late," said Mr. Kinder, "that proposition is too late; we have now made up our minds, like Mr. Gilbert Lincoln himself, to have all or nothing. The legitimacy of Colonel Lincoln can be no longer attached; therefore, that will places the property in that gentleman's hands: we will have all or nothing."

" Then you will have nothing," said Gilbert, and, springing towards the table, he snatched up the will before any one could stop him, and flung it into a blazing fire that was in the room, from which its rescue was impossible, and where, before any one could recover from the surprise of the act, it was entirely consumed.

" Now !" he shouted—" now !" he shouted, " with all your cleverness you are defeated, and I come back again to my doctrine of all or nothing. I will have all, and, before twenty-four hours are over, Colonel Lincoln, you shall lay rotting in a gaol."

" Capital," said Mr. M'Cormick, as he rubbed his hands together ; " capital—capital."

" Well," said the colonel, with the greatest coolness in the world ; " I am glad you are so easily pleased ; it was only a copy of the will after all."

" A copy," said Gilbert, faintly, " the devil !"

" A copy," groaned M'Cormick ; " we are done."

" Gentlemen," said Mr. Kinder, " you must really suppose we are uncommon fools. Do you fancy, for one moment, that we would lay down the real will on a table, before two such thundering rogues as you are, and a fire in the room ? No, gentlemen, no ; the real will is in the hands of a proctor, at Doctors' Commons, who will take good care of it ; and so, once more, we get pleasantly back to our statement of all or nothing."

Gilbert Lincoln could not speak, and the lawyer looked perfectly cadaverous, while the colonel and I put on our hats. Then Gilbert spoke, crying with fury,—

" It's false, all false—it's a mere trick ; I will not believe a word of it !"

" That's as you please," said Mr. Kinder, " we don't care whether you believe it or not, as long as we persuade the judges of it, and now, Mr. Gilbert Lincoln, your uncle is willing to allow you another chance of reformation ; and we will get back to where we started from before this suit commenced."

" You will be allowed a guinea a-day by calling for it at my chambers, which will be increased by a shilling at a time for good behaviour, and decreased in the same rate for bad."

Gilbert did not say one word, but seizing somebody else's hat—it turned out to be the lawyer's—he rushed from the place.

" He will go and murder Miss Cook," said the colonel.

" No, colonel, no ; she is in London, and in safety ; he does not know where to find her, and if he did, he would not get at her."

" Gentlemen," said Mr. M'Cormick, " pray be seated, and let us talk the matter over. I begin to think, do you know, that the young man who has just left us is no better than he should be."

" Then what must you be ?" said the colonel; " it so happens that Miss Cook identifies you as the party who bribed her to give false evidence."

" Come along, colonel," said Kinder, " this gentleman knows his situation and liabilities quite as well as we can tell them to him ; he knows that an indictment for conspiracy lies at his door, and that the least possible amount of punishment he would receive would be to be struck off the roll of attorneys, while the greatest might be a couple of years' imprisonment.

Upon consideration, an indictment was not brought forward against Mr. M'Cormick, because the colonel would not likewise prosecute Gilbert Lincoln ; but one day the Lord Chancellor made a few remarks upon an affidavit that was brought before him, which deprived Mr. M'Cormick of the privilege, for the future, of styling himself attorney-at-law.

Days, weeks, and months passed away, without anything being heard of Gilbert Lincoln, and at last it was ascertained that he had gone to sea, and at some foreign port had left his vessel with, it was believed, an intention of accepting service on board a suspicious-looking craft in the same harbour, which turned out to be a pirate.

Mr. M'Cormick, after he had been struck off the rolls, disappeared likewise, and I heard nothing more of him for a whole twelve months, until one day I was coming home from the city, and I saw standing up, with his back against a brick wall, in rather a lonely situation, a person apparently blind. Hung before him was a board, on which was painted the following inscription :—

"Please to pity the poor blind, whose eyes were picked out by fishes in the Indian seas in diving for pearls. The unfortunate object has a wife and eight small children, all under five years of age ; pity the blind, and Heaven will bless your store."

A glance satisfied me, and I cried out,

"Why, Mr. M'Cormick, is that you? when did you take to the pearl fishery?"

"Damn it," he said, as he opened his eyes, "I am always running against somebody that knows me," and then he took to his heels and ran off with amazing swiftness.

It was a long time before the colonel could be persuaded fairly to take possession and use the property that had been left him, but, when Linda got married, which in due time she did, he said to her,

"Now, my dear, Morden House, I consider, is mine, and my own income is quite sufficient for all my wants; so as regards this disputed property, which has given me so much more uneasiness than pleasure, you may take it all and do what you like with it."

CHAPTER XIV.

MY NEXT ADVENTURE BY NIGHT.—A MYSTERY.

It is now necessary that I should go back somewhat in time in order to place myself in a position to relate to my readers what occurred to me during the intervals that all these particulars concerning the story of the Lincoln family were in progress.

I had gone out in search of adventures several times unsuccessfully, but at length I did meet with one that amply rewarded my toil and perseverance.

It was one satisfactory to me, because it occupied but a short time in its action, and was satisfactory in its result.

It happened to be a very stormy night on the occasion that I had made up my mind to go in search of adventures; in fact, it was a night that almost deterred me, and, as my readers know it is not a trifle will do that, they may imagine that the elements were rather in a desperate state of commotion.

In point of fact, it was really difficult to get along in the streets, and although I did not like to give up the idea of meeting with something to repay me for my trouble, I despaired of doing so on that night, because I conjectured that few if anybody would be abroad who really had a home to go to.

I walked down and up several streets without meeting a single individual, and I began to fear that I should just get wet through for my pains, when I saw turn a corner a large old-fashioned rumbling hackney coach.

It was coming along at so slow a pace, although it did not face either the roaring wind or the dashing rain, that I felt certain it was soon about to stop somewhere, and I watched it intently.

Presently one of the windows was drawn down, and a man looked out to give some directions to the coachman, after which the poor worn-out horses were made to quicken their speed a little, and the vehicle stopped at the door of a house wearing a most portentous and gloomy aspect.

The coachman did not move from his box, but a man got out of the vehicle and let himself into the house with a key. Presently the door was cautiously opened again, and I saw a dim light burning in the passage, the man, for I knew him again by a peculiar jerking manner of walking he had, who had entered the house with the key, came again out of it, and looked cautiously around him. It took him many minutes to satisfy himself that no one was in the street, but at length he seemed convinced of that fact, and I completely escaped his observation by standing close to the other side of the coach, where he never thought of looking.

Having then satisfied himself that he was unobserved, he said to the man who was driving—

"It's all right, get down and give me a hand."

"I am afraid," said the man, "to leave these confounded old horses."

"Oh! they won't run away, it has been out of their power to do such a thing for this last twenty years."

"Well, then, I'll chance it."

The driver got off the box, and I saw at a glance that he was not an ordinary hackney-coachman. On the contrary, he was rather well dressed, and had the air of an idler, and not by any means one of the appurtenances of a driver about him.

He entered the house along with the other man, and to all appearance, the horses went to sleep. Probably they were glad of the opportunity, but certainly any idea of their running away, seemed most completely out of the question.

I waited with impatience for their reappearance, and tried to conjecture what circumstances they could be which induced such an immense amount of caution and mystery.

Ten minutes, perhaps, but certainly not more elapsed, when as I kept my eyes fixed upon the passage, I saw a dark mass moving along it, which at first I could make nothing of, but as it neared the street-door I found it composed of the two men whom I had before seen, and a dark mass of something which they were carrying between them.

They appeared very anxious, and moved along without speaking a word, showing by the manner in which they so moved, that whatever it was they were carrying it was of great weight.

They came down the steps, and then one said in a low tone—

"Quick, quick! open the coach-door, I'll hold her while you do so; she has never moved."

"Perhaps you have overdone it," said the other.

"Oh! no, no. I know better than that, but don't stand talking, open the coach-door at once."

While one opened the coach-door I crouched down on the other side of the vehicle, so that although it was not impossible I should be seen, it was extremely unlikely. Then they both resumed charge of their burden, and lifted it into the coach with considerable care. He who had formerly driven mounted the box, while the other one got inside, and then off they drove.

It did not take me many moments to decide upon what to do. I jumped up behind the vehicle where there was a very convenient seat, and accompanied it in its progress.

They took the road towards Camden-town, and then diverging to the right, proceeded at a very rambling leisure sort of pace towards Highgate.

It may be guessed that if the progress of the elderly horses was slow upon the hard ground, with what deliberation they would creep up such a hill as that leading to the ancient village of Highgate. A child of four years old might have distanced them as they went, and I began to think it would take a good hour before we reached our destination—if our destination was the village itself.

But in this I was agreeably disappointed, for the coach halted at the garden entrance of one of those cottages which are upon what is called Highgate Rise.

The weather had by no means abated its fury, and the man who was driving must have been as I was myself, completely wet to the skin. But the expedition he was on seemed to reconcile him to all such circumstances, for I heard not a word of complaint come from his lips.

I thought that the position I occupied was about as safe a one as I could very well have, as well as a tolerably good one to see from, and arguing upon the probability that they would not think of looking behind the coach, I determined upon remaining. The man who was inside got out, and as he had done in town, he with a key admitted himself to the dwelling. But this time he gave me none of the anxiety of suspense, for he paused upon the threshold only to prop the door open with a stone, so that it might not impede them in their operations.

A sudden thought struck me that, as the vehicle was upon such a hill and kept showing an inclination to roll backwards, he might take it into his head to come behind it and adopt some means of counteracting such an impulse, so I got cautiously down and hid myself behind a tree that was close at hand, and whose ample trunk afforded me abundant protection.

Then he who was driving dismounted, and the two together lifted from the coach the same burden they had put into it, which now I felt convinced was a human being, either in a state of insensibility or dead, and carried it into the house; they were gone nearly a quarter of an hour, during which time I carefully took the number of the hackney carriage, with the hope that that knowledge might assist me in solving some of the mystery in which the transaction was enveloped. Of course I fully expected to see the men return alone, and I was greatly surprised, when they did make their appearance, to see that they brought out with them the same, or what appeared to me to be the same burden with them that they had taken in.

This conduct seemed so strikingly inconsistent that I was surprised at it, and the more so that they seemed to do it quite as a thing of course, and not to be at all disappointed at the real or supposed failure of any project. A moment's consideration, however, imparted to me another idea with respect to this portion of the affair, and I said to myself,—

"Certainly this, to all appearance, is the same body which they brought with them, but still it really may not be so, and they may have effected some sort of exchange."

They placed then this second burden, whether it was the original one or not, carefully in the coach, and then the one getting in and the other assuming the situation of driver, they turned the horses' heads towards London, and trotted at a better pace down the hill, although it seemed to me little short of a miracle how the miserable old cattle kept their feet.

I had resumed my place behind, and was rather anxious to continue my progress with them, because I had neglected taking the number of the house in the street from whence the coach had come; and although I thought I should know it again I felt that if anything should arise to induce me to take steps in the affair thoughts would not do, but I must have certainties to go upon. The progress homeward was much quicker than that of leaving town, partly owing to being down hill, and partly, I presume, owing to that sort of perception which all horses have of the fact when they are going home. Certain it is that we reached the street and the lonely-looking house much earlier than I expected, and then the process of lifting out of the vehicle what was evidently a human body took place, but after that was over, on this occasion, one only returned, and that was he who drove the coach; and mounting on the box he took it away.

I had no motive in following him, but I stood on the opposite side of the way and took an accurate survey of the house. It was a large one, and I thought by what I saw about the windows that it was handsomely furnished, presenting every appearance of great respectability, although from its age it had in itself a dull look.

And what could I do? there was the whole affair just as it had happened, with all its secresy and all its mysteries, opening to my imagination a wide theme of conjecture, and yet not affording me the least clue by which I could be enabled to say that any hypothesis I might form upon the subject was correct. Was the body dead they took away? did they bring back the same one or another; and if another, was that a living or a dead person? What could be the object of the whole affair—was the man on the coach box a paid agent or an accomplice in fact? and last, but oh! not least in the chapter of inquiries, what was I to do to come at the bottom of the mystery and solve it to my heart's content?

And the idea that I should abandon the solution of such a mystery was not one tolerable to my mind, or that it was likely I should be able to endure for many minutes; my propensity to interfere with other people's affairs, as Martha called it, was powerfully called into action, and was it likely that I should sit down quietly with a knowledge that there might be something stupendous to find out, and not make something like a powerful effort to discover it?

It was some time past midnight now, but still I thought I might acquire some information as to the occupiers of the house if I could find a public-house open in the neighbourhood.

It was one of those quiet places where, if there be a public-house close at hand, it is only to be found in connexion with some mews, and depends principally for its custom upon coachmen and other servants belonging to the wealthy families of the neighbourhood.

I was fortunate enough to find a house of this description, and although it could scarcely be said to be open, yet it was not sufficiently shut to deter me or prevent me from entering it. Just as I reached the door a boy came out with a long pole and a hook at the end of it, with which he commenced poking up the sliding shutters, and which operation he had not completed as I entered the house.

At such a time nothing softens the heart of a publican but an order of brandy-and-water, and that hot, too, where the scalding nature of the mixture compensates for its want of alcoholic intensity and disguises the quality of the article.

" I'm afraid, sir," said the landlord, " we can't serve you."

" A glass of brandy-and-water, hot?"

" Well, sir, we don't like to refuse a gentleman though it is a leetle late."

The brandy-and-water was mixed and handed to me.

" Mix yourself another," I said, " I hate to drink alone."

The landlord looked astonished, but he by no means scrupled at obeying the order, and after he had tasted a drop and looked scrutinizingly up at the ceiling, preparatory, as I expected, to bursting out into some eulogium upon the liquor, I said,—

" Who lives at No. 7, round the corner?"

" Oh! Mrs. Darvell occupies that house with her little girl, and a very nice woman she is—been in the neighbourhood a matter o' eight years; Mr. Darvell died in Ingey, and now she's let in that scamp—saving your presence, sir—her brother, young Hutchinson, to sleep in the house, and there will no good come of that, sir, I'll be bound, for he's a bad 'un, if ever there was one. Now, you'd hardly think it, sir, here is the Crown and Cushion quite handy and promiscus, but he must go two streets off to the One-eyed Unicorn."

" A piece of desperate bad taste," said I, " I never go to the One-eyed Unicorn."

This was an assertion I might very well venture upon, for I didn't know at all where it was.

" Don't you, sir? then I means to say you know what a glass of good licker is. Now, sir, what do you really think of that one-eyed unicorn?"

" Well, I don't know," I said, " but perhaps he tumbled over head and heels and knocked the other out with his own horn."

The landlord stared at me, but I kept my countenance; and after a moment, as he slowly stirred up the sugar in the remaining liquor in his glass, he added,—

" They say that Mrs. Darvell has come into the Ingey property, and there's no end of money; but mark me, sir, no good 'll come of having that fellow Hutchinson poking about the place."

" What sort of a man is he?"

" Rather tallish and dark, dresses shabby, and has a fidgetty way of walking with him, like a cock on a hot shovel."

This description was quite sufficient to enable me to indentify the man who I had seen taking the greatest part in the affair of the mystery of the two bodies as Hutchinson.

" And how old is the little girl," I said, " that you speak of?"

" About twelve; but she's not Mr. Darvell's little child, you know, sir; Mrs. Darvell, they say, was the widow of a colonel, or a corporal, or a somebody, and was left with that ere blessed kid to purwide for, and nothing a-week to do it on; so then the rich Mr. Darvell married her, and she's been a trump ever since."

The landlord went on talking, but as he only repeated the information he had already given me, I perceived that I was acquainted with the alpha and the omega of all he knew, and therefore my object was to get away and think it over to myself.

I walked homeward, revolving the circumstances in my mind, but still I was completely at fault as the most inveterate enigmatist could wish me to be.   I had

acquired a certain amount of information, but there it stood in all its bold integrity suggesting nothing, but bearing in itself mysterious completeness, that while it abounded in mystery, baffled inquiry.

The stars were fading their ineffectual fires before the coming day as I reached home, for I had taken a long round, and during that period the storm-clouds had passed away leaving such a serenity and beauty in the atmosphere behind them, that I felt much induced to wander and inhale the bright oxygenated atmospheric draught which Nature presented to my lips.

I made my way to my own chamber, and flung myself, dressed as I was, upon

No. 16.

my bed; sleep crept over me, and I did not awaken until the bright sunshine was glaring in at the windows of my apartment, for my mind overnight had been so full, that I had forgotten to close them as was my custom. I found too, that I had had enough sleep, and upon consulting my watch, and seeing that it was near twelve o'clock in the day, I determined upon rising and astonishing Martha, by calling my dinner my breakfast. I sat down to that meal with some satisfaction, and after some usual conversation with her, which I need not trouble my readers by transcribing, I took up a morning paper, to while away an hour with.

I had not perused it more than ten minutes, when the following paragraph met my eye:—

"SUDDEN DEATH.—We have to record an awful instance of sudden death, which occurred last night at rather an early hour. It appears that a Mrs. Darvel, the widow of the late Richard Darvel, Esq. of Calcutta, was residing with her only daughter, at No. 7, Mortimer Street, Berkeley Square, and retired to rest at her usual time, in perfect health and spirits, requesting her maid, who was the only servant in the house, to call her at an early hour. Something, however, of a suspicious nature as to sound proceeding from the bed-room of the lady, induced her maid, who slept in the adjoining apartment, to visit her. She seemed to be sleeping, but it was soon ascertained that the vital spark had fled and that she was then in the presence of her Maker. Mr. Hutchinson, the lady's brother, was hastily summoned, and Dr. Runnythorp, of No. 10, in the same street, was speedily in attendance, who gave it as his opinion, that the lady had been dead some time, and that her decease in so sudden and mysterious a manner, was to be attributed to the rupture of some important vessel of the heart. We understand that an inquest will be held this day upon the body."

"Now what on earth," I said, "can be the meaning of all that—here's mystery upon mystery. How came Mrs. Darvell to have only one servant in the house?— Why did she die, and what did she die of?—How came they to hear a mysterious noise, and what on earth can be the meaning of these two bodies?"

"How should I know?" said Martha, who had come into the room to replenish the coffee-pot, "don't ask me your ridiculous questions, I don't know anything about it; and as for bodies, I'm sure it's enough to drive anybody mad to have to wait upon a person, who turns night into day, and who don't know the proper names of his own meals."

"I did not ask you, Martha," I said, "I was soliloquising."

"Was you?" said Martha; "I don't know what you mean by it, but I suppose it is some of your chemical nonsense."

"Now, Martha, you know I've given up the study of chemistry, but I've made some remarkable discoveries."

"Yes, you did, and I recollect one of them quite well; you found out how to make the smell of a choked-up water closet, a gas pipe in one small room, and was nearly the death of me—I did not get it out of my stomach for a week, and had to take lots of sul voily toity and continuously to smell at a bottle of pnuenomics."

"Now you're censorious, Martha, positively censorious; it was only a little sulphuretted hydrogen."

"You may call it what fine name you like, but it didn't stink a bit the less; I hate such messing, I do, though I will say you've given that up since you've turned night into day, and go poking your nose into everybody else's business."

"Upon my word, Martha," I said, "you're complimenting and flattering this morning. But now listen to me: I'll tell you what has happened, and it's one of the most mysterious and singular adventures I am certain that you have ever heard me recount. I should like to tell it you, in order that you may exercise your ingenuity in discovering what it means."

This flattered Martha a little, and induced her to lend me a favourable ear.

I related to her the whole of the particulars, concluding by saying,

"And now, Martha, what is your opinion? You know as much as I know about this affair, curious and interesting as it is; so tell me if you can form any reasonable surmise concerning it."

"Well," said Martha, "in my opinion, and to the best of my belief, I don't know, and really can't tell; there may be something wrong, and there may not; and if there is, you may find it or you may'nt, and if you don't, you won't, and if you do ——"

"Thank you, Martha; I am very much obliged for the extremely clear and lucid explanation; and I feel now that I can set about the adventure quite with an air, inasmuch as you have supplied me with such abundant materials for thinking."

"Oh, you're very welcome," said Martha, "but I don't believe you mean one-half you say."

Martha left me, and I lent my whole undivided attention to what had occurred, turning over in my mind, carefully and considerately, every circumstance, and trying to come to a conclusion which should place me in some rational course of action in the matter.

At length I hit upon an expedient, which required some impudence to carry it out, but which, at all events, promised to let me hear at first hand what should be said upon the inquest.

I thought that nothing would be easier than to go and knock at the door of the house, and boldly walk in at about the time when the inquiry was to be held.

Full of this intent, and feeling, most probably, that I had no time to lose, I speedily attired myself for the streets, and for speed took a hackney conveyance to Mortimer-street.

Just as I got out of the vehicle, I saw several persons ascending the steps of No. 7, and I followed them. The door was opened, and some one said something about being summoned on the jury, and then somebody else said "It's all right," and in we went.

The dining-room, which was a handsome and spacious apartment, was nearly full of persons, so that I felt I was quite at my ease as regards remaining.

A jury was sworn, and the investigation commenced.

The first witness examined was a girl, who gave her name Rebecca Smithson, and she deposed as follows:—

"There are only three servants kept in the house—myself for one, a woman of the name of Mary Day, who acts as cook and housekeeper, and a young lad, a footboy, who is her nephew. My mistress had given leave to Mary Day to go to the theatre, and William, the footboy, was to go and meet her at the door, and bring her home."

"At what hour did your mistress retire to rest?"

"Early, as was usual with her. I should say not later than half-past nine o'clock. I slept in the next room to her, and Miss Adelaide in a little room above."

"Who is Miss Adelaide?"

"My mistress's daughter, by General Bell, her first husband."

"State to the jury what occurred after your deceased mistress retired to rest."

"I was awakened about eleven, and I thought I heard an odd noise in mistress's room. I think I went to sleep a little after that, but it preyed upon my mind that something might be wrong, and I got up at last—and upon going into her room, I called her. She made no answer, and then I found she was dead."

"How was she lying?"

"In bed quite composed, as the gentlemen of the jury have seen her."

"What did you do then?"

"I gave an alarm, and Mr. Hutchinson, my mistress's brother, who slept on the first floor, came up stairs, and then he sent me for Doctor Pennythorp."

"Had anything happened to annoy or vex your mistress in the course of the evening?"

"Nothing, sir, that I know of. A hackney coach certainly came at about half-past ten, and some people wanted a Mr. Johnson, and would insist, for some time, that he lived at our house, but I assured them he did not, and then they went away."

"There was not noise enough to awaken your mistress, so as to give her a sudden shock of alarm?"

" Certainly not, sir."

" That's ingenious," I said to myself, " but it's not true, for the people in the hackney coach never asked for Johnson, and she has said nothing of the burden they brought out nor of the burden they brought back.   What ought I to do ?"

I was upon the point of getting up and deposing to all that I knew, but I feared that, if any villany was going on, the information I could give, defective as it was, would only just suffice to put the parties upon their guard without throwing any light upon the matter or in the slightest degree furthering the ends of justice. I therefore made up my mind to be silent, thinking that the best policy under the circumstances ; for it left me perfectly at liberty to glean what information I could, at the same time that it let no one know any human mind was active upon the occasion.

The next evidence was that of Mr. Hutchinson, and the moment I saw him I knew the man who, on the evening before, had taken the initiative in all the affair connected with the dead bodies.   The evidence he gave was such as completely to corroborate what had been said by the lady's maid, and he deliberately swore that he went to bed at ten o'clock, and had never been out of the house from that time till the present moment of holding the inquest, when I had actually followed him myself to Highgate Rise and back again in the midst of a pelting storm.

The inclination came over me again to interfere but I restrained it, and Doctor Pennythorp was called.

He was called in, he said, to a case of sudden death, and had no doubt that a heart affection was the cause ; he was quite willing to be present at a *post-mortem* examination, if the jury thought it requisite ; but as a physician he could not undertake it himself, which surprised one of the jurymen, who said he always thought a doctor was a doctor, and he didn't see what difference there was between them.

" Why a juryman's a juryman," said Doctor Pennythorp, " and there's a confounded difference between them sometimes."

" Well, gentlemen," said the coroner, " you have heard the evidence.   It appears there was only one other person in the house, and that was Miss Adelaide Bell.   I do not see that we need harrow that young lady's feelings by calling her forward at all ; nevertheless, if you think proper, I shall put her upon her examination, and likewise, if a *post-mortem* examination of the body be thought necessary by any gentleman of the jury, it is in my power to order it ; but really, gentlemen, although this is an afflicting case, it is but too common a one, and I do not myself perceive that such a course is necessary."

The jury fully coincided with the coroner, and in the course of another five minutes the most singularly stupid verdict of " Died by the visitation of God," was returned; but that is now altered into " Natural death," and the mingled stupidity and impiety of the first form of expression is exploded, except among the most ignorant.

And then the house began to be cleared, and in a short time I found myself in the street, not much wiser than I was when I went into No. 7 as a spectator and a listener to the evidence that might be adduced at the inquest.   I looked at the house, the windows, the area, the door and the shutters, and then, as I walked away, I said,—

" If I'm a living man to-night I'll visit that cottage at Highgate Rise."

*   *   *   *

I waited with impatience for the night.   It was a serene and quiet one, though very dark ; but that suited my purpose better than as if it had been one of those lustrous ones, when every object is so plainly visible.   I provided myself with a small pocket lantern, and ascertaining that my pistols were in good order, and loaded, as usual, one with ball and the other with shot, I started on my expedition.

Moreover, I carried with me a stout stick, in which was a sword blade I knew I could depend upon ; so I considered myself provided against all contingencies, and resolving to fathom the mystery, if I could, I walked briskly towards the place of my destination.

It was a pleasant walk to me, for the exercise was sufficient to circulate my blood well; so that, in a short time, the cool night-breeze came pleasantly upon my brow, and as I got towards the steep ascent on the left-hand side of which are the cottages, at one of which the coach had stopped, I felt ready for any adventure that might suggest itself to me.

As my readers may suppose, I had not been an unobservant visitor before of the place which I was now approaching, for I had taken especial notice of some of the old trees that grew around the spot, and, moreover, there was a particularity about some lattice-work upon the garden wall that, if once noticed, would always serve to identify the place by.

Such a pitchy darkness, as was around those cottages, I had scarcely ever seen, and aided, too, as that was, by dense shadows cast by trees, some of them more than a century old, and twining far aloft into the night sky, it became something perfectly tangible and opaque, and made me think that the phrase "a darkness that could be felt" was by no means an exaggeration.

In this state of things to see the lattice-work, with its peculiarity, was out of the question, unless I lit my lantern, which I did, and shrouding it carefully so that only now and then, like the faint glimmer of a will-o'-the-whisp, it showed itself among the trees, I hastened on.

At last I discovered, as I thought, the massive ancient tree, behind which I had hidden on the occasion of filling the coach, and, upon holding my lantern above my head, I caught a glimpse of the peculiar lattice-work, and, then, being satisfied, I instantly put out my light.

I like darkness among trees—that intense blackness, at first, which makes one feel as if in a cavern, or as if each step would precipitate down some yawning chasm—that darkness which, by degrees, the eyes become accustomed to, until at last the objects begin dimly and obscurely to assume their proper shapes and forms, and we can distinguish tree from flower, and the trim pathway from the untrodden green sward.

A light is destructive of all this—all the beauty and all the romance of darkness, amid abundance of foliage, vanished, and we are painfully brought back to an every-day world, which just extends to the limits around us, reached by the uncertain rays of a twopenny dip.

The short time I had my lantern a light a little composed me, and I was glad of the opportunity to put it out.

I soon found the garden-gate, but to find it and to open it were two very different things indeed. It was quite fast, and from the feel of the little sharply-made and well-defined keyhole, I could well imagine that no ordinary key would fit the lock.

If, however, it had been the commonest in the world, I had no means of picking it, and from the first I had made up my mind to climb the garden-wall to slaughter a dog, if I found him there, and then, at once plunging into the adventure *con amore*, trust to my own means of defence, and my rectitude of purpose to carry me gloriously through it.

The wall was old and decayed, and presented many a foot-hold by which I could easily climb it. It was above this wall, in order to make it higher either for the purpose for a more complete protection to the premises, or for ornament, that the curious lattice-work I have before-mentioned was placed.

It was not a very easy matter to climb this wall, for, although there were good foot-holds, it was by no means the easiest thing in the world to get such a hold with the hands as to draw one's self up. It was with no small degree of trouble that I did succeed at last in getting to the top of the wall, that is to say so far as to enable me to reach up one of my hands, and take firm grasp of the lattice-work which, from its construction, afforded abundant facilities for a good grasp.

I had, however, quite forgotten to ask myself if this lattice-work was likely to be strong enough to support my weight, and the moment I took hold of it I was reminded of that omission by a piece of it coming away in my hand, and, as a consequence, I was nearly precipitated into the road.

By a great scramble, however, I continued to keep my position, and trusting no more to the lattice-work, which had behaved so treacherously, I managed to get over it, and quietly to let myself drop into the garden.

I felt convinced that there was no dog, or else, of course, he would have taken instant notice of my intrusion, but the darkness was sufficiently great to prevent me from seeing how far I had to go before I should come to the house. I was rather surprised to find myself in a garden of any extent, because it had appeared to me when the coach, and its mysterious occupants, had stopped at the door, that the passage of a house at once presented itself.

But this appearance, I found after a little more examination, arose from the fact that there was a cupboard way proceeding from the garden-gate right up to the house, which, from the road, would have the appearance of a passage, but which, in reality, was quite detached from the building. I paused now, and listened with the greatest attention, in the hope of detecting some sound indicative of the presence of inhabitants in the house, but all was profoundly still, and I could perceive no lights, although the hour was not a sufficiently late one to justify the belief that the inhabitants had retired to rest.

There is something about the stillness of a place devoted to human occupation, but by some circumstances deserted, which is extremely melancholy, and as a light gentle air came sighing through the trees, it seemed as if the spirit of those who long before had made that habitation theirs were sighing over the devastation that had crept across the place.

Even in the darkness that reigned around, I could see that the garden was much neglected, that vegetation had been allowed to grow rank and luxuriant, and that what had once no doubt been clean and trimly-made paths were now overrun with all sorts of weeds, among which I carefully picked my way.

It was not long before I came in view of the cottage residence, and I seated myself at a window, close to which I placed myself again to listen for any sound that might direct me.

The stillness, as of the grave, reigned within the place. I could hear nothing. I could see nothing, so I determined at once to adopt some means of effecting an entrance.

I tried the window, but it was fast. As, however, there was no shutter, this was a trifling obstacle to my progress. I broke a pane of glass, and removing the fastening, which was one of those ordinary ones that keep a window in its place, I lifted the sash, and at once stepped into an apartment.

Now that I was out of the open air, I lighted my lantern, and by its beams I discovered that I was in a small parlour, which evidently had not been inhabited for a considerable period. There had been at one time a handsome paper on the walls, but from damage and neglect it was hanging down in long shreds and patches.

A great accumulation of black dust was upon the floor, which exhibited my footsteps with perfect precision, and as the only marks of that kind were those which I left, I felt certain that that apartment had not been entered for a long period, and that consequently I should find nothing that would repay my search.

I passed out of it into the passage or hall, and scarcely had I gained that when a low moaning sort of sound distinctly came upon my ears. It was so sudden and unexpected, and it was gone again so quickly, leaving not the faintest echo behind it, that I could not come to any decision as to the direction from whence it proceeded, but if anything I thought it was a human groan, and that it came from above. There was another door, opening from the passage, exactly opposite to that from which I had emerged, and before proceeding up stairs, I thought it would be as well to go into that apartment.

The door yielded to my touch, and I entered it, but judge of my intense surprise to find lying in the centre of the floor a coffin, which appeared to be nearly new, if not quite so, and to have been got up to adopt theatrical phraseology, regardless of expense.

I was perfectly astonished, and walked round, staring at it, and wondering what on earth could have brought it there. It was open, and the lid was lying by the side of it, and it seemed as if it were thoroughly repaired for the reception of the remains of same one, for it had in the inside all that kind of odd-fluted muslin decoration which fashion dictates as the proper adornment of those last homes of humanity.

I stooped down and read an inscription which was upon the lid, and found there the name of Mistress Susannah Bennett, together with her age and the date of her death, which latter circumstance had taken place within the last fortnight.

"Well," I said, "this is strange indeed, and I know not what to make of it. The more I inquire into this matter the more do I discover strange and inexplicable circumstances which completely puzzle me, and which from their apparently having no connexion the one with the other increase mystery, instead of explaining it."

But in proportion, as I found myself puzzled, my curiosity, as might be naturally supposed, increased, and with renewed energy I continued my search through the mysterious cottage, hoping and expecting soon to find something that would throw a light upon the matter.

My next step was to proceed up stairs, and a very narrow little staircase it was that presented itself at the end of the passage. When I had got half way up I heard a sound again, which could not be mistaken for anything but a groan.

It was not that sort of groan which a person utters when suffering bodily pain, but it rather seemed as if it were coming from some sensations of mental anguish, and I was more confirmed in my opinion that it came from above-stairs by the greater clearness with which I heard it now that I was proceeding in that direction.

It was quickly over, as before, and then the same profound stillness reigned throughout the house.

Carrying my lantern cautiously in my hand, and keeping myself fully prepared in case of any sudden attack being made upon me, I reached a landing-place, from whence several doors opened, the whole of which was fast locked. As I was debating in my own mind which I should burst first—for I could see from their slight make that I should have no difficulty in doing so—that sound of mental anguish which had before occurred to me came upon my ears more plainly and distinctly, enabling me to detect which room it proceeded from, and to direct my actions accordingly.

Without a moment's hesitation I placed my lantern on the landing, and then, drawing back a few steps so as to give a strong impetus to the movement I was about to make, I dashed forward with my whole force against the door, and it burst open with a loud crash.

A shriek of dismay came from some person within the apartment, and a female voice cried aloud—

"Spare me, spare my life; I will sign it, but spare my life."

It was necessary that I should go back for my lantern, which was only the work of a moment, and by its light I was enabled to discover the contents of the apartment. In one corner of the room there was a miserable looking mattress, and upon it lay a female form, whose hands were tied together behind her back, so that she was almost a hopeless prisoner.

"Spare my life," she cried again, "I have already endured enough. Spare my life, I pray you, and I will sign the document you wish; although I know not its import, I can guess it is one that will make a beggar of me, and place you in possession of all my property, but anything is better than continuing in this dreadful state."

"Madam," I said, "you mistake me for one of your persecutors. I know not who you are, or why it is you are placed in this melancholy situation, but if I can be of any service to you, be assured that I am ready with heart and hand to aid you."

"Can this be possible?" she said. "Has Heaven heard my prayers and sent me some one to assist me?"

"I trust," I said, "that I shall be able to render you effectual assistance ; and, in the first place, let me release you from your present bondage."

As I spoke I stepped forward, and, taking my penknife from my pocket, I cut the cord which fastened her wrists, so that she was in comparative freedom.

"Take me," she cried, "oh, take me from this place. I am sure that the intention is to murder me, whether I consented or not to pursue the course which my enemies pointed out. Save me, sir, save me."

"I know not," I said, "what can possibly have induced any one to persecute you, but be assured that you are now safe, and that I will protect you with my life. Do you feel yourself able to walk?"

"Oh yes, yes ! from here certainly ; take me anywhere, so that I no longer remain in his power, whose selfish wickedness I have now discovered."

"May I ask your name, madam ?"

"Yes ; my name is Darvel."

"What ! are you Mrs. Darvel who lived at No. 7, Mortimer-street ?"

"I am."

"Then for the first time I begin to have some sort of understanding of a number of mysterious circumstances which have hitherto been inexplicable to me. Come with me, Mrs. Darvel, and, as we proceed to town, I will detail to you some astonishing things that have occurred even during the short time—I believe during the short time you have been absent from your home."

"It is, indeed, a short time in reality, although it has seemed frightfully long to me. But, hark ! do you not hear something?"

Even as she spoke I heard a door closed in the lower part of the building with a loud noise, and, in another moment, the sound of voices met my ear.

"They come, they come," she said. "My brother Hutchinson and his companion come to kill me."

"Do not make so sure of that," I said, "I am armed."

"Give me any weapon that you can. I was once a soldier's wife, and have seen enough of warfare to be able to defend myself."

"Then," said I, "I have not the least doubt but we shall be able to hold out the garrison. Hark ! they are coming up the stairs. Take this pistol, but do not use it unless we should be hard pressed. I will try to get rid of them without bloodshed if I can."

That there were two men coming I could hear from their conversation, but, before I could reach the door, Mrs. Darvel said—

"Hold ! a thought strikes me : they have never yet thoroughly explained what it is I am required to sign, and besides there is a family secret that, by an affected compliance with their wishes, I may discover. There is another room opening from this in which you can conceal yourself. Do so, and listen to what passes."

"But the broken door ?"

"That I will endeavour to explain to them. Hush ! be quick."

Impelled by curiosity, and feeling that at any moment it was in my power to interfere, I went into the next room as she requested me, shrouding the light from the lamp as I did so, and she cast herself upon the mattress in much the same position as I had found her. These preparations were scarcely completed when a glare of light shot into the apartment, and a loud voice exclaimed—

"Holloa ! there has been somebody here ; the door is burst open ; surely she has not escaped ?"

"No," said Mrs. Darvel ; "I would that I had ! thieves have burst into the house, but upon seeing me they fled precipitately before I could implore their protection, as most unquestionably I should have done."

"Oh, you would, would you?"

"Yes, I have a right to implore the protection of any one to rescue me from the troubles I now endure."

"If you don't mind, your troubles will be sooner over than probably you will fancy ; but, come, are you in a more tractable mood than you were?"

"What is it that you require of me ? You ask me to sign documents the contents of which I am in total and complete ignorance of; what is it, I ask you again, you require of me?"

"Oh, tell her," said the other; "it makes no real consequence; tell her at once."

"It does make no real consequence," said Hutchinson; "and since you are so particularly anxious to know everything, you shall know it. Your life is in my

power; but I have set a price upon it which, if you like to pay, you may execute to me a deed of assignment of all your property, and you shall not only be free, but you shall have enough to live upon comfortably."

"And what is to become of my daughter, Adelaide?"

"Oh! bring her up as other people do their own daughters—to get her own living."

"And if I consent not to this arrangement?"

No. 17.

"Then you shall never leave this place alive, you shall assuredly come by your death here; and there is a coffin below, which you have already seen, that will answer the purpose of a last home for you, while a hasty grave in the garden will suffice to conceal the deed from observation."

"Alas, alas! can you be so inhuman?"

"Most certainly I can; and to show you how little I care for what you know and what you do not know, I will let you into a little family secret, the existence of which you are aware of, but concerning the particulars of which you know nothing. You fancy that I am your brother, and that consequently it is a very monstrous thing for me to use you in this manner; but I can tell you the family secret is, that your brother died while you were in India, as the wife of General Bell; but I have assumed his name, and successfully passed myself off upon you for him. My real name is Montrose, and it is in that name that I will have the deed of assignment executed; and I give you this necessary information in order that you may not be surprised if you see that name when you sign the instrument."

"This is, indeed, a mystery; but it is an intense relief to me to find that it is not a brother who is using me thus."

"It ought likewise to go some distance in convincing you that I am not likely to swerve from my word; and that, having you so completely in my power, you may be prepared for the worst."

"But surely I might sign such a paper, and it would be of little use to you if, when I gained my liberty, I detailed the means by which I was compelled to do so."

"Oh, you have thought upon that, have you? Well, you are quite right to be clear upon every point; and now I tell you that I thought upon that likewise, and most effectually provided against it. I shall realise the whole of the property before you regain your liberty, and nobody will interfere to prevent me, because I have adopted a means which it is needless to detail, but which will effectually prevent any one from being surprised at your non-appearance."

I understood this, but Mrs. Darvel did not; and I now understood with what consummate art the villain Hutchinson or Montrose, whichever was his name, had managed the sham death of Mrs. Darvel.

The whole affair became clear and transparent to me, and the mystery of the two dead bodies, or living ones, or the whole affair of the coach, became perfectly clear.

Under the influence of an opiate, probably, Mrs. Darvel had been carried from her home in the mysterious manner I have related, and the dead body which had occupied the coffin, on the lid of which was the name of Susannah Bennett, had been taken on that night when I watched the coach to Mortimer-street, and there placed in the bed of Mrs. Darvel.

Armed with such an assignment of all her property as Hutchinson required of her, and which, of course, he would have back dated, he would have had no difficulty in taking entire possession of everything, and I very much suspected that the murder of Mrs. Darvel was a measure already determined upon, and would have consummated the whole affair; so that he not only would have got rid of what he considered the only witness against him, but he would have achieved that object without causing the least inquiry into the affair.

These reflections passed through my mind as I heard that villain so unblushingly threaten the life of her whom he no doubt considered an easy victim.

"You must give me," she said, "until to-morrow to think; I cannot at once determine. Give me until to-morrow at this time?"

"Very well, as you please; but remember, that is the utmost limit that I can give you; and to-morrow, if you do not sign the paper, you will not live another hour. There is some food which will last you till then; and now you know what you have to depend upon."

"Be it so; I shall have no food, for I cannot endure the horrors of the confinement.

They turned, both of them, and abruptly left the room. I darted from my place of concealment, and, at the top of the stairs, listened to hear if they should make any remark, and I heard the man Hutchinson plainly say to his companion,—

"She will sign the paper to-morrow, and then I'll give her a dose that will pretty soon do her business for her."

"That's the only way," said the other; "I told you so from the first; but what's to become of the girl?"

"What do I care? we will turn everything into cash, and leave England with, I expect, about ten thousand pounds in our pockets; and the girl may go to the workhouse if she likes, for all I care."

By this time they had got down to the passage, so that I could hear no more, and in another minute I heard the slam of the door as they left the house.

I went back to the room and addressed Mrs. Darvel,—

"You see, madam," I said, "what a pretty scoundrel this fellow, whom you thought your brother, has turned out to be; and I have to add, to what you already know, the fact that he has announced his intention of taking your life, even should you consent to-morrow to sign the document he wishes."

"Let us leave instantly," she said, trembling.

"Nay, wait a little while until they have got clear off, and then let me go on to Highgate and procure some conveyance for you, for we should have to go at least a mile towards London before getting anything of the kind."

She was very loth for me to leave her, although she admitted she was quite incapable of walking far; but at length I prevailed upon her to let me go, and I hurried on to an inn at Highgate, where I knew parties were up all night to change horses for travellers proceeding on the great northern road.

I procured a post-chaise, and soon returned to the cottage, the door of which Mrs. Darvel opened for me upon my ringing for admission, and, lifting her into the chaise at once, I had the satisfaction of removing her from that place where she must have endured such a world of mental anxiety, and which it was a wonder indeed had not become her grave.

She was so pleased and elated at her escape that she wanted to drive at once to her own house, but that I would not permit, and said to her,—

"No, come to some hotel, and then let us send for some professional man in the morning, who will advise the best course to pursue under the circumstances, so that the guilty parties shall not escape."

She yielded to my persuasions, and, taking her to an hotel, I left her to get refreshment and repose, promising to be with her at as early an hour as possible on the following morning.

Then I repaired homeward myself; for, feeling that on the following day I should have to be actively employed, probably on Mrs. Darvel's business, I was anxious to snatch a few hours' repose before it became necessary to be up and stirring.

This I succeeded in doing, and, although by nine o'clock I left home again, I had had sufficient rest to feel quite alive and active.

On the road to the hotel I had the curiosity to pass down Mortimer-street, and it amused me amazingly to see two men, one leaning out of the second-floor window and another mounted on a ladder, busily engaged in fixing a hatchment to the front of the house, to signify the decease of Mrs. Darvel.

"We will soon alter all that," I said to myself, "and it is to be hoped such an adornment to the front of the house will not be required for many a long year."

Upon arriving at the hotel and asking for Mrs. Darvel, I found that she was up and anxiously expecting me. She gave me the address of a solicitor who had formerly transacted some business for her, and as he did not reside very far off, and was not likely to have left home at that early hour, I despatched a note to him in my own name, requesting his immediate attendance at the hotel on business of importance.

The style of the note was such that a professional man would be sure to attend to it at once, and half an hour brought the attorney.

I received him in a room adjoining the one where Mrs. Darvel had sat and was breakfasting.

"Sir," I said, "being a perfect stranger to you, but on business of importance, did you know a Mrs. Darvel, of No. 7, Mortimer-street?"

"Certainly; poor lady!" he said, "I have heard of her sudden and melancholy decease. Did she, sir, while in life, recommend you to me?"

"She recommended you very strongly, sir, about half an hour ago, and it is in consequence of that recommendation I have sent for you."

"Sir," said the attorney, "I never mix up jokes with matters of business."

"Nor I, sir; but I presume you doubt what I have said, as you consider it a jest."

"It is simply impossible, for a coroner's inquest was held upon Mrs. Darvel only yesterday."

"Well, sir, since I have made a statement, I am bound to substantiate it. Pray, Mrs. Darvel," I cried, as I stepped to the door of communication between the two rooms, "will you be good enough to come and convince this gentleman that you did recommend him this morning to me?"

The attorney gave a jump towards the door of the apartment, as Mrs. Darvel, whom he knew quite well, walked out of the inner room.

"Why, good God!" he said, "what's the meaning of this? are you not dead, madam, and now lying at home waiting for your funeral?"

"Not yet, Mr. Armstrong; this gentleman will explain all to you."

I briefly, but distinctly, detailed to the lawyer the particulars that are already before the reader. He listened with wonder and attention; and when I had concluded, he said, "This is the most extraordinary circumstance that ever came professionally to my knowledge. Mrs. Darvel, allow me to congratulate you upon your rescue from such a dreadful state of things; if you feel yourself capable of the exertion, we will get into a coach at once and go to a magistrate, for, in an affair like this, no time should be lost."

She signified her assent, and, a coach being sent for, we drove off to Marylebone Police Court, where considerable surprise and speculation were excited by our procuring a private interview of the magistrate.

That functionary took our depositions on oath of the circumstances, and then granted warrants for the apprehension of Hutchinson and the man who had accompanied him, and likewise of the maid who had given her evidence on the inquest, and who the magistrate said at once he had no doubt was an implicated party.

He directed, likewise, two of the oldest and most experienced officers to accompany us to execute these warrants, and we drove at once to Mortimer-street.

Mrs. Darvel was greatly agitated, for she anticipated the delight in a short time of clasping her daughter to her heart.

I thought of this part of the subject, and spoke to her saying,—

"Madam, would it not be prudent to prepare your daughter in some way for your sudden re-appearance? but of that you are the best judge, because you can be governed by a thorough knowledge of her disposition."

"I did not think of that," said Mrs. Darvel: "she is a highly sensitive girl, and a sudden shock might produce disastrous results. I really did not think of it, but will you arrange it for me, sir, according to your discretion?"

"Yes, I would recommend that you remain in the coach, while I and Mr Armstrong and the officers enter the house; you need not appear until all is over, and until I have explained to your daughter what may be some little tumult."

She acceded to this plan, and in a few moments more the coach stopped at the door, No. 7, all the blinds of which were down, while the hatchment, which the men had finished fixing, proclaimed to every passer-by what was supposed to have occurred.

We left Mrs. Darvel in the coach, and the party of four of us advanced up the steps, and knocked at the door.

The summons for admission was answered by a boy in the dress of a page, and the attorney, assuming the office of spokesman, said,—

" Is Mr. Hutchinson within ?"

" No, sir, he has been out about ten minutes, but he said he would be back in an hour."

" Very good, then we must wait for him."

" Oh ! it's quite uncertain when he will be back," said a female, approaching from the dining-room, " and it's no use waiting : there's death in the house, and Mr. Hutchinson can't attend to any business until after the funeral : you can call again in a week."

" Take her," said I, to one of the officers : " that's the female against whom you have a warrant."

" What !" she screamed ; " take me ! it's found out."

She made a rush to try and get past us, but the officer caught her in his arms, saying,—

" Come, come, it's of no use making a disturbance ; we don't do business in that sort of way : you are my prisoner, and if you don't make yourself quiet and comfortable, I shall have to clap a pair of handcuffs on you."

She sunk down upon one of the hall chairs, and began wringing her hands, and exclaiming,—

" It's not my doing ! it's not my doing ! Hutchinson persuaded me, and so did Brown. I'll tell all about it if you will let me off."

" We can make no promises," said the officer ; " you can use your own discretion as to what you tell ; I shall take you away at once, and lodge you in security, and then come back here again ; you can say what you like to the magistrates, but mind, nobody promises you anything."

" I know that, but I will confess everything. I'll tell you how it was I first came to know Hutchinson : I'll tell you when I first met him, and how it was he came to get me this situation, and then how he told me, if he could get hold of all Mrs. Darvel's property, he would take me abroad with him, where we should live like princes and princesses, and have lots of servants to wait upon us. I'll tell you then how he got the cook to go to the play, so as to be out of the way, and how he managed that the footboy should go and fetch her home, so that he should be out of the way likewise."

" You are running on at a nice rate," said one of the officers ; " but please yourself, it's no business of ours ; you can just say whatever you like, or leave it alone, and you may make up your mind that either way will suit us equally well, for we don't care one straw whether you tell anything or not ; there's lots of evidence to convict you, and that's all we need look to. I believe that's correct, sir?" turning to me.

" Perfectly correct," I said ; "and I, for one, should advise the prosecutors to show no mercy : it's a desperate and villanous affair from beginning to end ; and I don't see why any consideration should be shown to those who are implicated in it."

" Yes, but gentlemen," she continued, " I'll tell you where Mrs. Darvel is."

" We know," said Mr. Armstrong ; " we know perfectly well where she is ; and all you can get by running on in this way is just the doubtful merit of meaning to give information which we are already in possession of, and which your own danger prompts you to tender to us, and not really any wish to do justice."

She gave a groan, as much as to say that she felt there was no chance for her, and that she must give up to the circumstances which surrounded her.

" Oh, that I should come to this !" she kept exclaiming, " after being promised so much. Is this the management of the villain Hutchinson ? is this his cleverness ? when he told me it was quite impossible to be found out. Gentlemen, I'll forgive whatever you do to me, if you mind and take care that Hutchinson is hung."

" A benevolent wish on your part," said I ; " and if I might venture to give advice to so accomplished a person as yourself, I should say, most decidedly, your best plan was to be quiet, and say nothing."

"Well, I have said nothing; only I am sure Mrs. Darvel will speak up for me, and so will Miss Adelaide."

"Come," said the officer; who held her by the arm; "come, I can't waste any more time upon you, for I want to get back here again before your friend Mr. Hutchinson arrives."

So saying, he led her from the house; and my eyes accidentally falling upon the face of the page, I was quite amused to see the look of puzzled consternation that it bore.

He seemed in a perfect state of bewilderment, and the most suspicious person in the world, by one glance at him, would have been quite convinced of his perfect innocence in the whole transaction.

The waiting-maid was taken away, still proclaiming as she went the wonderful amount of information which she was willing to give us upon every subject connected with the affair she had so quickly guessed we came about.

The other officer sat down very composedly in the hall, and, turning to the page, he said,—

"I am going to give you a holiday for a little while, and shall answer the door myself; so you can just do what you like."

"Then show me," said I, "to the drawing room, and then go and tell Miss Adelaide that a gentleman, a friend of her mother's, wishes particularly to speak to her."

He preceded me up stairs, and showed me into a drawing-room, and that was all that he seemed to have understood of what I said to him, for he stared at me with all the stupidity in the world, as if waiting for further orders.

"Go and tell Miss Adelaide," I repeated, "that a friend of her mother's wishes to see her."

"Oh! Miss Adelaide, sir?"

"Well, she may be 'oh Miss Adelaide' for all I know; but take your message at once, and say that I am waiting here for her."

"Yes, sir, I will."

I waited for nearly ten minutes before any one came to me, and then the door was gently opened, and a very young girl made her appearance.

There was indeed dejection upon her countenance, and her eyes betrayed the sign of recent tears. She was plainly attired in a mourning dress, and presented a very pleasing and interesting appearance.

"I believe," said I, "that I have the pleasure of speaking to Miss Adelaide Bell?"

"Yes, sir," she said, "that is my name, and I am glad to see any friend of my poor mother's."

"Pray sit down," I said. "I suppose it was a great shock to you to hear of your mother's sudden death?"

I saw the tears start to her eyes as she said—"Sir, it is not kind to ask me such a question."

"Does not seem so at present," I said, "but you will find that it is kind; and I wish now to ask you another question, which, I dare say, you will think equally unkind, but which, in reality, is not so at all; I wish to know if you have seen your mother since her death."

"I have not," she said; "many and many a time I have thought of going to the chamber where she lies, to take a last look of her, but my resolution has failed me as often, and I could not do it."

"Well;" I said, "I am a friend of your mother's, and will you let me accompany you to the chamber where she lies, to look upon her remains?"

She hesitated and trembled—the colour went and came upon her face, and for several minutes she was irresolute; at length she spoke, saying—

"It is better than going alone; it is my duty to go before the grave closes over her. I will accompany you, sir, believing that you are a friend of my poor mother's, although you are to me a stranger."

She moved towards the door, and I followed her up the next flight of stairs to a chamber on the second floor. The room was completely darkened, with the exception of a small ray of light, which was permitted to enter from a dressing-room adjoining. Without any ceremony, I advanced to the window, and opened one of the shutters, so that a full light fell upon a coffin that was placed upon tressles, close to the foot of the bed.

Some white drapery was thrown over it, which I removed ; and while the girl stood aside with her hands clasped, and an expression of indescribable woe upon her countenance, I moved aside the lid of the receptacle of the dead, which was merely placed upon the coffin, and not fastened, and exhibited to her the face of the still occupant of that narrow home."

"My mother! my poor mother!" sobbed Adelaide ; and then she uttered a faint shriek, and added, "What is this ? What is the meaning of this? Whence comes this strange alteration? This is not my mother!"

"No, Adelaide, it is not your mother ; and if you could, before this, have gathered courage to look upon the face of the dead, you would have ascertained that fact beyond all doubt. This is not your mother, and I have persuaded you to come here and look upon this face, because I knew it was not your mother."

"Speak, speak to me!" she cried ; "there is some mystery, I am certain there is. Tell me all, sir; oh, tell me what it means."

"It means this," said I, "that you must learn to bear pleasurable shocks and excitements as well as painful ones. Your mother lives!"

"Lives ? Oh, sir, do not mock me ; that, indeed, will be cruel ; do not, sir, I pray you. But yet, let me hear those words again. Did I dream it, or did you really tell me that my mother lived?"

"Come away from this chamber," I said, "it is no fitting place for you to remain in ; come away from it at once, and I will tell you a story which shall astonish you."

I took her by the hand, and led her from the room ; and when we again reached the drawing-room from whence we had ascended, I bade her be seated, and related to her briefly and rapidly all that it was necessary for her to know.

She listened to me with a breathless attention that was almost painful, and when I had concluded she burst into a flood of tears, exclaiming,—

"Oh, take me to her, take me to her! let me look upon my mother's face again, or I shall die."

"Be patient," I said, "and you shall soon see her ; it was only fear that the sudden shock of her presence would be too much for you, so I took this mode of preparing you for her reception. Remain here, and in the course of about five minutes I will undertake to produce her to you."

Without waiting for her reply I hastily left the apartment, and proceeded to the coach in which was Mrs. Darvel. "Come now," I said ; "I have explained everything, and Adelaide expects you."

She hastily sprang from the coach, and accompanied me to the house. In another minute her daughter was in her arms, and I at once left the room, for I felt that no stranger should be present at that most affecting meeting.

I just reached the hall as there came a tremendous knock at the street door, and then a pull at the bell, which set it ringing as though it would never leave off, and the officer rose from his seat to open the door.

The moment he did so Hutchinson strode into the hall, and the officer closed the door and placed his back against it.

"How do you do, Mr. Hutchinson?" said I, "I have waited some time for you, but I am very happy to see you at last."

"What do you mean ?" he said ; "I never saw you in my life before."

"Probably not," said I, "but that has not prevented me from having the pleasure of seeing you before, and from going to some trouble and expense to meet you upon this occasion. Pray, Mr. Hutchinson, should you feel inclined to part with that little cottage on Highgate-rise?"

"Damn you!" he said, starting back; "who are you?"

"Why, strange to say," said I, "I am a friend of the living Mrs. Darvel, and I really think that the dead Mrs. Susannah Bennett has been decidedly ill-used."

He plunged his hand into his breast, and pulled out something which I could not at the moment observe. He made a dart forward at me, but the officer caught him round the waist, and at once disarmed him of a knife, or rather dagger, for it was double-edged and pointed.

With a celerity that seemed to me perfectly marvellous, a pair of handcuffs were clapped upon him, and the officer said,—

"You are my prisoner; resistance will be in vain."

He glared about him like a perfect demon, and muttered some unintelligible curses, which nobody cared one straw about, while the officer turned to Mr. Armstrong, and said,—

"I'll take him off, sir, as soon as my comrade comes back, and he, I think, had better remain here, in case the other man against whom we have a warrant should chance to call."

"Yes," I said, "we must have Mr. Brown as well."

"It's all found out, by Heaven!" said Hutchinson. "Why did I not kill her?"

"Because," said I, "you had no opportunity; for if you had attempted last night to raise your arm in a hostile manner against her, you would have found that she was not without assistance, and that every word you uttered was over-heard, and is already recorded as evidence against you."

"That explains the broken door," he said; and then he lapsed into silence, and would not utter another word.

Now the other officer returned, and the state of affairs being explained to him, he quite agreed in his companion's suggestion that one of them should wait for Mr. Brown; and, as it appeared a sort of etiquette among the officers for the one who took the prisoner to lodge him in safe custody, he who had arrested Hutchinson left the house, while the other took his place in the hall to wait for Mr. Brown.

When Mrs. Darvel, after half an hour's interview with her daughter, came down stairs, it amused me much to see the surprise that was depicted upon the countenances of the cook and the page, for both of those functionaries were in the hall, and, upon first sight of her, could not believe otherwise than that they looked upon a ghost.

They impeded each other in their frantic efforts to get down the kitchen stairs, and it required all our united persuasions to induce them to believe that their mistress was really in existence, and a being of flesh and blood like themselves.

I and Mr. Armstrong left the house; but we had the satisfaction to hear that, in about a couple of hours, Mr. Brown called, and was duly captured and marched off by the officer who had been placed in guard for him.

But little more remains to be told. It was ascertained that the coffin containing the body of Mrs. Susannah Bennett had been procured from a fashionable under-taker, to whose house it had been brought for the purpose of being inclosed in one of lead, previous to its being placed in a family vault some distance from town.

The undertaker could not deny the fact, and it had such an effect upon him and his business, that he was forced to remove from the metropolis.

Mr. Hutchinson and Mr. Brown took each a long voyage, advised by the Recorder of London as quite desirable for the benefit of people's morals, while the lady's-maid, who had leagued herself with them, was accommodated with a residence for two years in the Penitentiary.

CHAPTER XV.

ACCORDING TO MARTHA, I LIVED FOR A LITTLE TIME LIKE A CHRISTIAN.

SOMETIMES when I have had an adventure like the last one I have related, which has proved peculiarly satisfactory to me, by unmasking some villany, and restoring some persons to a position which their enemies would fain have deprived them of, I rest a while, and, for the sake of change, adapt myself to the usual habits and manners of society.

I did so upon this occasion, after the adventure I have related connected with Mrs. Darvel and the mysterious cottage at Highgate-rise.

I rose when other people rose, and retired to rest at an ordinary hour, and I did this more because I knew I should come back with new zest to my old habit of night-walking than because I fancied it.

No. 18.

It was some amusement to me to hear, however, the abundant communications of Martha, who, when she saw me thus behaving like other people, was always mightily well pleased, and took care to show me that I certainly had her entire approval.

This amused me much, and the expressions by which she gave utterance to her satisfaction were some of them extraordinarily original and rich.

But her principal notion of doing things properly, was to do them like a Christian, although what Christian among all the circle of her acquaintance she took as her standard of perfection I could never discover.

But it was quite clear that one of her great rules of doctrine, as regarded Christianity, consisted in a blind adoration of what the majority did, and a hatred of anything in the shape of innovation.

She considered, evidently, that what everybody did must be right, and all the foolish habits and manners which, from time to time, had been engrafted upon idle and unthinking people passed with her as quite correct.

During these intervals, when I conformed myself to the habits and manners of the world generally, I used to call upon my old acquaintances, whom, at other times, I had no opportunity of seeing, and so I renewed and kept up intimacies which otherwise, in consequence of my strange and solitary habits, would, no doubt, have, in course of time, merged into indifference, if not into complete forgetfulness; and when my readers bear in mind that this solitary and strange life I led was only in consequence of my conviction that at night I should find more adventures and more food for the imagination, they will acquit me, I am sure, of any desire to withdraw myself from the world, or to shake off old and much-valued connexions.

At these times, too, I availed myself of the opportunities that presented themselves of seeing the public exhibitions, and likewise of visiting a theatre or two occasionally, so that I might feel I took part in the every-day concerns of life, and in the common amusements of the world.

These sorts of alterations of conduct seldom lasted above a week at a time, and then some morning I would close my shutters, shut out the daylight and prepare myself for one of my nocturnal expeditions with renewed pleasure, like some one who returns to a welcome task after a brief period of relaxation, which has only served to show him the value to his own mind of his favourite occupation.

And when Martha saw that I was giving up my reasonable conduct, I always, of course, had a vivid remonstrance, and she would assert that it was quite possible for me to meet with as good adventures by conforming to the usual habits of society as not; and, certainly, what I now relate to the reader tells well for her argument.

The Abduction.

One evening I had gone to the Haymarket Theatre, with the intention of eking out the evening, and witnessing the performance of a new play, which was vaunted up in the play-bills and in some little paragraphs in the newspapers; but I had not sat above two hours before I got tired of it. There was nothing in it, and I determined to leave for an hour, and take an early supper at the Bear, and return to see a lively second piece.

This I did, and when I returned I found the curtain falling amid what the play-bills, and probably the papers too, would call the most gratifying applause, but which was in reality a small portion of plaudits, mixed up with, or drowned by, as much hissing, and groans, and cries of ' No, no.'

However, as a manager cannot afford to bring out a play for one night only, it was persisted in, and the second piece put on. This was somewhat of a favourite, there was much light humour in it, and one that pleased the house much.

I saw this out, but the last piece I had seen more than once, and I was tired and warm. The house was crowded and very hot. I arose and left the theatre, with the intention of strolling about in the cool streets till I felt tired of that, too, and then of retiring for that night at least.

As I walked under the piazza of the Italian Opera House—that part which runs into Charles-street, leading to Waterloo-place—seeing some cabs collected together, I had some thoughts of taking a country ride, and dispel the fatigue I felt, which was more caused by the heat I had endured that anything I had done.

Before I made my mind up, I heard two cabmen begin the following conversation—but I must premise that I was not seen, nor, before they spoke, did I see them. They were in the shadow of the arched way, and the first horse's head was about level with the shoulder of the driver, and the others followed on behind, as they do when they are waiting for the theatre to empty itself.

"Well, Bob," said one, "I haven't seen you since the night we had such a blessed row a-top of the Haymarket, that had liked to have been an ugly affair.

"Yes, but we got through it very well."

"So we did; but I have had a better thing than that turn up only last night: I had a rale, out-and-out good job."

"Had you?"

"I had, and no mistake about that, I can tell you; why, it was a sovereign and a night's work done before it was earned, so I had double luck on that night; besides which, the night before that, I picked up a swell, and I got thirteen sovereigns out of him, but he kicked at it."

"Did he?"

"Yes, and had me searched; but it was no go; I was not to be caught that way; but the fact was, Bob, I ripped open the saddle and put the sovereigns in among the stuffing; so when they came to search me I had nothing on me."

"Didn't they search your cab and horse?"

"That they did, all over, not a corner left unsearched; but they did not find my place of security, and I trotted away thirteen pounds the richer; at the same time I had a rare good pull at the swell who gave me so much trouble."

"You are in luck's way as regards jobs; you are always falling in with one or another," said the other man.

"Not for a long while before this did I get anything in the shape of a lift up but I expect one to-night, though not so good as the one I just told you off."

"About the thirteen sovereigns?"

"Yes."

"What job have you on to-night—a country one?"

"Why, partially so; but it is not far; but there are other things connected with it that make it a good job. I have got a good horse, you see, and a large cab; so that, if anybody as is a judge of convenience and cattle wants to go anywhere or do anything out of the way, why they will pick me out of a hundred, and that is a fact."

"What an uncommon kind of man you are! But this job to-night, what is it worth, do you think?"

"A sovereign at least."

"Well, that's lucky! you are determined, then, that you will do business of some sort or other. What, is it a plant?"

"No, no; but I think there is something a-going on, for a swell came up to me on the rank, and said to me,—

"Cabby, are you out at night?"

"Yes," said I, "I am."

"Well," said he, "if you have a good horse and this cab, I can give you a good job, if you can keep your own counsel, and do a little sharp work for a couple of hours."

"Well, yer honour," said I, "I just can do it; but what's to be the damage, yer honour?—that's a question."

"You shall have a guinea if you do the job well; but, mind you, there may be a lady," he said, "who may try to call out and get away, so you must drive like wind until you reach the place we are going to."

"Where's that, yer honour?" said I.

"You'll know when you get there," said he; "but until then you must ask no questions: it will be time enough to know where you are going to when I have got some distance on the road.   Will that satisfy you?"

"Very good," said I, "I am satisfied—it can't be far."

"How do you know that?" he inquired suddenly.

"Because you said you wanted me only for a couple of hours, and I reckon you are not going far by that."

"You will keep your counsel," said he; "and you may depend upon it if you take the job you will go where we want, if we take you twenty miles."

"Not for a sovereign," said I.

"We'll satisfy you," said he; "but if you repent, say so at once, but let us have no complaint after the job is done."

"I'm satisfied," said I; "but where am I to meet you, and when?"

"You had better be at the corner of Park-lane, Hyde Park, Oxford-street, at about a quarter to eleven, and wait till you see me, or some one who comes to you from me, and who will explain to you who he is; so be careful."

"You may depend upon that," said I; upon which he walked away, and I saw no more of him.   It's about ten now, and in another quarter of an hour I shall go and hang up at the end of Park-lane, and wait for him."

"I'm off," said the other man, as he shut the door after an old gentleman who had walked up the dark colonnade that runs from Cockspur-street or Pall Mall.

"Good luck!" said the other man, as his companion drove off.

I hesitated what to do—whether to engage the man for a short drive, and give him a gratuity to let me ride along with him while he had this job on, which he had been speaking about, or whether I would watch and endeavour to trace them out by myself afterwards.   I preferred this latter mode, and pursued my way towards Park-lane on foot, and meditating upon what I had heard.

I walked there at a sharp pace, as I guessed I should be none too soon for the cab.

What could be the meaning of all this I knew not, but it was evidently something that ought not to be; else, why so much secresy, and why so much paid? There is something that must be looked to—a matter that wants following out— I will follow it out too, if I can anyhow follow the cab.

Filled with these thoughts, I pushed onwards and made for Park-lane, where I arrived, at the same moment that I saw a cab drawn up a little way from the end of the lane, that is, the end of Oxford-street, where it joins the Uxbridge-road.

I immediately paused a moment, and then, when I saw the driver so far employed that he would not notice me, I walked leisurely past both cab and driver, and observed them so far that I could easily recognise them again.

Having done this myself I walked away and stationed, at the corner of a short street, and in the shade, so that I could not be seen by the driver, and hardly by any one who passed the street close by me, for the night was dark, the clouds hung heavily over the metropolis, and there are but few lamps in Park-lane.

I waited nearly half an hour before there was any movement on the part of the cab or its employers, when suddenly a well-dressed man with a cloak on, came up to the cabman and spoke to him.   I did not hear what was said, but the driver got upon his box, and slowly drove after the individual, who went on first.

They crossed the road, Oxford-street, and then went up Great Cumberland-street, and then they turned up one of the principal streets on the right.

At the corner of this place I paused to observe if they stopped at any of the houses in the first part of the street, but seeing they did not, I hurried onwards with all the speed I could make, lest I should lose them in the dark.

I stepped up to one or two doors to see which way the numbers ran, so as to form something like a guess which way they went, and the number they might stop at.

At the bottom of the street they turned to the left, and I hastened forward again, and then, when I came to the corner, they were nowhere to be seen.

I hesitated a moment, and then I dashed down the street, and had scarce got to the next corner when I heard the sound of wheels, and, directed by them, I made towards the spot, and had not gone fifty yards when I saw the driver get down and open the door of his cab and stand by it.

"Oh," thought I, " I'm just in time to see the place where they are going ; now if I can see who is going out, I can form some estimate as to what is going forward."

I went on the other side of the way and crossed over, and got up to the cab just as the door of the house, opposite to which the cab had drawn up as close to the kerb-stone as it was possible, opened ; then I saw two men muffled up, looking up and down the street, and then, seeing nobody, they returned for a minute or two, and then they came out again, urging onward some one who was struggling evidently against their will.

This person who came out between them, evidently forced on by them, was wrapped up in a long cloak—a very long cloak, for the wearer, whose form was completely enveloped, so that not even the feet were visible, and then, so struggling in the cloak, they pushed the third person down the steps.

"Without doubt that is a female," I thought, as I saw them push her into the cab.

There was a slight scream came from her—they urged her in with greater haste, and both got in with her. The further window was immediately pulled up, and then the driver shut the door, while he inclined his ear to catch the word as to where he was to drive to.

Having received his instructions, which I did not hear, he took the reins in his hand, and, jumping upon the box, he drove furiously away from the spot.

I know not the reason I acted as I did, but I suppose it was some blind instinct of the moment, for I got on the board that connected the two arms together upon which the cab seemed to rest, running parallel to the axles.

I sat on this and held on fast. It was a very uncomfortable seat, and the jolting was dreadful. The part on which I sat having no springs to support it, I received every jolt entire and fresh from the wheel, and at the rate he drove it was no joke.

But I was there, and worse difficulties than that would not deter me from following out an adventure when once I began to feel interested in the affair, [and I did in this.

On we went down the Edgeware-road for some miles, through the Pineapple-gate, and then onwards through Kilburn, and Heaven knows where, for I could hardly tell where I was.

After we had gone about six miles from Hyde-park Corner we came to a lane, or by-road, that ran up somewhere towards Hendon, or that way, I supposed, though I could not tell how far it might be off.

Up we went : we had previously passed over the river Brent, and proceeded, perhaps, about a mile; but nevertheless we went at a prodigious pace the whole distance.

" You have a good horse," I thought as we rattled along : up we went up the lanes, and I very soon lost all notion of whereabouts I was, my ideas of locality were entirely abroad.

Suddenly we stopped before a house where there was a light. The sound of the wheels appeared to have been listened for by the inmates, and the door was immediately opened, and then the iron gates in the front.

The cabman was about to get down when one of them called out to him to keep his seat, and he remained where he was, and the door was opened, and the two individuals got out still wrapped up in their cloaks, and still supporting the third between them ; indeed I thought they carried her out and into the house.

While they were thus employed I got down, and, taking a piece of chalk out of my pocket, I chalked the wall in front of the house with my own initials and a cross. I made moreover several other chalk-marks on the trees and palings as I slowly walked away down the lane.

I stopped at a few yards' distance, and then I returned to the cab, and had just got up to it when one of the strangers came out, put his head inside the cab for a moment, and then he went to the driver, and said to him,—

"Here is the guinea I promised you and five shillings for your speed—you came along well : now hold your tongue when you get to town—do you hear ?"

"Ay, ay, sir, I just do; and can mind what I hear too : never trust me if I talk of them as pays me well."

"Good night," said the stranger.

"Good night, your honour," said the driver, and he carefully put the money up in his pocket, and then, getting down, he let both the windows down, and then, jumping up, he turned his horse's head, and came down the same way he came up.

I walked down some distance, and after a short time the cab overtook me.

"Are you going to town ?" I inquired.

"I can go any way you please to hire me," he replied.

"Yes; but are you going to town, or any other way, supposing you are not engaged ?"

"I am going to London in that case."

"And why could you not have said so before? but will you take me to town for a crown ?"

"Very well, sir, I am empty, I'll carry you : jump in, your honour; my horse is warm, and I'll carry you back in style ; I'll soon get over the ground."

"I'll ride on the box with you if you have room enough for me up there," said I, and I began to climb up.

"Oh ! yes, your honour, there's room enough; it's a good large box, and, for a makeshift, would carry three easily, provided they were not all fat ones."

I got on the box, and we drove along for some time without making any particular remark, but at length I said,—

"Do you know the name of this place ?"

"No, I don't," said the man ; "the road we are going to turn into a few hundred yards further on is the Edgware-road, but I cannot tell the name of this out-of-the-way place."

"How far have you been down this road ?" I inquired.

"Not far, sir, to a great house there with iron gates ; I don't know the name of it, but there it is. I never was here before."

"Who did you leave down here then?"

"Don't know, sir ; there were three on 'em, but I can't tell anything about them ; they paid me well enough. They are of the right sort anyhow. I should like to carry them again."

"Where did you bring them from ?" I inquired.

"Can't well say," he replied, "because they took me to a street the name of which I do not know—a little short street—where they all got in, and I brought them down here."

This was all I could make out of the driver; he knew nothing more. I had every reason to believe he might suspect more, but I did not expect him to be very communicative to me upon that point, and I arrived in town without anything particular occurring.

I was very sleepy. The country night air I dare say caused this, and it was not long before I was in bed.

*   *   *   *   *   *   *

The next morning breakfast brought with it many odd reflections, amongst which were the following:—

What was the meaning of all this? What was the intention of the two men, who seemed to force the third individual away with them, evidently against her will ?

The third person I thought must be a female ; her size, and the slight scream, all told me so ; besides that, I remembered the words of the person who engaged the cabman, which indicated that one was to be a female.

Well, what can be done next?" I inquired. "What step to take is a puzzle which I cannot at this moment solve, and yet I think I may as well go and endeavour to make out the name and occupation of the people where they went from, and perhaps there may be something turn up.

With this notion I finished my breakfast, and then, taking some blank paper, a Post-office Directory, an ink-bottle fixed to the button-hole of my coat, I sallied forth.

I came to Park-lane, and pursued exactly the same route I had followed the cab on the preceding evening. I doubt much if I could find it under any other circumstances, and, as it was, I only come right by my calculating the distance and turnings, for I could not remember the appearance of the places.

I found out the house; I pulled out the Directory, and, putting my blank paper in form, I walked up to the door, and gave a postman's knock—a one-two, rapid and loud. This brought out a woman to the area.

"Who do you want?" she inquired.

"Does Mr. —— live here still?" I said, looking at the book. I left a blank for the name, which, of course, I did not know.

"Yes," she replied, "he does."

"But what is his name? I don't see it."

"Ah! you had better go next door."

"You don't want the name in the 'Directory,' then?" I inquired.

"No, nor the 'Court Guide:' our connexions can find us without such aid, I can assure you."

"Oh, very well," said I; "only, you know, respectable people usually like to have their names inserted."

"Very likely; but I tell you we aint such flats as that comes to; you may go about your business; we aint to be done, and that's the truth; we can smell a rat, though we can't see him; you don't come from the Post-office, it's all gammon; you are a precious goose."

"That's all you know about it," said I, in a huff, and I walked away; as I did so, I heard the laughter of the woman whom I had just been talking to.

This by no means increased my good humour. I had met with a rebuff when I least expected it—when, in fact, I thought I had acted with double cunning; and I returned home to replace my books, which had been so singularly useless to me on this present occasion; nay, they had brought ridicule down on me, which, though a simple matter, was annoying.

However, there was nothing to be done in that quarter I was convinced; and the possession of their names was of no consequence whatever, because the house was evidently one of a very questionable character, and, therefore, I could gain nothing there.

I will go at once to the very place I went to last night, and there reconnoitre, and endeavour to find out something that will at least give me a clue.

No sooner said than done. I left my home, having first taken the precaution of dressing myself as plainly as I could, so as not to attract any observation whatever, and then I made my way towards Oxford-street, and had the good fortune to get there in time to see the Watford coach and to obtain a place.

I mounted on the outside, and away we sped on the road until we arrived at Brent-bridge, and then we came in sight of a lane that ran to the right of the road.

"Well," said I, "coachman, this is the end of my journey."

"I thought you were going all the way, sir," he said.

"No; I told them I was going no farther than about six or seven miles from the Stone's-end."

"Very well, sir; I dare say it is all right."

"You may depend upon that," I replied, and I handed him his fare and a gratuity, and then pursued my way on foot until I came to the lane, and up I went and pursued it a wearisome way.

I thought that the distance was much less the night before, but I imagine the rate we travelled at made all the difference as to the supposed distance. I thought had either passed the place or had taken the wrong turning.

However, perseverance does many things, and presently I came to the first of my chalk-marks upon the trees and palings, which I had made the previous night.

"Oh, oh!" thought I, "then I have come upon it; at all events I am on the right scent. I must now be cautious, for I am near the fountain-head of all this mischief. I wonder what was the motive that caused the abduction, for certainly such it was, and I cannot believe anything else of it."

This was the thing to be found out, and so I obtained no answer from myself to my own question.

I now came to the spot where I had marked it with a cross, and where I had previously written my initials.

"This will do," I muttered, "this will do. I am here at last—there is no further toiling. I wonder where I can obtain any information respecting the inhabitants of that old house."

It was an old-fashioned place, built of what had been once red bricks, but which were now of a very dingy and weather-beaten appearance, and much of it was evidently built of wood.

It was an old place certainly; everything seemed to have run to decay—trees had been allowed to take their own shape, heedless of any desire upon the part of the tenants being manifested towards cultivating their luxuriant growth.

"To whom does this house belong?" I inquired of a countryman, who came by at the moment with his coat off.

"What! that ere house with the iron gates afore 'un, eh?"

"Yes," I said, "that is the house I mean."

"Well, then, I don't know."

I thought he had taken some trouble to make me know that he knew nothing about the house in question. However, he was gone, and I did not regret it, and there was a compensation in store for me. If he could or would say nothing, there was one who would, and that was a female.

"Can you tell me, my dear," I said, "to whom this large house belongs—that one with the iron gates to it?"

"No; I cannot tell you whom it belongs to," said the young woman; "it did belong to a family once, but that was many years ago, before I can remember."

"Indeed! and has it never had any owner since?"

"I don't know, sir, but there has been no one living in it these ten or fifteen years."

"When did these people come to live here?" I inquired; "for it is inhabited now you see," I said, pointing to the signs of its occupation, such as the blinds and smoke.

"Yes, sir, I know that, but these people have been here but a very few months at most; before they came it stood, I can't tell how long, quite empty and shut up."

"Then these are only tenants—do you know who they are?"

"That I do not know, sir."

"Can't you tell me what they are, or how many there are in that old house? It is a large place."

"We don't know anything about them hereabouts, sir; they never see or say anything to anybody. In fact, we see nobody but a man, a boy, and an old woman. There are other people, I believe, sir, but they are seldom seen—they come out late at night and are off early, or, if not, they are rarely seen."

"They are a strange set."

"Yes, they are, sir; nobody can get near the house, and even the servants won't say a word about them, being very close; indeed, we don't see anything of them but nobody thinks well of them about here—why, I can't say."

"Thank you," said I; "I wish you a good day: by the way, they have a large garden; at least I suppose so."

"They have, sir, and that wall you see is the wall of their garden; if you walk round you will see its extent. Ah! there is the boy coming out of the house."

" Good day," said I ; " I am much obliged to you."

" Good day," said the young woman, and she walked on.   I turned towards the boy who was coming towards me; he looked very red in the face, and seemed to have been much disturbed about the headand ears, as if he had been rather roughly used.

" Well, my lad, can you tell me the name of that house?" said I, pointing to the one he had just come out of.

" There's no name to it as I knows on," said the boy, rubbing his ears very hard.

" What's the matter with your ears?" I inquired.   " Has anybody been pulling them? they look quite red."

" No, not pulling them—a great deal worse nor that, sir. Our groom, curse him has given me two or three knocks on the head with a stick, and I won't stand it.

No. 19.

" Well, I should think not ; that is too much to put up with.   You are are big enough to be a groom yourself,"

" So I am," said the boy ; " but master pays good wages, and we don't like to leave a good birth, only I wish I could serve our groom out ; he's as cursed proud as he can be, but he's been here with master many years."

" Who is your master ?"

" Mister Beechy ; but there's more an that as belongs to his name, I know, besides, he don't live here, he only comes here now and then."

" Does he keep much company ?"

" I'll be bound he does at home, but he don't do so here ; he only keeps the house for—for—"

" Ay, for a lady, I suppose."

" Well, I suppose it is," said the boy, " for I can't see what use else it is ; for to be sure there was one brought last night but I haven't seen much of her, nor will they let me if they can help it."

" And why should they not like you to see her ? Surely you would do no harm ?"

" I should think not ; but I could see her when I liked, and they none the wiser for that, because I know where they have stowed her in the old house, and I know every nook and corner, and they don't."

" Do you, indeed," said I.

" Yes," said he, " I do. I'll lay a wager that I could get over the house and they be none the wiser."

" Well," said I, " I should much like to see this house and the lady too. I'm fond of making drawings and looking at old buildings ; do you think you could show me over ?"

" No," said the boy.

" Not for a couple of crowns ?" said I, holding up half a sovereign. " I don't care about being seen by any one, and should have no objection to creep into a loft or a coal-hole, or any place where one may not be seen."

" Don't you ?" said the boy, " then I'll show you over ; but you had better come by and by to the gate—my governor and his groom will be gone then, and there will be only the old woman in, and we shall have but little difficulty in going over the place."

" But the visitor—will she go away with them ?'

" Oh ! no."

" I will be with you in an hour then," said I.

" In two will be better," said the boy ; " they wont be out in one, come in two, and I shall be sure to be ready for you. Stop a little way on this side of the gate."

" I will do so," said I, and away I went without looking behind me, lest there should be any lurking suspicion in the boy's mind. I walked some distance, and came to a small ale-house, where I walked in and had some ale.

" Do you know anything of yonder old house ?" I inquired of the man who brought the ale to me.

" What, the house on the left hand down the lane ?"

" Yes.'"

" No, I don't ; it was empty many years, but some strangers have taken it."

" They appear a queer set," said I.

" Yes," he replied, " they are as far as I have seen on 'em, which isn't much, there don't seem to be many."

" Indeed, any females ?"

" There is one or two now and then," said the man, " but they either run away, or are sent away. I don't know what's the meaning of it at all—it's funny."

" Funny indeed," replied I. " I have some suspicion that there must be something wrong about the place."

" Don't know anything about the place, which I reckon might be good enough if they were to make it so ; it lies more with the people than the place."

" That is right enough," said I. " Do you know their names ?"

"No, but I have heard the name of Beechy made use of, but I don't know who it belongs to."

"I met a boy coming out there, and he told me there was a female visitor came there last evening."

"I dare say some one after the same fashion as before, who was glad enough to run away and seek protection here."

"Did they do so ?"

"It is a fact. A very beautiful young woman came out of the place and came here ; we sent her to town to her friends, and lent her money, which was returned to us afterwards."

"What did they say about it ?" I inquired.

"Nothing at all, sir, nothing at all. They knew very well that the least said was soonest mended, and they were wise enough to hold their tongues."

"I wonder the young lady's friends said nothing about the matter, and took no steps towards punishing them."

"I don't know how that was, sir ; but there may be more behind than we know of ; they may have done something, or have effected some fiction which we know nothing about, and which we never may."

"Very true," said I ; "I should like to ascertain where this young lady is, for something convinces me she has been carried there by force, and against her will."

"Very likely, sir ; but there is but little chance of doing that, the front gates are always locked, and you can be seen from the house when you ring the bell, so they can observe you well, and, if they think proper, refuse to answer it."

"So they may ; but I will endeavour to unmask them, if it be at all possible," said I.

"Well, you have my good wishes, I can assure you," said the man, "whatever happens, you may depend upon it, they will be ashamed to face it out."

*　　　*　　　*　　　*　　　*

I stopped for about an hour, and at the end of that time, I left the ale-house, and proceeded towards the house, and reached the garden-gate in time, for the boy had just opened it, and was looking about.

"Oh, here you are," said the boy ; "come in, they are just off. You'll find the old house full of all sorts of holes and corners, and if you are fond of them things, you'll have enough of them here, I think."

I entered the garden. It was a large place, but a perfect wilderness, and could be made a fine place of. It had capabilities, but they were lost.

"Keep under the trees," said the boy, "or you will be seen by that old cat—her eyes are everywhere ; the govenor and Joe are gone to town or elsewhere."

"Then you are alone ?"

"Yes ; I and the old woman."

"I see ; well, I'll keep out of her sight, and then we shall be all right enough. Is she fond of ale ?"

"She just is. She'd drink a pailful if you'd let her."

"Well, then, will you get some ? I'll give you some money ; you can say you'll pay for it, and that will employ her, so she will be out of the way, and we shall have no chance of being disturbed by her."

"Capital !" said the boy, who snapped at the idea as a funny one. "She will get so precious drunk that there'll be such a blessed row when they come home. I'll get the ale, and not tell her anything about it, and then she can't split upon me ; you stop here."

"No ; put me in safety in the house—why, if she come in the garden, I am sure to be seen."

"Aye, so you might ; well, tread lightly, and keep under the shade of the trees."

Following the boy's instructions I reached a kind of shed, into which I crept and then out at the top, and into a window where there was no sash, and then into the house.

"This," said the boy, "is one half of the house, which does not properly belong to the occupier, its a sort of double house; however, no lady ever comes here—they can't, the doors are all locked up, and so you are safe."

"Here is the money," said I, handing him half-a-crown; "leave the ale wherever you think best."

The boy gave me a knowing look, and then left the place in search of the ale, which, I was pretty sure, could not be procured in less than quarter of an hour at the least.

I immediately set about piloting my way from room to room, in the hope I should be able to effect something by the time he came back with the ale, which could not be immediately.

I walked cautiously from room to room without any let or hindrance whatever, until I entered one that was upon the second floor, and after a few moments I heard a deep sigh so close, yet so indistinct, that I could not account for it at all.

I looked about, but saw nothing; but presently I heard a light footstep cross the floor; this was in the next room—I was sure of it. There was a door which opened into it, and I found, upon trial, it was locked.

On looking round with an air of disappointment, I perceived the key hanging up above the door.

This will do, I thought, and immediately I took it down and gently opened the door, and then I saw a young female kneeling down by the side of the bed, as if in the act of prayer. I saw not her face, but she appeared eminently beautiful from the impression I received in only a momentary glance of the side face.

I entered the room, and I suppose, the noise of my footsteps alarmed her, for she arose in haste.

"Mercy!" she said, "mercy! have pity on me!"

"Hush! my dear young lady," I said, "hush! I am here by stealth, and unknown. Tell me what is it that ails you, and whom do you fear most? Be calm; I am your friend, if you need one, though I am a stranger to you."

"Oh! any one, however great a stranger, is a friend before the wretches of this house. If I remain here I am undone, and what to do I know not."

"Quit the house by stealth, and return to your friends."

"I have been threatened with such dreadful vengeance if ever I stepped outside the door, without their knowledge and consent, but to stay is destruction."

"You can escape if you will. Where have you come from?"

"They have kidnapped me away from my father's, through the instrumentality, I am sure, of Madame Milliere, the dressmaker; but I have only my own conviction to satisfy any one on that head, but I would my brother knew my situation."

"Why not come away at once?"

"I dare not."

"You dare not! What am I to understand by that?" inquired I, with some amazement. "Not dare, when there is no one to stretch out a finger against you?"

"I know it; but I have taken a solemn oath not to move or attempt an escape even from this room, to procure a few days' delay in the dreadful fate that awaits me."

"And you will not quit the house on that account then?" I said.

"I could not break such a dreadful oath; but, oh! sir, if you really be a friend to the unfortunate, inform my parents of my situation, and tell them what peril I am placed in. I would sooner die than submit to such a fate as that which seems to await me. Tell them they cannot come too fast to save their daughter—another night, and I am undone for ever."

"I will do what you desire," I replied. "Tell me who are your parents and where you live?"

"There is one of my father's cards, sir. I happened to have it in my pocket. My name is Amelia Beale, and as you see my father s a grocer and he sees many of the great people."

" Have you any knowledge of these people?"

" Nothing. That I have seen him on one or two occasions and he has addressed me with improper familiarity and I have resented it. But one evening I was watched, and when not far from Hyde-park Corner, I was seized and hurried into house where I was detained for a day and a night, I then was brought here, from which place God deliver me !"

" Have you any suspicion whether these people are only ordinary people, or he a man of rank ?"

" I think the latter—the usual course would hardly do against them ; it must be a force they cannot resist. But hark ! some one approaches, who can it be?"

" It is only the boy ; but I know enough. I will shut the door and meet him below and prevent his coming up."

I bade her be of good cheer and rest assured I would see her friends; and then I made the best of my way down to the floor below, and there I met the boy, who made a knowing grin, as he said :—

" I have just seen her dip her nose into the jug, and she won't give over very soon—her thirst always lasts while there is anything to drink and something beyond it."

That will do then. I have been up stairs; it does not contain much, so as the old house is filled with queer-shaped rooms there is more to see here."

" Well, there is to be sure more down stairs than up ; but it is just as you please—well, we can go down stairs now, since the old woman is in the front kitchen."

We descended the stairs and walked over many old rooms filled with dust and dirt—cobwebs there were in abundance ; and when I thought I could do so without exciting any surprise I intimated my wish to quit the house.

" I will not run any risk longer," I said ; " I have seen all I can see at this moment, but will do so again if you will let me into the house."

" Oh yes," said the boy ; " but I haven't got the half sovereign yet."

" Well, then, there it is," said I ; " and keep your own counsel and you may earn more crowns if you are careful."

The boy received the money with great glee, and led the way into the garden precisely as we had entered it, and then we walked down the path at a rapid rate taking as little heed as we had before been cautious in our approach ; but the fact was the old woman's love of ale made all the difference.

I got out of the garden by the door at which I entered ; then once clear of the house, I began my journey towards town at as rapid a rate as it was possible.

" I will see them immediately I get to London," I muttered to myself, " and then I will accompany them back to the spot and point out the very room in which she is placed."

I walked very fast to the Edgeware-road, and when I got there I was vexed to find there was nothing in sight in the shape of conveyance, and I had to walk, which I did, until I got to Brent-bridge, and then on looking back I saw a coach coming up.

Fortunately there was a place for one, and I mounted the roof, and we came merrily enough to town, and when I arrived at Hyde-park Corner I got down and began to search for the house of the parents of the unfortunate young lady whom I had seen in such a predicament of peril and distress.

After some little delay I found them out—a quiet and respectable-looking place, one in which people might live who had a good income; and by the appearance of it I should imagine they had a very decent property by them. It was one of those quiet, respectable shops in which there is nothing to catch the eye.

I entered the shop. The name was over the door—Beale was the name, and I was satisfied I was right. There was a shopman ; I applied myself to him.

" Is Mr. Beale within ?"

" Yes, sir, he is ; but not to be seen ; he is engaged."

" Has he not lost a daughter lately ?"

" Yes, he has," replied the shopman.

" Then tell him I have some news to communicate concerning her ; he will see me, I dare say."

" He will, you may depend upon that," said the shopman, and he immediately disappeared at a door, from which he soon after emerged into the shop, saying as he did so,—

" Will you step in this way, sir ?" keeping the door he came through open.

I walked through and entered a small parlour, where I saw a family evidently in great distress, for the whole of them had been, and, it may be said, were still weeping.

Mr. Beale had suffered much, as might be seen ; and there might be seen occasionally to betray an agitation he endeavoured to stay ; but nature was too strong for him, and the father would get the better of the man.

Mrs. Beale was weeping violently, and the children were in a state not far removed from that.

" You wished to speak to me," said Mr. Beale, " I believe, about my daughter, I think my shopman tells me, do you not ?"

" I do," said I ; " you have a daughter named Amelia Beale, have you not ?"

" I have or had, Heaven knows which is correct ; she has disappeared suddenly from us, and we know nothing of the cause or the means of such disappearance."

" You will be somewhat amazed as to the means by which I have become acquainted with the place of her detention ; but such is the fact ; it is about eight or nine miles from here."

" And has she been forced away or beguiled from her home ?"

" Forced away."

" I knew she would never have left her home purposely," said the mother ; " she only went out a short distance, and she has been forced away, and now she wants her father's aid."

" That is exactly the state of the case," I replied. " I saw some one hurried out of a house into a cab, muffled up, and evidently constrained, so that I was induced to follow the cab, and found where it went to ; and to-day I obtained admittance to the house ; I saw your daughter, and she requested me to obtain your aid. She dared not come when I saw her, because, to avoid some cruelty at the moment, she had taken an oath not to escape.'

" Poor child ! poor child !" said the mother.

" What had I better do ?' said Mr. Beale. " Go there and force the door and take her away by main force ?"

" I should recommend," said I, " immediate application to a magistrate for a warrant and proper officers. I will accompany you and tell them of what I observed, and my opinion decidedly is, that it is not safe she should be permitted to remain there any longer—another night and she may be ruined."

" Good God !" exclaimed the father, " you kill me with your intelligence, but come ; I am obliged to for your kindness—but come with me to Bow-street, we may be too late for the office, and we may be defied at this place."

" We have time enough," I remarked ; " but none to waste—we will go at once, if you please."

Mr. Beale seized his hat, and having placed it on his head, we both sallied out to make our way towards the office. In going along I told him all that had happened from the first to the last, which completely astonished the good man, who could not very well understand my motives in following up an adventure of this kind.

We now arrived at Bow-street and entered the police-office, where we were fortunate enough to find a magistrate sitting with nothing going on in court save newspaper reading, of which a very great deal usually takes place.

The application was made, and a warrant immediately granted.

" Do you apprehend much resistance to the warrant," inquired the magistrate.

" I cannot say I do," I replied, " but it will be a difficult thing to obtain-admission to so large and strong a place without something like force, for though they may refrain from offering any decided and positive resistance, yet they may oppose the progress of an officer by strong doors and iron gates."

"Then what do you consider sufficient force?"

"Two officers." I replied.

"Then you had better have two, and they must go at once, and endeavour to bring the young lady away by main force. This, of course, can be done."

With the aid of the two officers, the father and myself thought it must be bad, indeed, if we cannot accomplish our object in despite of two men, an old woman, and a boy.

"Now," said I, "the best thing we can do will be to take a coach down there, so that we can bring the young lady away with us, without trusting to any conveyance on the road, which are very few, and those few may be occupied, and no room left for a chance passenger."

We took a coach, and then rattled down the road, our lumbering machine making considerable progress, and raising a dust, too, as we rolled along.

"Well," said I, "here is Brent-bridge : another mile over, and we shall be there."

"Is it on the main road?" inquired one of the officers.

"Oh, no, we shall turn up the first road; and run up some distance, before we get there; it is very retired and quiet indeed; there is no other house near at hand."

"Just the place for such purposes."

"It is indeed; a cry for help in such a house would not be heard outside the walls; for there is a long walk with broad iron gates to prevent you going up there by accident, so that no cry could reach you."

"It is just the place," said the officer; "is this the turning."

"Yes," said I; and at that moment we turned up the lane towards the house; "we shall not be long before we are there; would you believe it that people could kidnap others in London streets, and yet carry them off with impunity?"

"Yes, I can, because I have known it to be done," said one of the officers; "I have known more than one instance of it; and even murder has been done, too."

"But found out?"

"Yes, the same as this has been found out; but not before it has been done."

"Would you have the coach drive up to the door?" I inquired, "or would you have it stop before you get there?"

"Before you get there," said the officer; "they need not know how many of us there are."

"I think myself it will be the better plan," I replied, "for there will be no preparation, and gives us an advantage. We will pull up here, then, for we have not fifty yards beyond the next turning." I pulled the check-string, and the driver drew up by the side of the pathway.

We all got out and walked on until we came to the gate, and then we paused.

"Now," said I, "it is a question as to the propriety of getting in at this side; there is a garden wall down below, where we may get over. A part of us can go round and get over, and let the remainder get in in the front of the house."

"Well," said the officer, "you and one of us can go in at that side, and the other two can wait for you, and you can let us in at the other entrance."

To this arrangement we all at once agreed, and away I went with one of the officers, until I came to the door in the wall, against which we set our shoulders, and in a very short time we had thrust it open and walked into the garden, and then into the house.

"Now," said I, "we may as well go in the way I went before, and get to the young lady's room without creating any alarm."

This was agreed to, and we got into the same room in which I had before been in, and then I opened the door. She was seated with her hands clasped and listening. She started, but, on perceiving me with another person, she exclaimed,—

"Oh! thank Heaven, you are come; they are below—I can hear their voices they will be here presently."

"Cannot we open this door?"

"No, it is locked."

"Well, then, we can descend here and get into the lower part of the house; take my arm : your father is in front, and when we get down we can let him in."

"My father! Heaven be praised! I shall be once again safe then. I did not expect this."

She took my arm and we walked out of the room, and descended to the ground floor, where, as we were passing the parlour, the door was suddenly thrown open.

A man immediately stepped out, and demanded what we wanted there?

"We want to get out."

"What was the reason of your getting in?"

"I merely called for this young lady, sir," said I; she is under my protection, and I shall only deliver her into the hands of her father, who will see what remedy he can take."

"Then I will see who you are, before you do," her gaoler said; "you shall be thoroughly well beaten before you go, and then pumped upon by my people."

At that moment there came a tremendous knock at the door, which made oth myself and him start; my companion opened the door, and in came her father.

"Amelia," he said, "Amelia, my dear child, are you safe—are you really here?"

"Father! father!" said the girl, and she was immediately in her father's arms, and had fainted away.

"Some water—water," shouted the father, and one officer went below and brought up some water, which was given her; the stranger standing in the hall, which was occupied by all the persons in the house.

"Who is the occupier of this house," I inquired, as I saw she was recovering; "who is master here—are you?"

I spoke to a tall, stout man, who had stood still and watched the whole scene which had been going on before his eyes, without a word being uttered.

"Well, and what do you do here? You are all intruders—get out, else I must use what force I can, and you may take the consequences upon your own shoulders."

"Stop, sir," said the officer; "I have a search warrant, and we are officers, we have a legal right here. I do not know, if, under the circumstances, I ought not to take you into custody, for your share in this deed of violence."

"Do you know who I am, fellow?"

"No, nor do I much care who you are; but I shall soon find out when I get you to Bow-street. You are, I dare say, known in the neighbourhood."

"Ha! ha!" laughed the stranger, "I am known, but no matter. This has been a failure—the girl is coy and she has given me much trouble. But you must get out of this place as fast as you can, and as for the young lady, you have no business with her. Leave her here."

"She is my daughter, monster, but you shall be punished for this. Officer, that is the criminal, take him into custody, I will have him punished."

"You had better leave the house before I have any farther provocation to have you roughly handled."

As he spoke he stepped back into the parlour and locked the door after him, so that we could not reach him, save after breaking the door open.

I could not but notice the coolness and contempt with which he looked upon the whole scene, and, I doubt not, that had there been more people by him, he would have rescued the girl from us; but we could have bound them hand and foot in a few moments, and he was, probably, well aware of that, for the officers were strong men.

Discretion was the better part of valour, and he left us to ourselves, and seeing nobody nigh we vacated the house and moved towards the coach, which was in waiting.

"My dear Amelia," said her father; "who was that man who spoke to us?"

"He is one whom I have met about in the neighbourhood of our house, and I am sure he must have been one of those who seized me and carried me away. I am sure he is some one of consequence by his manners."

"He is one of the dukes," said the officer; "else I should have taken him into custody."

"What! one of the dukes! what duke?"

" No matter," said the officer, " I cannot say more now ; I am forbidden."

This was news to us, but I returned with Mr. Beale and his daughter to their home, and was present at the meeting between mother and daughter, which was exceedingly affecting, and made me forget all the trouble I had to secure such a termination to such an adventure as this was.

No. 20.

CHAPTER XVI.

MY ADVENTURE IN THE STRAND.—THE TWO DEATHS.

I TRUST that my readers have hitherto been well pleased with the results of my various adventures ; I trust that from time to time, as I have detailed the various moving accidents that befel me, they have looked forward with some anticipation of pleasure to a denouement which should be gratifying to their feelings, and show that at all events, in some of the concerns of life a poetical justice is administered, and to use the language of a theatrical play-bill, virtue is triumphant and vice stultified.

But we cannot always expect these gratifying results—human life is but an April day, mixed of sunshine and of tears, and it is one of the evils of a highly artificial and civilized state of society, that greater individual injustices are committed than in a more barbarous state.

Man, as he advances in knowledge, and those refinements of intellect which make him feel what he is and what he ought to be, will no longer be governed by arbitrary dicta uttered by an individual, but he will have laws understood, or presumed to be understood, by the whole community, so that the path of a man's social duties shall be more defined than it can be under those circumstances when one person judges according to his sensations of right or wrong.

Now the great evil of this in individual cases, and the great argument in favor of arbitrary government, is, that legislation can never be sufficiently minute to meet all the cases which will arise in society, but that the arbitrary decree of an individual can search carefully into those minutiæ, and correct a thousand minor evils which the most enlightened legislature is unable to grapple with, for fear of intruding too much upon the liberty of the subject.

But do not let us suppose for a moment that in calling attention to this truth, we in any way put forth an argument for despotism. No ; we may point out an evil in any institution which in itself is commendable, and yet say nothing against that institution which we might expend our best heart's blood to perpetuate.

It says nothing really against the majesty of beauty to assert with a sigh that it is a dangerous gift, frequently abused by its possessor, and more frequently rendered an excuse for a kind of persecution which says little for the honor or the integrity of human nature ; but we are not to fly to ugliness and deformity because the possession of beauty is a gift which has produced dissentions and unhappiness, and by a purity of reasoning we are not to condemn our once free institutions because the law has been sometimes likened to a net, which while it will catch a large offender, lets a host of minor delinquents escape its meshes.

It will be found in the course of my adventures that I am a knight-errant of the modern times ; I have been enabled occasionally, to my own great satisfaction and pleasure, to achieve results which no written law could possibly reach.

And although it may be told me that we have proceecings in equity in this country as well as at law ; let not anyone affect to be so profoundly ignorant of what equity is, as to suppose that the tribunal of Chancery is a judgment-seat from whence shall flow words of consolation and of protection to oppressed poverty against arrogant wealth.

No, our court of Chancery, so far as equity proceedings are concerned, is deciding whether A be entitled to so many pounds, shillings, and pence, or B, may be all very well, setting aside some of its minor abuses ; such as the great cost entailed in putting it in motion, &c. but it interferes with nothing else. . Property is protected ; but morals—the feelings—the heart's dearest and best sensations, may wander loosely upon the wide world and find no champion.

In the incident which I am about to relate, although it is not strikingly illustrative of the remarks which I have just made, the reader will perceive how the highest an the noblest feelings may find a home in a lonely room, and be exposed to the greatest of temptations. Natural sensations of honour, and high integrity of purpose, will maintain a fine spirit through them.

It is but an incident, and one which we must look to more as descriptive of feeling than of action ; but still it is one with which, we think, our readers will sympathise, and one which at the time made a deep impression upon me.

Without further preface, then, I shall proceed to the relation of what affected me considerably, and awakened a train of reflections which I have endeavoured but weakly, I fear, to shadow forth in the few preceding paragraphs. But if they should become data and material for thinking to my enlightened readers who have more time than myself to enter into such abstraction. I shall not regret having indulged in this digression.

There is what is termed gaiety in the metropolis after dark, and that gaiety increases almost *ad libitum* until after midnight, and it goes on diminishing in the numbers of those who partook of it, but increasing in strength, and in many instances it becomes furious and uproarious, ending often enough in the cells of a station-house.

However, they who look closely and calmly into the promoters of this gaiety, few have found that it is not always the genuine exuberances of either youth or spirits. Old age, as well as sorrow, drive their votaries to these places of midnight resort; and while there they can by a false glare conceal from themselves the misery and wretchedness they feel at home.

Many of those who help to give a lustre to the hour and gaiety of the place do so only from necessity. It is well known that many a smiling face carries an aching heart, and very few are they who enjoy such pleasures unalloyed with bitter after thought.

There may be some who can enjoy the passing hour and receive no taint from such contact, in which they are obliged to come with characters and habits peculiar to such places. These few are rare ; but for them how many are there who, instead of tasting or gently sipping from the cup of pleasure, drink to the very dregs.

The man of the world who can pass through all the different scenes of a great city may have something to boast of; something he can talk about; recollections that may seem to guide the young and inexperienced with : but he who has fallen into excess only looks back upon the past with sorrow and regret, for he has everything to repent of—for what he then saw and felt he has now sorrows in abundance.

But of all those who suffer sorrow, and at the same time appear gay ; who hide a sorrowful heart under a gay exterior, there are some, perhaps, who sink more rapidly, and suffer more, than those whose occupation, unfortunately, calls them to minister to the wants and pleasures of others.

I have repeatedly had occasion to see and know this to be a fact, and one that is pretty well known—I may say for that unfortunate class it is too well known—it is a truth of which they are the living proof, to be pointed at any hour one may question it.

Enter what place you may, and you will find some gay-looking person who aids to give the place some of its pleasures, and could you wring from them the truth you would find they loathed their present mode of life so strongly that, had they the power, they would have left it any time, but cannot.

One evening as I passed down the Strand I had some such notions as these floating through my mind, when I saw two females turn out of a court, and walk a little way before me, they were both rather showily clad and jauntily set off, one much more so than the other, both in dress and manner.

There seemed to be more of a difference between them than would at first sight appear. They appeared to be well acquainted with each other, but of very different dispositions.

" If I were you, Margaret," said one, " I should not trouble myself about them. I should try and make a good thing for myself: they will cripple you all your life."

" My life is not a very pleasant prospect," said the other girl, in reply.

" Then why not make it so ? I would, I know. I never would or could be su
a simpleton as you are; why, as for daily labouring, and then at night si ngnrch
them ; why, I would see life and enjoy it."

" What ! and leave a poor mother to starve?"

" My mother got her own living; but if she didn't, I don't see why I should kill
myself to support her, especeially now that she is fit only for the hospital."

" Yes, that makes me more anxious than ever to do all I can for her ; for I fear,
poor thing, she will never survive many weeks ; and what to do for her burial,
Heaven alone knows; and how I am to work at all I cannot see]; sorrow and
labour go hand in hand ; and here am I no better than I was a twelvomonth ago."

" Nor ever will be ; why, if I had had your offer the other day, do you think I
would have refused it ? No, no, it isn't a handsome offer like that goes a begging ;
you don't like singing, you say ; and work is even worse."

" They give one nothing for it, I am sure; weeks and weeks have I worked for
the meanest trifle ; and, but for a few shillings I may make by singing at night, I
never could live."

" Then why such a simpleton as to refuse Mr. Smith's offer? I wish he would
give me the chance."

" No, no, I could not do it, even to save myself and dying mother from death
by starvation."

" Well, you are fonder of starvation than I am ; and there's nothing in life that
I wouldn't do to stop such an end to one's sufferings. I'd sooner drown myself.
And as to refusing Mr. Smith's offer—Lord bless me! ! I would fly to catch it.
And, after all, what is the odds? You have good' clothes 'to your back, you go
about and enjoy yourself, and who is to know how your money's earned ? nobody ;
and if they did, you have come by your money honestly, and what could they
say ?"

" That I had lost my character !"

" And who has a right to lose it, I should like to know? You may depend,
however, upon what I say—nobody loses their characters who can pay for what
they have and act honestly."

" Well, but one's old acquaintances would turn their backs upon one, you know,"
said Margaret.

" They might ; but what do they do for you now ?" inquired the other.

" Not much, to be sure ; and yet there are some whom one wish to be able to
meet with a clear conscience, and to be able to look them in the face."

" You may do that at any time."

" Not if one's heart tells one that one has oeen guilty. I must say that there
are those who would do me all the good they could if they knew I was so placed ;
but their means are limited, and I could not ask them, though I am sure I should
not ask in vain."

" Oh ! some sweetheart, I suppose?"

Margaret made no reply.

" I see how it is ; you have some silly notion of true love and all that stuff;
but it's all my eye, take my word for it. There's nobody will take you a lodging
and give you two pounds a-week and twenty pounds down. See if true love will
do that, and if it will, why then I admit true love is the love for my money."

There was a pause in the conversation, and I lost sight of them in a crowd of
persons who swarmed about. I endeavoured to find them out, but I could not.
They were lost entirely.

From the conversation I heard I felt persuaded they belonged to that class of
unfortunate persons who aid in the general amusements of town by lending their
voices at the taverns who have what is called a good night business.

Here they have rooms fitted up for the purpose, with a piano, and then they
hire a certain number of persons, who are called professionals, who sing songs
while the audience drink strong compounds of various kinds.

I came to one of these places where I heard the sounds of a piano being most industriously carried forward by the individual who presided at that instrument

After a few moments' hesitation, as to whether I should go up or go on elsewhere, I determined to go up stairs and spend an hour or so in search of adventure. I entered the house and paid my admission. There were very few persons present and there were but few of the professionals there.

I sat down, however, and having had a glass of brandy and water, I began to reflect upon the conversation I had overheard coming along, and regretted much that I had lost sight of the two young females who were so conversing.

It was evidently some young creature who had been cast upon the world by some unfortunate and fortuitous circumstances, such as she could not control. Her companion might, also, one day, be the same, but had now become vitiated by contact with the world, as all such must in the end.

Certainly, Margaret had preserved her virtue and her purity, which as a rare circumstance among people thrown into her class of life, and who had not only to support themselves but, as in her case, she had to support a dying mother.

I was just thinking that there were few such examples of excellence among people like her, placed in the midst of temptation, and were every act and thought of all others militated against her notions of rectitude and where hers were not only hard to be acted upon but where they were laughed at, produced nothing but distress and want, while the reverse brought ease and plenty for a time.

I was just thinking that I was sorry I had missed them, when the door opened and in walked the very two who were the subject of my thoughts, at that moment entered the room.

It was no easy matter to say which was Margaret or which was her companion. The latter was a strong girl, inclining to coarseness at the same time.

Margaret, on the other hand, was rather delicate, somewhat more than pretty, and yet her features where plain, good, and regular; it was only when lit up by her eye, or with a smile, that she appeared to advantage, to the full extent to what her features were capable of.

They sat still for a few minutes, both of them gazed around the room as if anxious to ascertain whether it was full or if they saw any one of the old faces that were in the habit of coming up to the rooms.

They came now and the room was rapidly filling. I could see, at times, there was a pensiveness steal over the face of Margaret, which she could not well conceal, even had she desired to do so, but it was at moments when she forgot the present and was wandering to her sad home, and the past.

What has she to think of, poor girl, thought I ; nothing that she can feel any pleasure in, for she has no pleasure, and her only consolation amid the afflictions she suffers is, she has preserved her integrity and her purity ; a rare boast.

The singing now began and one after another song was sung with plaudits, very decently indeed, and for such a class they were sung well. Margaret's singing was decidedly the best, not, perhaps, for such an audience. There was something so chaste and so pure in her singing that it would be judged, even among good judges, and her manners were, at the same time, so true to nature, that she won the good will of all who saw her.

After a time I changed my seat and went and sat beside her for the purpose of having some conversation with her. I saw she repulsed as gently as she could any of those attentions which were usually bestowed upon young persons at such places, while her companion appeared to enjoy and be pleased at such attention.

" You are very young to be at these places, my dear," said I, when I found she had time to attend to what I said.

" Misfortune does not respect age, sir," she replied.

" And how old are you ?"

" I was eighteen last December," she replied.

" Well, that is what I call very early, is it not ? And you speak of misfortune, too, surely you cannot have suffered much from that quarter beyond what is common."

"I hardly know sir, what is common, and seeing no two persons' cases are alike, and the nearest approach they can make is a similiarity—what more can be done?"

"Nothing," I said; "but do you mean to say you have seen much misfortune?—have you been driven to this mode of obtaining a livelihood by unavoidable events?"

"Most certainly I have."

"Have you a father?"

"I have not. I have lost him now nearly two years, and since then I have had misfortune enough; for I have been compelled to do what I never had occasion to do before."

"And what is that?"

"Earn my own bread. I never had occasion to do anything approaching to a day's work even in the house—but that time is past, the present is not like it; but while one can live, one must not complain of it, if it be ever so hard."

In some measure one ought not to do so certainly; but I do not ask you from any idle motive—have you no protector?"

"No, sir; and do not desire one," she said coolly.

"I did not mean anything of the kind; but are you living by yourself entirely," I inquired.

"Not at present, my mother lives with me."

"At present you say?"

"Yes, at present; for Heaven alone knows how soon she may be taken away from me."

"Is she so ill?"

"Yes, very ill, and has been so for some months, poor thing; it might seem a sin to ask her to live; but to part from my mother seems a greater misfortune than any I ever yet met with; but I feel painfully enough for her sufferings, and there must be a very speedy termination to them the doctor says."

"I am sorry to hear all this—is there anything in which I can aid you? I will, if I can, be of any service to you under such circumstances; you have only to say so."

It was near a minute before she made any reply, but seemed as if she were meditating upon what I said. At length she looked full in my face as she spoke, and saying—

"I do not know what may be your motives for this offer; but if you have any motives that are selfish, you have been unfortunate in the choice of your object."

"Believe me, I have none such; but you seem very suspicious, very suspicious, indeed. I hope I have said nothing that can justify you in having a bad opinion of me."

"No, sir, you have not; but you must pardon me for being cautious. I will tell you candidly I have had offers of aid before, but they did not spring from pure benevolence. You are a man of the world, and can understand me when I tell you that in such places as these it is not often one meets with a disinterested friend."

"I believe you are right," said I; "and your own heart will doubtless tell you how often is it that one meets with an object which is really worthy of such a friend."

"It is but just, sir, and yet it is hard for those who are borne upon by evils and misfortune, to be judged by the same standard as those who have none of these things."

"True again," replied I; "and to tell you a truth, I have heard your conversation as you came here to-night."

"What conversation, sir?"

"As you came here to-night I heard you and a female companion converse relative to some offers you have refused, and to the care you have taken of your aged mother."

"I recollect now, sir, we did say something about that."

" You did ; I heard her advice, and your opinions seemed to be of a class that is superior to such as that in which you now appear in."

" That can be of but little consequence, sir, to what I may be superior, and belonging to the class in which I am placed, and, at the same time, it is my duty to make the best of my situation."

" How, you refuse any assistance I can be to you ?"

" By no means, sir. My poor mother is in such a state that I cannot afford to do so. Should you really mean what you say in kindness, I shall ever be grateful to you."

" I will call upon, and see your mother to-morrow, if you will give me your address," said I.

" I will do so," she replied. At the same time she took a pencil from her pocket, and wrote the address upon a slip of paper, and handed it to me.

" There it is," she said ; " any time after ten in the morning, and before five o'clock in the evening, as of before and after those hours I am either out or attending to my home duties."

" You shall see me to-morrow," I replied.

* * * * * * *

I called the next morning about half-past eleven. It was at a chandler's shop where she lodged, in a back room at the top of the house on the second floor, for the house ran no higher.

The door stood ajar, and I knocked, but no answer came. I peeped in, and saw Margaret kneeling by a bed-side. I knocked again, and coughed, but I made no one hear. I then pushed the door open, but even this had no effect—all was still.

After pausing a few minutes, I walked in, and looked upon the bed, and there I beheld the corpse of a female, somewhat advanced in life. She was lying with her eyes open, as was her mouth. She had evidently died suddenly, or, rather, her death had been discovered suddenly by her unfortunate daughter, who had, no doubt, fainted, and fallen in the posture she was then in.

I could not forbear pausing and gazing upon them—they were both motionless !

" Poor thing ! poor thing !" I said to myself, " your suffering is over, but as for this young girl, why she has much to come ; the loss of her mother will be to her a source of great grief and sorrow—but for that her present life would have been much easier."

" But here am I," I thought, " moralising while the poor girl is in a swoon from which she may awake but to die, if proper remedies be not at hand for her recovery."

I left the room, and at once proceeded to the landlady's apartments—the shop and parlour.

" Do you know," said I, " your lodger in the two-pair back is dead ?"

" Dead ?" said the old woman, giving a start.

" Yes, quite."

" Good God ! and they owe me twelve and sixpence for rent ! Oh the wretch, to go out of the world without paying her rent ! What does she think she'll come to, the good-for-nothing creature ?"

" Well," but said I, " have you no care for the living ? for her unfortunate daughter ?"

" What ! is she dead too ?"

" Oh no," said I ; " not dead."

" What then ?" inquired the old beldame ; " what then—what then ?"

" Why she has fainted by the bedside of her mother and is there now, quite senseless."

" I think she must have been senseless at all times, else she would have done better than she has done, I am sure."

" That may yet be seen," said I, not liking the old woman's sneers ; " but if she have not aid, she will die of neglect in your house, and I will say so, if need be."

"And who's to pay me for what I do?"

"I will, you old hag"! I replied, in a great rage, for I really felt there was much to reprehend in the old woman's conduct.

"Oh! very well, it doesn't much matter what one does if one's paid for it."

"Well, then, make haste, or it will be of no use—she fainted, and may have been in that state for hours."

Urging the old woman on, I ran up stairs myself; and there the unfortunate female lay on the bed in the same state as before, while her daughter still remained by her bedside on her knees; the attitude of either might have been copied by an artist as a model of the death-bed scene of those who sink in poverty and wretchedness.

There were none of the solemnities which the rich find means of showing on such occasions. Poverty was imprinted upon every object around; at the same time there was an appearance of neatness and cleanliness in which the young girl lived.

"Come," said I, "take her up."

The old woman obeyed, she lifted her up and placed her in a chair; at the same time she exclaimed:—

"Why she is dead too! They are both on 'em hopped the twig."

"Good God! you cannot mean what you say," said I, and I went towards the unfortunate Margaret.

I looked at her—her eyes were almost protruding out of their sockets, and her mouth partially open; quite stiff and fixed. She had died no doubt in a fit of excessive grief. They were both buried in one grave—mother and daughter!

"Yes, one grave contained the bodies of both mother and daughter; and let us hope that those two souls, kindred in life and dear to each other, ascended together to Heaven, encircled with that glorious halo of immortality, which we may suppose to light the paths of the just from this sublunary and fading sphere, to those realms which are eternal—where the sun of joy never sets, and where the words grief and woe belong not to the vocabulary of articulate sounds.

And far happier was that young girl to have thus, even in the spring-tide of her life,

"Shuffled off her mortal coil;"

for a coil it is, and such a coil as those who know it most and know it best, most heartily wish to rid themselves of.

Her pure spirit had winged its flight to its native home from above; we will imagine it came to this world in one of those sweet missions of charity and love which, it is delightful to suppose, are undertaken by the gentlest of those heavenly hosts which in countless millions hover around the radiant throne of the Divinity.

It has often pleased me to imagine, when I see some fine young girl full of nature's best and holiest gifts, that even in her mortal guise she was something nearer akin to a better state than ordinary mortals; and when we have heard that the rude hand of death has crushed those early buds of beauty ere yet they had unfolded all their sweetness to the sun, it is melancholy, though pleasant, to fancy that they have completed their mission—that they have turned some wandering spirits from the downward path to realms of light and joy, and that having thus done Heaven's holy work, perchance amid poverty and all the squalor of absolute want, they rejoin the stars, exchanging that effervescent and mortal existence in which for a time they had clothed their purer, either for their own glorious home, where each word is music, and where eternal sunshine, the sunshine of the soul, is present.

Peace be to her who has induced us to enter into this train of reflections, and to wile away for a few short moments thoughts of earth—earthly by a contemplation of her existence.

CHAPTER XVII.

MY LAST ADVENTURE.

VARIOUS circumstances, with which I need not trouble my indulgent readers, began now to make me think that the daylight might be endured, and that possibly I might find a sufficient amount of happiness to chain me to the world, despite the sun shining upon it.

Probably my readers, from this slight exordium, may be tempted to set about guessing why it is that I begin to consider the daylight endurable, and that my housekeeper may be right in her strictures upon what she considered my unchris-tian manners and customs.

No. 21.

I have a strong suspicion that some of my fair readers, at all events, may have pretty shrewd thoughts upon the subject, and indeed, to repel the charge of inconsistency which otherwise might be brought against me, I am very glad to plead guilty to what I think they will guess to be the truth, viz., that there is a lady in the case.

Yes ; such is the fact. Somehow or another, about this period, I became acquainted with a certain Anna ——, the lady's surname is of little consequence to any but herself.

And so I was partly rallied, partly reasoned out of my night adventures, and that too, in the most insidious manner possible ; for first of all, a very wonderful amount of interest in them was affected.

After Anna and I understood each other a little, that is to say, I had given her a very candid opinion concerning her attractions, and had not by any means been turned out of doors in consequence, she pressed me very much to relate my most recent adventures.

One evening, therefore, I took with me what might be called my diary or log-book, and in pursuance of the invitation given and accepted, I professed my readiness to do the amiable, by reading some of the adventures therein contained.

This was acquiesced in, with the most amiable simplicity, and I quite pleased myself with the idea that I was making a convert to my opinion with regard to the attractions of the stilly hours of night.

Only consider, reader, for a man of my habits and accomplishments, what a very important thing it would have been, to have acquired a wife who would have acquiesced in my going to bed at breakfast-time, and getting up at eleven o'clock at night.

I certainly thought I had made a convert of Anna, and that the magic power of love had induced her to believe that night was day and day was night—provided the one object of her heart's best thoughts chose to think so likewise.

" I'm sure I shall be very much amused," said the little gipsy, as she seated herself in an attitude to listen ; " I'm sure I shall be quite delighted."

" Well, I hope so," was the reply ; " and it really is something to have found a sensible girl who is so completely of one's own way of thinking."

This compliment was received with a very gracious smile and I certainly thought I was getting on famously—I thought, with a degree of pardonable triumph, of how signal would be the defeat of my old housekeeper, when she should find that I had actually got a wife who did not disapprove of my night adventures, although she had often declared, that if I were to search the world through, I should not find such an individual.

Yet, here was one of the most charming girls it had ever been my lot to encounter, ready to link her fate with mine, I was quite sure, upon any reasonable notice being given her.

" Why don't you begin ?" said Anna ; " I am waiting for your night adventures."

Having thus received this most gracious persuasion, I commenced as follows :—

Walking down Harley-street one night—it was at that dull hour in the evening when few are about—thinking that there were few who strolled about for the same purpose, with the same ultimate object as myself, when my attention was attracted to the figure of a man, dressed in a long cloak, who appeared to be stealing along as if desirous of avoiding observation, with an evident desire of being unseen, and escaping from any one who gazed at him. He often looked round and stopped.

" What could he mean ?" I thought to myself, " no good, surely ; an honest man need not be so cautious ; his purpose is not mere gallantry, for in that case he would not be sneaking along the streets in such a manner as he is."

Convinced that something strange was about to be perpetrated, perhaps some evil deed—a good one would not require so much caution—I was determined that I would watch his motions and ascertain what it was that he was slinking about for; and why a man of his appearance was desirous of avoiding observation, as he evidently was endeavouring to do.

I therefore kept myself close to some area railings, so that where he was he could not see me very easily; while he was waiting thus, I saw him turn round, and believing he was not seen, he eyed, very carefully, the whole street; there was no one in it, save myself and the man in the cloak, at least, not within sight; and having done so, he hurried on for about fifty yards, and then turned up to the right; I immediately ran after him, and got there just in time to see him pass beneath the light of a lamp, and then hasten into a doorway.

After that I ran up as quickly as I could, and got into a door way as speedily as possible, and watched his movements to see what he was so intent upon doing. After about a minute, during which he looked carefully round, and yet he did not see me, he examined the door and the number, and then drew from his pocket a letter, after looking at which, he placed it beneath the doorway, and then left with much speed.

I ran away after him for some distance, until I saw him slacken his speed, then I did so too, but there was no pause; he continued his course through several streets, until he stopped at a house—a lodging-house—not far from Great Titchfield-street, where he paused, and entered a door, which he opened by means of a latch key.

The door was closed as I got up to it; I went up and took the number. I should know it again, I thought—there can be no doubt—but I tell you, my good friend, I instantly uttered to myself, I am convinced there has been something more than ought to have been done.

However, I could not make anything of what I had seen, and put it down as a case in which I could do nothing, and in which I had made no discovery, only a bare fact had come to my knowledge, which was merely this :—I had seen a certain individual put a letter under a certain door, and then go away and enter another house in another street.

Now, it is certain there were peculiar suspicious circumstances attending the whole transaction, and which I had noticed. These circumstances, indeed, were the only reason for my attention being attracted to the occurrence at all.

I thought it was a thing to be remembered, and which might some day or other turn up, and become an affair in which I might find some account in pursuing. At all events, if it died off, as it was very like to do, it would be of no consequence to me; as an absence of men and things, it would be neither a matter of pleasure nor regret.

There are many thousand little things in life which, taken of themselves, are essential and singular, but which are capable of instant and easy explanation; but taken of themselves, and accompanied by the many mysterious odds and ends of conduct, by which people surround them, they look strange indeed.

"Well," thought I, "I will dismiss this from my heart, and proceed to other matters, which are more prolific in incident."

*   *   *   *

About a week afterwards I entered a coffee-house at the West-end. I had been out late, and had, in fact, not been in bed the whole night; daylight had surprised me before I got home, and I determined to breakfast at an early house, thinking I should there meet with characters and incidents that might amuse me, or give food for future reflection.

I entered the rooms, and sat down in a seat which was unoccupied, and, for a few moments, gazed about me, and examined the place.

There were several boxes, which were about half-filled with substantial-looking people, such as those connected with the markets—salesmen of various sorts.

"Can you oblige me with the *Times* of this morning?" I asked of the damsel who waited upon this miscellaneous assemblage.

"Yes, sir, certainly;" she replied, and went away in search of it. In about five minutes more she returned, saying,—

"I have engaged it for you, sir; but here is yesterday's."

"Thank you," said I, "that will do for the present."

I was left alone, and began to turn the paper over to discover if there was anything that had escaped my observation on the preceding day, and, as is usual in such cases, having exhausted the body of the paper, I examined the advertisements, as a last resort.

"What have we here?" I exclaimed, as I ran my eye over the papers; "what have we here? plenty of ' Wants' as usual."

I turned my eyes to the first column, and there I saw plenty of shipping announcements—the second column began with rewards for things lost—on another I accidentally cast my eye, and then I became more deeply interested in one which had caught my eye, and the more I read, the more intense my interest became.

"This is strange," I muttered, as I read the advertisement through, " very strange—something will come of it, after all."

The advertisement ran as follows :—

"Fifty pounds reward. Whoever will give information respecting the writer of an anonymous letter, left at number ——, Harley-street, on ——, will receive the above reward. Any person giving any information, so as to bring the writer to light, will receive the thanks and gratitude of a respectable family. It is earnestly requested that this may induce some one to come forward, and in the event of any doing so, who has been an accomplice, will be free from any danger, save the concoction of the vile slander—any expense that may be incurred will be cheerfully paid.

"Address Smith and Mason, Howland-street, Tottenham-court-road."

"Well," said I, "this must be attended to ; I will go there myself this morning. Something has been done that cannot be easily explained. Little does the culprit imagine he is so near detection."

I partook of my breakfast and left the coffee-shop, and then made the best of my way to Howland-street. During my progress I could not but employ my mind upon the probable result of my communication.

After about half an hour's walk I found myself in Howland-street, and at once found out the office and residence of Mr. Smith. I rang the office bell, and was let in by the door opening by means of a bell-pull from the interior of the office; I walked in, and found several clerks there sitting round their desks, but not busily employed—in fact, they were thinking of the day's work, not beginning it.

"Is Mr. Smith in ?" I inquired of a pale-faced young man.

"He is in, sir," replied the man, "but he's not yet down."

"Will he be long ?"

"He has not yet breakfasted," he replied; "he is seldom down before ten o'clock, that is, in his office."

"And now it is just after nine ?"

"About twenty minutes," replied the young man ; "if you please to inform me of your business, I may be able to inform you of anything you wish to know."

"You cannot do that well," said I ; "this is my card—I wish to see Mr. Smith upon some important business."

"Very well, sir, I will take your card."

He did so, and retired to some other part of the house, while I sat down near the door to await his return. He was not gone long ; when he returned, he said to me in a civil voice,—

"If you will wait a few minutes, Mr. Smith will see you."

"Very well," I said, " I have not much time to spare, and if Mr. Smith exhausts it, I cannot wait to have the interview."

"He will not be long, sir," replied the clerk, civilly.

"Can you inform me," I said, after a short pause, "what is the meaning of the affair that has taken place in Harley-street. There has been an anonymous letter left there, and an advertisement has been inserted in the *Times ?*"

"Oh, yes, there has, sir."

"Can you inform me anything about it ?"

"I cannot, sir."

"Then I presume I must wait as long as I can."

"Is that the business upon which you wish to see Mr. Smith?"

"Yes, it is."

"I will go and inform him again," said the young man; "I know that he is particularly anxious about that affair. The fact is, sir, unless the business is important, Mr. Smith will not be seen out of business hours."

"Very well," I said, "tell him I have some communication to make respecting that matter, and the sooner he can see me the better."

"I will do so," said the young man, and he again left me. I thought there was a great deal of trouble to see an attorney, but I supposed he was well to do, and therefore he had it in his power to ape West-end airs. However, the business I had mentioned acted as a charm, and I was shown into his office.

"Be seated, sir," said Mr. Smith, civilly; "you have some communication, I believe, to make to me relative to an advertisement?"

"Yes," I said, "I only saw it this morning; I should not have been so urgent to see you, but I had no time to waste."

"Don't apologise," said Mr. Smith.

"I was merely telling you what was my motive for disturbing you. You speak in that advertisement of an anonymous letter being sent to No. — Harley-street."

"Yes, we did."

"Can you inform me of the nature of the occurrence?"

Mr. Smith paused, and, after some hesitation, said,—

"I cannot make any revelation to you, unless I know the amount of your knowledge and the object you may have in inquiring; for if I understood rightly, my clerk told me you had a communication to make to me, and not I to you, which, you see, materially alters our position. You must also see my knowledge is confidential—but I have of course a discretion to use."

"The matter is delicate," I said, "I am fully aware, but I do not wish to be the means of any vindictive proceedings for a trifling offence; should it turn out so, accident has placed it in my power to give you some assistance, but my curiosity is excited, and, by gratifying that, I may serve you."

"Well, sir, then I can say this much, that the letter alluded to was defamatory of the character of a young lady—one who is quite undeserving the dastardly attack that has been made upon her character."

"Have you any idea from whom such an assassin's blow could come from?"

"No, we have not the slightest suspicion, and only wait the chapter of accidents to turn up some information that may be made available for the purpose of restoring her mind to ease and serenity, and of doing her justice."

"Under those circumstances," said I, "I can have no hesitation to tell you all I know."

"In doing which you will earn the gratitude of more than one worthy person, as well as restoring the happiness which has been destroyed for the present by the means I have mentioned to you; I hope you will be confidential."

"I will," I replied.

I then circumstantially related to Mr. Smith all that had happened, and all I saw, ending with the information that I could swear to the man if I were to see him again, and told him where I had seen him go in.

"Well, sir, your information is not intended to cause any legal proceeding; it was intended by the parties injured only to expose the writer to shame, and to restore the character of the young lady, whose peace of mind is destroyed by the abominable falsehoods that were, by these means, conveyed into a family, in which were her best and dearest friends."

"And has so much been done?" said I.

"Yes, if you please to wait for half an hour, and will accompany me to Harley-street, I will introduce you to the family."

"I will await your convenience," I replied.

"Half an hour will be the most I shall require."

"I will wait," I replied.

He gave me the paper, and then left the room while I read it over ; and at the^e expiration of the half hour Mr. Smith came down and announced that he wa^s ready to accompany me. I arose, and we both went out together on our way to Harley-street.

"I will put you in possession of the circumstances," he said, " that have brought this unpleasant affair about. It will show the extent of mischief people are capable and willing to commit, when their revenge incites them."

"Indeed!" said I, "and is it so black an affair as that?"

"Yes, quite. You see Mr. James lives in Harley-street. He is an elderly gentleman, who has a large family, and a large fortune too, and is most anxious for the future prosperity of his sons and daughters, and will not permit them to form any alliance save with those who are their equals, especially in point of worth and station : wealth not being, as in many cases, the main object."

"He is a very sensible man."

"And a most kind and amiable man, too, he is ; so much so that his children obey him implicitly, and have the greatest affection for him that ever I heard of; and it is quite voluntary on their part."

"I am glad to hear it; for it shows the mildness of the parental sway, when it is so easily borne, and the great good sense excited in their education."

"It does so," he replied. "Well, Henry James is the second son, and he had made an advance towards a Miss Hathaway, a beautiful girl, the only daughter of a widow lady, who has but a small income, which dies with her. She is, however, a woman of rank, though not of property, for her husband was an officer in the navy, who had little more than his pay, but that was liberal."

"I see," I said, " she has but a widow's pension."

"Yes, she has—she has something more than that. She has some little property of her own, but not much ; however, that will be all her daughter will receive at her mother's death. Indeed, she is willing to give that up to her daughter Jane on her marriage, if with her consent, which is very liberal."

"Very," I replied.

"Well, then, it so happened that Mr. James had not any knowledge of this lady, and was somewhat averse to his son's continuing a suitor to the young lady ; which, however, he did not totally prohibit, believing, if his son could break the connexion, he would ; and if not, he felt convinced that it was not in his power to do so."

"A very reasonable conviction."

"Yes; well, suddenly, just as the elder Mr. James was about to give his consent to receive the young lady as his daughter-in-law, the very day he was about to make an arrangement for her reception, the servant entered the room and presented a letter to him, which was addressed to him."

"Whom is this from?" he inquired, as he took it.

"We don't know, sir; it was thrust under the door."

The old gentleman read it; but, as he did so, all noted the pain and surprise which it gave him, and after he had read it, he gave the letter to his son, saying,—

"Read this, Henry, and tell me what you think of it."

Henry took the letter and read it. You may imagine his rage and anger, and he indignantly declared the assertions to be false and dastardly, and that no man who dare face the innocent would have made the charge—it was a false and calumnious libel.

Of course, such a defence coming from him was no more than expected by all ; and the old gentleman shook his head, as much as to say, that one with a stain upon her character could not be his daughter-in-law by his consent. You cannot imagine the effect that such things have upon some minds.

"What was the gist of the libel?"

"It was a letter written in the most sorrowful style, declaring that the writer's only motive for concealing himself was to avoid more unpleasantness than even his communication could cause ; and that he only wrote because he could not bear the idea that so respectable a family as that of Mr. James should be sullied by a connexion that could bring nothing but sorrow and infamy with it ; solemnly assuring Mr. James that the writer knew too well both mother and daughter ; and conjured him, as he loved his son's happiness, to cause a separation by any means in his power, it mattered not how."

" It was an artfully concocted affair."

" It was, and has succeeded as yet ; for at the earnest solicitation of his father the son has promised not to marry until this affair, at least, is cleared up."

" And that might not have been done while they lived."

" Or even afterwards," replied the attorney; " but the young lady received a letter which cast imputations upon young James, and the result was an alienation between them, and at the same time it has caused both of them to be miserably unhappy."

" How much mischief from such a cause !"

" Yes. it is so; but I hope this matter may be settled now one way or the other. The fact is, Mr. James offered the reward in the hopes of quieting his son ; but, I am sure, he does not at alll anticipate any answer to it."

" He will scarcely be pleased at this discovery," said I.

" He is too good a man, not to rejoice in it," replied old Smith ; " I can answer for it, that it will be highly gratifying to him ; for I am sure that he will see it is ruining his son's health, to continue in the unhappy state he is now in."

We had now arrived at the house, and Mr. Smith, having sent up his card, Mr. James came down stairs to us, and entered the parlour where we were sitting.

Mr. Smith rose, and shaking the old gentleman by the hand, said,—

" I have brought you a gentleman, who, having seen your advertisement, has come forward to say that he saw the anonymous letter put under your door, and fortunately followed the person who left it, until he saw him housed."

" I am glad, we may have a chance of getting to the bottom of this mystery—if it be either to confirm or destroy the impression that has been made."

" You must not assume," said I, " that I saw the writer—I only saw a man thrust it under the door, and I followed him to a house—but that house might not have been his abode—but if I were to see him again I should know him."

" That is one object gained," said the old gentleman.

His son was afterwards called in, and a regular consultation was held amongst us; but as there was no one belonging to the family who knew the individual whom I had seen, or even made a guess of him, they determined that they would make what inquiries they could of Mrs. and Miss Hathaway, and learn if they could give any idea of the person who had done the deed that had caused so much unhappiness.

To give them time to do this, I agreed to call upon Mr. Smith, who would inform me what was done ; or he would write to me to tell me what was done, and when, if at all, my presence would be required.

This done, I left the house, and proceeded about my ordinary avocations and amusements, and that done, I waited impatiently the arrival of the letter from Mr. Smith's, which did not reach me until the third day, and ran as follows :—

" Dear Sir,   " Howland-street.

"Suspicion has at length rested upon an individual. Will you come to my offices by nine o'clock, and we will then call and breakfast with Mrs. and Miss Hathaway, where you will meet with this suspected party, and have an opportunity of examining him well, and of ascertaining if he is the man you saw leave the letter.'

        " Yours very truly,
          " J. Smith."

I read the letter over, and after a little reflection I was resolved that I would go and see these people, though I did not like the task, and yet I thought it was my duty to do so, that I ought not to allow two young people's happiness to be destroyed by the villany of any person living whatever, when I had it in my power to prevent it.

I went early next day to Mr. Smith's—I was there by the time appointed, and I was at once shown into his office without any delay.

"You are here in good time," he said.

"Yes, I like punctuality when it can be followed. What is the news with regard to the Jameses and Hathaways?"

"I have heard nothing since I last wrote to you."

"Who is this suspected person?" I inquired.

"Why he, if it be him, is a rejected suitor of Miss Hathaway's, and has sought by all means in his power to destroy the hope of young James, but has never succeeded in doing so; and it is suspected that he must have adopted this plan."

"And what is he?"

"There is some mystery about him. He appears, they say, in good society, but at the same time, no one knows much of him. That does not say much—it is very suspicious—in my mind very suspicious indeed; because, those who really are respectable are easily known as such, it always happens that somebody can speak for them."

"So there is, but there may be an exception, you know, but still it makes them appear to disadvantage."

We left the house and proceeded towards Mrs. Hathaway's residence, and were soon introduced to both mother and daughter by Henry James, his father also being present. He was then rather sad, and I described to Miss Hathaway the man whom I had seen; and she exclaimed,—

"That is his description exactly,—his very counterpart."

We had not much time left to converse on this singular affair, when the individual mentioned entered the breakfast room; and met Miss Hathaway with many expressions of regret at having detained her.

"Here is a friend of mine," she exclaimed, pointing to me.

"A friend of yours," he said, "I shall be very happy to make his acquaintance."

"I think," said I, "I have had the pleasure of seeing you once before, if my memory does not prove treacherous."

"Indeed! I do not remember it."

"And that very recently too," I replied; looking attentively at him for I remembered him well by a peculiarity of manner that at once stamped him the same, and I should have been safe in calling him the anonymous letter-writer at once, even if I had not seen his features, which I had. "It cannot be many days ago since I saw you put under the door of Mr. James in Harley-street a letter near midnight, and then walk towards Great Titchfield-street and enter a house close to that street."

* * * * * * *

The result was, though he denied all with the most solemn asseverations, yet his eye and pallid cheek proved to all that he was the author, his lips quivered, and he suffered all the torment of a convicted libeller. At length finding he could gain no credence, he left the house. Young James and Miss Hathaway were married in about a month, and I had an invitation to attend the wedding and witness their happiness, which I accepted.

* * * * *

The tale was over, and I looked into the sweet face of Anna; there was a glance f seriousness from her beautiful eyes which rested on me for a moment, and then I thought I discovered the slightest possible inclination to a laugh.

"Well, Anna," I said rather timidly; "now you have heard my night adventure, are you not decidedly of opinion that it is only when the sun has withdrawn its rays from the face of nature, that human character comes out in all its strangest aspects; are you not decidedly of opinion that I have adopted a right course in my studies of character?"

"No," she said.

I felt a little startled at the abruptness of the negative, and, as a sailor would say, I was certainly taken aback, at that moment.

"Why, why," I said, " you don't mean to say you have changed your opinion?"

" Not in the least," she replied, " it's you that shall change yours."

" No ; I'm sure I shall be able to convince you."

" Don't attempt it ; haven't you heard that women are never convinced of anything ?"

" Yes, but Anna—"

" Nonsense ! you've been going on at this sort of thing for a long time, turning night into day, until you look almost like an owl—what strange peculiarity do you suppose there is in human nature, that it should not exhibit itself in interesting

aspects, while the sun is shining, as well as under other circumstances ; certainly by going out at night, you may run a chance of being yourself deceived, and of seeing more of the worst side of the picture."

" Now, really," I said, " allow me to argue the question."

" I will allow no such thing ; I have made up my mind, that if I ever have a

No. 22.

husband, he shall be a man who likes the daylight for admixture with his fellow-creatures, and besides its quite adventure enough for a man to get married, to last him all his life besides."

" But I don't ask you, Anna, to go out seeking night adventures."

" Very likely ; but I won't have you go. I just wanted to see, by hearing you read of some of your adventures, how far your imagination was wrapped up in them, and now I find that you think of nothing else, for I have discovered by your manner how firm a hold they have had upon you. I am determined to break the charm."

"Alas, alas !" I cried; " I did not expect this from you. I really thought, that in you I had found a person possessing all the charms I had ever looked for in a wife, and at the same time not averse to my night adventures."

" Then you perceive how very wrong you are. I know I possess all the charms ; but I object to the night adventures—so you can take your choice."

Kind and indulgent readers, is it to be supposed for one moment I could think, for the most beautiful creature living, of giving up those little episodes of human life, to which I was so warmly attached—is it to be supposed I would deliberately do such a thing—no, I did it at once, without any deliberation at all ; thus commemorating myself as a notable example of the power which youth and beauty ever exercises over the poor sons of humanity.

Anna triumphed ; and I consented, although, perhaps, not with the best grace imaginable, to give up those night adventures which had been the solace of my bachelorhood.

*　　*　　*　　*　　*

And now the Night Adventurer bids adieu to his readers, with the hope that he has contributed, at all events, something to the philosophy and the morality of existence.

He hopes that in the strange scenes and adventures he has found it necessary to depict to his readers, he has shown, that while there is much evil in the world, there is likewise still lingering in it, some whose bright and beautiful feelings would remind one of primeval happiness.

It is just possible that in selecting the night-time for his adventures he saw humanity sometimes in that perverted shape which it assumes when the sun has sunk beneath the horizon.

It is an undoubted philosophical fact, and one which the philosophy of the human mind unquestionably proves, that great changes take place in the imagination and the feelings after sunset.

All physicians are well aware that there is a kind of fever in the blood during the time the sun is below the horizon, which induces men to do strange things, and to be guilty, sometimes, of follies, they would not have dreamt of in the full light of day.

Thus it may have happened that, in some instances, I got, as I say, perverted views of human nature, but I don't think these instances were very many; so I rather congratulate myself than not upon my good fortune ; and if I put aside one or two of my adventures, at the most, as episodes in which no great beneficial result to individuals or to society was produced, I may say that, with regard to all the others, some good certainly was done.

It will be seen that a species of rude poetic justice, if poetic justice can at all be rude, was carried out in most of those episodes of fortune, in which in was my lot to be engaged.

And now, perhaps, some of my fair readers may not feel disinclined to know if ever I repented making choice of Anna instead of Night Adventures.

To those ladies I can only say, that, as regarded giving up the Night Adventures, the whole affair was a fallacy, for five little cherubs, as I am told they were, in due time, graced my board, and my Night Adventures with one and another of them were so numerous, that if I had placed them all down in my diary, they would have made a most formidable volume indeed.

If little Fanny had not the nettle-rash, Susannah, of course, had the hooping cough, and if neither of them had anything, of course James, Marianna and Adolphus fell down flat with the meazles.

Then they all cried for three months after their birth without cessation, so that my usual Night Adventure was being awakened after about twenty minutes sleep by a squall that lasted until the break of day.

"So," said Anna, with a very cutting touch of irony, "you have plenty of Night Adventures, you see, without the trouble of going out."

THE END.

LONDON: PRINTED AND PUBLISHED BY E. LLOYD, 12, SALISBURY SQUARE, FLEET STREET.